TO AMERICA

"Do I have to go?" Jack pleaded.

"Sure, and your mam and me don't want you to go but it'd kill us if you were taken by the soldiers. Much better if we know you're safe somewhere. Anywhere."

Jack nodded, unable to speak. He gazed up at the dark sky, seeing the stars gleaming in the breaks between the high, flat clouds. The stars would be his map for the journey home to Kerry that he was certain he would make one day. "Michael . . . John . . . Brigid," he whispered to the night.

"Aye, lad, never forget them," said Father O'Sullivan. "Your brothers have joined the others who've fought for this land, giving their most precious gift of all to Ireland."

As they moved away from the cabin, Jack looked back once. His mother and father stood in the doorway, their arms around each other.

"Don't look back, son," the priest said quietly. "Never look back again. Remember what was but think now on what will be . . ."

ROBERT PERRIN

ALL THE RAGING SEASONS

TOR

A TOM DOHERTY ASSOCIATES BOOK

ALL THE RAGING SEASONS

A Tor Books edition, published by special arrangement with Pan Books Ltd. Previously published in Great Britain as NOONDAY by Pan Books Ltd.

First Tor printing: June 1986

A TOR Book

Published by Tom Doherty Associates
49 West 24 Street
New York, N.Y. 10010

ISBN: 0-812-58706-5

Printed in the United States

0 9 8 7 6 5 4 3 2 1

*For my dear friend and second father,
Bob Wyatt, who might read this elsewhere.*

"I have made their widows more in numbers
than the sands of the sea;
"I have brought against the mothers of
young men a destroyer at noonday;
"I have made anguish and terror fall upon
them suddenly."

Book of Jeremiah, Chapter 15, Verse 8.

BOOK
ONE

Chapter 1
August, 1822

Jack Keane stripped off his clothes and stood naked under the warm midday sun. The paleness of his trunk and thighs contrasted with the ruddy, weather-beaten color of the rest of his tall, husky body. He ran down the fine sands of the lonely Irish coast and laughed and whooped with joy as he kicked at the water. He walked out until the sea was up to his chest. Spluttering and gasping, he began to strike out with his own ungainly mixture of the breast-stroke and the crawl, arms and legs flailing. Soon, the sounds from the twin beaches of Ballybunnion faded behind him. To his right, once he'd left the headland at his back, he could see a huge, dark rock rising over 150 feet from the sea with a large, round tunnel running right through its middle. Here, the sea boiled and roared its way through. No man had ever swum the tunnel without drowning in its fierce undercurrents. Jack smiled to himself as he thought on the rock's name. A passage forced by no man, and thus the Virgin's Rock. He turned over to float on his back, raising his head slightly and looking down along his body, broad and long and without an ounce of fat, and then let his head fall back again, surrendering himself to the sway of the sea. He remembered his certainty that this day, 15 August 1822, was to be special.

Jack Keane had had the feeling ever since he'd been awoken that morning in the small cabin lit by the glow from the tamped-down peat fire. His mother and father were lying together on their straw bed in one corner; his older brothers, Michael and John, still asleep in the other. Jack quietly urged six chickens through the cabin doorway, pulling aside the brown hessian sack hanging across it. Next, he went to the large, wooden cage where the pig and sow lay with their four pigeens, opened it, and forced them out into the damp of the morning.

Outside, he dashed some cold water over his face and arms, scooping it from the wooden rainwater tub by the cabin doorway, alongside the bricks of peat, stacked neatly against the cabin's white-washed mud and clay walls. Now he felt ready for the day. He took a deep breath of fresh air, imagining that he could already smell the salt from the distant sea. Then he set off from the small huddle of cabins that made up the West Kerry townland of Drombeg, vaulting easily across dry-stone walls until he reached the broad track leading to Ballybunnion.

Jack could already hear the Atlantic rollers, now less than a mile away, and smell the salt in the air. He strode past the cabins that pointed the way to the sea. A woman in late middle age, a red shawl over her head and shoulders, looked up from the cow she was milking.

"Where are you from, boy?" she called. "Come a long way for the pattern, have you?"

"From Drombeg," Jack replied, stopping by the wicker gate set in the stone wall around her cabin.

"You must have a thirst on you."

"I am a wee bit dry," Jack conceded, a broad grin on his face, knowing that he would be offered a mug of warm, foaming milk. Custom dictated that he would drink only half of what he was offered.

When he'd finished his drink, he wiped his mouth with the back of his hand.

"Thank you, mother."

"Thanks be to God and His Blessings on this day. And not too much noise at the crossroads tonight, you mind," called the woman after him.

"I haven't even got a dancing partner yet," Jack shouted back as he started up the broad track.

"You'll have no trouble there, my young friend," muttered the woman to herself, continuing her milking. "Not with your looks, you won't," she sighed to herself. He'll break some pretty hearts, she thought, as she wearily rose from her milking stool and pushed her cow aside to grasp the handle of the brimming wooden pail.

The cabins ended thirty yards from the cliff-top and Jack saw the blueness of the sea stretching away from him; the ruined keep of Ballybunnion Castle on the headland and the curving bays of fine sand. He undid the knot in his red handkerchief, took out a large potato, and chewed on its cold, cooked flesh. The early morning sun was rising behind him, glinting off the small rock pools at the base of the deep grey cliffs shot through with streaks of red and yellow sulphur. Away to his left a lone figure worked amongst these rocks, picking mussels, lichens, and crabs from the small rock pools, and tossing them into a basket. The man's donkey stood patiently by, one filled basket already strapped to its back.

Now, his thoughts far away, he was almost lulled to sleep by the motion of the sea. If he floated long enough, would he be washed up in America, he wondered idly? Then, suddenly, something struck him hard in the side, pushing him off balance and under the water.

He coughed, struggling to the surface, arms and legs thrashing the water round him as he fought to keep afloat.

He heard a shriek of laughter and, blinking the salt from his eyes, saw a smiling face close to his, a girl's face with vivid green eyes, a snub nose, a generous mouth with red lips, all framed by long ringlets of gleaming black hair.

Angrily Jack grabbed at the girl's round bare shoulders, pulled her to him, and pushed her under the sea. He felt her firm breasts pressed against his body as she slid down under him. She bobbed to the surface, gasping for air, and Jack, alarmed that he might have gone too far, held her closely to prevent her going under again.

"You divil," she spluttered, her eyes blazing. Then she saw the genuine concern on his face and softened, feeling the strength of his arms around her.

"You dunderhead," she began to laugh.

"You started it, ducking me."

"No I didn't," the girl protested, her voice low and melodious. "I didn't see you lying there at all."

"Anyway, what are you doing way out here?" Jack asked, still clutching her close to him. "You'll drown out here, so you will."

"And why, pray? I could swim when I was only five. I'm as safe as you are."

Jack began to feel the warmth of her body against his, a disturbing, exciting warmth that he'd never known before. The girl, too, realized that he was still pressing close to her from her knees to her breasts. She felt his manhood lengthening and hardening against the soft curve of her belly.

"Now, get away from me," she cried, pushing at him. "A girl's supposed to have her privacy swimming from the women's beach."

Jack peered back at the shore and realized she was speaking the truth. He must have drifted with the current and was well north of the men's beach.

The girl laughed again when she saw his perplexed

expression. "You're coming ashore on our beach then are you, you brazen lummock?"

"No, of course not." Jack felt himself blush at the thought, aware of how the girl's soft body had physically excited him.

"Come on, I'm getting cold," said the girl with the green eyes. "I'll race you back to the headland."

She thrust out of the water. Jack glimpsed her slim body and full breasts for a moment and then she was pushing through the water away from him and back towards the shore.

Jack didn't follow her immediately, admiring with excitement the twin globes of her buttocks and the divide between them as her legs kicked her through the water. He realized that she was a strong swimmer with a smoother style than his. He began thrashing after her, pulling at the water with all his strength, and started to close the gap between them. As they neared the headland separating the beaches he was swimming level with her. Her eyes smiled into his, glad to have him alongside her.

"Where do you come from?" she asked.

"Drombeg," gasped Jack, panting with exertion. "The name's Jack Keane."

"Hello, Jack Keane. I'm Brigid Aherne from Gortacross-ane."

By now, the two youngsters were about twenty yards from the headland, near enough to hear the shouts and cries of the latecomers enjoying themselves on the beach. They realized that, for decency's sake, they would have to go their different ways, to the beaches reserved for men and women. Jack stood up, the water reaching halfway up his chest. Brigid swam a few more yards and turned to face him, the sea lapping the upper swell of her breasts.

"Thanks for the swim, Jack Keane," she smiled.

"Thank you, Brigid Aherne." Jack liked the sound of her name.

They began moving apart towards their respective beaches. "Brigid," he blurted, "are you dancing tonight?"

"I might be, and then again I mightn't be. Why?"

"Would you be my dancing partner?"

"And who says I haven't got one already?"

Jack's face fell with dismay. "I just thought."

She smiled softly at him. "And then again I might not have a partner."

"Meet me by the castle when you're dressed?"

"Perhaps, Jack Keane, perhaps."

Brigid glanced quickly over her shoulder at the eighteen-year-old. In one look she took in the details of his strong, lean body, from his broad shoulders to his firm waist, and lower. She walked ashore, her head high, two red spots bright on her cheeks, a smile playing around her lips.

Jack sat on the warm stone by the ruined castle staring out over the twin bays of Ballybunnion, now fairly crowded with people enjoying their holiday after having made their devotions. Many were youngsters, playing naked in the pools and shallows, but here and there were dotted family groups sitting against the rocks, the grandmother always at their center, invariably dressed in black with a shawl covering her grey head. He waited for more than half-an-hour, beginning to despair with each minute that passed that Brigid wouldn't keep their rendezvous. Perhaps she thought him just a farm boy with uncouth manners and at this very moment was giggling about him with some of her friends? He was torn with the uncertainty of youth.

Two hands crossed his eyes, blotting out the sunlight. "Hello, Jack Keane," said a soft voice in his ear.

He swung round on the stone. Brigid Aherne smiled down at him, her black hair fluffed in curls, a brown woollen shawl across her shoulders falling over her green blouse, the full, bright red skirt covering her legs to mid-calf. Her feet, like Jack's, were bare.

"Brigid! I thought you weren't . . ."

"You thought I'd break my word, did you then? And hardly knowing me, too," she exclaimed in mock indignation, putting her hands on her hips.

"Well, you didn't *promise* . . ."

"I'm here, aren't I?" She noticed his red handkerchief lying on the grass. "What have you there?"

"Some lumpers."

"That's good. I've got some seaweed to go with them." She plunged her hand into a deep pocket near the hem of her skirt and pulled out a handful of dried seaweed. Together they shared the food in silence. The bitter sweetness of the edible seaweed flavored the blandness of the large potatoes.

Brigid was the first to speak. "And how many more are there at home like you?"

"Just me and me brothers, Michael and John. And me mam and dad, of course. They've gone to the fair in Listowel today."

"So have mine." She looked at him keenly. "Have you much land?"

"Three acres or so with some wheat, some chickens and some potatoes. And we've got some pigs and pigeens and Siobhan."

"Siobhan?"

"That what me mam calls her. Says the cow reminds her of me dad's Auntie Siobhan."

Brigid laughed, a soft laugh that lit up her whole face. "Well, it strikes me that with Siobhan and all, you're well off."

"How many of you are there then?"

"There's Theresa and Bernadette, who are older than

me," Brigid ticked off her sisters on her fingers. "And Mary and May who are younger. Me dad's got a conacre, and what with a cow and him working for Sir James Watson, we survive."

Jack thought for a moment about Brigid's family. A man with a conacre was a cottier and was lower down the agrarian social scale than a tenant farmer like his father. A cottier, in return for his labors, was allowed by his landlord to farm a small plot by his rented cabin, invariably growing potatoes. The Ahernes would be a family, Jack thought, with little to fall back on in hard times.

"I suppose Jonathan Sandes is your agent as well, Brigid?"

"That he is and a hard man too. Me dad says he's got a smile like a brass plate on a coffin. It we didn't borrow ahead from the Cork butter men, or sell turf at the market, he'd have us out of our cabin as quick as a Kilkenny cat."

Jack nodded glumly in agreement. "The last time the potatoes failed, me dad had to go to the gombeen man for the rent, or the bailiffs would have had our roof off. What with his rates of interest, me dad's only just paid him off."

"Why's it allowed to happen, Jack?" asked Brigid, tucking her knees under her chin. "God knows we have little enough. Why do they always want more?"

"Because they're landlords, that's why," he said angrily. "Landlords are always like that. People like your man Sir James Watson sit in their fine houses in Dublin or London and let their agents like Sandes do their filthy work. They never see their land but they always want their rent on time. The most of them would rather see us living in the ditch first and the land turned over to cattle with no cabins in the way."

"Me dad says that some people are ready to do something about it," said Brigid.

"They are that. Me brothers, Michael and John, think so anyway." He lowered his voice. "They belong to the Whiteboys."

"The Whiteboys!" Brigid sniffed disdainfully. "And what do they do? All that burning and killing. Where does that get them?"

"It makes sure the landlords know that we're not beaten, that we'll fight them if needs be."

"I thought the Whiteboys were supposed to be secret. How do you know your brothers belong?"

"That's just it. I don't know for sure. But they keep slipping away at dusk and then the next day or so we hear the Whiteboys have done this or that. I'm guessing that Michael and John had something to do with the burning of the farm over at Duagh last week."

"I'm thinking you'd like to join them, Jack Keane," Brigid said, her face set with concern.

"They won't let me," he said, disconsolately. "They say I'm too young for such things. But I'm as strong and quick as they are."

Jack, like most young Kerrymen, held the Whiteboys in awe; a secret society with strange oaths and initiation ceremonies whose object was to harass and challenge the overwhelming power of the landlords and their agents. No one knew who they were, only that they identified themselves by wearing long white shirts when on their raids. They burned, stole, and killed, always directing their attacks at the landlords or those who supported them.

"Well, don't let me catch you running around in a white shirt, that's all," said Brigid, breaking into his thoughts. "You know what Father O'Sullivan says about all this violence."

"You mean you'd care what I did?" he asked, looking up into her face for reassurance.

She laughed and ran her hands through his thick hair. "And would I be sitting here jawing with you, if I didn't? You're a soft one, Jack Keane, that you are."

He put up his hand and touched hers, and then grasped it tightly. She responded to the pressure, running her thumb along his hand. But, after a moment, she pulled away and jumped up from the stone where she'd been sitting.

"That's enough of that, Jack Keane. You're taking a liberty, that you are. First you grab me when I'm having a quiet swim on me own, and now you're trying to hold me hand with everyone looking at us."

"But there's no one around," said Jack, looking guiltily about him.

"Sure, and what difference does that make?"

Jack sat bewildered on the grass as Brigid moved over to the stones of the ruined keep. He couldn't fathom her changing moods. In the distance, a fiddler struck up a tune.

"That'll be Michael Coffey from Doon," called Brigid. "Are you coming to listen to him?"

"I'd prefer to be here with you."

"Well, you can't. If you're not coming, I'll go on my own."

"Oh, all right then," he said reluctantly. He wished he could understand the ways of young women. One moment they were all affection and concern; the next, they were prancing away as if they didn't care. It was baffling.

By the time Brigid and Jack had reached the crossroads, a dozen other couples were already there, sitting on walls or on the ground, chatting quietly together. The men with partners stayed on one side of the road, while those without stood morosely across from them, only brightening when an unattached girl approached along the track. When she'd taken a partner and joined the other couples, the rejected men returned to stand in groups, making unflattering remarks about girls in general, though not in voices loud enough to carry across the road. No one wanted a fight at this stage of the evening. Later, perhaps, but not at dusk with the sky in the west glowing orange from the sinking sun.

When he'd judged enough people to be at the crossroads, a small, wizened man wearing a large, grey felt hat stepped into the middle of the track. From under his ragged tail coat, as if by sleight of hand, he produced a fiddle and bow. Michael Coffey, tinker and music man, was indispensable for any night's dancing at the crossroads. In fact, his fiddle went to every important event in the district, whether it was a birth, a wedding, or a death. He waited for the chattering to subside and then stroked a single chord of A out of his fiddle. Some at the crossroads dropped to their knees, others simply stood straight. All crossed themselves and waited in silence. Michael Coffey's fiddle had signalled the sunset "Angelus."

Brigid fell to her knees, pulling Jack down with her. There was silence and stillness everywhere without, it seemed, even a bird singing or flying. Jack looked towards the hills of Kerry in the east where yellow clouds drifted gently. In the falling light, the hollows of the hills were turning from blue to dark purple, and their fretted ridges to jet black. The high clouds changed color perceptibly against a sky glowing with an incandescent light that was almost pale green.

Brigid's eyes were screwed tightly shut, her lips moving as she silently recited a prayer. The sunset picked her face out in perfect profile, and in Jack's later years when the world had had its way he was to remember that this was the moment when he realized he was enduringly in love with her.

After two minutes or so, Michael Coffey stroked another

chord on his fiddle, and the spell was broken. Brigid's eyes opened and she looked directly into Jack's face. There was a misty sadness in her face and Jack knew that her prayer had been about the two of them.

He rose from his knees and held out his hand. Brigid grasped it tightly as he pulled her to her feet. For seconds, they stood closely together, pressing against each other. Then Brigid, still allowing Jack to hold her hand, pulled away to arm's length and dropped a deep curtsey. Her skirt formed a red circle on the grass by the side of the track as she sank before him and bowed her head, the ringlets of black hair dipping and bobbing. One or two of the girls standing nearby giggled shyly as they watched this open declaration of Brigid's love. It was a private moment of thoughts and vows, of overpowering warmth.

Michael Coffey saw Brigid's gesture and hesitated to begin playing his fiddle, not wanting to spoil precious moments for the young couple. But, as Brigid began to rise from her curtsey, he lifted his fiddle to his chin and, stamping his foot, launched into his first jig.

As the music rose into the evening, Jack pulled Brigid to him. "Why?" he whispered into her ear.

"Because . . . Well, just because for now," she answered shyly, standing on tip toe, pressing her mouth close to his ear.

Torches, made from damp bogland rushes dipped in candle grease, were lit and stuck in the walls on the four sides of the crossroads. Their smoky light flickered across the scene, casting wild, grotesque shadows as the dancers dipped and twirled into the eight-handed reel, "The Siege of Ennis."

Brigid's skirt flared up her strong and gleaming thighs, as she and Jack joined another couple in a four-handed reel, their feet pointing and darting in the complicated steps of the dance, their arms lifted above their heads. Wild cries came from deep in their throats as the tempo increased, never slackening, and Michael Coffey's fingers moved in a blur up and down the strings of his fiddle.

As the stars began to glisten in the dark blue sky, the dancing grew wilder with more and more couples joining in the reels. Eventually Jack and Brigid sank to the grass by the crossroads, thoroughly exhausted.

"Tis about time we started home, Brigid," said Jack softly. "We've a long walk yet."

"That's true, but I don't want this night to end. I'll always remember it."

"So will I. Until I die, and that's the truth."

The couple drifted off into the darkness and walked along the track towards Listowel in the east, hand in hand, letting the fiddle music and the whooping of the dancers fade behind them. Soon there were only the noises of the night for company. Brigid clung closely to Jack's arm, her head pressing against his chest.

"What happened to us today?" Jack whispered.

"I don't know, but I'm thinking it was blessed."

Jack smiled in the darkness and pressed Brigid closer to him, nuzzling her hair and smelling the sea still in it. It took more than two hours to reach the cabins of the townland of Gortacrossane, on the edge of Listowel parish, about a mile or so from where Jack lived.

"Shall I see you to your cabin?"

"No, it would be better not," Brigid replied.

"It's funny us living so close and never meeting before."

"We have now and that's the most important thing. The very most important thing."

Brigid stopped and lifted herself on to her toes. She kissed Jack lightly on the lips before he realized what was happening. Then she turned and ran off into the darkness.

"Brigid . . . Brigid," Jack called into the night.

"Hush, not so loud," came Brigid's voice, not many yards away. "Hush . . ."

"But you just can't go like that."

"I'll be at market next week."

"I'll be there," promised Jack. He could still taste her kiss on his lips.

"Goodnight, dear Jack Keane. Remember me till next week."

"That I will. Surely."

Jack wandered back along the track and across the fields to Drombeg, his mind whirling. He doubted if he would ever understand girls. He rubbed his fingers gently against his lips and smiled to himself. At that moment, he didn't care whether he understood or not. He'd known all along the day was going to be something special. And that's what really mattered.

Chapter 2
September, 1822

An insistent murmur below his bedroom window awoke Jonathan Sandes, land agent to Sir James Watson. He rolled away from the warm, musky nakedness of the girl beside him, pulled aside the curtains of his four-poster bed, and shivered a little as his bare legs and feet struck the cold air. He padded over to the window, parted the heavy dark green curtains, and looked down on to Listowel market square, still lit by pale moonlight.

The country folk were already afoot, arriving for the day's market. He watched a drover, bent over his stick, following his cows, calling from time to time in a low early-morning voice to his subdued dog. A donkey, knock-kneed under the weight of its load, plodded along, wicker baskets full of turf tied either side of its spiny back. A woman carrying a basket of dried seaweed, a sleeping baby of a few months tied papoose-like to her back by her shawl, pushed two other young children in front of her. Still half-asleep, they stumbled along, their thin bodies covered only by makeshift vests of sacking that fell to their thighs. The moon grew paler every moment, and the little chill wind that comes before the sun rattled the windows of Jonathan Sandes' house. The air outside grew grey.

Sandes turned back towards the bed, stretching his body, still vigorous and athletic in early middle age through constant riding and hunting. He smiled as he saw the bare back of the girl and her long, dark hair spread across the pillows. A pretty and plump serving girl called Finoola from his kitchen; a girl with some surprising tricks, he recalled. Yes, it had certainly been worthwhile letting his wife go to Dublin. He felt himself growing excited at the memory of the night's love-making and the thought of the coming faction fight. He slipped back into bed, put his hand on the girl's shoulder and rolled her over on to her back. Instinctively, even in her waking moments, the girl opened and raised her thighs as he plunged between their satiny smoothness. She began uttering small cries of delight as he moved rhythmically in her, her ankles and calves clasped tightly around his lean buttocks, thrusting upwards in unison with him, drawing him further and further into her. He groaned with pleasure.

Jack Keane thought nervously about the faction fight while he sat milking Siobhan the cow. He'd heard about it the night before, sitting with his family around the glowing red peat fire in the middle of their cabin, chomping on hot potatoes and drinking mugs of milk. His father had broken the news.

"I heard from tinker O'Brien that the Cooleens will be at market looking for a fight. It seems someone insulted your Cooleen man and it's being blamed on us Mulvihills."

"But why a fight, Joe?" exclaimed Mary Keane.

"Well, I'm guessing it's almost a year since we pulped the Cooleens at Tralee Fair and they're just finding any old reason to catch us out."

"How many will be there?" asked his wife anxiously.

"Your man O'Brien says no more than a hundred a side. That's why he was so late telling me. The Mulvihills had almost made up their numbers in Listowel alone. But they did their sums and decided on a few more, thanks be to God!"

Mary Keane grimaced with disapproval. "It's no thanks to Him that you couldn't work for two weeks after the Tralee fight, what with your sore head and cracked ribs."

"This one won't be like that, woman!" her husband said in exasperation. "This'll be a short spat, no more."

But, despite his father's cheery optimism, Jack had spent a fitful night. He had never taken part in a faction fight before, although he'd heard many gory tales about them. The Cooleens, he knew, were the descendants of old Kerry families, settled in the county for centuries. The Mulvihills were from the neighboring county of Clare and had moved to Kerry generations ago in search of better land. In the parishes south of the River Shannon, you were either a Cooleen or a Mulvihill, depending on your family's history. The Keanes were Mulvihills, and thus the sworn enemies of the opposing faction. It was as simple as that.

Joe Keane, a large man nearly six feet tall, wide leather belt holding up his breeches and containing his growing belly, was a veteran of many faction fights. Now he peered in the half-light at a broken piece of mirror pinned to the cabin wall, his chin raised, hacking at the last errant patch of stubble with a cutthroat razor.

"Are you ready yet, Joe?" Mary Keane called from inside the cabin, where she'd been carefully packing three dozen eggs and a round pat of butter in her wicker basket.

"Just coming, Mary. Is it all done?"

"It is that."

Joe Keane rubbed his hand over his craggy face and thought his rough shave would suffice. "Got everything, boyos?" he called to his sons. "Jack, get the pigeen and don't forget your stick, either."

"Must he, Joe?" protested his wife, wrapping her green

shawl firmly round her head as she came out of the cabin. "He's only a boy, after all."

"He'll have to learn some time, Mary. Today's as good a day as any. It won't come to much; a few split heads at the most."

"Father O'Sullivan won't be pleased. He'll be mortal angry, that he will. You know what he thinks of the factions."

"Sure, and the priest should look after things he knows about and keep his pointy nose out of men's business."

Joe picked up a thick, gnarled stick about three feet long that was resting against the cabin wall, and slapped it into his palm. He winced as the hard blackthorn wood, capped with lead, stung his hand.

His wife laughed at his discomfort. "That'll show you, Joe Keane. You and your shillelagh. It'll be you ending up with a split head."

"Not if I see a Cooleen first," said her husband gruffly as he jammed a shapeless felt hat on his head. He turned to his three sons standing by him and saw each was carrying his shillelagh. "That's good, boys. Now remember what I tell you. When the fight starts, stay together and then you won't get hurt. The Cooleens won't be pulping three big lads like you."

As they approached the market town, the sun rising in their eyes, the Keanes passed travellers more heavily laden than themselves. The greeting was unvarying and inevitable.

"A fine morning, it is."

"It is that, thanks be to God."

"And is it to the market you're going?"

"Indeed it is. And you?"

"We've a little to sell."

"And, sure, who has more in these hard days?"

Just outside Listowel, in sight of the town's ruined castle standing high on a hillock, the Keanes stopped for a few minutes. In front of them was the River Feale, shallow and clear in the gathering autumn. The grown-ups bathed their travel-stained feet in it, dried them roughly, and laced on their footwear. The sons looked at their father's shoes with envy, knowing that there wasn't the money in the family for them all to be shod. One day—not too soon, pray God, Michael thought—they'll be mine as the eldest son. He would treat his shoes just as sparingly.

In the market square hundreds of people were already milling about, getting out their wares for sale. Those with money enough were already gathering outside the coaching inn tucked away in a corner of the square, washing down a potato or two with draughts of black porter.

Jack began looking eagerly around for Brigid Aherne. At first he failed to see her in the crowd but then he spotted her standing by a large pile of turf at the far end of the square.

"Hang on to this, Michael," he said, handing his brother the squealing pigeen. "I've a call to pay."

His brother followed his glance and saw Brigid. She stood out vividly from the crowds around her, a bright red shawl framing her clear beauty.

"So that's your dancing girl, is it, young Jack? I'm thinking she needs an older man. Perhaps John or meself would fit her better."

Jack looked at him in alarm. Michael tried to keep a straight face but quickly broke into a broad grin.

"Go on. Off you trot and see your lady love. But mind yourself. Dad'll want you with us when the Cooleens arrive so just you watch out for their green ribbons. And listen for our shout."

Jack approached Brigid shyly, uncertain of his reception. Their day together seemed so magical in his memory that he wasn't even certain what to say. Brigid had seen him arrive in the square long before he'd caught sight of her, but continued to stack her pile of turf as if she hadn't noticed him. Then he was standing behind her, shifting his feet awkwardly. He coughed once and she spun round, as if surprised.

"Oh, I didn't see you there. Creeping up on a girl like that!"

"Hello Brigid."

"Just don't stand there, Jack Keane. Can't you see I'm having trouble piling this turf?"

Jack started nervously. "To be sure. I'm sorry. Let me help."

She handed him turfs from a cart and he piled them neatly on to the ever-growing stack.

"Haven't you anything to say then, you lummock?"

"It's good to see you again, Brigid. I've been thinking of you all week."

She slipped her hand into his and gave it a squeeze. "To be sure, I was awful worried that you wouldn't come today."

"A regiment of soldiers wouldn't have kept me away."

"Oh, it's just that boys are funny."

"So you know all about boys, do you?"

"Well, I've heard enough to know some boys think girls are just out to trap them."

"Trap them?"

"You know . . ." Brigid said shyly, lowering her eyes. "Trap them into marrying."

"And what if the boy wanted to be trapped?"

"Well, that'd be different, wouldn't it? That'd be fair."

"We can't wait a week again, can we, Brigid?"

"No, if you're asking . . ."

"What about meeting on Saturday at the old school?"

Before Brigid could reply, a woman, round and plump, came up to the pile of turf.

"Have you not finished yet, Brigid?" she snapped, angrily. "We'll never get these turves sold if you keep chatting to every Tom, Dick and Harry."

"Mam, this is the boy I told you about. This is Jack."

"Oh, your dancing boy, is it? Well, don't just stand there. Show me him."

"Jack, this is me mam. Mam, this is Jack Keane."

Jack held out his hand, then realizing it was grimy from the turf wiped it against his breeches before shaking hands with Brigid's mother.

"He has manners anyway, Brigid. I'll say that for him."

"Oh, Mam," Brigid protested. "He's been helping with the turf."

"Well, thank you for that, Jack. And I'm sorry I am that you had to do the work your man should be doing."

"Where is Dad?" asked Brigid.

"With the rest of his cronies, supping some courage for this fight. I've been trying to find Father O'Sullivan to see if he can stop it before it starts but he's nowhere to be found."

"Me dad says it won't be much of a fight," Jack volunteered. "He'll be in it too."

"Well, more fool him," said Brigid's mother. "Men have less sense than the cattle."

"Jack, Jack," the call came from across the square. He turned and saw Michael waving at him.

"That's me brother. I've got to go." He whispered, "Saturday, Brigid?"

"Saturday afternoon, Jack," she said shyly, looking at her mother for confirmation. But Mrs. Aherne had turned away to serve a customer.

* * *

The calls from the market drifted through the half-open window of Jonathan Sandes' living room in his house on the market square. The cries of the countryfolk selling their wares meant money to him, money to pay Sir James Watson's rents. Sandes, elegantly dressed in a chocolate brown jacket with rounded tails, matching knee breeches, and fine white silk hose covering his muscular calves, was entertaining his fellow land agent, Dr. Peter Church, who watched over the interests of Lord Listowel, the other great landowner in the area.

"Another glass, Peter?" he inquired, moving towards his guest with a decanter of his finest madeira. "It won't be long now before the fight starts and that's a sight I want to see."

"Gets rid of their energy, eh, Jonathan?" said Church, a stocky, red-faced man, dressed in black. "Few broken heads keeps 'em quiet, eh?" He held out his glass to be refilled.

"Well, it's a damned sight better than letting them use their energy for those accursed Whiteboys."

"Yes, I can imagine you're not too well pleased with them at present. Lost that farm over at Duagh a fortnight back, didn't you?"

"Yes, curse 'em. I gave the constabulary a stiff wigging over that. They didn't catch one of the devils. But I'm glad his Lordship has joined Sir James in asking for more militia from Dublin. The soldiers will soon stamp them out."

"I'm not so sure, Jonathan," said Church, rubbing his chin dubiously. "Remember we've thought before that they've been finished, everything's gone quiet for a while, and then there they are again, white shirts and all."

Sandes sank wearily back into the high-backed, silk-covered chair by the window. The dark rings under his eyes testified to the night's pleasurable exertions. "There's only one thing these peasants understand, Peter, and you know that as well as I. Strength! If once we let them suspect weakness, heaven knows what'll happen."

"I'm wondering if that's altogether right. The poor devils have little enough," replied Church. "They've to use all their energies just to find enough food to fill their bellies, let alone anything else."

"Well, they find enough energy to have these faction fights, don't they? And then join the Whiteboys."

Sandes moved to the window. "Ah, I thought so, Peter," he said over his shoulder. "There are the Cooleens at the far end of the square. They're putting the green ribbons on their shillelaghs. It won't be long now."

Church levered himself out of his chair. "Will the constabulary move between them?"

"Not if Inspector Kiddey values his rank. Faction fights are to be left alone. Those are his orders. Let them break their own heads open. If they weren't fighting each other, they'd be fighting us."

"True enough," Church agreed. "Can you see the Mulvihills yet?"

"Down there by the coaching house, tying on the white ribbons. Don't seem to be as many of them as there are Cooleens."

His eyes had not deceived him. About ninety of the Cooleens, ribbons fluttering from their shillelaghs, stood at the east end of the square, blocking the track leading to the bridge over the River Feale. Outside the Listowel Arms, about fifty Mulvihills were draining their mugs of porter and whiskey and handing them to the potmen, who were anxious to gather in all the inn's breakable property before the fight started. The last of the cattle were being herded out of the square and Jack Keane, standing nervously with his brothers, was glad to see Brigid Aherne and her mother move into a side alley, pushing their almost empty cart.

"Here, take these, Jack," said his brother, Michael, handing him three jagged stones. "Put them in your pocket. You'll soon be needing them."

"But what can we do?" asked Jack anxiously. "Can't you see we're outnumbered?"

"That's true enough, Jack, to be sure. But our boys know about these fights. They've got a few surprises yet. You just stand behind John and me and watch us."

Jack saw the Cooleens beginning to approach in two groups, one on each side of the church in the middle of the square.

"They'll rush us when they've passed the church," whispered John. "Then we'll show them a trick or two, I'm thinking."

"But we'll be cornered by the inn here," protested Jack, looking nervously around him.

"Better to fight with a wall at your back. They can't sneak behind us then," said Michael. "Now stop your blathering and get ready."

A strange sound began to fill the market square, empty now except for the fighters, as the Cooleens grouped into one body, no more than thirty yards from the waiting Mulvihills. It began low and grew in intensity.

"Coolee . . . coolee . . . coolee . . . coolee." Rhythmic and menacing, it grew to a shout.

Jack heard his brothers and the men around him begin to answer. Deep in their chests at first, and then louder in their throats, to the stamp of their feet, they began chanting, "Mmmulvi . . . mmmulvi . . . mmmulvi . . . mmulvi."

"Coolee . . . mmmulvi . . . coolee . . . mmulvi." The opposing chants mingled and grew to a crescendo. And then they suddenly stopped. For a few seconds the market square was silent, as if everyone was holding his breath.

Then the Cooleens charged, shouting wildly at the top of their voices.

"Now, Jack, now," said Michael urgently. "Get your stones."

The shrieking Cooleens were no more than ten yards away and Jack could see the distorted grimaces of hate and drunken anger on their faces.

"Now, me boyos," roared a voice from the side. Jack recognized it as his father's.

"Throw at their legs," shouted Michael, hurling his first stone with all his strength.

A hail of jagged stones flew low across the narrowing gap between the factions, some skipping up from the hard-trodden earth of the market square. They crashed into the unprotected knees and shins of the running Cooleens, gashing flesh and splintering bone. The front rank of Cooleens leaped and tumbled under the onslaught, screaming with sudden agony, their contortions tripping the men behind them. Twice more, the hail of stones hurtled into the mob of men at waist and knee height. Some Cooleens doubled up, shouting in pain, dropping their shillelaghs to hold on to their genitals where the stones had ripped into them. In seconds, the Cooleens were a mass of tumbling, shrieking men. But the impetus of the unharmed men behind pushed the injured further forward as they tried to retreat.

"Pulp 'em now, boyos," Jack heard his father cry. And the Mulvihills advanced, shillelaghs swinging at head height, into the disorganized mass of Cooleens, some lying groaning on the ground, other trying to hop backwards clutching their injuries, but all the time being pushed forward into their rivals' flailing shillelaghs.

For the first moments, as the two factions closed together, the unhurt Cooleens were unable to reach the Mulvihills because of the tangle of their own wounded. Cries of agony and panic mingled with oaths and the cracking sounds of the Mulvihill shillelaghs as they found their targets.

Jack felt his fear disappearing as the fight got under way. There was no time to think as the crowd of men pressed round him, cursing and grunting, wielding their heavy sticks. An irrational feeling of anger against the Cooleens grew inside him and he heard himself, almost involuntarily, mouthing the chants and shouts of the others.

"Mmmulvi . . . mmmulvi . . . mmulvi."

He saw a man lurch in front of him clutching a shillelagh with a green ribbon tied round it, blood streaming from his gashed legs. Jack struck out automatically feeling the shiver of impact run up his stick into his shoulders. His shillelagh caught the Cooleen in the angle of his neck and shoulder and Jack heard the sickening crack as the man's collarbone smashed. The Cooleen dropped his shillelagh and screamed with pain, grabbing his injured shoulder, his knees bending as he began to fall. Without thinking, Jack raised his stick again, holding it with both hands, and brought it down with all his strength squarely on top of the man's head. He dropped without a cry. Jack leapt over him to seek a new opponent. He saw a man trying to drag himself away on one good leg and thwacked him flat across his shoulders. The man looked round into Jack's face, holding up his arms in a mute appeal for mercy, but there was none in Jack's heart. He struck again at the man's upraised arm, hearing it break just above the elbow. The Cooleen screamed and began writhing in agony on the earth. Jack paid no heed to his suffering, kicking him in the ribs with his hardened feet as he stepped over him. A mist had descended over his mind.

All he could hear echoing in his brain was his father's shout, "Pulp 'em, pulp 'em, pulp 'em."

By now, though, the main throng of uninjured Cooleens had closed with the advancing Mulvihills. Jack glimpsed a thick-set man swinging his shillelagh at his head. He ducked, raising his own stick, and deflected the fearsome blow downwards. The Cooleens shillelagh thudded into him, skidding off the ribs on his right side. Jack could do nothing but bend double as the wind went out of him. He thrust out his own shillelagh and by luck, rather than judgment, caught the Cooleen a jabbing blow in the pit of his stomach. The man shouted with pain but raised his shillelagh again to strike at Jack, his features blazing with anger. But, before he could bring his stick down, his face went slack, his eyes glazing, and he toppled away towards the ground. Jack saw his brother, Michael, swing at the man again, striking him for the second time on the head.

"He almost got you, Jack," shouted Michael, above the din of the battle. "Start moving back now. And watch yourself."

The two factions were pressed so close together now that it was almost impossible to find room enough to swing their shillelaghs. The men jabbed at each other with their sticks or resorted to using their fists. Jack caught one blow high up on his forehead and staggered back, but the press of Mulvihills behind him saved him from falling. He jabbed out with the shillelagh in his right hand and swung his left fist. The stick caught a Cooleen under his ribs and, as he bent forward, Jack's fist cracked him under his right eye. He looked quickly behind him and saw the Mulvihills being pressed further into the corner of the square. There seemed no chance of escape as the greater number of Cooleens bore down on them, their anger inflamed by their heavy casualties.

"Coolee . . . coolee . . . coolee." Their cries had a triumphant note in them. They pressed forward until the Mulvihills could move back no further. The men at the back were crushed against the railings outside the coaching house and began to cry out in panic as they felt the breath being squeezed from their bodies.

Jack was pressed hard against a Cooleen, but neither of them was able to do more than hack at the other's shins with his bare feet and scrabble with his hands at the other's already tattered clothes.

"You bastard divil Mulvi." The Cooleen spat into Jack's face, his fetid breath nauseous and hot.

"Back Coolee . . . back Coolee." The shout came from the rear of the Cooleens. Jack realized that the enemy was going to retreat slightly to get space to use their shillelaghs against the helpless Mulvihills pinned in the corner. He looked wildly around him for any way of escape but could see none. Then he caught John's eye a few yards away. His brother saw the panic growing in Jack's expression and winked at him.

"Don't worry," he mouthed. "Don't worry, Jack."

And then the pressure of the Cooleens eased. Jack raised his shillelagh again prepared, as he thought, to face the final, devastating attack. The hope flashed through his mind that he wouldn't be too badly beaten or scarred or else he wouldn't be able to meet Brigid Aherne on Saturday.

Suddenly he heard his father's voice booming out across the square. "Now, boyos, at 'em. Get at 'em."

Jack couldn't understand. There was no way that the trapped Mulvihills could advance. Then he saw a flurry away to his left. He jumped up to get a better view, catching a glimpse of about thirty men waving shillelaghs bearing white ribbons. They were running out of the entrance to the

stables behind the coaching house, shouting the Mulvihill
battlecry.

The reinforcements caught the Cooleens totally unaware
as they attacked their rear lashing their shillelaghs into men
still turning to meet the new threat. Dozens fell under the
onslaught, limbs broken, scalps laid bare, their shouts and
groans reaching the Cooleens facing Jack and his brothers.
Bewilderment and then panic and fear flashed across their
faces, as they realized they were caught in a trap,
surrounded by Mulvihills on three sides with buildings on
the fourth.

"Attack now," cried Michael. "Thump 'em into the next
county."

Jack's shillelagh caught a Cooleen high up on his face,
splitting his cheek. The man reeled away directly into his
brothers' two flailing sticks which caught him high across
his back and shoulders as he tried to duck away from them.

"Holy Mother . . ." he gibbered as the blow caught
him. "No more, boys. No more. I'm beaten."

But now the Mulvihills sensed victory and were in even
less of a mood to give quarter. Jack watched Michael steady
himself and then smash his shillelagh flat across the man's
forehead. He collapsed in a crumpled heap on the ground,
blood from his head wounds dripping on to the hard earth.
The fight was turning into a rout with the Cooleens fighting
desperately to get away from the market square.

The ground beneath their feet was growing slippery with
blood and it was becoming difficult to reach those Cooleens
who were now in full flight. Within minutes, the last twenty
Cooleens were surrounded by more than fifty Mulvihills.
Some sank to their knees, holding their shillelaghs over
their heads with both hands, trying to ward off the blows.
Others, stoically, offered no defense to their attackers, ready
to accept the inevitable battering that would send them into

unconsciousness. Like a pack of wolves, the Mulvihills bayed their cry of victory as they savaged their opponents.

"Mmmulvi . . . mmmulvi . . . mmmulvi." There were no answering cries except those of pain and panic and fear.

The three Keane brothers surrounded one Cooleen who crouched low on the ground, his arms wrapped around his head and neck for protection.

Suddenly the brothers were thrust apart as a man burst between them, pushing them away with surprising strength. Jack swung round, ready to attack the intruder.

"Jack, Jack," cried Michael. "Tis the Father."

Father O'Sullivan, thin and wiry with a shock of grey hair, burst his way through the Mulvihills to stand amongst the small group of Cooleens still upright. He held his arms outstretched, as if putting a protective mantle above the fallen men around him.

"That's enough, boys," he shouted. "Stop it, I say. That's enough."

His strong voice, surprisingly deep and resonant for such a thin man, rose above the hubbub. "Stop this slaughter," he exclaimed, spinning round and seeming to pierce every Mulvihill brain with his blazing eyes. "Can't you see they're finished? Mercy on them!"

Shillelaghs hung in mid-air as the Mulvihills looked to their leaders for instructions. Jack Keane saw his father and two men with him nod their assent.

"Right, boyos," cried Joe Keane. "That's enough. The Father's right. They're finished. Come away now."

The Mulvihills turned away, exhaustion making their shoulders slump as their nerves relaxed and the blood lust drained away. Jack Keane felt curiously tired and dispirited for a moment, but then a sense of victory swept over him.

He lifted his head and, with the others, shouted a last Mulvihill battlecry.

"Mmmulvi . . . mmmulvi . . . mmmulvi . . ."

The victors began walking back towards the coaching house, stepping carefully over their fallen opponents, until they came to their own injured. Already the fallen men's womenfolk had hurried from their places of safety to begin tending their wounds.

Listowel market square seemed strangely silent after the violent noise of the fight. It had seemed to go on for hours to those, like Jack, who'd been in the thick of it. In fact, the fight had lasted barely twenty minutes.

"Didn't I tell you?" exulted Joe Keane, slapping his youngest son on his back. "Didn't I say it'd be no more than a short spat. To be sure, it was."

Jack smiled and began to untie the white ribbon around his shillelagh. It was red with blood, some of it his own.

Jonathan Sandes and Dr. Peter Church stood at the window, their glasses still in their hands.

"The viciousness of them," whispered Church in awe. "They're just like wild animals."

"And so they are, Peter. Wild animals. But cunning, too. Did you see how those Cooleens got themselves trapped. Good tactics by the Mulvihills. Cunning and vicious, that's what they are."

The two men watched people from the coaching house throw buckets of water over the scores of men still lying on the ground. Some began sitting up, groaning, hands pressed against their bleeding wounds. A few lay still. The priest in his sweeping, black cassock hurried among these, kneeling to feel their pulses and pressing his ear against their chests to listen to their heart beats. He rose from his knees after a few seconds to move on to the next injured man, satisfied that in time they would recover their senses.

"I wonder if I should go and help," said Church, who treated patients in his apothecary shop.

"Wouldn't bother, Peter. The priest is very experienced in these things. He's done all there is to be done. They'll all soon be on their feet."

They began turning away from the window when Sandes stopped. "Look here for a moment. Perhaps I was too hasty."

Father O'Sullivan was making the sign of the cross above a man lying on the ground. Then he bent down and began whispering into the fallen man's ear. Two women hurried across to where the priest was, the elder wearing a black shawl.

"There's one even you can't help, I'm thinking, Peter," said Sandes, sipping his glass of wine. "If I'm not mistaken, the priest's giving him the last rites."

"Do you think he's dead?" asked Church.

Sandes said in a bored voice, "They can't all have thick skulls. Short as the fight was, there were some murderous blows struck."

"To be sure," agreed Church. "That's true, I suppose."

"Not even that unusual as you know," said Sandes, watching the scene in the square with callous disinterest. "There were three killed in that fight last year, you remember. Part of the hazards and that's the truth."

The woman with the black shawl had thrown herself across the man's body, her back heaving with sobs. A younger woman knelt by the priest, her head bent low, praying and crying at the same time. Her red shawl contrasted vividly with the black of the priest's soutane.

Sandes rubbed his hands together. "Now what about

lunch, Peter? Watching that fight's given me quite an appetite. I've a brace of pheasant for us."

Church moved reluctantly from the window. "It really ought to be stopped, you know, Jonathan. Men getting killed for nothing."

"It'll never be stopped. The peasants enjoy it too much. Personally, I think it's a thing to be encouraged."

In the coaching house, the Mulvihills were drinking their fill, retailing their parts in the battle to each other. Jack Keane was flushed with excitement after having had three large mugs of whiskey forced down him.

"That'll ease your pain, me boyo," boomed his father, slipping his arm around his son's shoulders and turning him to face the assembled Mulvihills.

"Now look at him, me bonny fighters. What a fighting man he's going to be with some more weight on him."

The assembled faction roared with approval and Jack felt himself blushing. He felt no pain from his bruised face and ribs, nor from his split knuckles. He was on top of the world, accepted as a man who'd acquitted himself well in his first faction fight.

"Well, what do you say now, young Jack?" asked Michael. "Twasn't as bad as all that."

"I thought we were for it."

"Ah, and didn't I say not to worry? We pulped those Cooleens and no mistake."

Jack moved to the doorway, his brother still with him. They watched the injured being helped away, limping on sticks, or with arms draped around their family's shoulders. Potmen from the inn were busy sloshing water over the square, clearing the patches of blood away.

"Isn't that your dancing girl over there, Jack?" said Michael, pointing up the square. "There, where Father

O'Sullivan is with that cart. You want to go and show her your wounds. It'll be mighty impressed she'll be and that's the truth.''

"Do you think so?"

"I'm sure so. Off you go, but not too long else we'll be carrying your dad home with all the whiskey he's supping."

Jack tucked his shillelagh under his arm and strolled across the square, trying to appear as nonchalant as possible. Brigid, with her red shawl and skirt, had her back to him and was helping Father O'Sullivan push something into the cart.

"Brigid, Brigid," he called as he neared them.

She turned slowly round. Her face was puffy and lined with tears.

"Brigid, what's wrong?" He hurried the last few steps to her side. She said nothing, just nodded her head towards the cart. Jack moved round to stand between her and Father O'Sullivan. He looked into the cart. Two bare legs, grimy and covered with dried blood, protruded from under a pile of sacking.

Jack turned in bewilderment. First to the priest, who merely shook his head sadly, and then to Brigid. "What? . . . Who? . . ." he mumbled.

"Me dad," said Brigid softly. "He's dead. The fight. It happened in the fight." She looked at Jack, tears welling in her eyes. "The fight," she repeated, beginning to sob. "His head . . . oh, his poor head."

Brigid moved a step toward him. Jack dropped his shillelagh and put his arms around her, feeling her tears on his bare chest. She cried quietly for a few moments, then looked up into Jack's face, noticing the bruised lump on his forehead. She stepped back and saw his hand bandaged with a kerchief. Then her eyes moved down his body to rest on the stained shillelagh lying at his feet.

She didn't move her eyes from the shillelagh. She seemed transfixed by it.

"You were in the fight, Jack Keane?" she asked quietly.

"Yes . . . but . . . but I didn't . . ."

"You can't be a Cooleen else I would have seen you," Brigid reasoned aloud to herself, slowly. "You're a Mulvihill."

"Yes . . . but . . ."

"You're a Mulvihill, Jack Keane," she repeated softly, her green eyes fixed wildly on the shillelagh lying on the ground between them. Then, suddenly, she raised her head and stared into his face. "You killed him!" she shrieked. "You killed me father." Brigid leapt at him and began scratching at his face and chest, sobbing uncontrollably. "You killed him . . . you . . . you . . ."

Jack tried to push her away but her demented strength was too much for him. He staggered back under her onslaught. "Brigid, it was the fight," he exclaimed, gripping her shoulders, trying to hold her away.

"Murderer!" she screeched. "Murderer!"

She spat into his face as Father O'Sullivan thrust himself between the two youngsters, forcing them apart.

Suddenly, her strength dissolved. She crumpled to the ground, crying uncontrollably, hiding her face in her hands.

Jack moved again to comfort her, wiping the spittle from his cheeks.

The priest restrained him gently. "Not now, son," he said quietly. "Not now. It'll do no good."

Jack nodded, understanding, and turned away. He walked slowly back toward his family at the inn, his mind filled with the sounds of grief.

Chapter 3
September, 1822

The sullen sky wept gently with rain. The keening notes of Michael Coffey's fiddle gave Gortacrossane the sound of mourning. The fiddler stood close by the rough walls of the Aherne cabin, his sodden felt hat jammed firmly over his head. Michael Coffey's eyes were fixed rheumily on the distance as he stroked the fiddle tucked under his chin, voicing the almost physical sense of bereavement that hung over the cabin. Sometimes he bowed his head in recognition as a woman, black shawl pulled tightly over her head, moved past him, ducking to enter the low doorway of the cabin. Coffey heard the low murmuring of voices within the cabin punctuated by frequent bouts of sobbing.

He had already been inside to pay his respects to the dead Cooleen. The women of the township had done their best to clean and hide his wounds by wrapping his head in bandages, but they had been unable to cover the dark bruises under his closed eyes. The Aherne women sat in a semi-circle before Tom Aherne's rough coffin, the daughters dry-eyed in their grief, trying to comfort their mother as she swayed and sobbed on the only high-backed chair in the cabin, clutching a cross intertwined with smooth rosary beads. Cooleen men would come with bottles tucked under their arms. Then the cabin would become raucous with noise and the fiddler would stop his laments and help dance Tom Aherne to his grave.

39

From his position outside the cabin, Michael Coffey noticed a movement by the wall of another cabin fifty yards away. A young man with a shock of black hair peered round the wall, and then emerged to walk slowly toward the Aherne cabin.

Jack Keane presented a sorry sight; his hair plastered to his skull; his clothes clinging like a second skin; mud spattering his calves and covering his bare feet. The memory of Brigid Aherne's contemptuous spittle running down his face while she screamed at him in the square after the faction fight still seared his brain.

His father had been sympathetic but firm in his advice. "Sure, Jack, and it's a terrible thing to have happened," he'd said as the Keane family ate their supper the previous evening. "Tis a real shame what with you being stuck on his wee girlie. But think if it was me in the box and not him. Would you like a Cooleen calling here to pay a respect? I doubt so. I really do. Better let time pass, I'm thinking."

Jack had put down his mug of milk and gazed into the peat fire. "But, Dad, if I don't go now, I'll never be able to ask her to walk with me. She needs comfort, doesn't she?"

He looked toward his mother for support. She nodded. "He's right, Joe. The wound between them will fester with time, not heal."

"I'll not be telling you what to do, Jack," said Joe Keane, rising from his chair and hitching his trousers round his belly with an air of finality. "Tis your life and your girl. Remember you're Mulvihill and she's Cooleen, no matter what. But you're a fighting man now, not a boy. Do what is in your mind and I pray you're right."

Jack spent a restless night trying to decide whether he should visit the Ahernes. The next morning the rest of the family restrained themselves from giving him further advice. They let him wander around doing his chores and then watched him move off across the fields toward Gortacrossane.

As Jack neared the Aherne cabin, Michael Coffey recognized him from the night at the Ballybunnion cross-roads, and remembered his link with the sorrowing wom-enfolk inside. He stopped playing and moved toward Jack. "Tis only women in there, lad," he said quietly, almost conspiratorially. "Are you sure tis the right time?" Too well he knew the ritual of a wake; first women to comfort, then men to cheer. It was always that way.

"No," muttered Jack. "No, but when is it the right time for me? I have to go now or not at all."

"Then let me help," said the fiddler as they approached the damp sacking hanging across the cabin doorway. "I'll come with you. That's only proper."

Jack nodded dully. Michael Coffey pulled the sacking aside and entered the cabin first.

The two men stood inside the doorway unnoticed. Jack wiped the rain off his face, not knowing where to look first. Inevitably, his eyes were drawn toward the coffin in the corner of the tiny cabin. He crossed himself quickly as he peered through the half-light, desperately hoping that he wouldn't recognize the dead man as one of those he'd fought in Listowel. He searched his memory, remembering again the upturned faces distorted with panic and agony. "Thanks be to God," he murmured almost inaudibly to himself as he realized that he hadn't seen the dead Cooleen before. His shillelagh had not killed Brigid's father. Of that he was certain.

Jack's eyes moved away from the coffin and met those of the womenfolk. Two young girls sat on the earth floor looking at him curiously. They'd be May and Mary, he thought. His gaze flicked across Brigid's face, noting her surprised expression, to her elder sisters, Theresa and

Bernadette. They looked at him suspiciously as they crouched on the floor by their mother. Mrs. Aherne was bent over her rosary beads.

Brigid was the first to move. She rose from a wooden stool and crossed the cabin in half-a-dozen strides. She stood before Jack looking up into his face. "Why did you let him in, fiddler?" she asked Michael Coffey quietly, never once moving her eyes from Jack.

The fiddler shuffled nervously. "He just came. I said it wasn't time. I did say, to be sure. But he came."

"Well?" asked Brigid, still staring at Jack, pain and bewilderment in her dark-ringed eyes.

"I had to," he explained softly. "I just had to, Brigid." He looked over her shoulder at the coffin. "I'm terribly sorry. So are we all."

"Yes?"

"I had to tell you that now. We're all sorry." Jack saw a mistiness coming into Brigid's eyes. He leaned slightly toward her. "What can I do?"

"There's nothing." A tear formed at the corner of her right eye and began trickling down her cheek. "Nothing at all anyone can do. It's done, isn't it?"

"Brigid," Mrs. Aherne spoke without looking up. Her voice was low and flat. "Who is it here?"

Brigid half-turned away from Jack, her red skirt brushing his legs. "Tis the fiddler and Jack."

"Your young Jack? The one at the market? Bring him here for his respect then. And give the fiddler a mug."

Jack walked slowly across the cabin to stand before the coffin. "Rest in God, Tom Aherne."

"Amen," murmured Mrs. Aherne vacantly. Her eyes were red from weeping. "Thank you for coming, young Jack," she said, glancing quickly up at him. "It wouldn't be easy, I know. And don't be blaming yourself for it. We're not blaming anyone. Not even your man there." She nodded toward her dead husband.

Her daughters huddled closer to her as Jack returned to the doorway. He felt as if a great weight had been lifted from him.

The fiddler drained his mug of poteen and placed it back gently on the rough table. "All done, lad?"

"Done," said Jack, beginning to pull aside the sacking of the doorway.

Ten days later, Jack Keane, stripped to the waist, was rebuilding part of a dry-stone wall round the potato field near his family's cabin. In the warm midday sun he picked up the large stones which had fallen to the ground and fitted them back into place, stuffing in lumps of turf to make the wall secure before the fierce winter winds came off the Atlantic. It was a job he enjoyed. He worked steadily away, whistling to himself. It was some minutes before he realized he was being watched. He looked up and there was Brigid Aherne leaning on her elbows on the other side of the wall.

"Sure and aren't we busy now?" she smiled, her head cupped in her hands. "Perhaps too busy for someone who's walked all this way to see him."

Jack grabbed at his shirt, reddening with confusion. "How long have you been there?"

"Long enough to feel I'm being ignored."

"Wait. I'll come over."

Jack vaulted over the wall, brushing his hands together to rid them of the dirt from the stones and turf. "Tis glad I am you came."

Brigid plumped herself on to the ground, resting her back against the wall. She smoothed out the folds of her red skirt and looked up at Jack with an inviting smile. "Well, don't just stand there. Sit down." She patted the turf beside her.

"I've been thinking of you, Brigid," said Jack as he sat beside her. He looked closely at her. He saw that her eyes were once again clear and bright. "You look fine. Just fine."

"Well, life has to go on. Me dad's buried and that's that."

"I thought you were never going to see me again. After the fight you said . . ."

"I know. I am sorry for what I said, Jack." She reached out a hand.

Jack took it and gently squeezed. "Forget it now."

"Father O'Sullivan told me what I said. I don't remember at all. I must have gone half mad. I'm sorry."

"Tis over. How's your mam now?"

"She misses me dad badly. She was always going at him when he was here and now that he's away she misses him. I suppose that's the way of love, isn't it?"

"Sure and it is."

"But she's over the worst of it; and so are we all."

Brigid giggled suddenly, spreading her free hand over her mouth. "Truth, you should have been at the wake, Jack. That was fierce. I think the men were drunk for two days and me mam wasn't much better. Two of them fell in the dung heap and and nobody knew they were there until the next day. And then the fiddler's dog went and cocked his leg over the coffin."

She laughed out loud at Jack's shocked expression.

"You silly. Me dad would have enjoyed the joke looking down on it all. I just hope he had a bottle with him to join in."

Jack smiled. "Tis good to see you laughing."

"And why not, pray? We've cried enough."

"But how are you going to live now," Jack asked anxiously, "with you dad gone?"

"Well, the Cooleens gathered up some money for me

mam. Nearly three pounds, they did. It'll keep us for some months at least.''

"And then?"

"We'll see. Us girls can keep the potato patch going. That'll give us food and the Cooleen money will pay the rent.''

"That's a relief for a bit then," Jack said happily. "I feel better for you.''

"Just better?" Brigid whispered, glancing down at her hand still clasped in his. "You feel just better? And don't you remember the crossroads, you big lummock?"

"I do that, Brigid.''

They smiled at each other. Brigid leaned towards him. Jack released her hand and put his arm round her shoulders, pulling her to his chest. He felt her breath on his skin where his shirt was unbuttoned.

"You smell nice," she breathed against him. "All warm and nice.''

"And you feel nice," he muttered into the ringlets of her hair. "All soft and round and nice.''

"Do I, Jack?" Brigid raised her head and looked up at him.

They gazed deeply into each other's eyes. Jack felt himself tremble as their faces were drawn towards each other. Their lips met, softly at first, then harder. Brigid's mouth opened under the pressure and Jack felt the tip of her warm tongue push between his teeth, gently exploring. They kissed until they were breathless, Brigid's eyes looking hugely into his. They were like green pools of Erin fire.

For long moments they gazed at each other. Then Brigid moved her head back on to his chest. "There," was all she said. And then again, "There.''

The two youngsters rested against the wall, warmed by the sun and their love, both too happy to speak.

"I always knew this would be." Brigid's quiet, wondering voice broke the silence. "Ever since I first saw you, I just knew."

"When I ducked you in the sea?"

"No. No, long before that."

Jack started with surprise, pushing Brigid slightly away from him and turning her face to him. "Before that?" he asked.

Brigid smiled mischievously. "Oh, a year or so. Ever since I saw you with your mam and dad at market. It took a time to find your name, that it did."

He grabbed her shoulders, feeling their firmness under her green blouse. A broad grin spread over his even features. "You little divil! You . . ."

"Now aren't you glad, Jack Keane?" she interrupted. "You said you didn't mind being trapped."

Jack threw back his head and laughed. "Trapped? That I am, but I'm wondering who trapped who?"

"We both did, didn't we?" said Brigid gently, putting her arms around his neck. "And it's not bad. Tell me it's not bad."

"No, not at all."

They kissed again. But this time it was a different embrace. There was a sureness about it, a certainty. It was a kiss that sealed a bond as yet unspoken. They both knew that now their lives and loves were committed.

Jack pulled away first and stood up.

Brigid pouted, "You're tired of me already then?"

"No, but I'm thinking you must be as hungry as me. Come to our cabin and eat. I'm sure me mam will have enough for you."

He offered her his hands and, as she took them, pulled her to her feet.

"Are you sure it'll be all right with your mam and dad?" asked Brigid.

"I'm sure, mavourneen." Jack savored the endearment. "Mavourneen Brigid," he repeated.

"Avourneen Jack," she whispered, smiling at him.

Together, hands clasped, they strolled towards the Keane cabin. Jack's mother was putting some washing over the cabin wall to dry and realized that her son was with the girl Cooleen. They made a handsome couple, she thought proudly. At the same moment she knew a strange sadness. Her youngest child was now grown up, she realized, and the long parting had begun.

Mistress Keane went forward and stood before Brigid. "Welcome, little one."

Tentatively, she bent forward and kissed the girl's cheek, noting the happiness shining in her eyes. She felt a twinge of envy, remembering suddenly when she'd first been in love with Joe Keane. She took Brigid's free hand and led her into the cabin.

Jack's father and brothers soon warmed to Brigid's infectious gaiety. By the time they'd finished their meal there was an unspoken but complete acceptance that here was a new member of the family.

Eventually, Michael, a broad grin on his face, spoke the words that were in everyone's thoughts. "I'm thinking, Mam, we'll need feeding up like this through the winter if we're to build a new cabin in the spring."

He looked directly at Jack and Brigid. "If that's not too long a time, that is."

The family laughed as they saw the two youngsters blush beet red. The small cabin was filled with happiness.

* * *

The winter winds howling off the pounding Atlantic transformed West Kerry into a bleak wilderness. People huddled around their peat fires, only half warm, as the relentless wind found every chink in the walls and windows. They rarely ventured out, hibernating like squirrels and living on the meagre supplies of potatoes and corn they'd managed to harvest during the summer and autumn. Their animals spent the winter inside the cabins too, bringing some precious warmth along with the pungent smell of fresh dung. To survive was enough. Sickly babies and frail old folk died from pneumonia and were buried with little ceremony in shallow graves hacked from the frozen earth. Those families which ran out of food begged handfuls of corn from their neighbors and searched potato patches for any leftover lumpers. Even wrapped in sacking, they froze to their bones as they scrabbled with stafans—large bent hoes—in deserted fields under the fast-moving, grey clouds from the west that brought biting rain or flurries of snow. By St. Stephen's Day, the workhouse in Listowel was crowded to overflowing with families who had given up the struggle. Here, at least, was warmth and a daily chunk of bread and a bowl of thin gruel. Their deserted cabins were soon torn apart by the ever-searching wind.

For Jonathan Sandes, the winter was an equally difficult time. Rents went unpaid and he had either to reprieve families at a properly burdensome rate of interest on their arrears, or condemn them, with the workhouse full, to a makeshift home in a ditch with an inadequate roof made from branches covered with sods of turf. Thus it was, in early January, 1823, that the plight of the Aherne womenfolk came to his notice. Jonathan Sandes sat at a desk by a crackling log fire in the study of his home at Listowel hearing the weekly report from his rent collector, Finn Bowler.

"Tis my opinion, sir, that we shall get no more rent from them," said Bowler, a stout figure in heavy, rough tweeds. "I'm believing we should have had them out after their man died in last year's fight."

"Is that so, Bowler?" said Sandes, his voice drawling with sarcasm and mulled wine. "And, pray, would we not have aroused some wrath if we'd done that? I'd have had the Whiteboys through my front door and no mistake. What grounds would we have had for putting them in the ditch? The Cooleen's woman was able to pay her quarter's rent."

"Well, that's not the case now, sir. They've no money, precious little food, and no prospect of getting either when spring comes. I'm thinking we should cut our losses."

Sandes drained his pewter mug and poured himself some more wine. He rose from his desk a trifle unsteadily and walked over to the fireplace, picking up a glowing poker which had been thrust into the burning wood. This he pushed into his mug of wine with a sizzle. As he did so, he reflected yet again on the harshness of Irishman to Irishman. The peasants call me heartless and cruel, he thought, and yet here's one of their own, a man only marginally higher in station than them, who'd be as ruthless as any land agent. The peasants were their own worst enemies, he reckoned. Squabbling among themselves, killing each other, betraying one another. What chance did they have? But what if they united against a common enemy? The thought made Jonathan Sandes shiver inwardly even in the sweating warmth of his study.

"So that's what you think should be done, Bowler?" he said aloud as he resumed his seat behind his desk.

"It is, sir. It is."

Sandes looked at him curiously as he stood before him, perspiring in the heat of the fire. Bowler's judgment was usually correct. The rent collector drew on the cunning that had carried him unscathed through the wars against Bonaparte.

"I just wonder, Bowler. Remind me, how many there are?"

"The mother, sir, and five strapping girls. One of them is set to jump over the broom in the spring with a lad from Drombeg, so it's really only four."

"A marriage, eh? And the lad's family can't help?"

"Tis Joe Keane's boy, sir. The Keanes have little enough to spare, as you know. They've only just paid off the gombeen man."

Jonathan Sandes smiled blearily at Bowler. "Well then, we shall have to do something, won't we? The first fine day and we'll ride out there together and have a look at this gaggle of women."

Four days later, Sandes, astride his favorite bay hunter, trotted among the battered and sorry-looking cabins of Gortacrossane. His high-crowned, silver-grey riding hat perfectly matched his thick coat. His brown leather boots gleamed with polish.

Finn Bowler, beside him on a shaggy, ungroomed horse that had seen better years, pointed out the Aherne cabin. "Shall you be going in, sir?" inquired Bowler, his breath whitening on the sunny but still cold air.

Sandes raised a pained eyebrow. "In there, Bowler?" He pointed disdainfully with his riding crop. "Indeed not. Call the women out."

Finn Bowler sidled his horse as near to the doorway as he could and, bending in the saddle, shouted into the cabin. "Mistress Aherne. Tis Bowler here. I have Master Sandes with me. Will you be coming out now, woman?"

The two men heard a sudden chatter of female voices. A few moments later the sacking across the doorway was pulled aside and Mrs. Aherne appeared, a black shawl over her head. She stood, her arms folded across her, gazing up at the men high on their horses. She'd been expecting this call ever since she'd told Finn Bowler that she was unable to pay the next quarter's rent. One by one, her daughters stepped through the doorway behind her, all muffled against the cold, their faces pinched and grey from lack of food and warmth. Jonathan Sandes surveyed them with distaste.

"Well, Mistress Aherne," he said coldly, "and what are we going to do about this rent you're owing?"

"I don't know, sir," she replied quietly, after a moment's hesitation. "It has been terrible hard since me man was killed last year. The girls have done their best . . ."

"But not well enough, I fear," interrupted Sandes. "The rent must be paid, you know, if you're to stay on. Sir James is most clear on that point."

"Sir, things will be better when the winter is over. We'll plant the patch and have a few things to sell at market."

"Perhaps so, Mrs. Aherne. Perhaps. But until then, what? How's the rent coming?"

"Can't you wait until next quarter, sir?" Mistress Aherne asked desperately.

Sandes smiled without the least warmth in his expression. "If it was me, Mistress Aherne . . . if it was only me . . . but Sir James would have my hide. Let you off with the rent and they'd all want the same. You must see my position."

"I don't know, sir. I just don't know," she whispered, her eyes lowered. She was near tears as she searched her mind for some way to postpone the inevitable sentence of eviction.

"Can't your daughters find other work?"

"They've tried, sir, but there's none. No one has any money to spare."

Sandes looked more closely at the girls standing protectively by their mother. Two were too young, two looked old before their time, but the fifth . . . now that's the prize of the litter, he thought, as he noted Brigid's fine beauty. He pointed his crop at her. "You, girl, step forward."

Brigid's green eyes flicked up at him defiantly. Mistress Aherne turned and gave her daughter a push. Reluctantly, she moved out of the group and stood by Sandes' horse.

The land agent looked down at her. A pretty one this, he decided, with a good spirit as well. An idea began forming in his mind. "Can't she find service in a house?" he asked Mistress Aherne, looking over Brigid's head.

"But, sir, Brigid's getting wed in the spring."

"Well? She has a few months to wait. Time enough to work if she wants to keep the cabin."

Mistress Aherne didn't reply.

Sandes spoke directly to Brigid. "Do you want to work, girl?"

"Yes, sir," Brigid said quietly. "I'll work . . . but where?"

Sandes made up his mind. It would solve the problem. "There's a girl needed in my kitchens. You'll get food and somewhere to sleep. Work for a full quarter and I'll reckon the rent on the cabin is paid. What do you say?"

She looked round at her mother, a mute appeal on her face. Mistress Aherne dropped her eyes to the ground and shrugged her shoulders. Brigid turned her head slowly and gazed up at the land agent. "All right, sir," she said resignedly. "If working for you is the only way, then I'll work."

"Good. That's settled then. Come to the kitchens on Monday."

"Yes, sir."

"A good girl you've got there, Mistress Aherne," Sandes

called as he took up his horse's reins again. "She'll do you credit, I'm sure."

Brigid's mother nodded dumbly. Tears were running down her full cheeks. As Sandes and Finn Bowler trotted away, Brigid ran into her mother's arms. "Twas the only way," sobbed Mistress Aherne. "The only way."

Brigid Aherne arrived in Listowel just as the first grey January light was breaking the darkness. The streets of the small town were completely deserted. Everywhere there was the eerie silence that preceded a new day.

The castle ruins, picked out in the dull light, looked more foreboding than usual. It was hard now to imagine that once, near the end of the thirteenth century, the castle had been all there was of the town. That'd been when the all-conquering Norman family of Fitzmaurice, the Lords of Kerry, had started the construction to protect the strategic ford across the River Feale.

At her ditch school, Brigid had learned something of the violent history of the North Kerry plain; how it had once been inhabited by a Celtic people called the Alltraighe, later to be known as the O'Connors; how learned monks had built an abbey at Rattoo, nine miles from Listowel, fortified against the Norsemen who raided and plundered from their settlements along the Shannon, until the Normans had arrived and overwhelmed the native populace in their turn.

For the Kerry people, like most Celtic Irish, it had been a history of raid and rape, conquest upon conquest, death and terror at the hands of alien races. And finally, of course, it had been the English who conquered all.

Sir Charles Wilmot, for Queen Elizabeth the First, had besieged Listowel Castle in the winter of 1600, taking it after a month from the rebellious descendants of the Normans. They, and their native Kerry supporters, dozens of them, had been hanged from the parapets, dangling till their flesh had been picked to the bone by grateful carrion. The thought of that time, the awful images, made Brigid shiver even more in the sharp cold of the morning.

She stood in the market square, gazing round, apprehensive. Her feet in Loipins, soleless stockings, were frozen nearly solid from her two-mile trudge over frost-hardened tracks and fields. She walked down an alley by the side of Jonathan Sandes' house and saw the glow of an oil lamp in a basement window. She went down three steps and knocked at the kitchen door, timidly at first and then harder. After some minutes Brigid heard bare feet padding up to the door, bolts being drawn, and a key turning. The door was opened by a girl with long, dark hair, not much older than herself, dressed only in a white shift that emphasized the plumpness of her body. Her voice was full of sleep.

"So what are you wanting this early in the morning?"

"I'm to work here," Brigid said nervously.

"Oh, the new girl, is it? Well, come in quickly. Tis perishing I am with no clothes on." The dark-haired girl beckoned Brigid inside and locked the door behind her.

"What's your name then?"

"Tis Brigid Aherne."

"Welcome then, Brigid. My name's Finoola Gaughan. I'm thinking you're to work in the kitchens with me."

"That's what Master Sandes said." Brigid shivered with cold.

"Here now," said Finoola. "Here's me blathering on about being perished and sure you must be real frozen. Come into the warmth. I've just lit the range."

The sight of the kitchen took Brigid's breath away. She had never seen anything so luxurious before. It was the size of her family's small cabin with a long wooden table and chairs and a cooking range running almost the length of one wall. By the range was a rocking chair filled with cushions.

"Well, sit yourself down and have a warm, Brigid," said Finoola as she went to the range and dipped her finger in a large bowl of water which was warming over the range.

Brigid moved toward the rocking chair. She'd never sat in such a chair in all her life.

"Not that one," said Finoola sharply. "Only the cook, Mistress Stack, sits there. Pull up one of the others."

"Is Mistress Stack . . . ?"

"No. She's not up yet. She sleeps the sleep of a good widow woman, that she does. And the master and mistress were out hunting with the O'Mahony yesterday so they'll not be rising yet awhile."

"What is it I have to do, Finoola?" asked Brigid.

"Just warm yourself for now. Mistress Stack will tell you herself. Humping water from the pump in the square, cleaning dishes and pans, carrying food to the dining room, and such like." Finoola went on, smiling mischievously, "There's one or two other duties but you'll be learning about them soon enough."

"Where do I sleep? Do you know?"

"There's a room in the attic for us. Tis quite cosy enough. Warmer than the cabin you're coming from, I'm thinking."

"It couldn't be any colder," Brigid conceded with a smile.

"Good. Tis glad I am you're smiling. We'll get on well enough, I'm sure."

Brigid spent her first day in a welter of bewildering activity. Mistress Stack, a tiny, dried-up woman with a sharp tongue, ordered her from this task to that. She watched wide-eyed as meals that were feasts to her were cooked and carried upstairs without any comment. That evening she tasted beef for the first time in her life as Mistress Stack carved at the remains of the joint left at dinner by Jonathan Sandes and his wife. By the time she'd finished eating, she was almost asleep in her chair with exhaustion.

"To bed, girl," ordered Mistress Stack, a slightly friendlier tone in her voice. "You've had a hard first day. I made it like that so that you would know that although we have warm beds and full bellies here, we have to work for them. You're a lucky girl being here. And don't you be forgetting it. Now off you go with Finoola."

The two girls climbed four flights of narrow back stairs to their room with Finoola lighting the way with a smoking candle. The room was tiny with a low, sloping ceiling and a small uncurtained window.

Finoola unbuttoned her skirt, letting it fall carelessly to the floor, and shrugged off her blouse. Then she lifted the hem of her white shift and pulled it over her head. Without a trace of embarrassment she stood naked before Brigid for a moment and then climbed under the blankets. "Come on then, Brigid," she said quietly, patting the bed beside her. "'Tis cold here without you."

Brigid had never undressed before a stranger in her life. She turned her back to Finoola as she quickly pulled off her blouse and dropped her skirt. She blew out the candle on the windowsill before getting into bed. She'd often slept with her sisters but the feel of a strange, warm body against hers was different, somehow exciting. Finoola put her arms round her and pulled her close. Brigid, to her surprise, realized that Finoola's nipples were erect as they pushed against her breasts. She tried to move away but there was little spare room in the narrow bed. Brigid felt Finoola's breath against her cheek.

"A goodnight kiss, little one?" whispered Finoola,

pressing her lips against Brigid's, moving her hands caressingly down her back toward her firm buttocks. Brigid could feel her bed companion trembling against her. Finoola's lips pressed insistently on hers and her tongue prised open Brigid's mouth and darted between her teeth. She tried to push Finoola away with her knees, but the dark-haired girl gripped one firmly between her legs and began pressing down on it rhythmically.

Brigid pulled her face away with an effort. "What are you doing, Finoola?" she gasped.

"Just a cuddle, little one. Just a goodnight cuddle," Finoola crooned in her ear.

"Well, I'm tired out. Go to sleep," said Brigid, pulling out of Finoola's grasp and turning her back on her.

"All right," sulked Finoola. "But it's sure I am that your pretty body wants a proper cuddle."

The last thing Brigid heard before sleep overwhelmed her was Finoola's voice speaking to no one in particular. "And so innocent too. Master Sandes made a proper fine choice in her."

When Brigid awoke the next morning she didn't recognize her new surroundings. She gazed at the ceiling and wondered why it wasn't thatched. And then she remembered where she was.

"I bet you were thinking you were still in your mam's cabin," whispered Finoola beside her, noticing Brigid's confused expression.

"I was that." She felt Finoola's arms encircle her, her hands gently squeezing her breasts.

"And isn't this a sight more comfy?" murmured Finoola, her caresses becoming more urgent.

In her half-wakened state, Brigid felt a warmth inside her that she'd never known before. She pressed her back against Finoola and shivered slightly as her companion's hand wandered over her body. She could stay like this for ever, she thought dreamily to herself. Then Finoola's hands slipped between her thighs and tried to push them apart.

"What are you doing?" Brigid asked angrily, pushing the intrusive hands away and sitting upright in the bed.

"Just warming you," said Finoola softly.

"Well, you can stop it," cried Brigid angrily, now fully awake.

"Oh, don't say you didn't like it," muttered Finoola crossly. "Look at those." She reached up and tweaked Brigid's firm-pointed breasts.

Brigid blushed in the half-light as she realized that the caresses had excited her. She jumped out of bed and pulled on her skirt and blouse. "I'll see you in the kitchen," she muttered to Finoola as she left the attic room in some confusion.

In the days that followed neither girl mentioned the incident again although Brigid took to sleeping fully-clothed, much to Finoola's annoyance. After the strange-ness of her surroundings wore off, Brigid began to enjoy her work. She wasn't allowed to serve meals in the dining room yet but Mistress Stack, recognizing her interest, began to give her little hints about cooking and even allowed her to do simple jobs at the range like par-boiling potatoes or frying eggs. Her relations with Finoola were easy enough outside the confines of their shared room and the two girls discovered they had a deal in common. Finoola, too, was in service because her father had met an untimely death from pneumonia. Her mother and younger brother and sister remained in their cabin at Shanacool, near Listowel, simply because Finoola worked for the land agent. Brigid learned that, like Finoola, she would be allowed one free day each month when she could visit her home. She began counting the days until she would see Jack and her family again.

One morning, three weeks after she'd joined the household, she entered the kitchen to find Mistress Stack hard at work on her own. The cook was wrapping cuts of beef and ham, pies and cakes, in muslin cloth and packing them in a large wicker hamper.

"Tis the mistress going away," she explained to Brigid. "Her sister in Cork has been brought down ill so the mistress will be off visiting for a few days. You can give me a hand."

Together they had the hamper of provisions ready in time for Finn Bowler to carry it, puffing and blowing under its weight, to the daily stage coach that trundled the rutted tracks between Limerick, Listowel, and Cork.

After saying goodbye to his wife, Jonathan Sandes worked in his study and ate alone, served, as usual, by Finoola. Brigid was doing the dishes when Finoola told her that she was to serve a meal that evening for the first time.

"Master Sandes wants to know how much you've learned," Finoola said, a quiet smile playing around her mouth. "Oh, not to worry, I'll be here to help you. And, by the by, the master says you've got to bathe this afternoon and put on some of my clean clothes before serving him."

"Why should that be?" asked Brigid.

"He wants you looking your best, I'm thinking." Finoola put her arm round Brigid's shoulders and squeezed affectionately. "Twas the same with me when I started here. You'll be all right."

That afternoon, while Mistress Stack was resting in her room, the two girls filled as many pans as they could with water and heated them on the range. Finoola dragged a tin hip-bath into the kitchen and began filling it with warm water. Brigid watched in amazement. She'd heard about people bathing in such things but she'd assumed they were only used by the very rich. Until now, washing in cold rain water had been good enough for her and her sisters.

Finoola tested the water with her finger and added a little cold water. "Now that's about right," she announced. "In you get, little one, and I'll be bringing some towels and fresh clothes."

Brigid undressed and stepped gingerly into the bath. Steaming water slopped over on to the wooden floor as she lowered herself into an awkward and uncomfortable sitting position. Finoola returned to the kitchen with her arms full of clothes and towels.

"Holy Mother of God. You look as though you're being tortured," she laughed, seeing the worried expression on Brigid's face as she sat stiffly in the bath covering her breasts with her hands. "Relax, little one. The water won't hurt you. Here, I'll soap your back and then you can wash yourself."

Finoola leaned over the hip-bath, splashing Brigid with the warm water, and then rubbed soap over her smooth back, working her hand in a circular motion. Brigid sighed as a delicious feeling of relaxation spread over her. She smiled gratefully up at Finoola.

"Tis nice indeed, this bathing."

"You look all pink and fresh—like a new-peeled prawn, that you do," smiled Finoola, standing back and looking admiringly at Brigid. "Now to make you smell sweet as well." She produced a small glass vial from a pocket in her skirt, uncorked it, and sprinkled the contents into the bath.

"A touch of the mistress' perfume," she explained. "She won't miss it and it'll remind the master of her when he smells it on you."

"Won't he be angry?"

Finoola looked pityingly at her. "So beautiful you are and so innocent." She shrugged as she picked up a towel.

"Still, it's none of my business. Here, out you get and dry yourself."

That evening Mistress Stack cooked a meal of roast mutton with dumplings and roasted potatoes. Finoola showed Brigid how to lay out the table in the dining room; the way to uncork a bottle of claret; and the correct procedure for serving the meal.

"The master'll do his own carving of the meat but you'll have to give him his vegetables and then wait outside the door while he eats," she instructed Brigid. "When he's finished, he'll ring his little bell and you clear away and serve the pudding and then wait outside again. That's all there is to it. Then he'll expect you to take him his brandy and baccy later on."

Jonathan Sandes greeted Brigid with a long, admiring look when she carried in the covered meat platter. The white blouse she'd borrowed from Finoola emphasized the raven blackness of her hair; the green skirt matched her eyes almost exactly; and a wide, buckled belt showed off her slim roundness.

"Welcome to the dining room, Brigid," he said, pointing to the space on the table where the platter had to go. "You're looking a sight better than when I last saw you. It shows you what good food, hard work and a warm bed will do, eh?"

Brigid merely nodded.

"Come along girl. Lost your pretty tongue?"

"No, sir."

"Good."

Sandes lifted the cover off the platter and sniffed the aroma rising from the mutton.

"Just the meat to build a man's strength, eh, Brigid?" he smiled.

He didn't speak to her again until he'd finished his meal and was halfway through his second bottle of claret.

"Wait fifteen minutes, Brigid," he ordered. "And then serve me in my dressing room upstairs. Finoola will tell you where."

When Brigid reached the kitchen, she found that Finoola had already prepared a tray carrying a decanter of brandy, a bowl of tobacco, a clay churchwarden pipe, and two crystal glasses.

"Two glasses?" Brigid asked. "But the mistress is away."

"The master will probably offer you a glass," said Finoola, a strained, curt note in her voice. "He usually gives me one when he's on his own. And it's no good refusing him because he'll be insisting you drink with him."

Brigid walked carefully up the stairs, balancing the tray, and knocked quietly on the brown mahogany door. Sandes swung it open, looming over her, dressed now in a long, dark green dressing gown with quilted lapels. He stood aside to let Brigid squeeze past him with the tray. The drawing room was lit by two candles, casting flickering shadows over the heavy maroon curtains and the two easy chairs in the room. Through a second door, Brigid glimpsed the bedroom, looking rosy and warm from the wood fire she guessed was burning in the grate. She placed the tray on a low table and turned to leave.

"Not so fast, little Brigid," said Sandes sharply. "You have two glasses on the tray so I'm guessing Finoola has told you I like my serving girl to take a drink with me before retiring." He lifted the stopper off the decanter and poured out two large glasses. He handed one to Brigid. "Take this and sit down."

Brigid huddled back in the upholstered chair furthest away from Sandes.

"Have you ever tasted brandy, Brigid?" he asked, trying to inject a trace of gentleness into his normally sharp voice.

"No, sir," she whispered. "But I have sipped a little poteen."

"Well, drink your glass then. This is much better than that cabin-brewed poison."

She smelled the sweet brandy fumes before she tasted the amber liquid. It warmed her stomach quickly without burning her throat like poteen. "Tis good, sir," she agreed.

"Good? That's the finest French brandy, Brigid. Good?" he repeated jocularly. "Tis the very best." He hovered over her, filling her glass to the brim again. Brigid tried to stop him but he brushed her protesting hand away. He put his glass down and moved his chair nearer to Brigid's.

"I hear good reports of your work, Brigid," he said expansively. "From the way you served table tonight you've not been idle. I can always tell a girl who'll learn to her advantage."

"Thank you, sir," said Brigid, gulping a large mouthful of brandy in her surprise at the unexpected sincerity in the compliment. Master Sandes could be quite pleasant, she thought. She found his face slipping a little out of focus. The room was terribly hot all of a sudden, she noticed. She wiped her hand across her brow.

"Anything the matter, Brigid?" inquired Sandes, anxiety apparent in his voice.

"Just a little dizzy, sir. Tis the heat in this room."

"Well, come and lie down next door. You'll be better soon."

"No, sir," protested Brigid, trying to struggle from the depths of the chair. "I'll get to my bed."

"I insist, Brigid. Remember I'm your master. I know best."

Sandes rose from his chair and lifted Brigid around her waist as if she weighed nothing.

"Put me down," she cried, twisting in his arms. "Put me down."

Despite her efforts, he carried her easily into the bedroom and sat on the four-poster bed. Brigid, now thoroughly alarmed, prepared for a further struggle, but, to her surprise, he moved away from her toward the door.

"Now just lie down and have a rest, little Brigid," he said quietly. "Don't be alarmed. I'll be next door."

He left the bedroom, shutting the door behind him. Brigid fell back across the bed and giggled to herself. She'd been prepared for the worst and now she was alone on the most comfortable bed she'd ever lain in. She gazed into the flames of the roaring fire in the grate for a few moments, her head still spinning, then fell into a deep sleep.

Next door, Jonathan Sandes, still smiling, poured himself another brandy.

Soon there came a low knock on the door. It opened slowly and Finoola came into the room. "Where is she?" she whispered.

Sandes put a finger over his lips and pointed at the closed bedroom door. Finoola nodded and tiptoed over to his chair. She looked down at him for a moment and then bent and kissed him on the lips. Sandes grasped her round her waist, pulling her on to his knee.

"Have you . . . ?" Finoola breathed in his ear.

"Not yet. The drink got to her too quickly. She's mighty innocent, is little Brigid."

"So was I once."

"But not any more, eh, Finoola?" murmured Sandes, fondling her breasts through the thin blouse and kissing her.

Finoola pulled away and stood up. She unbuttoned her blouse quickly and let it slip off her shoulders. Then she unbuckled the belt round her waist to allow her skirt to fall to the carpet. She stood naked before him, caressing her full breasts with her hands, smiling down at him. Sandes half-rose from the chair to untie the sash of his dressing gown. Finoola knelt between his thighs, running her short finger-nails over his bare chest. Then, with deft fingers, she opened the waist of his grey breeches, lifting his swollen manhood into the flickering candlelight. She rested her head on his thigh, her long hair falling over his flat stomach, as she caressed and kissed him. He moaned with pleasure.

"Next door," he gasped. "Let's go next door."

Sandes stood up and took off his dressing gown. His open breeches fell to his knees. "Get her prepared," he muttered thickly. "Don't worry, you vixen. There's enough for both of you."

Brigid was still fast asleep as Finoola entered the bedroom. She scarcely felt practiced hands opening her blouse and slipping off her skirt. Brigid murmured once in her dreams and that was all. Sandes stood by the bed as Finoola caressed the sleeping girl. His excitement hardened as he looked at the two young, naked bodies lying close together on the bed. He could bear it no longer.

"Is she ready?" he whispered to Finoola.

Finoola's insistent hands wandered over Brigid's smooth thighs, parting them gently. Brigid began to stir under the pressure, coming out of her sleep. She tried to sit up as she felt her legs jerked firmly apart, but the weight of Jonathan Sandes pinned her to the bed. Her eyes looked wildly into his face, distorted with passion. Her mouth opened to scream but Finoola's hand clamped across her lips. She tried to beat Sandes away with her fists only to find her arms held by the wrists as he began to thrust into her. She tried to twist away but was held fast. Suddenly, she moaned as she felt a sharp pain between her legs and then Sandes was in her and the pain had dulled. His body pushed her thighs achingly wider than they'd ever been. He pumped urgently into her. She moaned in anguish as she saw Finoola next to her watching with wild excitement in her eyes, fingers busy between her own thighs.

Brigid thought she was being torn in half. She could feel Sandes quickening his plunging strokes. Then he stiffened above her, groaning deep in his throat. Brigid's insides flooded with pulsing liquid warmth and then there was only blackness as she fainted.

Brigid regained her senses to find herself still in the four-poster bed. Finoola was cradling her in her arms, an expression of relief mingled with concern on her face. For a moment Brigid couldn't remember what had happened but then the aching soreness of her limbs brought it all back to her. "Oh, God," she sobbed. "He's taken me. The bastard divil has taken me."

"Hush, Brigid," crooned Finoola, feeling her companion's tears on her skin. "Tisn't the end of the world. It happened to me as well . . ."

"You . . . you . . . you helped him, you did," Brigid complained bitterly, heaving with sobs.

"If I hadn't it would have been even worse for you," said Finoola matter of factly, no trace of contrition in her voice. "He was much rougher with me."

"But you were enjoying it."

"So will you one day."

"Never. Never. Help me get dressed and out of this divil's house," Brigid pleaded, sitting up on the bed.

"And, sure, and what good will that do?"

"I have to get away."

"If you leave it'll be the worse for your family."

"But I'm getting wed in a few months to me Jack."

"Who'd have you as a bride now, little one," said Finoola coldly. "I don't want to hurt you but there's no mistaking that."

"Oh, Holy Mother of God. Why? . . . . Why? . . ." Brigid sobbed into the bed. She turned and looked directly at Finoola. "Is there nothing I can do? If there's not, I'll kill myself."

"And, sure, that's a mortal sin. You won't be doing that."

"But what can I do?"

"Nothing, as I told you. From the minute you stepped into this house you were the master's property, you poor little one," said Finoola, shaking her head sadly. She put her arms round Brigid to comfort her. "All that's happened tonight, Brigid, is that Master Sandes has put his brand on you, and that's the truth."

Chapter 4
March, 1823

The only sounds in Jack Keane's ears were the beating of his own heart, the burring of the nightjars, and the spluttering of the rush torches that lit the small clearing in the copse of yew trees. He stood alone in the circle of white-shirted men. His eyes still ached from the tight blindfold that his brothers had put on him before leading him the last half mile to the meeting place of the Whiteboys. Jack knew it was to the east of Listowel, somewhere near the township of Duagh, but he didn't know exactly where. He had been warned by Michael and John about the blindfold after he had persuaded them, much against their better judgment, to let him be initiated into the Whiteboys. But Jack was still frightened by the aura of menace in the silent gathering of men. He shivered slightly in the cold night.

Suddenly, a man stepped forward from the circle and walked slowly towards him, stopping a few yards away. "Who brought you here to a meeting of the association, Jack Keane?" he demanded in a clear voice that echoed around the copse.

"My brothers did," Jack said as loudly as his dry throat allowed.

"Is that so?" said the man, turning back to the circle.

"It is so, Master Whiteboy," chorused two voices from the circle. Jack recognized them as belonging to his brothers.

The man took another pace towards Jack. "And is it so that you wish to join this association?"

"Yes, it is so."

"Tell why then, that we may examine you and judge whether you are suitably fitted."

Now the man was nearer to him, Jack could see in the twilight that he had a vivid scar across his forehead and a badly misshapen nose that seemed to spread over his entire face.

Jack began to reply, "I have been done . . ."

"Speak up, I tell you," interrupted the man. "All the brothers here gathered will hear you."

"I have been done harm by Master Jonathan Sandes and wish to be avenged."

A murmur ran round the circle of men at the mention of the land agent's name.

"What harm, Jack Keane?"

"I was to be married but he took the girl into his service and has so twisted her opinion of me that she will not even meet me anymore. He has cast a spell on her and she is no longer mine. She turns her face from me."

"And you wish to revenge yourself on this man?"

"I do."

"What say you, brothers?" called the man, raising his voice. "Is his cause worthy?"

A low mutter of assent came from the assembled Whiteboys.

"Then, Jack Keane," said the man, "you can join the association when you have taken the proper oath."

A second man moved from the circle. In the flickering half-light, his billowing white shirt made him look like a giant white moth. He walked up to Jack carrying a shallow bowl. He grasped Jack's right hand and pushed the bowl into his left. Then he pulled a knife from his belt and drew it sharply across Jack's palm. Jack winced at the sudden pain. The man held his hand over the bowl, which Jack could see was half-filled with water, letting the blood run into it. He let go of Jack's hand after a minute when the water in the bowl had turned red. The bowl was taken from Jack and handed to Master Whiteboy.

"Jack Keane, this is the oath and article of the association. Be knowing that if you disclose them you will be cast into hell from a high place and your remains, such as they may be, consumed by the swine of the field. Are you knowing this?"

"Yes," Jack gulped.

"Know this also," cried Master Whiteboy in ringing tones. "This secret association shall fight the soldiers of the foreign oppressor. We shall drive the usurpers from the island of our fathers. We shall not bend in subjection nor shall we hold in honor those that most cravenly do. Rather shall we torment them from their ways. We declare that the bones of Erin's martyrs crack under the weight of the foreign repression; that the eyes of Erin's saints weep at the sufferings of their faithful servants. We swear that we shall do our utmost to ease that weight and dry those tears. And we further swear that to do so we shall willingly give up our lives and forego all ties of family and kinship. Do you so swear, Jack Keane?"

"I do."

Master Whiteboy held up the bowl of bloodied water.

"This is the blood of Erin's martyrs reborn in this most worthy association of Whiteboys. It is the blood of the Fianna, resurgent and scourging this land."

He handed the bowl to Jack.

"Drink this blood and be born into the association."

Jack raised the bowl to his lips and sipped the mixture of water and his own blood.

"In your own blood you are baptized a Brother Whiteboy," said Master Whiteboy, a smile breaking across his mutilated features as he stepped forward and clapped Jack on the shoulder. "You're one of us now and mighty welcome you are at that."

He gripped Jack's bleeding hand tightly in his large fist. "I'm Paddy Quillinan from Knockamoohane. Tis good to have you with us. If you're half the fighter your brothers are, Master accursed Sandes will soon be ruing the day he took your girl from you."

The other men in their white shirts crowded round Jack, patting him on the back and shaking his hand.

"Is this all there are?" Jack asked Paddy Quillinan, amazement in his voice.

"That's right, boy. Just forty-two of us now that you've joined."

"But, I thought . . . well, I thought there'd be many more what with all the raids and that."

"We don't need any more, Jack. Our weapons are surprise and secrecy," explained the Whiteboy leader. "If we had more men then we'd be afeared our secrets would soon reach the likes of Sandes and his cronies."

"What use can I be? What can I do?" asked Jack eagerly. "When can I go out on a raid, Master Quillinan?"

"Not so fast, young Jack," laughed his brother, Michael, punching him affectionately in the chest. "You're in too much of a hurry to be caught by the soldier boys, I'm thinking."

"But I want to fight," Jack persisted.

"And sure if John and I weren't awful certain of that, we wouldn't have brought you here tonight."

John interrupted. "But to fight you've to have a cool head, Jack. If you've anger like you have, you're only going to get captured and transported to Botany Bay or even stretched on a rope after the Sessions at Tralee."

Jack felt deeply disappointed as he trudged home across the fields with his brothers. He had thought that as soon as he had joined the Whiteboys, he would be able to go with them on their raids. He had dreamt of fighting against overwhelming odds and dying romantically, gloriously, with Brigid's name on his lips. They had been comforting dreams and had helped soften the blow of the message he had been given weeks before by Theresa Aherne—that her younger sister never wanted to see Jack again.

"But why?" he'd asked Theresa. "Why, when we're set to marry in the spring?"

"I'm not knowing why," Theresa had replied. "Brigid hasn't been home for weeks. But we're all thinking that she's in the power of Jonathan Sandes."

He had been inconsolable for days afterwards, moping around the cabin, hardly speaking to his family. The one thought in his mind was revenge on Jonathan Sandes.

Now, he thought, as he neared Drombeg with his brothers after the initiation ceremony, he would have to wait even longer for his revenge. The sour bile of disappointment was in his throat.

Captain Eugene de Vere Pearson, resplendent in the red and gold uniform of the 12th Dragoons, was quite adamant. "Gentlemen," he declared, "I don't think it matters whether these murderous ruffians are called Whiteboys, Ribbonmen, Carders or Rockites. The simple fact is that they have to be stamped out."

The men sitting round the table at Gurtinard House, the home of Dr. Peter Church, nodded their approval. Jonathan Sandes banged his pewter mug of ale on the table enthusiastically. "Hear, hear, Captain. You're absolutely correct."

"Ever since this unsuccessful rebellion and the Act of Union twenty-five years since," the officer continued, "these cursed associations have terrorized the countryside. They might have different names depending on where they're sprung from, but they're all repealists at heart."

"I doubt if the Whiteboys know the word 'repeal,' dear Captain," drawled Sandes. "They're just damned murderers who destroy farms and ruin our revenues, simple as that. Nothing more."

"Hush, Jonathan," murmured Dr. Church quietly. "Let the officer finish. After all, he's come all the way from Dublin to address us."

"The secret of this exercise will be intelligence," Captain Pearson continued, wearied already at interruptions from men whom he regarded as little more than country bumpkins. "We can chase around after every raid like your local Volunteers but that, I would hazard, is somewhat without purpose. We've got to discover these ruffians' plans before they're carried out."

"Easier said than done," ventured Dr. Church mildly.

His friends nodded in agreement. Inspector McMahon, who commanded the police in the Listowel area, had nothing to say, preferring to take his lead from others.

"I understand, gentlemen, that you have access to funds denied to me," Captain Pearson said curtly. "Your patrons have wrung these monies out of the government to pay informers, I believe."

"That's correct," said Sandes.

"What success then?"

"Little, I'm afraid," replied Dr. Church. "We have placed a man in the association but he's not been made privy yet to any of their plans. We know their leader is called

Quillinan of Knockamoohane, and that's about all. We've tried to follow him but he's as slippery as a Shannon eel."

"Is that all?" Captain Pearson sniffed disdainfully.

"Oh, and another thing," Sandes broke in. "Seems they all cut the palms of their hands when they take their blasted oaths. We could look for scars, I'm thinking."

"Not the quickest solution, I fear," said Captain Pearson flatly. "No, the answer is intelligence. And to contain them, an immediate imposition of martial law. Anyone outside their cabins between sunset and sunrise without special reason goes before a drumhead court martial."

The 120 dragoons drafted into Listowel were split into small units to enforce the imposition of martial law. In the smaller townships, like Drombeg, only two men were needed to make certain that everyone stayed indoors during the night hours. In the larger parishes, like Ballybunnion or Bally-longford, units of ten men commanded by a corporal patrolled the curfew. The remainder—some thirty men—were stationed permanently in Listowel or detailed to set up check points with the Volunteers on the main arteries of northwest Kerry. Large notices threatening transportation or death to anyone breaking the martial law regulations were posted liberally throughout the area and, at first, served as an effective deterrent.

Paddy Quillinan realized immediately that a special watch had been mounted on his cabin on the outskirts of Knockamoohane township. Night raids would be too dangerous. It was a time to wait and plan.

Eventually, Quillinan decided that the Whiteboys would have to risk attacks in daylight. They would strike at more than one target simultaneously, hoping to cause maximum confusion to the military. He travelled to Listowel market to spread his plans by word of mouth. His "shadows," a pair of dragoons, didn't even try to conceal themselves as Quillinan walked towards Listowel, driving a pig before him and carrying a pigeon under his arm. They were thoroughly bored with their assignment, much preferring to be on ceremonial duties back in Dublin. Quillinan exchanged cheery greetings with the people he passed on the way to market and the soldiers were too far away to hear the occasional order muttered from the corner of his mouth as he met another Whiteboy. Two days later, in the copse near Duagh, about twenty Whiteboys who had heard of the meeting, gathered to receive their orders.

"Master Whiteboy can't be here for reasons that you know well enough, brothers," said Padraig Broder, the burly and affable second-in-command. "But his instructions are clear enough. While he's being watched we're to carry out two raids at the same time. The Master thinks tis necessary to give our reply well and clear to this Captain Pearson and his dragoons for putting on this damned curfew." Broder looked at the expectant faces pressed around him. "Today, we'll be burning a grand house and helping His Majesty's mails on their way to perdition. Get your weapons and then divide yourself into two groups."

"Come on, Jack," said Michael Keane to his younger brother. "Under this tree. Help me lift this turf," he called as he knelt on the grass. His brother helped him pull it away and then watched as he scrabbled at the black earth underneath. "Ah, here we are."

Michael pulled a long, slim parcel from the ground, dusting the earth from it. Jack saw it contained something wrapped in oilcloth. His brother undid the cloth and carefully lifted out a flintlock pistol.

"There we are," Michael smiled. "You see, Jack, tis not only taters that grow in the ground."

Inside the cloth was another packet, double wrapped for

protection. Jack undid this to find some lead bullets, firing caps and a small box of gunpowder.

"You carry those, Jack, and I'll take the pistol," ordered Michael. "Push them under your shirt."

Jack pulled up the voluminous white shirt he was wearing and stuffed the ammunition in his breeches. The shirt was much too large for him. It really belonged to his brother John but it had been decided that it would be better for one of the brothers to remain at the cabin in Drombeg in case the dragoons came by and noticed that only their father was working in the fields.

When the Whiteboys had dug out all their weapons and covered up the hiding places again, they split into two groups to receive further instructions.

Padraig Broder pointed at the group containing the Keane brothers. "You'll be after the afternoon stage to Cork, me boys. I'll be leading you." He turned to the second group. "And you'll be making your way to Riversdale and burning the mansion of Samuel Raymond. Master Whiteboy thinks he should be concerning himself with something other than brewing ale and using his profits to support the soldier boys in the Volunteers. You'll be having no trouble, I'm thinking, since there'll only be servants there and they'll be supporting you. But remember to travel there singly and keep off the main tracks to avoid the dragoons.

"Finally, brothers, when we've finished our work, don't come here," said Broder. "We're not to use this place again. Take the weapons to your own cabins and listen out for the next orders. Now off you go and God be with you in your enterprises."

Jack walked with his brother for well over an hour to the rendezvous. They took the necessary precaution of bundling their white shirts under their waistcoats. The other Whiteboys arrived in ones and twos, until they were all gathered out of sight of the track leading from Listowel to Cork.

Padraig Broder shielded his eyes as he peered at the position of the bright April sun. "I'm thinking we've got maybe an hour to wait before the stage comes but we can't be too sure, me boys." He pointed to Jack. "Now you, young Jack Keane, are going to have a mighty important task here. Give him your pistol, Michael. You needn't bother to load it."

It was the first time Jack had ever held a weapon. He found it heavier than he had expected.

"Get your shirt and waistcoat off, lad," ordered Broder. "You've got some acting to do. You're to lie in the track and pretend you're mortal bad. That'll make the stage stop when the driver sees you lying there." Broder grinned hugely. "At least, it'd better make him stop or you're *really* going to be mortal bad." He laughed out loud as he saw Jack's worried frown. "Don't be alarmed, lad," he said gripping Jack's shoulder. "We'll be on hand to help."

Jack walked from the shelter of the wood, and stood alone on the rutted track. He dipped his hand into a drying puddle and smeared mud over his face and chest, then lay down on his stomach with the pistol concealed under his body. Into his mind came distorted images of Brigid, of Sandes kissing her like Brigid and he had kissed. He concentrated on listening to the sounds around him. The birds in the wood whistled their calls of alarm, the long grass rustled in the sighing breeze.

His body felt the approach before the sound reached him. Then the rattling, rumbling sound was upon him. Jack pressed closer to the earth of the track, his face turned away from the approaching coach. Would it ever stop, he wondered? If it didn't would he have time to roll out of its path? He tensed his body as the coach's noise overwhelmed him. Then came an urgent shout, the screeching of wooden brakes on iron-covered wheels, the creaking of leather harnesses, and the protesting neighs of horses as the bits sawed hard into their mouths. Then silence, followed by the clumping of heavy boots toward him.

"What have we here then?" a gruff voice said alarmingly close to him.

"Looks like a sick lad," a voice called.

A boot prodded into Jack's ribs, trying to turn him over. Then a hand pulled at him and Jack knew he could act no longer. He pushed himself away with all his young strength, rolling over and thrusting the pistol upward into the startled face of the stagecoach driver, a man of about fifty with reddened, weatherbeaten features. The driver's expression of amazement changed to anger as he grabbed at the pistol stuck in the belt of his thick coat.

"Blast you . . ." he cried.

"If you move, you're dead," Jack shouted, pointing the unloaded pistol.

The driver's hand rested on the wooden butt of his weapon. Their eyes locked together for a moment and then a piercing blast from a horn made both Jack and the driver look toward the woods. Broder and the eight other White-boys came bounding out of the trees, some waving rusty swords, others carrying muskets and pistols. The driver backed away from Jack, fear in his eyes, as he saw the men in their flapping white shirts. His empty hands shot up into the air. "Mercy . . . Oh God, mercy," he stammered in a strangled voice.

Jack got up from the drying mud of the track, keeping the pistol trained on the driver who stumbled away from him, hands still raised, until his back was pressed against the heaving flanks of one of the stage's lead horses.

"Keep him there, lad," called Broder, waving his musket in the air. "We'll take care of them in the stage."

The Whiteboys gathered around the coach while Broder pulled open the door.

"Out, out," he shouted, poking his weapon menacingly into the coach. "All of you, me pretties, out for the Whiteboys."

Four men, dressed in topcoats and high-crowned hats, stumbled from the coach. They huddled together uncertainly in a group, gazing fearfully at the Whiteboys.

"Right, gentlemen, empty your pockets," ordered Broder. "Master Whiteboy says no harm should come to you but he says to lighten your loads. I call that mighty considerate, too, thinking on the walking you'll be doing later."

"This is an outrage," stormed one of the passengers, a stout, middle-aged man, florid of face from rage and self-indulgence. "I refuse to hand over anything."

"Is that so?" murmured Broder, still smiling. "Now aren't you the brave one?"

Without changing his expression he reversed his musket swiftly and crashed the butt against the man's face, catching him on the bridge of the nose with a sickening crunch. Blood gouted from the man's face as he staggered back against one of the coach's wheels, falling senseless on the track.

"Now, gentlemen, is there anyone else with an argument in him?" said Broder. He walked over to the unconscious man and kicked him casually in the ribs.

As one man, the other three began frantically turning out their pockets, tossing clinking leather bags of money on to the track. One of them pulled his watch off its chain; another tugged at the ring on his index finger.

"Not your jewelry," said Broder evenly. "What would the likes of us be doing with such pretty things. No—your money will do." He stooped and picked up the purses.

"Now, while we attend to the mail, you can all be taking

off your fine boots. Master Whiteboy doesn't want you to walk too fast, after all."

One of the Whiteboys clambered up into the driver's seat and began tossing sacks from the roof of the stagecoach. Broder poked them with his musket until he found the one containing the mail. He gestured to a Whiteboy with a sword to slit open the sack. The letters tumbled into the dust.

"Right, me boys," he called, "you know what to do." Broder looked over at Jack who was still menacing the now-barefoot driver with the empty pistol. "You all right, lad?" Jack nodded. Three Whiteboys began tearing the letters into little shreds, tossing them up into the air and into the hedges.

"Nothing upsets people more than not having their mail delivered," Broder observed generally. "Really makes them mad, so it does. And that's the truth."

When all the letters had been destroyed, Broder ordered his men to unhitch the horses. He lifted the driver's long whip off the stagecoach and cracked it over the lead horses' withers, making them bolt. "Off you go then," he said flicking the whip at the feet of the stage's erstwhile passengers. "And take the driver with you. You've a fair step to the next township."

"What about him?" asked one of the passengers, pointing at the unconscious man.

"No matter to me, gentlemen," smiled Broder. "You can either carry him with you or leave him where he's resting. But if he stays there, he'll be stripped as naked as he was born. Such fine clothes are a mighty rare sight for the people hereabouts. They'll probably slit his throat from ear to ear for good measure."

The passengers looked at each other, shrugged their shoulders, and began walking off down the track in their stocking feet, picking their way gingerly between the sharp stones. The driver, feeling a twinge of duty, hesitated for a moment and then hurried off to catch up with the others.

"That's fine gentlemen you are," Padraig Broder taunted their retreating backs. "Leave him to be murdered, would you . . . and him the bravest of you all?"

Broder turned to his men. "That's the sort who are bleeding us dry. Mark them well, the cowardly swine. They're not so high and mighty when it's their miserable skins they're after saving."

He went over to the bleeding and unconscious man and began lifting him under the shoulders. "Give me a hand, one of you," he called. "We'll put your man back in the stage. It'll be more comfortable for him when he wakes from his sleep I'm thinking. He'll be found soon enough, if he's lucky."

The man was eased on to the coach floor. He started to groan as he began to regain consciousness.

Broder surveyed the torn-up letters all round the coach with a satisfied smile. "That'll show them soldier boys. Now let's be off through the woods before anyone claps a sight on us."

Once the party of Whiteboys were well away from the coach, deep into the safety of the woods, Broder called a halt.

"So you won't be needing any more instructions, boys, let me tell you what Master Whiteboy has decided. Two days from now we're to raid one of the Palatine farmers over at Knockanure. We'll meet by the cross there, three hours before dusk."

"What about the others? Will they be coming?" asked Michael Keane.

"No, they'll be away burning another big house. Master Whiteboy wants to keep the soldiers hopping around. For the next few raids we'll be in two groups. That way the soldiers won't know how many we are or where to guard. We'll learn them to leave Dublin and hunt for us, that we will.''

The Whiteboys split up as they left the woods to make their way back to their cabins.

"Why the Palatine farmers?" Jack asked his brother when they were well on in their journey to Drombeg.

"Because they don't belong here, that's why. They're on some of the best land round here, paying little enough rent just because they're Germans settled on us by an English king. We're going to make sure that they don't stay.''

"But they don't cause any trouble," persisted Jack. "They were persecuted out of their own homes, weren't they?"

"That's as may be. But now they've taken over our land. They help the landlords, they do. We want none of them.''

"'Tis strange we should attack other farmers.''

"We'll attack anyone," said Michael grimly, "until Ireland's for the Irish.''

"The farms of the Palatines near Knockanure, eh?" mused Captain Pearson the next evening. "You sure of that?"

"That's what the informant says," replied Dr. Church. "He passed the news to me at the apothecary shop.''

"I must confess to some surprise, Doctor. I'd have thought holding up the stage and burning out Raymond would have been enough for them." He slapped his kid leather gloves in his palm. "So they want all-out war do they? Well, we'll see. We'll see.''

"You'll occupy the farms then, Captain, and ambush them?"

"I think not, Doctor." The officer rose from his chair in the shabby Listowel police barracks, and looked at the map on the wall behind his desk. "The farms of these Germans are all to the east of here?"

"A few of them. Most of them are on the Blennerhasset estate near Tralee."

"But there are some near Knockanure?"

"Two or three, I believe."

"Well, I don't think I'll move my men there. They'll be too conspicuous and the Whiteboys will change their plans."

"But . . ." Dr. Church started.

"But nothing, Doctor," said the officer sharply. "From our information some of them must come from the townships to the west of Listowel. On this map, there are only two tracks they can take. We'll try to surprise them on their attacks at the farms, they'll run in panic, and snap." Captain Pearson clapped his palms together. "When I've got 'em, I'll teach 'em a very quick lesson."

He turned back to Dr. Church with a grim smile on his face. "I just pray your information is correct."

Jack Keane and his two brothers crouched under the hedge by a wooden farm gate bearing the sign "Swizer" in rough, Germanic writing. The air was still in the late spring afternoon as if the whole world was holding its breath. Jack held the pistol, loaded now, pointing carefully away from him. John and Michael Keane were carrying ancient muskets which they'd primed during their walk to Knockanure. Jack felt uneasy. He'd been worried ever since the previous evening when the Keane family had been sitting around the peat fire in their cabin. Jack had peered through the gloom and seen a frog leap away from the glowing peat, straight between his brothers and into some straw in a dark corner. He'd jumped up, grabbed his shillelagh and beaten at the place where he'd last seen the frog but it vanished.

"Tis an omen," he'd told his family who were highly amused by his antics. "A frog came right out of the fire."

"Hush, Jack," his mother had said, patting his arm. "And what sort of omen is that, pray? Just a hedge frog keeping warm if you ask me."

"But it came straight out of the fire, I tell you."

"Sure and you've been thinking on the little people too much," said his father. "Tis no omen at all except maybe to a foolish boy like you."

But nothing could rid Jack of the certainty that it was an omen, and a bad one. He hadn't liked the idea of attacking another farmer simply because he happened to be a foreigner from the start. But if he refused to go on the raid he knew full well that the Whiteboys would have had little further use for him.

The brothers waited for a few minutes while the other Whiteboys got into position and then Padraig Broder's horn signalled the attack. They scrambled over the hedge, guns at the ready, and raced toward the neatly whitewashed cabin. Other Whiteboys held smoldering pieces of turf wrapped in sacking as they ran toward the farm's two outhouses. One howled in anguish as he tripped over a pigeen and fell on to the hot sacking he was clutching.

The door of the cabin flew open and a tall, bearded man, wearing a black wide-brimmed hat, emerged with a musket at his shoulder. He aimed carefully at the Whiteboy rolling on the ground, trying to disentangle himself from the lump of burning turf at the same time as beating away the squealing pigeen trapped between his legs. The gun went off in a cloud of smoke with a thunderous clap. The Whiteboy heaved into the air like a hooked fish, reaching for his shattered breastbone, blood already spattering his white shirt, and then fell back, dead.

For a moment there was a silence then, with shouts of

rage, the Whiteboys flung themselves at the farmer. He showed not a trace of fear as he whirled his empty musket around his head like a club. Two Whiteboys toppled to the ground under its blows before Padraig Broder managed to get a sword thrust into the farmer's body, catching him high up on his right shoulder. He dropped the musket with a cry of pain but still closed with his attackers. He gripped Jack and John Keane round their necks, pulling their heads across his broad chest. John dropped his musket as he tried to punch the farmer away but Jack's pistol was trapped between himself and Hans Swizer. "Ihr mordenden schweinehunde," shouted the farmer.

The blood running down his arm and chest made them so slippery that Jack's head pulled out of the farmer's grip. But as he backed away the farmer grabbed at his pistol. Jack's index finger tightened involuntarily on the trigger and the pistol exploded into the farmer's face at point-blank range. The lead ball smashed upward through his brain and out through the crown of his skull. The air was filled with a pink mist of blood, brains and skull fragments. He fell away from Jack and lay on the ground, his legs twitching. Then he was still, eyes staring blankly upward at the sky.

"Oh God," Jack moaned as he stumbled away vomiting over the ground. "Oh God, I've killed him."

The Whiteboys gathered round the body, stunned and silent at this grotesque act of violence. Suddenly, they were pushed apart with demonic force by a woman who ran shrieking from the cabin. She flung herself across the body, looking wildly up at the men standing above her. Tears ran down her round, plump face.

"What have you done? Me man, you've killed him. Me man," she kept shrieking. "Me man. Me poor man."

The Whiteboys turned away, shame and pity in their

hearts. John Keane comforted his younger brother who was kneeling on the ground, heaving and retching.

"Come away, boys," called Padraig Broder. "Twas an accident. Nothing more. Let's finish the job we came to do." He tore one of the glowing sods away from a Whiteboy and hurled it high into the rush thatch of the cabin. "Come on, boys," he urged. "The soldiers will be here with all the shooting. Hurry up."

More lumps of burning turf were flung into the thatches of the cabin and the outhouses. Tiny licks of flame spread around them and the thatch crackled fully alight. The flames engulfed the roofs, sending plumes of dark grey smoke into the sky. Then with a roar the roofs collapsed and the screams of burning pigs, chickens, and a horse filled the farmyard, joining with the sobbing shrieks of the farmer's widow in a cacophony of horror. The Whiteboys looked dully at the awful scene, fascinated yet totally dismayed by the devastation they had caused. Their eyes and ears were so numbed by the dreadful sounds all around them that it was some moments before any of them realized that their look-out was standing by the farm gate, shouting and waving frantically.

"Horses are coming," he bellowed. "For Holy Mary's sake, tis the soldiers. Get away. Tis the soldiers."

"Quickly, boys!" shouted Padraig Broder. "Make for the woods. Quickly now."

Without apparent effort, he heaved the dead Whiteboy across his shoulders and, bowed under the weight, ran toward the gate. The other Whiteboys scrambled through the hedges, pulling their shirts over their heads as they went and disappeared into the nearest cover. The three Keane brothers hid in a ditch, pressing deep into the undergrowth as the sound of galloping horses grew nearer and then passed. John peered cautiously out and saw four dragoons, their sabres drawn, jump down from their mounts and run into the farm which was now almost totally obscured by a pall of smoke.

"Come on," he whispered to his brothers, "tis clear now." They left the ditch and ran along the track that led back to Knockanure Cross and Listowel. For a quarter of a mile they kept to the track before crossing fields and copses toward the lower track leading westwards. Only when they reached it did they begin to relax.

"What about the guns?" asked Jack breathlessly. "We surely can't carry them all the way back to Drombeg."

"Tis right he is, Michael," agreed John. "Let's bury them."

"They'll get rusty."

"We can wrap them in our shirts. That'll protect them a little and get rid of our shirts at the same time."

The brothers looked for a suitable place and chose a ditch under a broken dry-stone wall. They pulled away tussocks of grass to make a large enough hole to bury the pistol and the two muskets. Then they marked the spot with a small cairn of stones from the wall.

"We'd better hurry," said Michael. "We don't want to be caught in the curfew after getting away by the skin of our teeth."

They began running again, their bare feet pattering on the hard earth. Then they rounded a sharp bend in the track to find a farm cart and horse barred their way.

"Halt, in the King's name," came a gruff shout as the sergeant of dragoons stepped from behind the cart, the bayonet on his musket pointing at the brothers.

They looked quickly around them for a way of escape but saw two more dragoons clambering out of the ditch behind them.

"And what might you three fine buckos be running

from?" asked the sergeant menacingly. More dragoons rose from the ditches on either side of the track and surrounded the brothers. The points of their bayonets pressed lightly against the chests of the three young men.

"Sure and weren't we just running to get home before curfew?" replied Michael, trying hard to appear nonchalant and at ease.

"Sure and weren't we just running to get home before curfew?" mimicked the sergeant. "So that's your story, is it? Where do you live?"

"Drombeg."

"And what are you doing so far this side of Listowel?"

"Just visiting a friend, that's all."

"Shut your gob, farmboy," snarled the sergeant. "Search them."

The dragoons ran their hands roughly over the brothers' clothes. One of them turned to the sergeant and shook his head. "Nothing on them."

"So they've got rid of their shirts, have they?" drawled Captain Pearson as he walked from behind the cart. "And their weapons as well, no doubt."

The brothers shrank inwardly at the sight of the officer in his resplendent uniform, his height emphasized by his black stovepipe uniform hat with its curved peak.

Michael put on a bold front. "Sure, and I don't know what you're talking about, your honor."

The butt of a musket crashed into his stomach, driving the breath from his body. He doubled over, gasping for air.

"I said shut your gob," said the sergeant evenly. "You speak to the officer when you're told to."

Captain Pearson strolled up to them. "You see, lying won't help you now," he remarked pleasantly. "We know what happened back at the German's farm. I must say I didn't expect you Whiteboys to go as far as murdering him."

"Whiteboys? And who's to say . . ." John started, then went silent as the dragoon who'd hit his elder brother drew back his musket.

"You were going to reply, I think, 'who's to say we're Whiteboys,'" said Captain Pearson. "Well, no one is going to say you are until we look at your hands. You see, a friend told us all Whiteboys had a scar across their palms."

He smiled as he saw the brothers clench their fists. "Ah, yes," he murmured. "That's what's going to say you're Whiteboys. Not your shirts, not your weapons, but your own dirty, stinking bodies." His tone sharpened. "Sergeant!"

"Suh."

"Their hands."

Strong fingers gripped the brothers' wrists and prised their palms apart, turning them upwards.

Captain Pearson leaned forward casually and ran his gloved finger softly along one of the three scars. "The newest recruit, wouldn't you say, Sergeant?" he said, holding up Jack's hand with the red raw scar vividly on it. "Who are you, Whiteboys?"

"We're the Keanes; Jack, John and Michael Keane," said Michael defiantly. "And we're not . . ."

"Not Whiteboys, eh?" the officer interrupted. "Well, I think you are. Your scars prove it. So there's no use pretending any more, is there?"

Michael dropped his head.

"No, I thought not. The problem is who to make an example of. All of you . . . ? No, I think not. Someone has to tell the Whiteboys what sort of punishment they're going to receive in the future."

"I shot the farmer," Jack blurted out. "I shot him, not the others. Twas an accident but I was holding the pistol."

"Well, well. A volunteer, eh, Sergeant?" remarked Captain Pearson. He looked closely at the three brothers standing sullenly before him. For all the emotion he showed, he could have been appraising cattle at the market. "I think the eldest should have the honor, Sergeant," he said quietly. "The first-born son is a little special after all. And I've little doubt he recruited the other two. Tie him."

"No, you want me," protested Jack, struggling in the soldier's grip. "I'm the one."

Captain Pearson ignored his cries. "The rope, Sergeant. Fix the rope."

The sergeant took a long, thick rope from the back of the cart and flung it over a branch of an elm tree which hung out over the track. The end had been fashioned into a noose.

"Tie him," ordered the officer.

Two dragoons pulled Michael away from his brothers and, while one held him, the other tied his hands behind his back. They carried him to the cart, pushing him up into it. Michael looked up at the noose dangling above him and ducked away, pressing himself against the dusty floor of the cart.

The sergeant lifted him without any difficulty, pulled down the noose and fitted it around his neck. "Pull up the slack," he shouted and two dragoons heaved on the other end of the rope.

Michael twisted his head as the sergeant hung a large card around his neck. He tried to see what was written on it but the rope stopped him. The sergeant jumped down and then the cart jerked forward as the officer slapped the horse across its quarters. Suddenly, there was nothing beneath him. He choked for breath and tried to kick his legs upwards but there was no escape.

His brothers ceased their struggles as the cart pulled away leaving Michael dangling from the rope. Struck rigid and silent by the horror before their eyes, they saw him arch convulsively, kicking his legs wildly, and then swing limply under the tree, his tongue swelling out between his darkening lips. His body turned gently in the twilight breeze, blood oozing from its ears, a stench of human waste filling the sweetness of the air as all muscles relaxed in death.

Tears ran down Jack's face as he looked up at his dead brother. He could hardly make out the sign around his twisted, bent neck. It bore only two words, "A Whiteboy." "British murderers," he screeched and lashed out with his feet, catching a dragoon in the groin. "British murdering bastards," he shrieked again, just before the butt of a musket crashed between his shoulders. As he fell forward, diving into unconsciousness, he thought he heard the officer shout, "Beat them but don't kill them."

His voice, Jack thought, croaked just like a frog. The frog . . . the frog . . . and then another musket cracked across his skull and he heard no more.

Chapter 5
April, 1824

The news of Michael Keane's death spread over the district like a rain cloud off the Atlantic. The Kerry people, with little between survival and starvation in their lives, had a close kinship with death. It was not something to be offered a glass of hospitality round their peat fires, but death was more than a nodding acquaintance and so was usually accepted with the minimum of ill grace or resentment. What feeling there was would be blown away by the grief-absorbing rituals of the wake and sooner or later the everyday consideration of living would take over. But the manner of Michael Keane's dying was different. It was not even softened by the procedures of justice, long enough for a man to adjust gradually to the notion of his execution, accepting it finally as a welcome release from the torment of his own uncertainty. Nor was it in hot blood. The treatment of Michael Keane's body, too, repelled them. After the deed, whispered the Kerry folk in the darkness of their cabins, it should have been returned to the sorrowing family for a proper wake and burial, not left hanging under guard of the dragoons until the crows and ravens had pecked out its eyes and eaten its tongue; until the flesh, muscles and bones had given way and the body had toppled out of the noose, not even then to be buried but only flung carelessly into the ferns for the carrion eaters to finish their work.

"They shall pay for this foul deed," vowed Paddy

Quillinan, as he sat in the Keane cabin at Drombeg. He'd denied all caution in his rage at Michael's death and had joined the dozens of others who'd called on the family to try to ease their grief.

Master and Mistress Keane sat close by the fire, their hands clasped as they huddled together in their shock. Near them, on a pile of straw and sacks, lay John and Jack recovering from their beating by the dragoons, their faces and bodies swollen and mottled with bruises.

"I swore eternal vengeance when the soldiers beat me nigh to death and left me with this scarred and misshapen face," said Quillinan grimly, running his hand over his battered, bristly features. "For Michael Keane, they will pay double. And for the sufferings of his brothers and parents, they will pay threefold."

"And what about the person who told the soldiers so that they could lay their trap?" John asked, raising himself on his elbows with difficulty.

"Tis true. He is the foulest and blackest of all for didn't he betray his solemn oath?" Quillinan agreed gravely. "He is the first to be rooted out else none of us is safe. Padraig Broder and meself have already been thinking on it."

"Who is the traitor?" asked Jack eagerly.

"We're not sure yet but have a plan to reveal him. You're not to worry about him yet. I promise you the satisfaction of meeting your brother's Judas."

As John and Jack slowly recovered from their beatings and time began to numb the pain in their memories, Quillinan and Broder went ahead with their plan. They had reduced the possible informants to two.

"It's either Paddy Stack or Jimmy McElligott," said Broder.

"And both of them recent members, too," Quillinan observed. "Tell both of them that the Whiteboys are going to raid the police barracks at Ballylongford. Then we'll watch for the one who tells the dragoons."

Broder passed on the false information to the men after arranging for two trusted Whiteboys to watch their cabins and follow them wherever they went. Within a day, they had the identity of the informer. Stack had remained in his fields, but McElligott had hurried off to Listowel and entered Dr. Church's apothecary shop in the market square. If confirmation was needed, it came when McElligott immediately repaired to the Listowel Arms coaching house and began spending lavishly on whiskey and porter.

"A foolish man as well as a cursed one," was Quillinan's satisfied reaction when he heard the news. "Since the blasted Captain Pearson saw fit to make an example of Michael Keane, bless his tortured soul, then the Whiteboys shall do similar to his spy."

"How many men shall we be needing?" asked Broder. The two Whiteboy leaders mingled with the crowds at Listowel market, keeping a wary eye open for constables or the soldiers who ineffectively followed Quillinan.

"One thing is certain, Padraig," said Quillinan. "I shall be there, soldiers or not. I'll give them the slip somehow. You come too and bring the Keane brothers. Tis their right to be present."

Three afternoons later, Jimmy McElligott, a thin-faced, scrawny man, was in the fields about two hundred yards from his cabin at Coolagowan, desultorily hoeing the weeds along the rows of potatoes. He didn't regard himself as a traitor to his own people. What he was doing was born out of necessity. He felt sorrow for what had happened to Michael Keane but, after all, the money helped pay for a few delicacies for his sickly wife and guaranteed him security of tenure at his poor farm. Some of the money was put by in what he called his "travelling fund" so that one day he could take his family away from Kerry, perhaps to England, maybe even to the Americas. The thought of capture and exposure didn't trouble his mind too much since he believed implicitly in Dr. Church's guarantee of his safety.

"Hello there, Jimmy."

He looked up from his work and saw Padraig Broder alone by the hedge, leaning on the shafts of a hand cart. McElligott waved and began tramping across the field towards the visitor. This must be the instructions about the next raid, he thought.

"Padraig, tis nice to see you. Tis fine weather is it not, thanks be to God?"

"It is that, Jimmy," replied Broder, a wide smile across his face. "I've brought something for you."

"And sure, what would that be?"

"Come over the hedge and have a look. Tis in the cart."

McElligott scrambled over the stone and turf hedge and went up to the cart.

"Tis under the sacking," said Broder, standing away from the shaft.

"Now what could this be?" puzzled McElligott as he leaned over to pull the sacking aside. Broder's shillelagh caught him twice squarely on the back of his head before he slumped unconscious over the side of the cart.

McElligott came to under the pile of sacking as the cart was being pushed along a rough track, its wheels squeaking and grinding. He tried to sit up but found he was bound hand and foot. A gag was fastened over his mouth.

"Your man's awake," he heard a familiar voice say. It sounded like Broder.

"And just in time too. We're nearly there and I'd have been hating for him to miss our little surprise, Padraig."

Oh God, thought McElligott, the voice of Master

Whiteboy. He realized it could mean only one thing; his spying activities had been discovered. He moved his mouth trying to shout an alarm, an explanation, a plea, but the gag was too tight. He could only lie there and shiver with terror.

Soon the sounds of the Atlantic rollers grew louder. Suddenly, the cart stopped and the sacking over him was pulled away.

McElligott blinked his eyes, adjusting them to the still bright and clear light of the late afternoon. He raised his throbbing head and saw Quillinan, Broder, and to his deepening horror, John and Jack Keane. They stared down at him grimly.

"So there's your spy," growled Quillinan. "There's your man who broke his oath and put the noose around your poor brother's neck. Look on him and see the abject terror of him."

The prisoner shook his head from side to side, attempting to dislodge his gag.

"He wants to speak, does he?" said Broder. "Well I'm thinking he's talked too much all his life. Let's sit him up so he can see where he's going."

Rough hands grasped McElligott and propped him up against the side of the cart. He stared wildly round him and realized he was by the ruins of Doon Castle, high up on a green promontory jutting into the sea.

Quillinan leaned over the cart and spat into his face. One by one, the others did the same.

"Curse you to hell," cried John Keane, slapping him across the eyes. "May you rot just as our brother did."

"Amen to that," muttered Quillinan, lifting the shafts of the cart. The others helped him push it to the edge of the cliff. McElligott's eyes widened in terror as he realized what was about to happen. A strangled, gurgling noise came from behind the gag.

The four Whiteboys pulled the cart around so that McElligott could look down over the cliff to the rocks and stones far below, washed by the angry sea.

"Now," grunted Quillinan. The cart swayed and tipped. With his last effort, McElligott somehow pushed himself over the side of the cart but it was too late. It fell away from him over the cliff, tumbling downwards. McElligott rolled a little way down a gentle slope and then pitched forward. His body twisted and turned several times before it hit the rocks with a thudding crash which could just be heard above the breaking waves. It lay there for a moment before being lifted gently by a wave which began drawing it out to join the rest of the flotsam in the breakers. The body rolled over and, just for a second, it seemed that the pale face of Jimmy McElligott gazed upwards at his executioners peering down over the cliff.

"An eye for an eye, eh, Doctor?" remarked Captain Pearson as he reclined on a chair in Jonathan Sandes' drawing room. "So much for your spy, what?"

"It's an outrage!" spluttered Dr. Church. "You take it too lightly, sir. That you do."

"If you'd hanged the other two Whiteboys you caught, this might not have happened," agreed Sandes. "I thought you were being too lenient."

"Gentlemen," protested the dragoons officer, "you must expect casualties in a war. This man McElligott was bound to have been discovered and killed sooner or later. In his unhappy case, it happened to be sooner."

The three men stopped talking as the door opened and Brigid Aherne came into the room carrying a silver tray of glasses and a decanter of wine. She curtseyed slightly to

Sandes before placing the tray on a side table for him. Her figure had filled out with the months of regular food from Sandes' table. Her hair shone blackly under the white, frilled mop cap that framed her oval face. Only the dark rings under her eyes betrayed the fact that Brigid was unhappy. Sandes smiled up at her with real warmth. For weeks now he had mistaken her dull submission as real enthusiasm for his increasing desires.

"Thank you, Brigid. You may leave us."

She bobbed again before him and left the room. Captain Pearson followed her with his eyes radiating open admiration and desire.

Sandes noticed his look. "Kindness and perseverance," he said. "That's what makes a good servant, eh, Captain? Who would have thought that that girl was a dirty, ragged, starving little wretch only a few months back?"

"And what did you do for her, Master Sandes?" asked the officer with an easy smile on his lips.

"Taught her how to serve."

"Deuced if I'm not wondering who's been serving who by the rings under her eyes and the look on your face, Master Sandes," replied Captain Pearson, laughing out loud.

"See what you mean, Pearson," Dr. Church cackled venally. "Who's serving who . . . very good . . . very good indeed."

"Gentlemen, gentlemen," said Sandes, joining in the laughter. "No more, I pray. All I will say to your sallies is that I find Brigid's service a pleasure to us both."

The three men laughed together as Sandes filled glasses with wine and handed them round.

"Enough, enough, of all this tittle-tattle," said Dr. Church, wiping his eyes with a red silk handkerchief. "We were discussing more serious business?"

"Right enough, Doctor," agreed Captain Pearson. "The Whiteboys."

"Well then, Captain, what's your next plan? Do you think they will continue with their plan to raid the police barracks at Ballylongford?"

"I doubt if such a plan ever existed. I feel that it was simply the sprat to catch the mackerel, but it's an interesting thought . . . attacking a police barracks. They haven't done it before and its very boldness might tempt them."

"But not Ballylongford, surely?" interrupted Sandes.

"No, I think not. That would be hoping for too much. Bluff and counter-bluff isn't their strongest suit."

"So?" said Dr. Church.

"So, my dear Doctor, I am reinforcing all the police barracks except at Ballylongford and here in Listowel. I haven't enough men to go round and thus I'll have to gamble a little."

"I pray you gamble correctly this time, Captain," remarked Sandes sourly. "Your previous wager in letting those two scoundrels go free cost dear to us. Dublin wouldn't like any more failures, I'm thinking."

The police barracks at Lixnaw, a few miles to the southwest of Listowel, was a squat, single-story building standing greyly on the edge of the village of poor cabins. It was manned by three constables and a sergeant whose standards of living were scarcely better than those of the local population. This brought a feeling of ease between the police and policed, so that there was rarely any trouble in the village. There were the drunks and the wife beaters to admonish; the disputes about land and creeping hedges to sort out; the occasional eviction. But in all these duties the police managed to retain a friendly relationship with the peasant farmers. This changed when, in early June, 1824, six dragoons were drafted unwillingly to Lixnaw to be received with equal ill grace by the villagers and the incumbent policemen. For a start, there simply wasn't enough room in the barracks for all ten men to sleep in comfort.

"If one turns over, we all have to turn over," grumbled Corporal Hogg, who was in charge of the dragoons. "Ever since we left Royal Barracks in Dublin we've had to live in pig sties or worse."

"Tis a poor nation we are, Corporal," agreed the police sergeant, Michael Sheehy, sadly. "But then I'm wondering if it's not all the people who've ruled us who have made us so."

"Now careful, Sergeant," warned Corporal Hogg. "That's the sort of talk these blasted Whiteboys are putting about."

"Maybe there's a bit of Whiteboy in all us Kerrymen. Maybe most of us are too afeared to know it."

"If you're all so poor then, why don't you go and work in England?"

Sergeant Sheehy managed to snort with disgust at the same time as sucking his clay pipe alight. "Wouldn't you know, Corporal, that that's already the curse of Ireland? All the men of spirit are going away, leaving just the women and children and old men to look after the land. What there is of it after you English landlords have had their way."

"On my oath, that's all I need. A hutch to live in and a constable who supports the Whiteboys."

"A sergeant, Corporal," said Sheehy quietly. "Remember that . . . a sergeant, whatever I may believe."

The police and the soldiers lived together in an uneasy and uncomfortable truce for the next two weeks. Each day, the police went out on patrol while the dragoons stayed at the barracks. At first, Corporal Hogg tried to keep them occupied with drill but soon gave this up under the derisory comments of the local children who took to aping the drill movements. Finally, the dragoons simply lolled around the barracks, guarding them against something none of them believed would happen.

All they heard as they sat in the June sunshine outside the barracks after a lunch of dried beef and lumpers was a blast on a horn. As they began scrambling to their feet, a fusillade of shots came from behind the nearest cabins thirty yards away. One dragoon fell, cursing, with a ball in his thigh but the rest of the shots thudded harmlessly into the barracks, sending chips of brick flying in all directions.

"Inside," shouted Corporal Hogg. "For Christ's sake, back inside."

The dragoons pulled the injured soldier inside, then slammed and bolted the stout wooden door of the barracks before knocking out the glass windows at the front and sides of the building with the butts of their muskets. After the first noise of the attack, an unreal silence fell on Lixnaw as the Whiteboys reloaded their weapons and the dragoons searched for targets.

"There! By the cabin!" called the corporal as he saw a musket appear round a wall. A dragoon loosed off a shot, raising a puff of dust near the cabin. The Whiteboy musket fired and a ball crashed into the wood of the barracks door.

"Christ, they can shoot at that," said Corporal Hogg in grudging admiration, still cursing himself for the dragoons' unpreparedness for the attack. "There's another one," he cried, spying a young man in a billowing white shirt run from behind a cabin holding something wrapped in sacking. The muskets cracked out and dirt flew up around the man's feet but he vanished out of sight behind the barracks without a shot apparently hitting him.

"Where the devil are the constables?" muttered the

corporal. Then he heard another fusillade of shots and realized the constables were under attack elsewhere in Lixnaw. In fact, the Whiteboys had chosen the time for their attack after watching the constables' movements closely for more than a week. They had deliberately taken up positions between the troops and the police, reckoning that to divide was to conquer.

The Keane brothers were in the contingent of Whiteboys ordered to concentrate their attack on the barracks. Jack had watched fearfully as his brother ran into the open under the sights of the dragoons' muskets. Now he saw him crawling around the side of the barracks out of sight of the troops who peered from the windows above him. John reached the door and unwrapped two lumps of smoking peat from the sacking he carried. He piled them carefully against the door, then waved back at his companions. The dragoons ducked back from the windows as the Whiteboys' volley smashed into the barracks and John ran, crouching low, towards the shelter of the cabins. Jack could see a grin of triumph on his brother's face as he neared safety. Suddenly, it changed to a grimace of pain as a ball from a dragoon's musket caught him in the small of the back. He stumbled but his momentum carried him behind the cabin wall where he collapsed headlong into Jack's arms.

"Oh, God," he cried. "They've done for me. Oh, Holy Mother of God."

Jack clasped him, turning him gently so that he rested in a sitting position against the cabin wall. John's face was grey with pain, sweat dripping from his forehead. As he held him, Jack could feel the wetness of blood seeping under his palms.

"Rest there, John. Rest there," he mouthed into his brother's ear. "We'll get you safe away. You'll be safe."

The excitement of the battle, the thirst for revenge filled

Jack. Without thinking of his safety, he moved out from cover and took careful aim at the police barracks. The musket thumped into his shoulder as it exploded. Smoke was now billowing about the front of the barracks with flames curling around the door.

Inside, the dragoons coughed and rubbed their smarting eyes, hardly able to see through the windows. One began to sob with panic.

"Shut your noise," bawled Corporal Hogg, desperation now beginning to press in on him.

"We'll be burned alive," shouted a dragoon, throwing down his musket and clawing at the heavy wooden beam across the blackening door. "We've got to get out."

"Steady men," cried the corporal. "If we run out there we'll be cut to pieces. Don't panic."

He looked around the barracks. "Grab hold of that," he ordered, pointing at the rough table which had been thrust back against a wall. "We'll use it as a shield."

Two of the dragoons, coughing deep in their chests with the suffocating smoke, pulled the table upright.

"Right," exclaimed Corporal Hogg. "Move away from the door all of you. When I open it, you two get the table through."

He pulled at the beam securing the door, feeling the heat of the flames burning on the other side. The door swung open and the corporal staggered back from the flames. For a second, he presented a perfect target to the Whiteboys. A musket ball thudded into his chest, hurtling him back across the barracks. He cannoned off the table and crashed to the floor, dead. His men hesitated for a moment, shocked by his death, before their training and instinct for self-preservation took over again.

"Come on, lads," called one of the older dragoons.

"Let's do what poor old Hogg said. Through the door with the table."

Shots thudded into the table as it was thrust outside, splintering the wood, but it proved an effective enough shield for the two dragoons. They carried it away from the flames that were now threatening to engulf the entire barracks, knelt behind it and started giving covering fire to enable their two unhurt companions to crawl from the cabin pulling the wounded soldier between them. Corporal Hogg was left where he had fallen.

By now, the Whiteboys attacking the barracks had begun to look uneasily over their shoulders as the firing from the other side of Lixnaw came closer. They realized their other group was being forced back by the advancing constables. Paddy Quillinan, ducking low as he ran between the cabins, slumped breathlessly beside Jack Keane.

"Tis looking like we'll have to leave here, lad," he panted. "The constables are getting too close." Then he noticed John Keane leaning against the wall, his breath coming in wrenching gasps that shook his entire body.

"A dragoon got him," explained Jack. "But he set the barracks alight first. I'm thinking we shot two of the dragoons, too. There are only four still fighting that we can count."

Quillinan peered quickly round the wall. Before a ball spattered the whitewash of the cabin above his head, he saw that the roof of the barracks was now alight. The dragoons were firing from a kneeling position, protected by the table. The Whiteboys' leader could see that there would be casualties amongst his men if they tried to close with the dragoons across the open ground. He had no alternative.

"We're going now before it's too late. Start moving away one by one so the soldiers don't rush us." He turned to

Jack. "I'll help you with your brother. We'll get him to your cabin all right."

Quillinan pulled John Keane upright. "Put an arm round my shoulder, boy, and the other round your brother. You'll have to try to walk out of here. We can carry you later."

With the gravely injured man between them, frothy blood dribbling from the corner of his mouth, they stumbled away from the cabins of Lixnaw under the Whiteboys' covering fire that effectively kept the dragoons cowering behind their makeshift barricade. Once, a bullet from a musket thudded into the trunk of a tree a dozen feet from them but soon the sounds of battle faded behind them. John began coughing up gouts of blood and phlegm and they were forced to rest until his paroxysms were over.

"The ball's pierced a lung," Quillinan muttered to Jack. "That's why he's bringing up all this blood."

"Is there nothing we can do?"

"Just get him to his cabin and then it's up to Father O'Sullivan and God, though I'm guessing the priest can do little except ease your man's passing."

"Hush, John might hear you."

"He's too far gone to be making any sense of what I'm saying," Quillinan replied.

John tried to gasp a few words. "Michael . . . Michael," he spluttered before lolling into unconsciousness.

"Come on," urged Quillinan. "We'll take turns to carry him across our backs. It'll make little difference now."

It took them nearly two hours to reach the Keanes' cabin at Drombeg. As they neared the cabin in the gathering dusk, Jack saw his mother waiting anxiously outside. As soon as she saw the burden Quillinan carried, Mary Keane began hurrying towards them across the field. Jack ran forward to meet her.

"Tis John, Mam," he blurted. "A soldier's ball got him. He's awful hurt."

An expression of pain crossed Mary Keane's face but she said nothing. She moved behind Quillinan and lifted her son's head, smoothing his black hair from his eyes and brushing away the blood that was still coming from his mouth.

"Tis awful sorry I am," muttered Quillinan. "I'd rather it was your son carrying me with what happened to Michael and all."

"Oh, son," murmured Mary Keane. "Oh, son. Carry him gentle."

They laid John on some sacking and straw in the cabin, turning him on his side to allow his mother to staunch his wound. She ripped off part of her petticoat and thrust it into the gaping hole in his back.

"We should get Father O'Sullivan," advised Quillinan. "If you'd like, I'll run for him."

"Would you, Master Quillinan?" said Mary Keane. "That's a good man you are. And while you're at it, would you see me man in the fields and tell him what's gone on?"

"Tis my duty, lady. Your lad bleeding there was doing my bidding after all."

"No—don't be putting the blame on yourself, Master Quillinan. My sons fight for your Whiteboys because they believe in what you stand for."

She knelt by her son, a tear trickling down her cheek. "If Ireland has to take them, then let it be so."

Less than two hours later, Father O'Sullivan knelt by John inspecting his wound. John was breathing shallowly and with great effort. The priest shook his head sadly as he turned to the family standing anxiously around him in the small cabin.

"Tis in God's hands, I fear," he said quietly. "There's little man can do for him." He took a purple sash from inside his cassock, arranged it around his neck, and began administering the last rites, bending close to the mortally wounded man.

"He is at peace and in a perfect state of grace with his Maker," the priest declared finally, rising from his knees. Mary Keane held her son's hand, crooning a lullaby. Her husband knelt by her, his arm comfortingly around her shoulders as her sweet voice filled the room.

Jack stood by them remembering in vivid flashes times long past. How John had taught him to swim in the shallows of Ballybunnion amid much ducking and splashing and laughter; how they'd hunted for birds' nests in the hedge-rows; how they'd learned together at the itinerant teacher's school in the ditch. As he remembered, a great sadness filled him.

Towards the end, as the dusk lit the cabin with a gentle, grey light, John awoke from his unconsciousness for a moment. His eyes were soft and free from pain as he gazed up at his family. "Tis Michael there," he whispered. "There . . . in the shadows by the door. The soldiers didn't . . ." His voice faltered and then choked. "Oh, Mam," he cried once, his eyes staring wildly at that instant. Then his head fell back.

"He's gone. God take him and bless him," said Father O'Sullivan. "He made a good death, that he did."

Joe Keane leaned forward and pulled some sacking over his dead son's face. Then he turned to Quillinan who was standing away from the family at the back of the cabin.

"And what happens now, Master Whiteboy?" he asked bitterly. "That's two of me boys you've had. Will you be wanting the youngest now? And what about me? And will you be taking this poor woman, too?"

Quillinan shifted uneasily, for once at a loss to find the right words to say.

"Well?" said Joe Keane, rising menacingly to his feet.

"Now, Joe," said Father O'Sullivan gently. "Sure and can't you see that Master Quillinan shares your grief? God knows, I've preached often enough against the Whiteboys and I feel like you do that two young lives have been wasted. But isn't it time we thought on the living? God is seeing to Michael and John now."

"Amen to that," added Quillinan.

"Will the soldiers be coming for Jack, do you think?" asked the priest sharply.

"I fear so, Father," said Quillinan. "They know that Jack is a Whiteboy. We'll have to get the lad away."

"Oh, no. Not Jack," cried Mary Keane. "Not Jack now."

"But where to?" asked Jack. "England?"

"You'll find no friends nor safety there," said Quillinan. "Tis the Americas that'll be best for you."

"That's true," Father O'Sullivan agreed.

"But how?" said Jack, bewilderment in his voice. "There's no money for a passage and the soldiers will be watching the ports."

"The only way will be a boat from the Shannon," said his father. "One of the timber ships lying off Tarbert Island. You'll be able to work your passage."

"Do I have to go?" Jack pleaded.

"Sure, and your mam and me don't want you to go but it'd kill us if you were taken by the soldiers. Much better if we know you're safe somewhere. Anywhere."

"When?"

"The sooner the better," said Quillinan. "The soldiers will be coming on their horses at first light."

"Not so soon, please God," sobbed Mary Keane, burying her face in her husband's shoulder.

"Tis for the best," said Joe Keane, his voice gruff with emotion.

"Wait till it's fully dark in an hour or so, then Jack can walk as far as Ballylongford with me," said Father O'Sullivan. "He'll be safe from the soldiers. They'll not question anyone with me."

An hour later, Jack clasped his mother to him as he said goodbye. "I'll be back, Mam," he whispered into her hair. "I'll be back some time."

"Be safe, son. You're taking my heart with you."

"Will you get a message to Brigid for me? Tell her what's happened. Tell her I'll be back."

"I will, son."

Jack moved gently from her arms. He knelt in front of his father with head bowed. Quillinan turned away, unable to bear the sight of the farewell.

"Take the blessing of your father," said Joe Keane, placing his hand on Jack's head. "And the blessing of this home which will always be yours. And the blessing of your dead brothers, resting with the merciful God."

"Amen," said Father O'Sullivan, making the sign of the Cross with his right hand.

Quillinan took Jack's hand in his gnarled fist. "God be with you, lad. Be sure your sacrifices won't be wasted. The Whiteboys will keep fighting till this land is free and safe for you to return."

Jack nodded, unable to speak. He took half-a-dozen potatoes wrapped in his father's best green handkerchief. In his pocket were two gold sovereigns from the family's meagre savings, and the wooden crucifix from the tiny shrine to the Virgin Mary fixed to the wall.

He had one last look around the cabin, then ducked

through the doorway into the night. As he waited for Father O'Sullivan to join him, he snapped a twig of hawthorn from the hedge outside and slipped it into the pocket of his waistcoat. He gazed up at the dark sky, seeing the stars gleaming in the breaks between the high, flat clouds. He concentrated hard on the sky, trying to blot from his mind any thoughts of what might lie ahead. The stars would be his map for the journey home to Kerry that he was certain he would make one day. "Michael . . . John . . . Brigid," he whispered to the night.

"Aye, lad, never forget them," said Father O'Sullivan, who'd emerged quietly from the cabin to stand by him. "Your brothers have joined the others who've fought for this land, giving their most precious gift of all to Ireland. May they be blessed for that, because they died for their beliefs, whatever priests like me may think of the terrible waste of it all." He put his bony hand on Jack's shoulder.

As they moved away from the cabin, Jack looked back once. His mother and father stood in the doorway, their arms around each other.

"Don't look back, son," the priest said quietly. "Never look back again. Remember what was but think now on what will be."

Chapter 6
July, 1824

The cawing of rooks in the trees woke Jack Keane from his deep sleep. The night before he had walked with Father O'Sullivan to Ballylongford without encountering any army patrols and then had continued his journey alone until reaching the River Shannon. The moon had painted the wide river in dancing silver. Jack had sat for a long while listening to the waves lapping quietly on the shore and almost fell asleep at the water's edge, lulled by its insistent, hypnotic motion. But he had shaken himself awake again, realizing that he needed to be under cover when first light came. He had found a hiding place in the deep undergrowth of a thick wood along the shore. When dawn came, Jack ate one of the lumpers in his handkerchief and continued along the riverbank. He kept to the edge of the wood as much as possible, always ready to duck into it if he sighted any soldiers or other early-morning travellers. He had no clear plan except to reach Tarbert where the ships that crossed the Atlantic discharged and took on cargoes.

By mid-morning Jack had reached some cabins on the outskirts of the small port. He could travel no further under cover. His clothes were grubby and stained from sleeping the night in the open; his legs and hands were dirty, his chin rough with fine stubble. He realized he painted a suspicious picture. Jack summoned up all his nerve as he approached a cabin outside which a grizzled old man sat mending a fishing net.

When he was still a few yards away, the fisherman looked up. "Been travelling long, lad?" he asked gruffy.

"Some . . . some distance," Jack stammered.

"Rest a while here," said the fisherman. He gestured at the water-barrel by the cabin door. "Wash and freshen yourself. A stranger shouldn't be looking like a running man in these parts, not with soldiers and militia as thick as fleas on a mangy dog."

Jack's heart jumped in alarm but he hid his nervousness as he splashed water over himself.

"Need a razor, lad?"

"I have a few bristles."

"There's one on the window ledge inside the doorway. Use it carefully. Tis sharp."

Jack went into the neat little cabin and shaved without a mirror, feeling the blade pull at his soft bristles.

"I'm not a man to be pushing his nose into any man's business," said the fisherman. "When you're as old as I am you've learned to keep your silence. But tis sometimes better to share a problem."

Jack felt that he could trust the old man. "I must find a ship to get me to the Americas."

"And what would a young lad be wanting to be away for?" asked the fisherman, his fingers still busy at his net.

Jack hesitated.

"Have the little people got your tongue then? Or is it something that might be shaming you?" the old man persisted.

"Tis nothing to be ashamed of to fight the English soldiers," Jack said hotly. "Me brothers have died fighting and now the soldiers are after me."

"So tis a fighting man you are then. Well, that's a surprise for one with so few bristles. Well, if I was a few years younger I'd be there helping you fight the soldier boys." The fisherman laid down his net. "Now, that's tight enough to catch the salmon." He smiled conspiratorially at Jack, peering at him from beneath his eyebrows. "Can you be paying your passage?"

"I've only a little money. Two sovereigns in all."

"Ah, then, tis a fine problem," said the fisherman, rubbing his chin thoughtfully. "That's not enough for a passage. You'll have to stow away and then throw yourself on the mercy of the captain. There's the *Grannia* of Captain Higgins making ready to sail tonight to fetch some timber from the Americas. She's lying just where I was thinking of laying my nets." The fisherman winked at Jack, and clapped him on the shoulder. "Well, if we're to be shipmates you'd better be knowing I'm called Sean McManus."

"My name is . . ."

"No, better not be saying, lad. Though you remind me of me own boy who's a long time away working in England."

The fisherman took a stub of a pipe from his pocket and filled it with shag tobacco. "You rest the day with me, lad, and I'll be seeing if any of me boy's clothes will be fitting you. If you're to cross the Atlantic, you'll be needing stouter clothes than you have now."

When the heat of the day had passed, Jack and the fisherman made their way down to Tarbert Harbor. A patrol of soldiers in red and black uniforms lounged by the quayside watching the activity in the small port. A number of tiny one-masted fishing smacks were being prepared for their nightly expeditions to the mouth of the Shannon where the fish were plentiful. Jack was prepared for the shout of discovery at any moment, but in fact, he was indistinguish-

able from any of the dozens of fishing folk making ready for
sea. He was now wearing a thick blue sweater, heavy
canvas trousers, and boots that reached nearly to his knees.
With a net swung across his shoulders, he looked every inch
a seafaring man as he walked alongside Sean McManus.

After stowing the nets, the old fisherman pushed his boat
off from the quay and began rowing out of the narrow
harbor. "You just be sitting there and look busy, lad," he
told Jack. "I'm thinking you're a country boy who might
not be too much at ease pulling a pair of oars."

When they were clear of the harbor, the fisherman
shipped his oars and hauled up the boat's single sail. The
soft summer breeze pushed them out into the river. Ahead,
Jack could see the low, grey shape of Tarbert Island rising
from the Shannon, its outline tinged with the sun's orange,
and the tall masts of the ocean-going ships lying safely at
anchor in its lee.

Sean McManus pointed to a two-master. "See, the one
with the red deckhouse?"

Jack nodded, peering through the haze.

"Well, lad, that's the *Grannia* bound for North America.
A fine ship that'll carry you safely across the Atlantic."

Jack helped him throw out the nets as the fisherman
steered his boat out in a circle. The corks on top of the nets
bobbed in the gentle swell out in the river. The fiery sun
sinking beneath the horizon transformed the Shannon into a
scarlet carpet.

After drifting for an hour, hardly speaking, content with
nature, they pulled in the net and a dozen silver, wriggling
salmon tumbled into the bottom of the boat. The fisherman
was delighted. "You brought luck with you tonight, lad. Tis
a fine catch."

But Jack's thoughts and eyes were firmly on the *Grannia*,

looming hugely over the small fishing boat as it drifted, seemingly without purpose, closer to her hull.

"See those ropes hanging from her rails?" said Sean McManus. "When we get closer, you slip over the side and swim to one of them. Pull yourself up and slide into one of the ports. After that tis up to you to stay out of the way until the *Grannia*'s well into the Atlantic. If Captain Higgins discovers you before he clears the river, he might put you ashore with a few lashes across your back."

Jack nodded apprehensively. The fishing boat slid under the bow of the timber ship. Jack stood up, ready to clamber overboard.

"Best be taking those boots off, lad," called the fisherman. "They'll fill with water and send you straight to the bottom of the river. Put them between your teeth."

Jack did as he was told. Then he slipped quietly over the side of the boat.

"Thank you for your help, Sean McManus," he said, holding on to the side for a moment. "One day I'll return and pay you back."

"Don't be thinking on it, lad. May God go with you in your travels."

Jack raised a hand in salute and swam into the shadow of the timber ship as she swung gently on the rising tide. He grasped one of the ropes hanging down nearly to the water and started to haul himself up, hand over hand. The first port he reached was securely battened down. The second was open and he swung through it.

He was in a hold stacked high with barrels lashed together to stop them rolling around when the ship met the open sea. Jack concealed himself behind the barrels in a corner of the hold and peeled off his sodden sweater, shivering slightly as the night air played over his body. Above him he could hear orders being shouted, feet running on the deck, the creaking of ropes, and then the rattle of the sails being hoisted. Away from him, towards the bow, he heard the heavy clanking of the anchor chain as it was pulled up. Almost imperceptibly, the motion of the ship changed as she began to make headway towards the mouth of the Shannon. A slurping noise came from the barrels around Jack. He guessed they must be filled with drinking water for the voyage.

He took a last look out of the open port. Tears formed in his eyes as he watched the river banks, hardly more than a smudge against the sky slipping by. He thought about his dead brothers; the gentleness of his mother; the reassuring strength of his father; the happiness that had always seemed to fill the cabin at Drombeg. Jack was suddenly filled with a terrible loneliness, and the tears rolled down his cheeks. Then he felt in his trouser pocket and pulled out a package wrapped in oil cloth by the old fisherman. Inside were the crucifix and the twig of hawthorn from the hedge by the cabin. Somehow they comforted him. "I'll be back," he murmured. "One day. One day."

Then, he heard a noise directly above him. He scuttled back to his hiding place just as the hatch was pulled back and a seaman began clumping down the ladder into the hold. Jack shrank back into the darkness of his corner.

"'Tis right you are, Captain," the seaman bawled. "Some lazy begger didn't close the port."

Jack heard the seaman move to the port, only a few feet from him, and slam it shut before securing it with an iron bar.

"Now that would have been a nice state of things if the sea had got to the barrels," the seaman muttered. "All battened down, sir," he called up through the open hold and, satisfied, climbed the ladder and pulled the hatch back over the entrance to the hold.

* * *

Jonathan Sandes was in exultant mood as he dined with his wife that evening. Everything seemed to have worked out to his advantage. The battle at Lixnaw had ended in a bloody draw. One Whiteboy and one soldier killed, a few on each side wounded, a police barracks razed to the ground; but most important, the leading Whiteboys had scattered into hiding and Captain Eugene de Vere Pearson had been ordered to return to Dublin to explain his actions. The troops in North Kerry had been left under the command of Robert Leslie, the head of the local militia, a man whom Sandes knew he could easily dominate.

"You look happy, dear," remarked his wife, helping herself to two slices of roast beef.

"Not happy," replied Sandes. "Just thoughtful. With that Dragoon popinjay on his way back to Dublin we've got to consider our next actions against these accursed White-boys."

"From what you were saying before dinner, dear, they don't seem to pose much of a threat now."

"Far from it. They're slippery and cunning. They'll lie low for a few weeks and then they'll strike again. We must tighten the curfew and go on searching the cabins for weapons, that sort of thing."

"I know I shouldn't feel sorry for them but I can't help but feel a little sympathy for that Drombeg family who've lost two of their sons."

"All three of them, by all accounts," snorted Sandes. "The youngest is well away in hiding by now, I'm thinking. If we find him he'll be the first to dance on a rope at Tralee. There's ample proof he was at Lixnaw. He and his brothers went everywhere together."

"I'm sure you know best, dear."

"Well, that may be so," said Sandes expansively, stretching across the table to ring the tiny bell. "Certainly I know better than that fool Pearson with his soft tactics. Things are going to be harder from now on. And that's the truth."

Brigid Aherne came into the room to clear the table. Her eyes still showed the signs of the tears she had wept after hearing in the market square about John Keane's death and Jack's flight.

Sandes barely glanced at her. "I have some late work to do tonight," he told his wife. "So I'll be wanting some brandy and a pipe in my sitting room after you retire."

"As you wish, dear."

"Did you hear that, Brigid?" asked Sandes, smiling at her. He was in such an expansive mood that he'd decided to risk an hour or so with Brigid even with his wife in the house.

"Yes, sir," said Brigid dully. "Whatever you say." Her mind was so numb with grief and shock that she didn't even experience her usual feeling of self-disgust at Sandes' command and all it would mean. "In your sitting room later, sir."

When Jack Keane awoke, the ship was yawing and pitching as it ploughed through the heavy swell of the Atlantic. He stood up, stretching his cramped, aching limbs, and looked round the hold. Slivers of light filtered through the port and the hatch above him. He paced up and down for a few minutes, trying to adjust to the motion of the ship. If he could put up with hunger perhaps he could remain undetected for the whole voyage. Then a queasiness began to fill his throat. A sudden cramp in his stomach bent him double and he retched up bile. He slumped to the deck, clutching his stomach and moaning in agony. Fresh air, he must have fresh air, he thought. Jack crawled over to the closed port. He pulled the iron bolt from the port and pushed it open. A rush of sea spray spanked into his face as he gulped air into his lungs. He felt as if he was going to die as he retched again and again, bringing up almost colorless liquid. He swayed and slipped in his own stench and misery for hour after hour as the ship, with little ballast in her holds, continued its rolling. He was barely conscious when the hatch was pulled open above him. He moaned and turned his head away from the shaft of bright light.

"Ye Gods and what have we here?" a voice shouted. Rough hands grasped him and pulled him upright. "A stowaway, eh, and won't the Captain be right glad to see you."

A hard face swam into Jack's vision and he moaned again as his body was racked by another bout of retching.

"You're learning the hard way about the sea, and that's the truth," said the seaman. He hauled Jack upright, pushing him toward the ladder. "Up you go, lad. The captain will be wanting to meet you."

Jack crawled up the ladder on his hands and knees, until a final shove sent him sprawling on the deck. He lay there unable to move.

"Well, well, Flannery," a gruff voice said above him. "So you found a hidden piece of cargo, did you?" A heavy sea boot crashed into Jack's ribs, lifting him almost off the deck and thrusting him on to his back.

"Belay that, sailor," a voice roared. "Can't you see your man's half-dead already? What are you kicking him into hell for?"

"Aye, aye, Captain," the man standing above Jack replied. "Flannery found him in the water hold."

"We won't be getting any sense out of him yet awhile, Flannery."

"I'm guessing not, Captain."

"Well, strap him to the mast for his own safety and let him suffer his sickness until it's out of him. He'll be better before the day's out and then maybe we can be teaching him what happens to stowaways."

"Aye, aye, sir."

After six hours on the open deck, Jack felt weak and empty but, at least, the motion of the ship wasn't making him dizzy anymore. He began to take an interest in his surroundings, watching the crew climbing the rigging to adjust the sails which billowed and cracked in the strong wind driving the *Grannia* westwards. By twisting his head he could just see the coxswain straining at the wheel on the raised afterdeck, trying to give the ship every advantage of the prevailing wind. By the wheel, Jack could see the man he presumed to be Captain Higgins; a tall, gaunt man with a dark beard shot through with grey, wearing a navy blue reefer jacket and a peaked cap. A shiny brass hailing tube for shouting commands was tucked under one arm. Jack noticed that the captain's spade beard was divided in half with each side cut at a different length. The captain saw Jack watching him and approached the mast.

"Feeling better now, laddie?" he said.

Jack nodded, a weak and guilty smile on his pallid face.

"Aye, well I think we can be unstrapping you since you won't be falling overboard now in your sickness."

Jack stood up, rubbing his arms where the rope had bitten tightly.

"Now, laddie," said Captain Higgins. "You've got some reckoning to give about how you came to be in my ship."

"I . . . I . . ." Jack coughed as he tried to speak.

"Get some water for the boy," ordered the captain.

When Jack had supped two mouthfuls of brackish water from a mug he tried to speak again. "I came aboard from Tarbert," he began.

"I'm aware of that," snapped the captain. "From one of those fishing smack that were skipping around like mosquitoes on a stagnant pond."

Jack nodded agreement. "I had to be away from Ireland and your ship was the only one ready to sail. Tis sorry I am for any trouble I've caused you."

"You've caused me no trouble at all, laddie," said Captain Higgins grimly. "But I'm wondering if you know how much trouble and pain you're going to cause yourself."

Jack looked puzzled. "I feel better now," he said.

"Not your seasickness, you bilge rat," roared the captain. "Stowaways have to be punished or we'd have every guttersnipe sneaking aboard. Since you've suffered a mite already, I'm not going to be harsh on you. But you have to be punished."

The captain turned to a burly seaman standing by him. "Tie the stowaway to the rails."

"Aye, aye, Captain."

The seaman deftly slipped a rope around Jack's wrists and pulled him toward the rails on the after deck. Jack was too weak to resist. The seaman looped the rope around the rails above his head and tugged on it so that Jack's arms were jerked high into the air. He was forced to stand on tiptoe to ease the excruciating pressure on his arms. His face was pressed against the timbers of the ladder leading to the afterdeck.

"Right," he heard the captain bellow. "Administer the punishment, if you please."

"How many, Captain?"

"Six will be enough, I'm thinking."

"Aye, aye, sir."

Jack heard a whistling sound behind him and then an agonizing blow laid his back bare. He screeched in his agony as he felt the hot blood running down his back. Jack rocked his head from side to side, screaming all the time, as the lash tore into his flesh five more times, ripping and cutting.

"That's enough," shouted Captain Higgins. "Cut him down and take him below. And swab down the deck. The lad's bled like a stuck pig."

Jack slumped to the deck and lay moaning and writhing in a spreading pool of his own blood. Another sailor picked up a bucket of seawater and flung it over him, making him sob with renewed pain as the brine bit into the open wounds. Two sailors lifted him under the arms and dragged him across the deck to the ladder leading to the crew's quarters.

"You either walk down, lad, or you fall down," one of them muttered in Jack's ear. He summoned all his remaining strength to stumble down the ladder. At the foot of it he collapsed in a heap. The sailors picked him up effortlessly and laid him face down across the wooden slats of a bunk.

"Let him rest there," said one of them. "He's near done in."

"No, tis better if we get it over with now," said the other. "He's as near senseless as makes no difference."

"Hold him then."

Jack felt the weight of a body press across his lower back, while other hands grasped his arms and held his head in a vise-like grip. A rough gag of sail cloth was thrust between Jack's teeth and a sailor began rubbing salt in the long stripes of his wounds. The gag turned his screams into agonized groans. The sailors needed all their combined strength to hold Jack down as he quivered and bucked. His mind filled with the glowing redness of his suffering. Finally, mercifully, he slipped into unconsciousness.

For the next two days Jack hovered in and out of delirium as he lay on the rough bunk. Occasionally he was aware of someone lifting his head and pouring cooling water between his lips but for the rest of the time he was in a deep sleep. On the third day he awoke, his head clear, aware of the creaking and swaying of the ship. He raised his head slowly and looked at his surroundings.

The crew's quarters were long and low and narrow. On either side of a rough table were bunks filled with lumpy-looking sacks. A candle in a lantern swung from one of the beams, bringing some light to the gloom below decks. Jack saw two sailors sitting on a bench by the table. They were carving slices off what appeared to be a leg of pork and eating them with square biscuits. He tried to speak but only a croak came from his parched throat.

One of the sailors looked up from his eating and gestured toward Jack with his knife. "Sounds as if the stowaway's come to his senses," he said. He stabbed the knife into the top of the table and walked over to Jack's bunk, bending to peer closely into his face. "Are you better then?" he asked.

Jack tried to speak again but the effort was too much. He nodded weakly.

"Right then, tis best we get you out of there or else you'll be permanent stiff. Can you move at all?"

Jack pushed himself up a little on his arms and rested on his elbows.

"Come on, Martin," the sailor called to his companion. "Give us a hand."

The two of them lifted Jack off the bunk with surprising gentleness. His whole back ached dully but the hurt was no longer jaggedly painful. The sailors supported him as he limped to the table, his arms around the sailor for support. He sat gingerly on the bench and rested his head in his hands. The sailors watched him with concern until Jack lifted his head and smiled gratefully at them.

"Thanks be to God," he muttered hoarsely.

One of the sailors banged his fist on the table and roared with laughter. "You be all right now, stowaway. Just awake and already giving thanks."

The other thrust a lump of meat in front of Jack but he pushed it aside. "Water," he whispered. "Any water?"

A mug of water was put on the table. Jack picked it up with shaking hands and gulped it down. He wiped his mouth with the back of his hand. Then, painfully, he began to eat.

"How long?" he asked eventually, his voice still low and thick.

"Two days, lad, you've been laying there since your lashing," said the sailor who'd given him the water. "The carpenter was getting all set to sew you in canvas and slide you twelve fathoms deep. Twould have been unsettling not knowing what name to bury you under."

"Tis Jack Keane."

"Well, I be Patrick Deane," said the friendly sailor, a huge man, well over six feet tall with a round, moon face. He gestured at his companion. "And this mate of mine be Martin Flannery. Twas Martin that found you baulking your belly up with seasickness."

Flannery smiled apologetically at Jack. He was as tall as Deane but as thin as a begging priest. "Sorry, Jack, but if it hadn't been me, twould have been someone else."

Jack nodded understandably. "What happens next?"

"Well, by rights," said Flannery, "we should be taking you to Captain Higgins right away but just you be resting a bit and find your strength, shipmate."

Jack began walking unsteadily around the crew's quarters, knocking himself painfully against the bunks, but soon he had adjusted to the roll and life of the ship. Surprisingly, he found, he no longer felt any sickness. The two sailors watched him carefully as he eased the stiffness and soreness out of his limbs.

"You'd better be cleaning yourself up before you meet the captain," said Patrick Deane. "You can use my razor on your bristles but be preparing yourself for a shock when you look in the glass."

Jack took the broken piece of mirror from Deane and looked blearily into it. A face he hardly recognized stared back at him. It was no longer the face of a young, untried man. The cheekbones were more prominent in the thinner, gaunter features. The eyes were gleaming hard, reflecting the extreme pain he had suffered. But, most apparent of all, there was now a streak of snow white hair on his head, about an inch in thickness, running back from his widow's peak.

Jack brushed his hand back through his hair, and studied his new face as he tugged at the bristles with Deane's blunt razor. It wasn't unpleasing, he thought; definitely the face of a man to be reckoned with.

When he'd finished, Deane handed him a thick red shirt woven out of soft wool. "That comes from the Frenchie trappers along the St. Lawrence River," he explained. "Twill keep you warm and be gentle on your back until the scars harden."

"I'll take you to the captain now," Flannery volunteered.

"He can be a hard man, Captain Higgins, but I'm telling you he'll be mighty glad to see you up and around."

He led the way up on to the deck. The sky was grey and sullen but it was one of the most welcome sights Jack had ever seen, and he breathed the spray-filled air deep into his lungs. Captain Higgins was by the wheel of the afterdeck. As he approached him, Flannery raised a knuckle to his forehead.

"The stowaway, Captain. He tells us he's named Jack Keane."

"So, Jack Keane," remarked the captain with a welcoming smile, "you're up and about again." He offered Jack his hand. "No hard feelings, I hope. A captain dare not be making an exception to the rules on stowaways."

Jack shook the calloused hand. "I didn't understand at the time, Captain."

Captain Higgins laughed throatily. "No, I reckon you didn't. But there be very few men at sea without some scars on their backs."

Jack looked around him. All he could see was water; foam-flecked green waves to every horizon, pounding under the bow of the *Grannia* as she rolled and bobbed like a cork in and out of the troughs. "Tis green, not blue," he observed. "The sea's green."

"Aye, lad, out here and under this sort of sky, tis green. I can tell you've never been on an ocean before."

"Nor have I, Captain. I'm a farmer if anything."

"So, lad, what are you running away from to come to sea?"

Jack gripped the rail to steady himself as he told Captain Higgins the story of how he had been forced to flee from Ireland. The captain listened in silence, merely grunting with disgust when he heard of the hanging of Michael Keane.

"So you're a bit of a rebel, are you, lad?" he said when Jack had finished.

"Sometimes you've got to fight," Jack replied simply.

"Aye, and isn't that just the truth? Twas what me dad used to say when I was a youngster. He was hung in Wexford in the '98. But that was a proper rebellion that was. Not like your Whiteboys dashing around the countryside."

"You've got to start somewhere," Jack said lamely.

Captain Higgins laughed and slapped him on the shoulder. Jack winced at the sudden pain. "Sorry, lad, I'm forgetting," the captain apologized, still chuckling to himself. "So now you want to go to the Americas?"

"I can pay, Captain." Jack fumbled in the pockets of his canvas trousers and pulled out the two gold sovereigns.

Captain Higgins looked at the money in Jack's hand with a surprised expression. "Still got them, have you? I must have a more honest crew than I was thinking," he said, smiling broadly. "Put them away, lad. True they'd help towards a passage but you'll be needing them when you reach the Americas. You can work your passage. Put some muscle on you, so it will, and the more hands I have crossing this ocean the better I like it."

"Where are you bound?"

"Boston town, lad. That's where we'll be taking on some more provisions and then we sail up the coast to Canada picking up timber. You can leave the ship where you will, but I'm guessing Boston's as good a place as any. There be quite a few Irish settled there, although I hear tell most of them are from Ulster rather than Munster like you."

At first, Jack was put to scrubbing decks and polishing the brass, but his new friends, Deane and Flannery, began teaching him how to splice ropes and tie knots and soon he was allowed to climb dizzily into the rigging of the ship to help reef the sails. The work was hard and unremitting, as the *Grannia* ploughed ever westwards. Jack enjoyed it, although at first he hardly had the energy left at the end of the day to climb into his bunk. Later on, as his muscles hardened and he became used to the work, he stayed some nights on deck with the rest of the crew, watching the gamblers playing pitch and toss, throwing coins into the air and guessing which side up they would fall, or joining in the shanties sung to the accompaniment of Flannery's mouth organ. Sometimes he would listen entranced as one of the sailors told of the far distant lands he had visited and the exotic women he'd known. Jack blushed at first at some of the bawdier tales and was glad the night hid his innocence from his shipmates. Occasionally he would stand by himself at the ship's rail looking up at the stars and thinking of his home. It was then he would feel totally alone in the world, alone with the sea, and yet very close to his family and to Brigid Aherne. The harsh thoughts about Brigid and Jonathan Sandes had faded from his memory to be replaced by a deep, warm longing to hold her again as he had the first evening they'd met.

Once Flannery came up to him as he stood gazing up at the stars pinpricking the dark blue coverlet of a clear sky. "Sure, Jack," he'd said, "and doesn't it make you wonder? Looking up there at all those tiny lights, you sometimes think you're the only person in creation, so you do. And then you wonder if there might be sailors on a sea up there looking down on you and wondering the same."

"Tis true, Martin."

"Aye, Jack, and that's why the men who go to sea are very different. They see things others don't. Out here on the ocean you're terrible close to the secret of life. And because you are, you live happier and harder than most others, I'm thinking. You belong to no one but you belong to everyone. You've no home but everywhere is home."

"Is that why you go to sea?"

"Didn't me dad go to sea and his dad afore him? We Flannerys have been putting to sea ever since Grannia was Queen of the West."

"Queen of the West?"

"Of course, you wouldn't be knowing about the greatest she-pirate of them all. A handsome woman she was, by all tell, but she could fight down any man or three. Hundreds of years ago Grannia was the terror of the west coast, raiding and plundering all the Dagoes and Frenchies and Portugee who traded into Cork and Limerick. She even took on Turkish merchantmen, and made then haul down their flags to her. And wasn't she a true queen as well? Didn't Elizabeth of England, that cursed Protestant, receive her as an equal when Grannia sailed into London to offer her help to beat the Armada? And didn't Grannia chase all the Dagoes on to the rocks clear around Ireland? Sure, and tis lucky you are to be crossing the ocean in a ship named after her. Tis a lucky charm."

Jack was fascinated by Flannery's tales and his cavalier approach to life. Flannery sensed this admiration and tried to persuade his young friend to stay with the ship.

"Tis a good life, Jack, and you'd be enjoying it," he urged.

It was tempting for Jack but he had the feeling that if he became a seaman, he would never see his home again. That was the driving thought in his mind; to return eventually and claim Brigid Aherne. He was explaining this to Flannery one day, the forty-second of the voyage, while they were busy on deck coiling ropes.

"Tis probably true, Jack," conceded Flannery. "Once a sailor, always a sailor, and once a landsman, always a landsman. Tis weaned into you at your mam's breast."

Just then, from high up the main mast, came a shout, "Land ho! Land ho! Two points on the port bow."

With the other sailors on deck, Jack and Martin Flannery rushed to the port rail and peered into the distance. At first they could see nothing but then, as the *Grannia* rose on the crest of a wave, there, running along the horizon, was a grey smudge.

"Where are we?" asked Jack excitedly. "What land?"

"Tis too early to know," said Flannery. "But Captain Higgins being the navigator he is, it won't be too far off Boston town. Somewhere along the New England coast, to be sure. It has been a good voyage for charting the stars, even if the wind's been against us a deal of the way."

Jack noticed that even the most experienced sailors were excited at the prospect of land. They went about their routine work with a new bounce in their step, talking among themselves like womenfolk at market.

In another two hours, the coastline was clearly in sight. Occasionally, a flash of white was visible as a wave broke upon the rocks along the low, featureless shore.

"Tis New England without a doubt," observed Flannery. "I be reckoning we're just a mite south of Massachusetts Bay, just as we should be. The captain'll want to run up into Boston around Cape Cod rather than beat down past Salem from the north."

"You'd be right, Martin," said Patrick Deane. "The last time I made fall at Boston, the captain found the coast north of Salem Harbor and had the divil's own job coming down the shore. The wind was howling from every point of the compass, so it was."

For three hours, the *Grannia* stood well off the coast as she ran northwest with the prevailing wind. Then the coast fell away, as the ship rounded a rocky headland and entered a wide bay. By now, dusk was beginning to fall.

"We'll be staying out another night," Flannery explained to Jack. "There be islands between us and Boston Harbor and the captain won't be risking them at night. He'll lie well off until first light. You be ready to get into the rigging to shorten sail."

Sure enough the order came to reef back all sails until the *Grannia* was wearing only enough canvas to maintain the slightest headway. From high in the swaying rigging, Jack could see small, twinkling lights along the shore, and above them one steady, stronger light.

"The lights of Boston town," said Flannery, hanging in the rigging beside him. "The light above them all is what's called 'Bullfinch's Pillar.' In the old days it was called the Beacon Light till the Yankees renamed it."

Hardly anyone slept for more than a few hours that night. At dawn, the *Grannia* took on more sail and under a brightening sky began moving towards Boston Harbor. She slid past large, wooded islands on her port side before Jack got his first real sight of the town. From the buildings along the quays, bristling with the masts of ships, Boston rose, undulating on hills, along a promontory, clearly separated from the mainland by a wide river. As the *Grannia* nosed into harbor, she was taken in tow by three rowing boats which pulled her to a berth. Even at this early hour, the quays were thronged with men, loading and unloading other vessels in the port, moving cargoes between wooden warehouses that stood only a few yards back from the cobbled quayside. Lines were thrown from the *Grannia* and tied to bollards. When she was secured, her anchor dropped into the murky water of the harbor with a loud splash and a rattle of iron links. As gulls mewed and swooped above, the crew was assembled by the bosun on the quarterdeck.

"We have a day before we take on provisions," Captain Higgins told them. "Apart from one watch, you can go ashore, but be back aboard at first light tomorrow. I need not be reminding you that those who go adrift forfeit all their pay under the ship's articles." He pointed his telescope at Jack. "You . . . report to me before you go ashore."

"Right, Jack, since you've determined not to be a seaman," said Flannery, "at least you can see your new home for one day in the company of your old shipmates." He winked at Deane. "We'll be showing you some sights, I'm thinking, that you didn't see in Kerry. Now off with you and talk to the captain."

Jack clambered up the ladder to the afterdeck. Captain Higgins was standing by the rail watching the activity on the quayside. He swung around at Jack's approach.

"Ah, the fighting man, eh?" he smiled. "All ready to be starting your new life?"

"Aye, Captain."

"Well, in the absence of your father, let me be giving you a little advice, lad."

"Captain?"

"This is a new country you're coming to. The Yankees threw off the English yoke just as the men of '98 tried to do. But that doesn't mean it's all that different here. There's them that serve and them that are served. Just like anywhere else. Keep to your kind, work hard and curb your spirit. They've had enough rebellion here to fill their stomachs for a lifetime." He smiled warmly. "But I'm guessing you'll adapt. You've learned to be a passable seaman quick enough. It might have given you some white hairs but it's also built you some useful muscles."

Captain Higgins reached inside his waistcoat pocket and pulled out a gold sovereign. "Here's your wages for the crossing. I'm reckoning you deserve them."

Jack took the coin and shook the captain's outstretched hand. He didn't know quite what to say in the face of such kindly generosity. "I'll never forget you, Captain, and that's the truth."

"No, lad, I doubt if you will. Every time you undress, you'll have the scars on your back to remind you." The captain guffawed. "Now be off with you and God watch over you."

Jack Keane strode down the bouncing gang plank behind the tall figures of Flannery and Deane, his three gold sovereigns jingling in his pocket. He felt ready for anything that Boston had to offer.

Chapter 7
August, 1824

A definite odor came to Jack's nostrils as he walked along the quayside with Martin Flannery and Patrick Deane. Later, he was to recognize sewerage and mud from the marshes of Back Bay, the oxides belching from the iron works and the smell of raw cotton from the textile mills. The smell suggested people and industry on a scale he had never encountered before. There was a bustle among the people that was strange to him. They scurried about their work purposefully, speaking in a burring accent with an indefinable nasal harshness. They dressed more sturdily than the Irish but not as finely as the land agents like Doctor Church and Master Sandes. There were some men in high crowned hats, men obviously of high station, but many still wore the tricorn hats which even Jack knew had passed out of fashion on the other side of the Atlantic. The buildings too were immediately different to his eyes: constructed more of wood than stone, two stories high with narrow, latticed windows. Such large, brick buildings as there were, clearly great centers of commerce or worship, dominated the cobbled streets and alleys that rose and fell, higgledy-piggledy, behind the quayside.

Flannery and Deane seemed familiar with the town, and pushed past people, bumping shoulders, in a way that was quite new to their young companion. Down one street, up an alley, under an archway, they made their way to a two-story, wooden building in a narrow cobbled street which was divided by an open gutter.

"Now, Jack," said Flannery, "this is the most important place for you in all Boston town. If you're a wise lad, this is where you'll make your life for tis here you'll meet all the people you should be knowing."

He unlatched the wooden door and flung it open. "Mother McCarthy's groggery!" he announced loudly.

A torrent of noise flooded out of the low-beamed room to greet the three men as they stood in the doorway. It ceased for a moment as the men and women inside, seated at rough tables, turned to look at the newcomers and then it swelled again as they settled back to their chattering and drinking. Jack coughed as the fetid smell of spilt drink and rough tobacco hit him. Flannery laughed sympathetically and gave Jack a push towards a wide plank set on two upturned barrels. It was covered with bottles and empty mugs and clearly served as the bar. Jack stumbled over someone's feet and nearly fell to the sawdust-strewn floor. He gripped the bar to save himself and stared directly into the leer of a dried pig's face, the color of a moldy lemon with salt caked in its ears, which lay morosely on the end of the plank.

"Flannery and Deane!" a voice shouted raucously above the din. "Tis me favorite sailor boys back to see their old Mother McCarthy."

A large, lumpy figure in black with a grimy, once-white mop cap swept past Jack and gripped Flannery and Deane round their shoulders in a tight hug, planting smacking kisses full on their lips. Jack's two companions whooped with joy and, together, lifted the woman off her feet, swinging her high into the air. Her stained petticoats fluttered up, revealing a pair of thick, knobbly legs encased in black stockings.

"Tis not for long, mother," exclaimed Flannery. "We've only a bit of a day and a night here so we've to be getting down to serious business straight away."

Deane caught Jack's eyes and winked. "Mother," he cried, "we've brought a new friend for you, fresh from the old country he is too."

The woman turned round and looked up at Jack.

"His name's Jack Keane and he'll be staying on in Boston town, that he will."

"Welcome then, Jack Keane," shouted Mother McCarthy. She was at least fifty years old, thought Jack; thin, grey hair straggled from under the mop cap; tiny broken veins in her nose and cheeks betrayed her taste for hard liquor. "My, my . . . and tis a handsome young friend you've brought me, boys," she said, her voice punching loudly through the hubbub in the room. Her arms reached up and encircled Jack's neck, pulling down his face to her own level. Her lips devoured his.

Flannery and Deane guffawed at his squirming unease. They patted the woman on her ample shoulders.

"Come on, mother. Tis cradle snatching you are. Let the lad be."

Mother McCarthy released Jack and stepped back, a broad grin on her face. She gestured towards the bar. "Come on, now, and get some grog down you. You've had a mighty long voyage to build up a thirst that you have."

Flannery reached out and picked up a dusty bottle lying by the pig's head. He slopped the contents into three earthenware mugs.

"Come on, lads. Let's join the party!"

Jack and Patrick Deane lifted their mugs. Deane drained his in one gulp and Jack, still embarrassed from Mother McCarthy's embrace, did the same. The undiluted alcohol, oily and sweet tasting, coursed down his throat like a stream of red-hot lava. He gagged on it and was almost sick on the floor. "By the Holy Saints," he spluttered, red in the face once more, "what's this concoction?"

"The juice of the juniper," said Flannery calmly, picking up the bottle and pouring another mugful for each of them. "Mother McCarthy's gin brewed by her own sweet hands."

Jack followed his friend's example in draining the second mug. This time the room took on a cheerier, less sordid, atmosphere. Everyone gave the appearance of enjoying themselves. The women at the tables laughed vivaciously, attractively. Many of them, Jack saw, wore paint on their faces, emphasizing their eyes and lips. Occasionally a man and a woman would get up from a table and walk towards the stairway at the back of the room with their arms around each other's waists. He nodded towards the wooden stairway as Flannery filled his mug again. "Where does that lead to, Martin?"

"Paradise, lad. But get in the proper mood first or you'll be thinking it's more like hell when you climb them stairs."

Jack looked puzzled.

"Women, lad," explained Deane with a lopsided smile. "There's more to this groggery than gin. You can find anything you want at Mother McCarthy's from a business deal to a sturdy wench."

"Have you any friends for us?" Flannery called over to Mother McCarthy who was now deep in conversation with a tall, well-dressed man in a stovepipe hat.

She waved over at Flannery. "The best, lads. Only the best." She hurried around the tables with surprising agility, whispering in the ears of three young women and nodding over at Jack, Flannery and Deane who had by now seated themselves at an empty table by the stairway.

The girls walked over to the table, mugs in hand, swaying a little. Two of them were flaxen haired; the third was very dark, her hair the shade of a raven's wing. Jack, now sipping his third mug of gin, felt a pang of memory, and thought how similar her hair was to Brigid's.

"Sit you down, girls," invited Flannery, grabbing one of the fair-haired girls around the waist and pulling her on to his lap. "Which one do you want, lad?" He noticed Jack's eyes flick towards the dark-haired girl. "Right, Patrick, tis you for the other then," he told Deane. "Tis only right the lad should be having his choice on his first visit to Mother McCarthy's."

Without hesitation, the dark-haired girl sat down next to Jack. "And would you be getting a girl a drink, Irisher?" she said, putting her hand on his forearm.

Close to her, Jack could see that the paint on her face helped conceal the fine lines around her eyes and at each corner of her mouth. Her eyes sparkled; her features were pleasant, if not beautiful, her perfume was fresh and light. There was a sense of vulnerability about her, an eagerness to please, that attracted Jack.

"Sure I will," he said. "But first be telling me your name."

"Meg."

"I'm Jack Keane."

"Hush with your name giving," the girl said. "You're my Irisher with the white streak of hair."

She reached up and touched his hair. "They say a man with a streak like that has fortune on his side."

Jack laughed. "You wouldn't think that if I was telling you how I got it." He drained his mug and pulled the pitcher of gin on the table towards him. By now, he was feeling relaxed and happy. Flannery and Deane were whispering into their companion's ears, making them giggle. Jack leaned closer to his girl. "And what would you be doing in this groggery, Meg?"

Her eyes widened a little. "Tis your first time here, Irisher?"

"Tis indeed. I was leaving Ireland only a month back."

Meg hesitated for a moment. "Then I guess you weren't being the sarcastic one. I work here, earning a living—such as it is. Twas this or the mills."

"Don't your mam and dad mind?" asked Jack.

Meg giggled into her mug. "Aren't you the innocent one with the questions? I come from a farm up in Maine, a way from here. There wasn't enough to support us all so I had to make my own way."

Jack suddenly felt protective towards her. His head was beginning to feel a little muzzy, but he decided it was because of the smoky air in the room. He swigged another mouthful of gin, peered over at Flannery and noted, with surprisingly detached interest, that he was now kissing his companion, passionately. One hand had disappeared under the folds of her skirt. Deane, too, was embracing his girl. Somehow, such private behavior didn't appear out of place in the free and easy atmosphere of the groggery. Flannery stood up, lifting his girl off his lap.

"And who's for the stairway to dreams?" he asked.

Deane broke away from his girl. "Why not, shipmate? We've not that long before the captain will be wanting us back aboard. What say you, young Jack? Ready for a taste of Paradise?"

Jack, still slightly puzzled, looked at Meg. She nodded. "If you like, Irisher," she said softly.

Flannery overheard her reply. "If he likes . . ." he guffawed. "I doubt, lass, if he knows what he likes yet."

He leaned over the table and pinched her cheek. "But you'll be teaching him, won't you?"

Meg took Jack's hand and led him towards the stairway. The floor of the groggery tilted and swayed just like the deck of the *Grannia*. He stumbled on the stairs and would have fallen but for Meg's support. "Just a few steps more, Irisher," she said, encouragingly. "Then you can lie down."

Jack smiled at her blearily and nodded, feeling queasier with every moment.

It was dark at the top of the stairs. A long corridor lit by only two dim oil lamps stretched the length of the groggery's upper floor. A dozen or so cubicles led off the corridor. Jack could still hear the sound of the drinkers below but now there were other noises as well; low rustlings, creakings and soft moans came from the occupied cubicles. Flannery and Deane disappeared with their girls into the first two empty cubicles but Meg led Jack further along the corridor. The curtain was pulled aside and through the narrow entrance Jack saw that the cubicle contained a narrow bed and a wicker chair. Nothing more. Meg gave him a slight push and he tumbled gratefully on to the bed. He lay on his front, his head spinning, and then looked around over his shoulder.

Meg had drawn the curtain across the doorway but enough light filtered through from the oil lamp outside for Jack to see her beginning to undress. She pulled her brown blouse over her head letting her full breasts tumble free, and then she slipped her black skirt down over her hips and stood naked at the foot of the bed. Jack blinked as his eyes were drawn to the triangle of dark, tight curls in the shadow of her plump belly. It was the first time he'd ever seen a woman so brazenly naked and, even in his inebriated state, felt a stirring in his loins. He rolled over on the bed and tried to prop himself up on his elbows but they slid away from him. He fell back on the blankets, smiling up at Meg.

"Too much gin for such a young lad," whispered Meg, half to herself. She knelt on the bed and unbuckled the thick belt around Jack's waist. Her fingers opened the trousers and pulled them down to his knees. "But perhaps then not too much gin, eh?" she added as she grasped Jack's thickening, lengthening maleness for a moment. She pulled off his sea boots, dropping them on the floor with a thud, and slipped his trousers off completely. Then she unbuttoned his shirt and ran her fingernails over his hairless chest.

Jack reached up and squeezed her soft, bare shoulders, pulling her down to him. Her lips met his in a long, fierce kiss. He felt her belly grinding gently from side to side and tried to raise himself, but as soon as his head left the blankets the cubicle began to spin around him.

Meg pushed him back, shaking her head. "You rest there, Irisher, or I'm thinking you'll be awful sick and Mother McCarthy wouldn't be pleased with little Meg if that happened. She told me to gentle you and I'm guessing tis the first time you've been with a woman. Am I right? Now tell the truth?"

Jack nodded, not daring to speak.

A smile of delight crossed Meg's face. "And aren't I a lucky one? They say a man never forgets the first woman he beds." She bent forward and kissed him again. Then she knelt back and straddled his body. Jack could feel her warmth and wetness against him. She pushed a hand between her legs, grasping him again and guiding him into her as she lowered herself to him.

Jack threw back his head and gasped. Meg supported herself on her arms and began moving up and down on him, slowly at first, savoring every sensation as he filled her, then faster, moving her hips from side to side. A mist of pleasure closed over Jack as he lay passively beneath her but then he reached out to hold Meg's waist to steady himself as he began thrusting upwards into her. There was nothing except the sensation welling up inside him until, finally, he exploded into her. Meg groaned as she felt her insides dissolve in a torrent of burning liquid and collapsed across Jack. They lay close together, panting, slippery with perspiration.

Meg looked directly into Jack's face. "And was that nice, Irisher?" she whispered. "Was it worth crossing the Atlantic for?"

Jack nodded and impulsively gave her an affectionate kiss on the cheek. "'Twas like nothing before nor since," he mumbled. His head fell back and he was fast asleep.

He was still asleep, hours later, snoring gently, when the curtain of the cubicle was pulled back. Flannery and Deane, both fully dressed, stood in the entrance gazing down on the couple intertwined on the bed. They grinned at each other.

"Well, the lad seems to have broadened his education, and that's the truth," said Flannery with a wink. He squeezed into the narrow cubicle and shook Meg by the shoulder. She murmured protestingly in her sleep, then awoke.

"What do you want?" she asked, looking up at Flannery, not in the least embarrassed by her nakedness.

"Just this, pretty one—and don't you look sweet enough lying there to tempt a saint?—just tell the lad goodbye from Flannery and Deane. We're off back to our ship now. Tell the lad we'll go to his folks and say he's safe. And tell him also to see Mother McCarthy when he's fit because she has something that might be interesting him."

Meg nodded sleepily before turning back and burying her head in Jack's shoulder.

When Jack awoke some hours later, his head ached and his mouth tasted foul. He groaned as he lifted his head off the bed and looked around the cubicle. In the light of day he could see just how shabby his surroundings were. He gazed at Meg with distaste and remorse. No longer was she the alluring person of the night. Her mouth hung open slackly as she snored loudly. Her body appeared white and slug-like to Jack as it curled around him. A vivid image of the clear, unsullied beauty of Brigid Aherne flashed into his mind. He felt ashamed of himself. He rolled quietly off the bed and began pulling on his clothes. The first thing to do, he thought, was to find Flannery and Deane and get away from this place.

He was just leaving the cubicle to search for them when Meg, who'd been watching him dress, noting the scars on his back, spoke.

"They've gone. Your friends are gone some hour back, Irisher. They told me to tell you their goodbyes."

Jack was bewildered. What was he going to do without their guidance and support? His head was hurting so much that it was difficult even to think.

"But you're to see Mother McCarthy before you go," Meg continued, swinging her legs over the side of the bed and reaching for her clothes. "That's what your friends said. Something that might interest you, they said."

Jack swayed slightly in the doorway, wiping cold sweat from his forehead. "Where . . . where is she?" he asked in a voice still thick with drink.

"'Tis a bit early for her yet," replied Meg, buttoning her skirt and pulling her blouse over her head. She fluffed and patted her dark hair into some order. "I'll be cooking some breakfast while you wait. You can wash up in the kitchen as well.''

She led the way down the dark corridor. Sounds of snoring and coughing came from the curtained cubicles. A half-naked girl appeared at the entrance of one of the cubicles by the stairway, and smiled at Meg as she stretched sleepily. "How was your young Irisher?" she asked, ignoring Jack completely.

"Well enough," muttered Meg, grabbing Jack's hand and pulling him past the girl.

All the customers had left the groggery. The door to the street was open while an old man swept up the sawdust and cigar butts. Jack coughed as the pungent dust caught the back of his throat. The man with the broom glanced up at them, winked slyly, and continued his work. Meg led Jack into a small room behind the bar. Inside was a cooking range, a long table, and half-a-dozen stools.

Meg busied herself cooking bacon and beans as Jack washed himself. He felt slightly steadier after he'd splashed cold water from a wooden bucket over his face and chest.

"Sit yourself down," said Meg briskly, putting two filled plates on the table alongside a round loaf of bread. "You'll feel better with something inside you to soak up all that gin you guzzled." She smiled at Jack and patted his hand. "I'm guessing how you feel, Irisher. Not too proud of yourself, eh?"

Jack shook his head as he chewed on a thick rasher of bacon.

"Bet you left a girl behind in the bogs," Meg chattered on between mouthfuls of food. "Bet you think she'd be proper ashamed of you if she could see you now. That's what I thought me mother would be feeling after my first time. Well, what the eye doesn't see, the heart doesn't grieve at. That's what I say."

Jack smiled gratefully at her, touched by her desire to put him at ease. She was clearly a woman of kindness and understanding.

As they were mopping up the fat and juices from their plates with hunks of bread, Mother McCarthy swept into the kitchen.

"Me pretty little Meg and her handsome Irish boy," she boomed. "Very nice. Very domestic-like." She went over to the range and poured herself a steaming cup of black coffee. "Did you get the message from those two rascal shipmates of yours, Jack Keane?"

Jack nodded.

"A good head for names, that's what you need in this business. And a good head for figures, as well." She sat down beside Jack with a loud sigh. "Trouble is I'm not getting any younger and running a business like this is becoming a might difficult for a poor old woman like me."

Meg giggled behind her hand.

"Now, none of your cheek, young lady," said Mother McCarthy sternly. "Didn't I take you from the streets and treat you just like me daughter? Shame on you. Now off you go and help the other girls tidy upstairs while I have a little chat with young Jack here."

Meg flounced out of the kitchen. Jack watched her with an affectionate smile.

Mother McCarthy drained her mug of coffee and thumped it down on the table. "Now, lad, to business. So you're going to stay on in Boston, are you?"

"I can't go back to Ireland."

"You can tell me all about that later," interrupted Mother McCarthy, brushing a straying lock of grey hair under her cap. "You'll be needing a job that's for sure, and since Flannery and Deane reckon you're a good shipmate, that's enough. Will you be working here for me?"

Jack looked doubtful. The groggery was so unlike anything in his previous experience that it frightened and overpowered him.

Mother McCarthy sensed his hesitation. "You'll be helping me in the business, Jack Keane, not drinking and wenching all night and day. I need someone young like you to help me make the gin and keep order in the house. I'll be teaching you the tricks of the trade and a lot besides. You'll learn about keeping the books and banking the cash and paying our dues. Why, if you're half as smart as I'm thinking you are you'll be a proper businessman in no time, and that's the truth."

"But what about the girls? What about them?"

Mother McCarthy began to laugh. "So that's it, is it?" she cackled loudly. "I should have known too, what with you being fresh from the old country. The priest's teaching still in you, eh?"

She leaned forward and ruffled his hair affectionately. "Holy Mother, if only I'd had a son like you to keep me in my old age . . . Tell you what, young Jack, you can have a cubicle upstairs all to yourself, then it's up to you what you do about the girls, though from the way little Meg was looking at you you'll have a problem keeping to yourself."

"Well," Jack said. "Well, I'm not sure . . ."

"I'll be paying you five dollars a week and all you can eat," Mother McCarthy continued quickly, sensing that Jack was weakening.

"How much is five dollars?" asked Jack.

"More than you'd be getting in a month back in the bogs."

"'Tis settled then," said Jack. "What would you be wanting me to do first?"

"Well, seeing as you had such a hard night, by the look

of your eyeballs,'' Mother McCarthy smiled, "you can have the day off. Take Meg and have her show you Boston. That way you won't be getting lost when you venture out on your own.''

When Meg heard the news, she rushed back upstairs to put on a brown bonnet and borrow a black shawl from one of the other girls. As they went through the door of the groggery, she thrust her arm through Jack's. She smiled up into his face. "Now we'll be looking like any other couple taking the air. I'm thinking we'll walk to the Common. The sight of the cows will make you feel at home.''

"You've got to show me Boston town,'' insisted Jack.

"Well, we'll see it on our way. I'll take you the roundabout route.''

They stood in the narrow street outside, just by the open gutter.

"Now see behind the groggery,'' Meg pointed. "That's called Fort Hill and we're in Bread Street. So if ever you're lost you can always head for the hill and you'll fetch up not far away from the groggery.''

They strolled along a network of narrow, cobbled streets, standing aside to let men on horseback trot past them. Jack peered down each turning, trying to memorize its name scrawled on the corner of a house. He kept looking back towards Fort Hill to fix his position.

"They're all black people down there,'' he exclaimed in amazement as he crossed the entrance to one street. Jack stood for a minute looking at the first Negroes he'd ever seen as they sat on the stoops of their tall and narrow houses.

"Aye,'' said Meg. "That's where them Nigras live. Southac and Belknap streets. The old Boston people have taken to calling Fort Hill 'Nigra Hill.' Still, they don't treat

them like they do in Virginia and the other states. They
don't have bond slaves here. Nobody owns anybody else in
Boston."

"Not like back in Ireland," Jack muttered. "The landlords own everybody there. That's why I had to leave."

"Is that how you came by those wicked scars on your
back?" asked Meg.

As they walked along, Jack told her briefly of how and
why he'd come to Boston. Meg squeezed his arm sympathetically when he'd finished his account. "Well, that's
all behind you now, Irisher. Here, you're free."

"Now look here," she said as they approached a squat,
handsome, three-story brick building with a balcony opening out from tall windows on the second floor. "That's the
old State House where the Britishers used to have their
headquarters. When we'd beaten them, the Declaration of
Independence was read from that balcony up there."

"One day," said Jack grimly, "we'll read our own
declaration of independence in Dublin."

"Of course, you will, Jack," said Meg soothingly,
sensing the bitterness within him.

By the time they reached the Common other couples were
enjoying the warm early autumn sunshine, strolling on the
open land. Barely a mile from the groggery and the
congested heart of town families sat in leafy glades just off
the cow trails or watched the cattle grazing on the fenced
pastures. Meg led him through a thicket. "There you
are . . . water!"

Before them stretched the marshy fens of Back Bay. In
the distance the sun glinted off the River Charles and the
windows of the homes and farmhouses across the river.

They sat down on the shore of the bay. "Tis different
from the shore in Kerry. Tis much wilder there," said Jack.

The sickly-sweet smell he'd noticed the day before when he'd left the ship came to his nostrils again.

"Phew!" he sniffed. "It smells like the dungheap back of our cabin."

"You get used to it," said Meg, amused at the expression on his face. "After a time you don't notice it at all. There's talk of filling in the bay with other than dung. Some of the work has started, too. But I don't reckon they can fill in the whole bay. It's too big."

"Where's this place you come from? Maine, didn't you call it?" asked Jack.

Meg pointed back over her head. "About thirty miles to the north. A little place called Kittery, or just outside it."

"All farmland is it?"

"Oh, no. They build ships up there and what farms there are have been hacked out of the forests. It's rough land. Not so many years back, me pa kept his rifle by him in the fields in case the Redskins attacked."

Meg led him along the shore of Back Bay until they could see a high column of grey stone rising above the trees. "That looks familiar," Jack said.

"Well, you would have seen it out at sea, I'm thinking. That's Bulfinch's Pillar on Beacon Hill."

"Oh, yes," Jack remembered. "The light that guides ships into harbor."

They came to the edge of the Common. Before them was a wide cobbled roadway with tall, elegant houses standing in spacious grounds on the far side. Women in pretty bonnets, carrying parasols to protect them from the sun, clattered past in gleaming open carriages. Their coachmen, usually Negroes, wore uniform livery with high crowned hats brightened by feathers stuck in their sides.

"Them's the ladies of the swells," said Meg, jerking her

thumb at the carriages. "Anyone who's anyone lives around Beacon Hill."

Jack looked wonderingly at such outward signs of wealth. He caught the eye of one young woman in a carriage, sitting opposite an older, bearded man wearing a high stovepipe hat. For a second, her cornflower blue eyes appraised Jack before she turned away. The carriage stopped further up the roadway outside a four-story house built of brick and fronted with wood. As the man got out of the carriage, Jack thought for a moment that he recognized him.

Meg, who had been watching Jack's face, broke into his thoughts. "High and mighty he is up here. But you should see him upstairs at the groggery."

Then Jack realized he was the man he'd seen the previous evening talking with Mother McCarthy.

"That's Master John Patrick Kilfedder," said Meg, a contemptuous note in her voice. "The richest Irisher in Boston, and didn't I carry his marks for weeks? To look at his prissy wife, you'd think butter wouldn't melt in his mouth."

"He lives in grand style . . ."

"On the interest he charges his own countrymen," said Meg bitterly. "None of the banks will give loans to Irishers when they arrive here so they have to bend the knee to J. P. Kilfedder for the money."

"Did Mother McCarthy . . . ?"

"Aye. That's why none of the girls dare complain about his treatment of them. He all but owns the groggery. If he snapped his fingers, Mother McCarthy would have to close down or hand the business over to him. Not that he'd want it. Wouldn't do for someone living on Beacon Hill to be seen connected with a groggery in Bread Street. Wouldn't do at all."

They passed the domed Massachusetts State House before heading back towards the crowded alleys and streets of Boston. High above the reddish brown roofs of the houses, the steeples of half a dozen churches poked upwards. Meg pointed out one. "That's the cathedral for you Irishers; the Holy Cross in Franklin Square. All good Catholic girls get their learning at the nun's convent next door to it. Even Mother McCarthy goes to hear Bishop Fenwick preach sometimes, not that he's Irish, but she says he's nearly as good as the priests you've got back in the bogs."

At the corner of Ann Street, Meg stopped to admire the bow window of a shop selling bonnet ribbons and pieces of lace.

"Would you like one?" asked Jack.

"Oh, yes, they're so pretty. Can I?"

"Sure and you can. I'm thinking you're deserving a present from me."

Meg blushed. "Twas a pleasure, Jack Keane. Every moment."

Inside the shop Meg behaved like an excited schoolgirl as she picked her way through the ribbons and lace. Eventually, she chose two lengths of silk ribbon—and a strip of finely worked lace. Jack grandly handed over one of his gold sovereigns and received a handful of dollars and cents in change.

"Now what about something for you to wear, Jack Keane," said Meg. "You can't stay dressed like a sailor just down from the rigging. Remember, you're going to be an important man at the groggery."

Jack looked down at his red shirt, canvas trousers, and heavy sea boots. "Tis right you are, Meg."

Further along Ann Street, they spied a shop selling men's

clothes. Jack broke into his second gold sovereign to buy a white shirt, brown breeches and stockings, an emerald green waistcoat, and the first pair of shoes he'd ever owned in his life. He told the shopkeeper to set his trousers and seaboots against the bill for his new clothes but insisted on keeping the red shirt he'd been given by Patrick Deane.

"Tis a keepsake," he explained to Meg as they left the outfitter's shop. "Its redness will remind me of the lashing on the ship long after the scars have faded. Tis something I shouldn't be forgetting."

They stopped to eat at a tavern a few streets away from the groggery, and used their fingers to dip into a large earthenware pot of corned beef stew with potatoes, turnips, carrots, and cabbage.

"Tis a dish we eat all the time here," said Meg, licking her fingers with relish.

Jack, who'd been careful to pick out as much meat as possible, was amazed. "All the time?" he exclaimed. "Sure and back in Kerry, it would be a feast even for St. Stephen's day. All this meat . . . you live like lords here."

"We haven't finished yet. There's 'heaven and hell' still to come."

"What?"

"'Heaven and hell,' tis very sweet, made with molasses, corn meal and milk."

"Tis delicious whatever its name," exclaimed Jack after finishing a large portion of the pudding. "Sure and I feel bloated out like a cow in calf, that I do."

"We'd better be going," said Meg anxiously. "Mother McCarthy will be thinking I carried you off."

The groggery was busy even in mid afternoon, the air thick with tobacco and Irish voices. Mother McCarthy greeted them in a booming voice like her own long lost children. "My, you look smart, Jack Keane. That you do. And have you been shown Boston properly?"

"Sure and it's a fine town," said Jack, successfully side-stepping her attempted embrace. "Only a day here and I'm feeling at home already."

With a sense of well-being from his full stomach and new set of clothes, he looked around the groggery with something of a proprietorial air.

Chapter 8
December, 1824

As Boston's autumn gave way to the fierceness of winter, Jack Keane worked long hours under the tutelage of Mother McCarthy. He learned how to deal with fighting drunks— how to use a shillelagh to knock them unconscious rather than risk a brawl by accepting an invitation to fight. Down in the cellers he was taught how to distil gin from juniper berries, watching the clear alcohol drip from the maze of pipes that made up the still. He learned a crude form of book-keeping and paid in the takings once a week at the Massachusetts Bank, where as much as sixteen per cent interest was paid on deposits. He came to recognize which of the town's constables were sympathetic toward the small Irish community, who could be treated with confidence and a mug of gin and who should receive the deferential approach. Similarly, he came to know which selectmen from the town's council liked to spend an occasional day's drinking and whoring away from the prying eyes of their voters.

"Discretion and hard work make a successful groggery," Mother McCarthy would tell him. "But most of all discretion. See all, hear all, but say nothing."

As the months passed, Mother McCarthy spent more and more time drinking with her cronies, leaving Jack a virtually free hand to run the business. The groggery's customers gave Jack the respect due to someone who held sway in an important Irish meeting place. He was called on to arbitrate in disputes about rates of pay, about rent levels and about who should be the ganger in a team of laborers.

Many of the Irish who'd settled in Boston during the early nineteenth century found it easier to earn a wage by laying aside their skills and relying on laboring jobs, either along the harbor wharves or in the public construction works beginning to spring up all around Boston, which tried to link the town more securely to the mainland with better and bigger toll roads, or to expand the area of the town by filling in the fens and marshes on the outskirts. This work was shunned by the native Bostonians as being too menial and so gave an opportunity to Negroes and settlers from Europe. Much of the money earned by the Irish laborers found its way into Mother McCarthy's coffers. As Boston grew, so did the credit balance of the groggery at Massachusetts Bank.

The one problem which caused Jack headaches was controlling the dozen or so girls who used the groggery as a place of business. He went on sleeping with Meg when she didn't have a customer but soon discovered the other girls saw this as unwarranted favoritism. The dilemma was clear to Jack; either he had to sleep with all the girls in turn or else he had to end his relationship with Meg.

"Tis a terrible problem, to be sure," he told Mother McCarthy when he confided in her. "I'm very fond of Meg and getting used to her ways. But tis mighty clear it cannot go on like this."

"You've another choice if that's the case, Jack. You could always marry her and then the other girls would have no cause for complaining."

Jack shook his head emphatically. "No. My word is given to a girl back home and I shall return one day and claim her."

"Well then, Jack," said Mother McCarthy, gulping down the last of a mug of gin, "tis certain what you've got to do. You must find a friend outside the groggery."

The first thing Jack did after accepting her advice was to pay a carpenter to fit a wooden door to his upstairs cubicle. Then he had an uncomfortable half an hour breaking the news to Meg.

"Let's still be the best of friends," he urged as he saw tears welling into her eyes. "But no more can we be sharing a cubicle when you've no business. We can still walk out together but nothing else."

Meg sulked for a few days and some of the other girls, thinking Jack was looking for a new friend, began calling on him in his cubicle in various states of undress to make it clear that they were his for the asking. But at last it became accepted that Jack wanted to be on his own. Not that he didn't regret his decision. Many nights he lay behind his secure door listening to the sounds of love making in the cubicles adjoining his, wishing he had Meg beside him to slake his lust. But his self-imposed celibacy gave him an added inner strength that enabled him to deal successfully with men and women older and more experienced than himself.

It was that strength he needed when Mother McCarthy fell ill during the early spring of 1825. Her considerable constitution had been weakened by her increasing drinking and by a troublesome cold which had failed to respond to any remedy.

Her physician, Samuel Dillon, who was called to the groggery, shook his head sadly as he came down the stairs after seeing Mother McCarthy in her room. "Tis her tubes," he told Jack. "They're awful congested. Over the years the atmosphere in here can't have helped, nor her liking for her own gin."

"What's to be done then, Master Dillon?"

"Tis a rest she needs well away from this place. She says she can stay with friends on a farm at Dorchester and that would be the best thing, to be sure. If she spends the spring in good, clean air it'll aid her a deal, but she's not a young woman. She'll have to take care if she's to survive many more winters."

But Jack found Mother McCarthy in ebullient spirits when he went upstairs to see her. She was propped up on pillows, grey hair fluffed out, a pink shawl across a nightgown that failed to hide the outlines of her pendulous breasts.

"Ah, Jack," she wheezed. "Did that quack tell you I had to be going away a wee while?"

"He did that. He said you were needing some good air."

"Tis a mug of gin I'm needing. Send one up to me, will you?"

"He says you're to take care."

"And sure I will." She began to cough. "By the saints," she spluttered, thumping herself on the chest. "Tis the dampness of the winter that's brought me low. Get me the gin, lad, for Holy Mary's sake."

When Jack returned with the gin, she sipped at the mug as if it contained the foulest of medicines. "Sure and you can lose your taste for this without regular practice," she smiled. "But I can feel it easing me already."

She put down the mug on a bedside table. "I'm thinking I can leave here without worrying about it. You'll take charge, lad, and to show my confidence in you I'm set to make you my partner. I've been thinking on this for a time so while I'm resting up for my journey the lawyer can draw the proper papers."

"Is that necessary?" asked Jack, overwhelmed at the offer.

"Tis fair. Only fair. You've been running the groggery for six months past while I've been in my dotage." Mother McCarthy grinned. "And besides it'll be mightly galling to Master J. P. Kilfedder, so it will. I'm surprised he's not already perched on my bed waiting to pick the groggery clean when I'm out of the way. He'll be surprised to find a spalpeen like you in control."

Two days later, Jack and Mother McCarthy signed their partnership agreement and a day after that she set off for Dorchester.

As she sat in the carriage, well wrapped in blankets and rugs, she gave Jack some last words of advice. "Remember what I was telling you before, lad. Discretion is the word. Be discreet, watch Kilfedder close and don't be drinking too much of our own gin." She winked at Jack. "After all, look what it's done for me." She gave a last wave to Jack and the girls standing outside the groggery before settling back into the seat as the carriage rattled away over the cobbles of Bread Street.

That night the groggery was full to the doors. Jack and his three potmen were run off their feet trying to serve all the customers. Two men—one with a fiddle, the other with a tin whistle—added to the hubbub by playing lively jigs and reels. Evenutally Jack cleared a space in the middle of the floor so that the girls could dance with the customers. He was standing beside some drinkers who were avidly watching the girls' skirts swirling up their thighs when he felt a tap on the shoulder. He looked around and found himself staring directly at a man's chest, matted with dark, curly hair. He raised his eyes and saw an unshaven face split by a large, hooked nose, its right eye covered by a black patch.

"Master Keane?" The man looming over him by some six or seven inches spoke in a high, squeaky voice.

"Yes, who's wanting him?"

"This is for you." The man handed over a note sealed with wax.

"And who are you?"

"I'm called Hawk. I'm Master Kilfedder's man."

Jack moved away from the men watching the dancers and slid open the note with his thumbnail. The message was to the point. Would Master Keane call on J. P. Kilfedder in his office in State Street at ten o'clock the next morning?

"Tell him I'll be there."

"Then I bid you good night, Master Keane."

Jack watched Hawk thread his way through the customers to the door. He walked with a lightness of foot uncommon in such large men. Jack could see the muscles bulging under his black shirt.

When most of the evening's customers had gone, Jack left the potmen to deal with the remaining few and went to sit in the kitchen. He took with him the box of business papers handed to his care by Mother McCarthy. He searched through them for the agreement with J. P. Kilfedder. As he read the document, drawn up several years previously in 1818, he began to realize the extent of the hold Kilfedder had over the business. Jack began jotting down figures on a scrap of paper.

The document showed that Kilfedder had loaned Mother McCarthy 3,000 dollars at an interest rate of thirty per cent per annum, payable every quarter. In default of payment, ownership of the groggery would pass automatically to Kilfedder. Only in the last year had Mother McCarthy managed to begin repaying the capital of the loan in addition to the quarterly interest of 225 dollars. The amount of the loan still outstanding was 2,600 dollars.

Jack felt anger as he studied the figures. J. P. Kilfedder, he decided, was nothing more than a thief who battened on other people's desires to build their own businesses. "A leech," he muttered furiously to himself. "Nothing but a blood-sucking leech."

What made him even angrier was the knowledge that Kilfedder was as Irish as the overwhelming majority of his customers, yet still he exploited mercilessly their lack of capital.

At nine o'clock the next morning he stood on the white-washed steps of the Massachusetts Bank as its doors opened for business. He advanced to the cashier's grille and asked to see one of the bank's partners. Five minutes later he was in the sombre office of Oliver P. Dunwoody.

The banker, a small middle-aged man, peered benevolently over his half-moon glasses at the agitated young man standing before his desk. "Master Keane," he said, rising to shake Jack's hand. "And how is Mistress McCarthy? Is she recovering?"

Jack's surprise showed in his face.

"Boston is really only a small village," said Dunwoody by way of explanation. "Mistress McCarthy is one of its better-known characters. I am told she is planning a convalescence in the country."

"She's gone," said Jack shortly. "I'm running the business as her full partner."

"Congratulations, sir," said the banker. "You're making your mark swiftly in the community. What service can I be to you?"

"Are we in good standing with this bank?" Jack asked, settling back into the upholstered chair by Dunwoody's large desk.

"Indeed, sir. Oh, indeed." The banker looked down at a document on his desk. "A credit balance of more than four hundred dollars. Regular payments in, a healthy balance. Most commendable."

"Then Master Dunwoody, look on these documents."
Jack pushed the agreement with J. P. Kilfedder on to the
banker's desk.

Dunwoody studied it for a few minutes and then leaned
back in his chair and coughed. "I fear this sort of thing is
not unknown, Master Keane," he said, fingering the agreement with an expression of distaste. "Master Kilfedder's
methods of business are known only too well to me."

"Well, I want no more of him." Jack stood up and bent
over the desk, looking directly at the banker. "Will you
help me? Will you loan me the money to settle his
agreement?"

Dunwoody put the tips of his fingers together and looked
thoughtful. "Security, Master Keane. There must be security, you know."

"What about my share of the business? I'll sign it over to
you."

"But without you, sir, there is no business. That's not
particularly good security . . . But you'll have your
money. In this particular situation, an honest face will
suffice, sir . . . and your share of the business assigned to
the bank till the debt is paid."

"At what interest?" asked Jack suspiciously.

Dunwoody laughed drily. "We pay you 16 per cent on
your balance, Master Keane, so I fear it will be 18 per cent
interest on the loan. That, sir, is banking."

"I'm to see Kilfedder at ten o'clock this very morning,
and would like to pay him off then."

"I understand." The banker adjusted his glasses, a half-
smile playing around his mouth. "Then you can have it now
and return here to sign the agreement." He scribbled on a
piece of paper with a scratchy quill pen. "Take this to the
cashier and he will give you 2,600 dollars."

Jack shook hands with Dunwoody. "I cannot thank you enough."

"It's business, Master Keane. But a word of advice before you leave. Master Kilfedder will be far from pleased at losing his hold on your business. I'm advised he can be an ugly man if he's crossed."

Twenty minutes later, Jack was being ushered into J. P. Kilfedder's office on the first floor of a tall, narrow building on State Street. Kilfedder had his back to the door when Jack was shown in. He was standing with his hands clasped behind him, gazing up at a portrait of the woman Jack had seen in the carriage on Beacon Hill.

Without turning around, Kilfedder spoke. "A woman, Master Keane, is the most important attribute in a man's success." He swung around. "Don't you agree?"

"I . . . I . . . I'm not sure," Jack stammered nonplussed at this approach.

"Not sure, Master Keane?" said Kilfedder sternly. "Why, you should know as well as I do. Without Mother McCarthy, you'd be carrying a shovel on your back. Without my Elizabeth, I'd probably be down there digging with you."

Kilfedder carefully parted the tails of his dark grey jacket and sat in the high-backed chair behind his desk, gesturing to Jack to sit down at the same time.

"When I arrived here ten years ago, Master Keane, I was as penniless as you are. Until I met Elizabeth I had no ambition but to survive. Certainly her father's chandlery business was prosperous enough but it was she who showed me how to make money work. Without her inspiration and my desire to give her the best of lives, why there would be no J. P. Kilfedder of any standing in Boston today." Kilfedder stroked his beard, evidently well satisfied with himself. "Let that be a cautionary tale for you, Master

Keane. Stay close to Mother McCarthy and you will not go far wrong."

"I intend to, Master Kilfedder."

"Good." He smiled thinly at Jack. "I asked you here simply to ascertain that that was the case." His tone sharpened. "You are aware, of course, of my place in Mother McCarthy's business affairs."

"I've read the agreement," Jack replied simply.

"Excellent—so there'll be no need for me to be worrying myself about the payment while Mother McCarthy is regaining her full health with God's help."

Jack stood up. "None at all, Master Kilfedder. Twill be no worry at all." He reached inside his shirt and pulled out the wad of notes he'd been given at the bank. "Tis your money, Master Kilfedder. All of it. All 2,600 dollars." He placed the notes carefully on the desk, pulled the agreement from his pocket, tore it in half, and put both halves beside the bank notes. "You've no hold over the groggery any more."

Kilfedder's lean jaw slackened in amazement. "But how . . . the money? . . ."

"Tis not your concern. Check your accounts and you'll find it is the correct amount."

Kilfedder gazed balefully at Jack for a moment, then rose from behind his desk and strode quickly to the office door. He flung it open and shouted into the outer office, "Find me Hawk."

He turned to Jack. "Before it's too late, you upstart bog-trotter, it would be better if certain facts were made clear to you."

Hawk knocked on the door and came lightly into the office. His presence, towering over both Jack and J. P. Kilfedder, made the room seem overcrowded.

"You've met Hawk, haven't you?"

"Yes."

"Well, Hawk plays a very important part in my organization. You could say he protects my investments. He helps persuade people that they should stick to the letter of their agreements with the House of J. P. Kilfedder. Don't you Hawk?"

"That's right, sir," came the answering squeak.

"Good," said Kilfedder. "Well, let me explain, Master Keane, my fine young friend. Apart from financing the establishment at which you work, I take it upon myself to offer it my protection. Fort Hill is notorious, is it not, for containing some of the rough elements of our fine citizenry?"

"We've never had any trouble at the groggery," said Jack firmly, beginning to catch the drift of Kilfedder's words.

"Precisely. And I suggest tis because anyone who causes trouble knows they would have to explain their actions to Hawk here."

"But . . ."

"Please not to interrupt, Master Keane, while I'm instructing you in the ways of business. If you terminate our agreement, then I fear I shall have to withdraw my protection from your business. You already have enough white hairs for such a young man. You wouldn't want more, would you? I urge you to reconsider your hasty action."

Kilfedder walked to the desk and picked up the bank notes and torn-up agreement. He offered them to Jack, an ingratiating smile on his face.

"Here, take them and let's forget all about what's happened this morning."

Jack shook his head. "No, Master Kilfedder. Our agreement is at an end, paid up, finished. I shall bid you good day."

* * *

Jack walked back to the groggery deep in thought. He stood on the corner of Bread Street and looked up at the cinder colored sky. Some time soon, he knew, he could expect a visit from Hawk and his friends. But how to protect himself and the groggery? He couldn't rely on his customers, he realized, and anyway it was hardly fair to involve them in a private battle.

When he reached the groggery, he was delighted to find Martin Flannery and Patrick Deane waiting for him.

"Tis a mighty auspicious day you've picked to sail back into Boston," he told them, signalling a potman to bring over a fresh jug of gin.

"Well, we're only here for a day and a night again," said Flannery, "but weren't we agreed that we had to see how our old shipmate was faring?"

Jack brought them up to date with the happenings at the groggery.

"Now, didn't Captain Higgins spot you aright," exclaimed Deane. "He said you were a man with a future. We'll have a proper tale to tell your mother when we reach the Shannon again in the summer."

"You've seen her?" asked Jack eagerly.

"Aye, Jack, we passed on the news about your reaching here and finding a good berth."

"How are me mam and dad?"

"Just fine. Fine. Though missing you a deal, I'm thinking." Flannery reached inside his shirt and produced a stained, crumpled letter. "You mam bade the priest to write you."

Jack seized the letter and opened it. Flannery and Deane kept silent as he read.

"Dear son," the letter began, "Your friends from the sea brought us the news of your safe arrival and your start in Boston, for which we thank God. Your dad and me are well, considering all. John had a proper funeral and the neighbors were mighty good. Your dad is managing the extra work and we have enough to live on and some over to sell at market. Before St. Stephen's Day we saw your Brigid in Listowel and passed her the news. She works still for Master Sandes and sent her kindest felicitations and thoughts to you. All your other friends are safe and have come out of hiding. The militia is mighty busy searching and patrolling but there's been little trouble hereabouts, thanks be to the Holy Mother. Must end now as your friends are waiting to return to Tarbert. You have our love and blessing, Jack. Remember all your teachings and your mam and dad. With kisses from your loving mam."

At the bottom of the letter was a note. "Think not on returning yet, my son, since Master Sandes has rewards out for you. God's blessing and comfort on you." The note was signed simply "O'S"—from Father O'Sullivan, Jack presumed.

He put the letter down with a smile. "Tis as you said, Paddy. The folks seem well enough. Before you go, I'll give you a letter for them. That's presuming you intend to spend your time in Boston as my guests here."

"Where else? Tis you have the finest gin and the prettiest girls in the whole of this town. What more can a body want after a month at sea?"

"Then I shall give the day to you," Jack laughed. "Though you'll have to be taking care of the night yourselves."

"Is that dark-haired friend of yours still here?" asked Flannery, his eyes shining in anticipation.

"Meg, you mean? Meg Griffiths? Aye, she's still here and no doubt glad to entertain you."

Deane lowered his voice. "Tis true you could be in

trouble with this gombeen man Kilfedder you were mentioning?"

"Looks likely, Patrick. Tis a call his bully-boys will be making before long, I'm thinking. And wouldn't it have been nice to have had all Captain Higgins' crew here to meet them?"

"Twould be a true brawl, that it would," agreed Deane. "But why don't you find a crew of your own?"

"And haven't I been wracking my brains about just how to do that?"

"I remember once in New York someone having the same problem," volunteered Flannery. "He found his own crew, he did."

"How?"

"Well, he organized a money tournament to find the best bare-knuckle fighter in the town. And didn't he hire on all the best fighters. Strange to tell, not only did he get a crew of men but the fights were so popular that he's still holding them to this day."

"Tis a grand idea," said Jack excitedly. "We could hold the fights here and charge money to see them. That way we'd win both ways."

"And isn't he just the man of business?" said Deane. "Making his fortune while his friends sit here with empty mugs."

That day Jack first took the precaution of writing a note to Father O'Sullivan for his parents before getting drunker with Flannery and Deane than he had on his first day in Boston. He had to be carried off to bed by two potmen while his two friends stumbled behind him up the stairs, Deane with a fair-haired girl and Flannery clutching on to Meg. Jack awoke with a blinding headache but with the conviction that Flannery's idea was the solution to his problem of defending himself against any action by J. P. Kilfedder. He hurried around to O'Hanlon's the printers to order one hundred posters advertising a forthcoming tournament. When the posters were delivered a day later he distributed them to the staff and the girls at the groggery with instructions for them to be placed all over Boston. He himself took some into the Negro district. Jack approached Southac Street with some trepidation. At first everyone pointedly ignored him as he stuck a poster to a wall using flour and water paste. But as soon as the poster was up, crowds gathered round to read it.

GRAND PUGILISTIC CONTEST
AT MOTHER McCARTHY'S
IN BREAD STREET
SATURDAY SATURDAY
ALL WELCOME TO FIGHT
PRIZES FOR ALL FROM
$10 TO $100
SPECTATORS $1
PROMOTER AND REFEREE
MASTER JACK KEANE
SATURDAY SATURDAY

"Hey, white man," a tall, husky Negro called to Jack. "Does that 'all welcome' on your poster include us Nigras?"

"Sure and it does. And isn't that why I'm putting the posters down this street?"

"You'd let an Irisher fight a Nigra?"

"Why not?"

"Well, Irisher, that ain't usual even in this town," said the Negro, shaking his head. "Why, I ain't never heard of it before nowhere, nohow."

"You a pugilist then?"

"That I ain't, mister. But I reckon I can lick most anyone hereabouts."

"Enter the contest then. You might win."

"I will that. Tell your man he'll be hearing from Homer Virgil Socrates Penquick."

"Is that really your name?" Jack asked with a wide smile.

"My given name by the slave master. I know you white folk find it right amusing so I ain't taking any offense at your humor."

"Nor should you. Tis a fine name; a name surely to remember, Master Penquick."

With a wave, the Negro sauntered off down the street. Jack watched him thoughtfully. Now, he reckoned, half a dozen men like that would certainly give Hawk and his thugs more than a bloody nose if they dared to call at the groggery.

The tournament was held that Saturday evening. Even by late afternoon, the groggery was crowded with more than three hundred people who'd paid their dollars to watch. Two of Jack's regular customers, Timmy Brehoney and Padraig Costelloe, both Irishmen who worked along the wharves, had decided to enter the tournament and three Bostonians had also announced their intention of taking part. Jack had cleared the tables and benches in the middle of the bar and roughly roped off a ring, covering the floor liberally with sawdust. As the time of the tournament grew closer, Jack started to get a little anxious about having only five contestants. Then he saw the black face of Homer Penquick appear in the doorway. The Negro spotted Jack and pushed his way through the packed bar. Another Negro, thin and barely five feet tall, was with him.

"A good evening to you, Irisher."

"Master Penquick."

"Where be this Master Jack Keane who's running this here tournament?"

"And aren't you just looking at him?"

"Well, well, so all along you were the boss man."

"That's right Master Penquick, and tis mighty glad I am to see you."

"When do we start then?"

"We?"

Penquick gestured to his undersized companion. "He's entering the tournament too. His given name is Horace Archimedes Plato Penquick."

"A relation?"

"Nope. We come from the same plantation in Viginia run by . . ."

". . . Master Penquick, I'm guessing," interrupted Jack.

"Ain't you catching on then?" smiled Homer Penquick. "He was a devil for them Greek and Roman folk was Master Penquick. Even spoke their languages, or said he did."

Jack looked doubtfully at Homer's companion. "Isn't he a bit small?"

"Small he might be but he's quick and wriggly as a swamp snake."

"He'll be tangling with bigger men."

"That ain't never worried him, Master Keane. Nope, never had."

"Right then, we'll get started."

Jack took the shillelagh from behind the bar and banged it repeatedly on the floor. "Silence! Quiet!" he shouted. The hubbub in the groggery declined. "The draw for the tournament is about to take place. Are there any more wanting to take part?" There was no response. "For the last time, is there anyone else who fancies himself as a fighter?"

There was a commotion at the back of the crowd and a squat, sunburned man, wearing a coonskin cap and clothes made from leather, jumped up on a table.

"Look here for a fighting man," he cried, slapping his broad chest. "I've fought with redskins, swum with alligators, wrassled with bears . . ." The crowd around him began guffawing.

"If that be so, friend," Jack shouted across the room, "then you be mighty welcome, though there be no alligators or bears in this groggery. Only a few bilge rats . . ." The room exploded with laughter.

The man jumped off the table and stuck out his hand. "Augustus Hawkins, sir, at your service."

"Well, Master Hawkins, we shall put your name in for the first bouts of the tournament."

The draw matched Hawkins against one of the Bostonians; Homer Penquick against Padraig Costelloe; Horace Penquick against the second Bostonian, with the third fighting Timmy Brehoney.

"Come to scratch," shouted Jack, standing inside the ring, when the first two men were stripped to the waist and ready to begin.

The first fight was over almost as soon as it had begun. Augustus Hawkins, four long white scars running vertically down his back, rushed at his opponent, gripped him in a bear hug, and squeezed him for almost a minute. The Bostonian struggled unsuccessfully to free himself, growing redder in the face every second before Hawkins the trapper disposed of him by throwing him on the floor and jumping on his stomach. Even those who had wagered on the Bostonian realized the fight was over when they heard the breath whoosh out of their favorite's body.

The second fight didn't take much longer. Costelloe swung huge roundhouse punches at Homer Penquick's head but the Negro ducked easily out of their way and hit the Irishman two fierce blows to his overhanging belly. When Costelloe bent over, gasping for breath, Penquick brought both his hands together and clubbed him on the back of the neck, smashing his knee upwards into the Irishman's face. He slumped unconscious to the floor, blood pouring from a broken nose.

Tiny Horace Penquick turned the third bout into more of a running race. His opponent lumbered after him swinging blows but the Negro took to his heels and ran around and around the ring. The crowd in the groggery shouted derisively at the Bostonian and cheered wildly when Penquick suddenly turned and tripped the larger man to end the first round. When the two men came to scratch for the second time, the Bostonian was so out of breath that he merely stood still swatting blows at Penquick who continued to run round him. The bout ended suddenly when Penquick jumped on to his opponent's back like a little monkey and throttled him into submission with his forearm wrapped around his wind pipe.

The last fight was more conventional, with Timmy Brehoney eventually pounding the Bostonian unconscious after both men had knocked each other down at least a dozen times.

After a short break to enable everyone to refill their mugs, another draw was held. Jack breathed a sigh of relief when the two Penquicks were drawn against separate opponents. He had feared that the Negroes would have refused to fight each other and he wanted another opportunity to watch them both in action.

Augustus Hawkins had as great difficulty as the defeated Bostonian in getting to grips with Horace Penquick. Again the tiny Negro ended the first round by tripping his opponent, but when he tried to climb on to the trapper's back he was thrown right across the ring by Hawkins, who shrugged him off with a heave of his broad shoulders. The fall badly winded the Negro and when the men came to scratch for the third time Hawkins was able to slow him down even further with a solid blow to the side of the head that knocked him to the floor. It was clear to the jostling crowd in the groggery that, this time, Horace Penquick was outmatched. He struggled back to scratch but quickly succumbed when the trapper caught him in another bear hug. The Negro lay panting on the floor for more than a minute trying to get the breath back into his crushed ribs, but, after recovering, seemed little the worse for wear. He was cheered resoundingly from the ring.

The sixth fight of the evening was again a battle of attrition, with Homer Penquick swapping blows with Timmy Brehoney. At one stage, it appeared that the Irish-man had the Negro beaten, when a particularly vicious punch knocked him senseless. But a spectator bent through the ropes and emptied a mug of gin over him. The alcohol stinging into the bruises and cuts on his face brought Penquick around before Jack called the fighters to scratch again. Somehow he absorbed more blows from the Irishman before butting him across the bridge of the nose. As Brehoney staggered back, roaring in agony, Homer Pen-quick kneed him in the groin with all his remaining strength. It seemed that all the spectators winced. The Irishman writhed in the sawdust, moaning loudly, one hand between his legs, the other clutching his face. Jack didn't even bother with the formality of calling both men to scratch. It was obvious that Brehoney wouldn't be fit to fight again that evening.

To give Augustus Hawkins and Homer Penquick time to recover from their earlier bouts, Jack announced that there would be an hour's delay before the final contest. He had never seen such scenes in the groggery before. Clutching handfuls of dollar bills, the customers were striking bets with about a dozen spectators who'd set themselves up as bookmakers. The given odds seemed to favor the trapper, who was surrounded by his cronies in one corner of the bar. Hawkins was unmarked in contrast to the big Negro, who had left the groggery telling Jack he wanted to breathe some fresh air and get some balm for his cuts and bruises.

"You'll default, Master Penquick, if you're not back when I call you to scratch," Jack warned.

"Even that trapper's alligators won't be keeping me away, Master Keane," Penquick replied through swollen lips. "He might have wrassled bears but he ain't yet tangled with the likes of me."

"Whoever wins, Master Penquick, I'll be wanting to talk business with you and your little friend after the fights are done."

An hour later, the yellow light from the oil lamps on the walls flickered over the gleaming torsos of the two men on either side of Jack in the middle of the ring. It was impossible to see from one wall of the groggery to the other through the cigar and pipe smoke. Jack tried to introduce the fighters but the noise was so great that only the spectators pressed around the ropes could hear him. He shrugged his shoulders helplessly and began to give instructions to Penquick and Hawkins.

"By now, you should know what the rules are. Just fight clean and fair."

"How's that?" interrupted the trapper.

"I'm thinking you're not to kill each other or tear each other's limbs off or gouge the eyes."

"That be fine with me," exclaimed Penquick, spitting on his palms.

"The loser be the one who can't come to scratch after a

knockdown," said Jack finally. "Go to it on my cry and good luck to you both."

The noise in the groggery rose to a crescendo as the two men squared up to each other. They began circling each other warily and Jack called for the fight to begin.

The Negro was the first to strike, rapping a blow into Hawkins' face that sent the trapper staggering back, almost colliding with Jack. A trickle of blood began running down Hawkins' nose. He shook his head and brushed the blood across his face with the back of his hand. Suddenly he rushed at Penquick trying to grasp him around the body, but the Negro stepped nimbly out of the way and clubbed Hawkins on the back of the neck. The blow carried the trapper into the rope around the ring. His head caught a spectator under the jaw. The man fell back into the crowd while Hawkins rebounded straight into a vicious punch to the kidneys from Homer Penquick. He dropped, groaning, to his knees and Jack stepped quickly between the fighters. Hawkins crawled into a corner where a spectator tossed a bucket of water over him, then painfully pulled himself upright on the rope.

"To scratch," shouted Jack above the excited clamor.

Hawkins, obviously in considerable pain, tried to keep away from Penquick but the Negro pursued him, throwing out straight punches that cracked into his face, drawing more blood. The trapper turned his head after one blow and spat two teeth on to the sawdust. Under the barrage of blows he sank slowly to his knees again. The second round was over. His face and shoulders were now covered with smears of blood. He groped his way into a corner and gulped down a mug of gin handed him by one of his supporters. Penquick stood nonchalantly in the other corner blowing on his bruised knuckles and talking through the uproar to his diminutive friend, Horace Penquick.

When Jack called the men to scratch for the third time, Hawkins staggered towards the center of the ring. Penquick, perhaps overconfident, strode forward, hands at his side, ready to settle the fight quickly. He was totally unprepared when the trapper, summoning his last strength, launched himself backwards into the air with a shout and kicked out with his bare feet. The blow caught the Negro squarely in the stomach. He reeled back, bounced off the rope, and crashed to the floor. Hawkins flung himself down on him, snarling with rage and pain. He gripped the Negro around the throat, squeezing with both hands, at the same time banging Penquick's head up and down on the wooden floor. Jack leapt forward and gripped the trapper around the waist, trying to pull him off. Hawkins, maddened with blood lust, butted his head backwards, catching Jack on the forehead and knocking him to the floor. Horace Penquick was under the rope in an instant. He pounded Hawkins on the top of his head to try to make him release his friend but to no avail. Other spectators who'd bet on Hawkins began clambering under the rope to reach the tiny Negro. Jack scrambled up again in time to see Horace Penquick jab his first and index fingers into Hawkins' eyes. The trapper reared upwards, hands across his eyes, and began staggering around the ring, colliding with the invading spectators. Within seconds the ring was a mass of people swapping punches with each other. Jack stood above Homer Penquick to protect him as the Negro retched and heaved some air back into his lungs. He desperately sought some way to end the fighting which had now spread all over the groggery. Suddenly, a shot rang out. The noise of the explosion reverberated under the low beams. The men stopped fighting; some dropped to the floor not knowing where the shot came from.

"Haven't you seen enough broken heads tonight?"

shrilled a female voice above them. They looked up and saw Meg Griffiths standing on the stairway, a smoking flintlock pistol still pointed above her head. She lowered the pistol, beginning to blush as she realized that she was now the center of attention.

"And didn't me mam say I should only use a pistol to protect my virtue against a man?" she said, dropping her eyes in embarrassment.

The silence in the groggery was broken first by a titter from Jack. "Your virtue, Meg?" he laughed aloud. "You'd need a musket and a blunderbuss to protect that!"

The men near Jack began laughing, slapping each other on the back. The laughter spread throughout the groggery. Jack saw his chance and moved quickly to the bar.

"The gin's on Jack Keane," he bellowed. "A free mug for everyone."

There was a shout of jubilation as the spectators surged towards the bar. Jack pushed through them to reach the Penquicks and Augustus Hawkins. They were all sitting dazedly in the tangle of rope that was all that remained of the ring. Horace Penquick was massaging his friend's neck gently while Hawkins tried to prise open his swollen eyelids. Jack helped them to their feet.

"Gentlemen," he shouted. "Your attention, if you please."

The crowd packed near the bar turned around clutching their refilled mugs.

"Tis the result of the fight I have to announce," Jack called. "Since neither man was able to come to scratch for the very reason that the referee was on the floor with them, the contest is declared a draw. They each win fifty dollars, as much gin as they can drink, and the girl of their choice. That's if they've the strength left."

A roar of approval greeted Jack's decision.

"Don't I deserve them both?" whispered Meg Griffiths, sidling up behind Jack with the pistol still in her hand.

"You deserve almost anything you want, lass, for stopping that brawl," Jack replied. "Murder would have been done, I'm thinking."

"Almost anything?" asked Meg, with a pout.

"That's right. Now find me Brehoney and Costelloe and bring them to the kitchen."

Jack guided Hawkins and the two Negroes to the kitchen behind the bar, trying as best he could to protect them from back-slapping customers.

In the comparative quiet of the kitchen, the fighters slumped exhaustedly on the benches around the table, streaks of blood and sweat across their shoulders and chests. Meg ushered in the two Irishmen and then began washing the men's bruises and cuts. Jack produced a bottle of rum and poured them all generous tots. Then he went around the table placing the men's winnings in front of them, peeling the bills off a large wad of notes.

"Meg," he said, handing her thirty dollars and another bottle of rum, "go and find them Boston men and pay them off with my compliments. Then tell the potmen to make sure no one comes in here while I have a quiet talk with these gentlemen."

When she had gone, he stood at the head of the table and surveyed the men around him. All of them displayed signs of their recent fights—black eyes, swollen lips, cut and bruised knuckles. "Friends," he began. "First I'd like to thank you for taking part in the contest tonight. All of you showed that you're fighting men out of the ordinary." Then he explained about the threat from J. P. Kilfedder and the reason why he had organized the contest. "And I'm guessing I've found the right men to help me," he concluded. "I'll be paying each of you two dollars to come here every day. You get your food, as much as you can drink without losing your senses, and the pick of the girls if they're willing, and I'm betting they won't mind pleasuring such fighting men as you."

"How long for, Jack?" asked Timmy Brehoney.

"Till Kilfedder's men pay us a call or I'm satisfied that your man was just blathering. What say you?"

The five men nodded their agreement wearily.

"Sure and it'd be a pleasure," smiled Brehoney. "Wouldn't it, Padraig?"

His friend grinned. "Twill be the easiest money I've earned, Timmy, since we pinched that man's pig and then sold it back to him."

Jack poured another tot of rum for each man. "A toast," he said.

"Who to?" asked Hawkins.

"Why, who else but your man, J. P. Kilfedder? He's found each of you a job and given me the five best fighting men in Boston town."

Chapter 9
July, 1825

The half-filled glass of claret sang as Jack Keane tapped his finger against it. He held it up to the light from the candelabrum in the middle of the table, admiring the rich red of the wine through the sparkling lead crystal glass.

"Pretty, isn't it, Master Keane?" said Elizabeth Kilfedder across the table from Jack. "You should be flattered. It's the best crystal in the world and it comes all the way from Dublin."

"Sure, and don't you live in fine style?"

"Master Kilfedder has worked hard," his wife said simply. "Not that you haven't benefited as well from your short time in the Americas."

Jack looked down at his maroon coat, white stock, lace ruffled shirt, and grey breeches. Yes, he thought, his new outfit, chosen with Meg Griffiths' help, was a far cry from his ragged clothes of nearly a year before.

Her low, husky voice broke into his thoughts. ". . . and everything was going so well until you came to Boston and chose to defy us."

"Defy, is it?" said Jack, gazing directly at her. He felt for the yellowing bruise under his left eye. "The word I would be using would be defend . . . not defy."

"My husband said you were a stubborn man."

"I'm thinking he might have also called me other things after the wee fight last week."

Elizabeth Kilfedder laughed, her ringlets of blonde hair dancing in the candlelight, but there was little humor in her voice. "A wee fight, you call it? If that was a wee fight then I understand all the tales I hear about Ireland."

Jack sipped his wine, not replying immediately. She was right, of course, he thought to himself. By any standards, it had been a memorable brawl while it had lasted . . .

Jack had been sitting with the Penquicks and Augustus Hawkins at a table near the bar, listening with fascination to their tales of life in the less civilized parts of America.

At first, it seemed just like any other drunken brawl among four men at a table. Voices began to be raised, mugs clattered on the table and, suddenly, fists began whirling. One of Jack's potmen hurdled over the bar, shillelagh in hand, ready to settle the fracas with a few sharp cracks around the head. Jack watched with idle amusement. It was a scene often witnessed in the groggery. But this time the apparently drunken men didn't scatter before the shillelagh. One of them calmly slid a knife from his jacket sleeve and slashed it across the potman's face. The potman dropped the shillelagh and staggered back with a scream of agony, clutching a gaping wound that ran from his cheekbone to the corner of his mouth. As Jack and his three companions jumped up the brawlers lifted their table and hurled it through the leaded window opening on to Bread Street. As the glass crashed on to the cobblestones outside, the wooden front door splintered off its hinges and half a dozen men, led by the giant figure of Hawk, poured into the groggery. At the same time, three more strangers, until then seated quietly by the stairway, pushed their table over and produced shillelaghs from under their coats.

"Lord Almighty," muttered Homer Penquick. "There be enough of them varmints!"

"Like Redskins from the bushes," whooped Augustus Hawkins, slipping a large-bladed hunting knife from its sheath inside one of his tasselled boots.

One of the girls in the groggery screamed. The other customers scattered away from the three groups of men advancing on Jack and his three friends, who retreated into the corner between the bar and the door to the kitchen. That way no one could get behind them.

Little Horace Penquick began picking up empty mugs and hurling them at the advancing mob. One caught a man next to Hawk square on the forehead and he dropped to the floor without a sound, but most of the mugs missed their targets, bouncing harmlessly off the walls.

"Throw at their legs, Horace," urged Jack, remembering the faction fight in Listowel. The tiny Negro needed no second bidding. The mugs were soon landing on unprotected shins, and Hawk's men began to hop and shout with pain.

Hawk himself was squeaking with excitement as he brandished a thick wooden club, its end bristling with nails. He twirled it around his head as he advanced on Jack's party, his one good eye glittering with enjoyment. But his height and bulk were disadvantages in such a restricted space. The men around him were unable to get in any blows or even approach within striking distance. Roaring and shouting, two of them began picking up benches and stools and smashing them to pieces on the floor.

Suddenly, Hawkins darted forward under Hawk's swinging club. His knife stabbed upwards in a silvery blur catching Hawk along the ribs. A wide sweep of red welled up through the rip in the black shirt. The knife thrust must have cut through muscle as well as skin because Hawk's arm dropped helplessly to his side. The club impaled itself in the shoulder of a man beside him who fell away, shrieking in pain, pulling frantically at the shaft of the club to try to dislodge the nails from his flesh. As he cannoned into the others behind Hawk, Jack and Homer Penquick saw their chance. Penquick lowered his head and charged forward. His skull cracked into Hawk's damaged ribs, sending him reeling back into the already disorganized mob behind him. Squealing like a pig, Hawk tried to keep his balance but his feet slipped on pieces of broken pottery. He fell sideways, making the floor shudder with his impact. Jack moved swiftly forward and kicked him twice in the head, his heavy shoes smashing into Hawk's long, matted hair. The high-pitched squeals changed to groans and then silence.

With the fall of their leader, Kilfedder's thugs retreated into the center of the groggery, smashing everything within reach. Hawkins dashed around them, like a circling sheep-dog, occasionally slashing out with his knife at an arm or leg which came within reach. One man, holding a stool above his head, dropped it with an oath as Hawkins' knife caught him across the forearm. Little Horace Penquick curled himself into a ball and dived at knee height into Kilfedder's men, sending two of them to the floor.

The tide was turning: only seven of Kilfedder's men remained in the fight and they were quickly losing any stomach for it as Jack, Homer Penquick, and Augustus Hawkins began landing solid blows with their fists. But they fought on, trading blow for blow, until they were set on from above by Jimmy Brehoney and Padraig Costelloe. After being roused from their pleasures by the sounds of breaking furniture and the howls and shouts of the injured, they had quickly dressed and vaulted over the stairway, crashing down into the middle of Kilfedder's men. Jack and his two friends dived into the pile of struggling, cursing bodies on the floor, striking out with fist and foot. Two of

Kilfedder's men began yowling with pain and shock when Augustus Hawkins bit through the lobes of their ears. Others staggered upright, hands clutched to their eyes, after being jabbed by the fingers of Horace Penquick who, somehow, had managed to continue fighting even while pressed under the combined weights of a dozen big men.

As it became obvious that Jack's men were gaining the upper hand, the groggery's customers began to join in. They pulled Kilfedder's men from the mess of bodies on the floor, stood them upright against the walls, and then battered them unconscious with pieces of broken furniture, mugs, fists, indeed anything they could lay their hands on. Two of the thugs managed to break free and made a run for the door only to bounce off an incoming patrol of constables who promptly knocked them to the floor with their truncheons. As soon as they saw the blue uniforms of the town constables, the rest of Kilfedder's men gave up the fight.

"Jesus, we've had enough," one shouted. "No more," pleaded another as he lay on the floor under a threatening truncheon.

Gradually the defenders began sorting themselves out and taking stock of their injuries. Jack's left eye was closing rapidly where he'd been struck in the face by an elbow; Homer Penquick's face was covered with blood, some of it his own from a bleeding nose. Augustus Hawkins clutched his right side, muttering that he thought he'd cracked a rib; Horace Penquick nursed a hand broken by someone stepping on him during the fight; Brehoney and Costelloe were unmarked except for bruised knuckles.

"You're a fine pair," Jack chided them. "You were almost missing the fight altogether."

"And weren't we busy when it started?" replied Brehoney.

"Well, you could have stopped what you were doing sooner," Jack continued, pretending anger.

"And maimed ourselves for life?" said Costelloe. "The women had too close a hold on us, and that's the truth. Indeed, we couldn't have stopped what we were at even if the Angel Gabriel had tapped us on our shoulders."

As the constables carried or led Kilfedder's men out of the groggery, Jack surveyed the damage caused by the brawl. Nearly every piece of furniture was smashed; the floor was littered with broken bottles, mugs, and pitchers; the bar was overturned and splintered; every window was smashed; the door hung off its hinges.

"Well, they succeeded in wrecking the place, that they did," said Meg Griffiths, who had watched the fighting from the stairs.

"Aye, but we certainly damaged them somewhat as well. I'm doubting if Master Kilfedder will be sending his men down Bread Street again."

"What about that son of a whore mother?" demanded Costelloe, keen to continue fighting now his blood had been roused. "Sure and wouldn't it be the proper thing to give him a taste of his own medicine? Why should it just be us left to pick up the broken bits?"

"Tis right he is," agreed Brehoney. "Let's be paying him a call, Jack."

"Aye, let's settle it once and for all," said Augustus Hawkins. "When you've wounded an animal, it's only fair to track him to his lair and put him out of his misery."

"You're right," Jack conceded finally. "Your man Kilfedder has to be settled."

The six of them were joined by a dozen customers as they strode through the streets and alleys towards Kilfedder's office on State Street. The flames of the oil lamps cast grotesque images on the cobbles and on the walls of shuttered houses that were soundly, and, in the main, respectably asleep; the flickering shadows of giant, elongated men carrying shillelaghs and table legs.

"Will he be at his office? Let's go to his home instead," said Costelloe as they tramped along.

Jack shook his head. "Knowing Master Kilfedder, he'll be behind his desk awaiting news of how we were battered in the fight. He won't want his brawlers calling at his high and mighty house on Beacon Hill."

His judgment proved correct. From the street below they saw a light shining palely through the windows of Kilfedder's office on the first floor. Jack put his finger to his lips. The door to the office building was unlocked. They doused their lamps before going in. Even on tiptoe, the stairs creaked as they crept upwards to the office. The glass door stood ajar. It squeaked open at Jack's push.

"Would that be you, Hawk?" Kilfedder called from his inner office. "Come in and tell me the news."

Jack said nothing. He was standing with his men around him outside Kilfedder's inner sanctum. Hawkins bent down and slipped his hunting knife from his boot. It glinted in the yellow half light.

"I said come in, Hawk," called Kilfedder again. "Damn you, man, have you no ears?"

The men outside the office heard the sound of a desk drawer slamming shut and then footsteps.

"Hawk, Hawk," shouted Kilfedder, flinging open his door. "What the divil is the . . . ?" His voice died as he saw Jack and the men around him. "Holy Mother of God . . ." he muttered, beginning to back away.

As Jack advanced toward him, Kilfedder overcame his shock and tried to slam the door. Homer Penquick took two steps forward and effortlessly leaned into the door with his shoulder, sending Kilfedder staggering back across his office.

Jack moved into the room. "Good evening, Master Kilfedder," he said pleasantly. "Tis obvious you weren't expecting me, but I won't apologize for coming. I'm afraid," Jack continued quietly, "that your gang of thugs won't be helping you for some time. They weren't as good fighting men as you were thinking."

Kilfedder stumbled around the desk until it stood between him and Jack, then sat down in his heavy chair. A muscle began twitching high up on his right cheek. "How much?" he croaked. "Money . . . how much?"

Jack moved around the desk. Kilfedder cowered before him, holding both hands in front of his face.

"Come along, Master Kilfedder," said Jack. "No one's going to hurt you."

Kilfedder slumped in his chair. "How much?" he repeated, his dark beard contrasting with the shocked whiteness of his features.

Jack sat on top of the desk swinging his legs nonchalantly. "The damage at the groggery, you mean? Well, tis hard to tell but I'm thinking two hundred dollars would put it right."

"Here," said Kilfedder, reaching forward toward a drawer low in the desk. Jack raised his leg and pushed him firmly back into the chair.

"Homer, see what our man wants to show us."

Penquick, a broad grin across his battered features, knelt by the drawer. He pulled out a small polished wooden box and placed it on the desk.

"There," muttered Kilfedder. "Take what you want." He unlocked the box and spilled some notes onto the desk. Jack carefully counted out two hundred dollars and then slammed the box shut again.

"Witness that, friends," he said. "No more, no less than he owes us. I wouldn't want your man telling the constables that we came here to rob him."

Kilfedder shook his head. "Just take what you want and leave," he said wearily.

"Not so quick," Jack replied. "You sent your men to wreck me so I'm thinking you should be taught a lesson."

The men standing around the desk murmured in agreement.

"Go to it, boys," ordered Jack, not taking his eyes off Kilfedder. He saw the eager flare in his eyes as the men began smashing up the furniture, tearing open cupboards, ripping and scattering business papers all over the floor. Then the anger was replaced by dull despair as Jack slid off the desk to allow Homer Penquick and Hawkins to pick it up and carry it over to the window.

"One, two, three . . ." chanted Hawkins, ". . . and away!"

The desk sailed through the window with a splintering of wood and a crashing of glass to smash on to the cobbles below.

"That's enough," exclaimed Jack. "By the saints, that must have woken the whole town. Let's be going before the constables arrive."

Jack stood in front of J. P. Kilfedder and pulled his hands away from his face.

"We've finished now, Master Kilfedder," he said, staring into the despairing eyes. "You might be thinking twould be healthier for you to leave Boston for a while. Some of my men might not be so soft-hearted as meself."

". . . a wee fight?" Elizabeth Kilfedder went on, awaking Jack from his reverie. "With the constables called, five men in hospital beds, a mob rampaging down State Street to ransack my husband's office . . . is that a wee fight, Master Keane?"

Jack shrugged. "If tis so bitter you are, mistress, why ask me to Beacon Hill for supper?"

"Ever since I was a small girl I have been versed in the ways of business, and now you have ruined my husband I must salvage what I can from those ruins." She smiled disarmingly. "Quite frankly, Master Keane, you and I have to reach an accommodation."

"An accommodation?" asked Jack in a puzzled tone.

"Yes, in short, you must manage my husband's business."

Elizabeth Kilfedder raised her glass of wine. "To the victor, the spoils, Master Keane. We must ensure that some good comes out of it, otherwise all that blood will have been spilt in vain."

Jack sipped his wine, responding to her toast. "I'm not sure I would be wanting to run Master Kilfedder's business," he said, placing his glass carefully on the white linen table cloth. He looked across at Elizabeth Kilfedder, admiring the smooth shoulders revealed by her low-cut, powder-blue silk gown.

"Oh, come now, Master Keane," she smiled. "Everyone says that you have ambitions. Surely you want to be as powerful as my husband?" She looked at him from under her eyelashes, a half smile playing around her mouth. "Now you wouldn't refuse me such a small thing? A woman would be hard put to run an enterprise such as Kilfedder's. Surely you'll help me?"

Before, Jack had been needed for his physical strength, his honesty, his good nature. Now, a mature and beautiful woman—a woman who attracted him—was virtually begging him as an equal to join her in a business which had held him in its hands a few weeks before. And, as he felt his own power, he also began to feel stirrings of anger at the way Elizabeth Kilfedder was using her femininity.

She persisted. "Think of what we two could achieve, Master Keane." She reached across the table as if to touch his hand. Until that moment, she'd employed her wiles purely to persuade him into the business. She had no qualms whatsoever about doing so. Elizabeth Kilfedder had enjoyed her luxuries for too long. She had no intention of reducing her standards because of her husband's flight. Although she'd enjoyed a relatively comfortable upbringing among Boston's middle class families, her life on Beacon Hill, the privileges of real wealth, had become very precious to her. And, undoubtedly, she'd decided, Jack Keane was the person to help sustain those privileges.

She'd been quite cold blooded in her efforts to enmesh him. But during the dinner, she'd begun to sense within herself a growing physical attraction for the young Irishman, particularly when she sensed his depth of feeling.

"God's teeth, mistress, do you know what you're asking?" he muttered. "Your man hardly away and you already making plans without him. What happens when he returns?"

"He won't. Not ever," she snapped back at him.

"But why? I gave him a warning. He only has to keep clear for a few weeks."

"He won't be back," Elizabeth Kilfedder said flatly. "You might merely have warned him, but it was I who told him to go. He's weak and beaten and finished. Oh yes . . . a mighty strong man with the likes of Hawk around him, but a snivelling cur on his own. And do you think I don't know about his nights at Mother McCarthy's with your trollops? Coming to me all grogged up and smelling of cheap scent . . ."

"Enough," Jack cried, pushing his chair back from the

table and standing up. "What sort of wife is it who says these things? Have you no modesty, no shame?"

Elizabeth Kilfedder's eyes hardened. She rose from her chair and walked swiftly to the dining room door. As she opened it, a plump Negress, listening at the key hole, almost fell on to the rug. "Clear the table, Naomi," she snapped. "And if I catch you eavesdropping again I'll cut your ears off."

"Yes'm," muttered the Negress as she scrambled to her feet.

"And show Master Keane to the door. He's leaving."

"Not so fast, Mistress Kilfedder. I have some more to say." Jack took four steps to her side and gripped her waist. "I haven't . . ."

She shook his hand away. "If you have further insults, at least have the decency not to utter them in front of a servant," she exclaimed, not turning her head to look at him. Jack followed her as she moved swiftly into the hallway and then into the salon at the front of the house. She walked to the mantelpiece and stood for a moment with her back to him, both hands clenched to her mouth. "Well," she said, swinging around to face him. "What else does the big brave Irisher have to say of my virtues?"

"'Tis clear that I misjudged your . . ."

Jack stopped as he noticed tears running silently down her cheeks, streaking the powder on her face.

"Go on," she said furiously, brushing the back of her hand across her eyes. "Spare nothing. Damn you." A sob escaped from between her lips. "Say what you will and leave. Get out!"

Jack stepped forward and she was in his arms, sobbing wildly, her head pressed against his chest. He felt her body shake and her tears wetting his shirt. He heard himself crooning words of comfort into her sweet smelling hair. "Hush now. Hush, Elizabeth. Dry your tears now."

She looked up at him with wet eyes. "Oh, Jack Keane," she sobbed. "Tell me you'll help me. Don't leave me now."

"No, I'll stay."

She raised herself on tiptoe, closing her eyes, offering her lips to him. He bent his head and kissed her. Her mouth tasted salty from her tears, sweet from the wine at supper. At first, her lips were pressed firmly together but then they opened and their breaths mingled. Their tongues touched delicately, tentatively.

Elizabeth Kilfedder shivered in his arms and pulled her head sightly away from his. "Truly I have no shame nor modesty," she whispered. Then she smiled. "But then I suppose I never did have."

"What now, Elizabeth?" said Jack, cupping her face in his hands and gazing into her eyes. The tears drying on her cheeks made her seem more vulnerable, more childlike. Her eyes shone up at him.

"Let me show you."

She led him by the hand to an ornately carved bureau in a corner of the salon. From a drawer she took out a ledger bound in red leather. "This contains the real secrets of Kilfedder's business. Everything is written in here—the loans, the bribes . . . everything. It was too important to too many people for it to be left in the office." She handed the ledger to Jack. "What is in there will make you one of the most feared men in Boston. Let me show you." She opened the ledger at the first page. It was covered with spidery writing. "Now this is the index," she explained. She ran her finger down the page. Her nails were long and finely manicured. "Look here—'Bread Street,' page 29. We turn to the page and here's your business."

She handed Jack the open ledger. He read the details of

Kilfedder's agreement with Mother McCarthy and saw that all the repayments were entered neatly column by column. At the bottom of the page, scribbled in the margin and encircled, were the initials "D.P." "What does that stand for, Elizabeth?" he asked.

"That's what will make you powerful. Look back at the index."

Jack did as she suggested and found the initials again with "Page 75" written against them. He turned to this page. On it were dates and figures, ranging from fifty to five hundred. He looked quizzically at Elizabeth.

"I've no idea what it can mean," Jack said.

"Well, it's a record of payments made by Kilfedder . . ."

"To D.P. whoever he is," Jack interrupted.

"Well, only Kilfedder and I know who D.P. is . . ."

"And who might he be?" Jack asked, a note of impatience entering his voice.

"Daniel Proudlane. The selectman whose ward includes your groggery."

"Why should he be paid?"

"You silly . . . If he wasn't paid, why he'd have been on his feet in the town meetings telling the world and his wife what a sink of iniquity the groggery was. And then the constables would close the business and if that happened a fat chance Kilfedder would have had of making you pay him his interest."

Jack whistled through his teeth, shaking his head in amazement. "So that's how tis done."

For the next half hour, Elizabeth, pressing close to him, explained the full extent of Kilfedder's business. There were seven groggeries under his control, two bakeries, a tailor's shop, and three coffee and eating houses. On the payroll were four selectmen, all responsible for wards bordering the harbor and Fort Hill, and twelve constables.

When they had finished examining the ledger, Jack leaned back in his chair, rubbing his chin thoughtfully.

"I can see now how you can live in a style like this and why Kilfedder held such sway in Boston."

"Oh, I knew you would understand, Jack. But you see why you must help me with the business. Kilfedder took all the money before he fled and there's all this money still owing."

"Tis as I said before, Elizabeth. I don't care for such a business and now you've told me about the bribes and all, I care for it even less." He shrugged his shoulders. "But I did say I'd help . . ."

"You have to, Jack," Elizabeth pleaded. "If we don't carry on collecting the money, then we can't pay the bribes, and then the groggeries would be shut down."

"But bribing selectmen? They should know better than to be taking money. The people who voted for them would be mighty angry to hear it."

"It's the way it's done," Elizabeth said simply. "No one gets hurt by it and everyone profits in some way. And anyway it's only Daniel Proudlane who matters. The others are very small fish."

"Well, I don't like it at all. I shall think on it for a day or so and then decide what to do." He stood up, reached inside his waistcoat pocket and pulled out a small roll of dollar bills. "In the meantime, take these to see you through."

Elizabeth waved them away. "My credit is well enough for a few more days." She smiled mischievously. "It's other than money I need from you."

Jack moved toward her, put his hands around her narrow waist and pulled her to him. He looked down into her face.

Her lips were slightly parted. Her tongue flicked out and moistened them.

"Truly shameless," she murmured. "And to think I hardly know you."

They kissed deeply, standing together in the middle of the salon. Jack could feel himself becoming excited by her warm, perfumed softness.

"So long," she whispered, her eyes shining up at him. "So very, very long, my sweet Irisher." She moved from his embrace and walked to the door. "Just wait a few minutes and then come to me," she said quietly as she opened the doors of the salon.

Jack picked up Kilfedder's ledger from the chair and leafed through it. He suddenly shivered despite the warmth of the room, realizing what power lay in its carefully annotated contents; what an extensive web of intrigue and greed was revealed by the spidery names, dates and figures. He shook his head sadly. How could he use it? He placed the ledger carefully back inside the bureau and then strode into the hallway.

A single oil lamp was burning on a table. He took the stairs slowly, enjoying the richness of the paintings hanging on the walls and the feel of the polished wood of the banisters under his hand. Everything around him spoke of money and influence. He drew strength from it, knowing that such things were now within his grasp. At the top he saw a slightly open door and flickering candlelight in the room beyond.

"Sweet Jack in the dark." Elizabeth Kilfedder spoke from a dim pool of light at the far end of the room.

Jack closed the door behind him and pressed his back against it. The smell of her perfume was everywhere. As his eyes adjusted to the darkness, he saw her standing beside a large four-poster bed, its curtains drawn on three sides. The candle on the table reflected in the highlights of her blonde hair. She had unpinned it and let it fall across her shoulders and down the front of her long white negligee. She took one pace toward him. Jack's breath caught in his throat as the candlelight shone through the lacy material and outlined the curves of her body. "Dear God," he muttered, half to himself, wondering at her loveliness.

"Dear Jack," she replied dreamily. She held her arms out toward him, palms raised upward, offering herself. The next moment her arms were around him and his face was buried in the curve of her neck. She pushed him gently away and stood against the side of the bed. Without taking her eyes from his, she raised her hands slowly to the front of the negligee. He watched, mesmerized, as she undid a large silk bow. With the slightest whisper, the negligee fell apart, the candlelight catching and playing on the fullness and roundness of her pink-tipped breasts. She shrugged her shoulders and the negligee drifted filmily to the floor. He grabbed for her but she pushed her hands flat against his chest, restraining him. "So ardent, my Irisher," she smiled. "But let me enjoy you first."

She stood on tiptoe, her breasts rising tautly, and slipped his coat from his shoulders. She untied the stock from around his throat, tossing it to one side, then began unbuttoning his shirt, at the same time pulling it free from his breeches. Jack groaned deep in his throat as she ran her fingernails lightly down his chest. She bent her head and kissed both his nipples in turn. Then she unbuttoned his breeches and slipped her hands inside to grasp his hard maleness. She gasped as she felt its warmth and strength. His breeches fell to his knees and there was no longer any pretense nor softness in their desire for each other. He felt her pulling him backward and allowed himself to fall with her on to the bed. Her thighs opened beneath him, her knees rose to grip him round the waist, and, instantly, he slid into her velvety, sucking warmth. Her nails bit into his lean buttocks, urging him ever closer and deeper as their bodies began moving rhythmically together. Their desire for each other was so strong, so urgent, that their climaxes were quickly upon them. Jack's body arched upward as he felt himself flow into her. Elizabeth's eyes opened wide, staring unseeing upward into his face, and then she moaned and thrashed her head from side to side until the overwhelming paroxysms had passed. Jack knelt by her to lift her into the center of the bed. In the half-light, her eyes were mauve rather than blue.

"Oh, my Irisher," she whispered, her lips a few inches away from his still erect, shining hardness.

"Pull the curtain," she said, rolling away from him. He gazed lovingly at the smooth twin muscles running down her back and bent forward to kiss her between her two dimples. Then he drew the curtain that shut them snugly away from the rest of the world in their own cocoon of desire.

Toward morning, as they lay quietly content, hands clasped, Elizabeth Kilfedder turned her head on the pillow. Her eyes, bruised now with fatigue, looked softly at Jack. "Oh, it's so beautiful to be loved," she said.

Chapter 10
September, 1825

Jack Keane paused outside the State House and looked up at its massive round dome. It always raised a sense of wonder when he saw it on his way to Elizabeth Kilfedder's house on Beacon Hill. For him, it was the one building which summed up the spirit of his adopted country. Everything about the building spoke of ordered democracy where the cries of ordinary supplicants would be equal to the voices of the rich and influential.

The outer lobby of the State House was thronged with people; some scurrying here and there, others talking or arguing in groups. Jack stood bewildered in the entrance for a moment, trying to take his bearings. One or two people looked around at him casually and, not recognizing him, turned back to their conversations.

He swung on his heel and collided with an elderly man who was hurrying past. The man staggered back a few paces and would have fallen if Jack hadn't reached out to steady him.

"My apologies, sir," Jack blurted out.

"That's the trouble with this place, isn't it," said the elderly man, slightly winded by the collision. "Everyone in a hurry to catch the eye or ear of someone or other."

"Indeed I wish it were so, sir."

"I beg your pardon?"

"Well, I'm trying to talk to Master Daniel Proudlane on most urgent business but I don't know where to find him."

"Proudlane, eh . . . a friend of his? A supporter, perhaps?"

"No, sir. My name's Jack Keane and I simply have business with him."

The man, plump and bald but for a few whisps of white hair fluffing out behind his ears, smiled and held out his hand. "I am Josiah Longman, sir. By your accent I presume you're an Irisher not so long on these shores . . ."

"'Tis right you are, Master Longman," Jack said.

"Well, Master Keane, let me help. Follow me, if you will."

He set off with twinkling steps, hands clasped under the tails of his green jacket, nodding to his left and right at those who sought to greet him. The elderly man, Jack realized, was someone of importance at State House. He led Jack across the lobby toward a group of six men who were deep in conversation, standing under a large canvas depicting a scene from the War of Independence. He addressed a small, weasel-faced man at the center of the group. "A young Irisher to see you, Proudlane," he said curtly. From his tone, he was no friend of the selectman for the Fort Hill district. But he turned to Jack with a smile. "A pleasure to bump into you, Master Keane, as it were. Perhaps we'll meet again one day under more formal circumstances." Without waiting for Jack's thanks he scurried off again back across the lobby.

"Well?" said a voice behind Jack. He faced the man spoken to by Josiah Longman.

"Master Proudlane?"

"Indeed . . . and I don't see any of my constituents without an appointment. You are a constituent?"

"I come from Fort Hill, sir . . ."

"Write to me of your troubles then, though I fear you Irishers bring so many problems on your own heads that I can be of little help."

One of the group behind Proudlane tittered. Jack flushed at the studied insult. The selectman was turning back to the group as Jack gripped his arm. He bent slightly to whisper in his ear. "I come from Kilfedder's, Master Proudlane."

Jack felt the selectman's muscles tighten under his grip. He let go of his arm as Proudlane turned to him again. His narrow eyes bored into Jack's face.

"Not here, you fool," he hissed.

"Here," Jack insisted in a loud voice.

Proudlane stared at him for a moment and then nodded. "A moment, my friends," he said over his shoulder to the group behind him. "This Irisher does have an urgent problem indeed."

He guided Jack into an unoccupied part of the lobby, well out of anyone's hearing. "Damn you," he said furiously. "What do you mean by coming here? And, anyway, who are you? I've never met you before."

"I'm Jack Keane."

"Keane?" Proudlane looked thoughtful for a moment. "The spalpeen from the groggery in Bread Street?"

"You know your people, Master Proudlane," Jack said sarcastically.

"What's all this about Kilfedder? From what I hear your cronies sent him packing from Boston. What concern is it of mine?"

Jack smiled. "I would have thought you were worried about where your funds were coming from."

"Funds?" Proudlane snapped. "What funds? You're mad like all the other Irishers. I bid you . . ."

"I have a ledger, Master Proudlane, which lays out all the kindnesses shown to you by J. P. Kilfedder."

"A ledger? How . . . ? What ledger?" Proudlane spluttered, his bleak eyes flickering around the lobby to make sure he couldn't be overheard. "I know nothing of it. It's a ruse by my opponents. I should have known that you're a friend of Longman."

"So be it, Master Proudlane," said Jack, turning away from him. "Your opponents, as you call them, can have the ledger then . . ."

"No . . . wait . . . wait . . . come to my house in Salem Street before dusk this evening."

Jack walked down the steps of the State House feeling less than proud of himself. His meeting with Daniel Proudlane had confirmed everything that Elizabeth Kilfedder and the entries in the red ledger said about him. Every word, every gesture from Proudlane had been those of a conniving, corrupt politician. Jack glanced back at the State House as he strode briskly up Beacon Hill. He wondered how many more politicians like Proudlane defiled the building's proud architecture with their shabby dealings.

"They have to be stopped," he declared to Elizabeth Kilfedder as he sat in her salon an hour later.

"Stopped? Why stopped, dearest Jack?" said Elizabeth, perching on a small stool at his knee gazing up at him. "In every barrel of apples there are always some rotten ones—and always will be. You can never change that."

"I know, Elizabeth. But when you find the rotten ones you don't leave them in the barrel to ruin the others. You throw them away."

"If you stop Proudlane—as you term it—then what of your business? And what of Kilfedder's? You'll be bringing them both crashing down. If you expose Proudlane and the others, then you expose us as well. Yourself for running a disorderly house and myself as the wife of a criminal who bribed public servants and officials.''

Jack bent down and gently kissed her warm lips. ''I promise I'll do nothing that will harm you, and that's the truth. You know that.''

Her arms encircled his neck, pulling him from the chair to kneel beside her. They embraced, their kisses becoming more ardent.

''You'll stay for lunch and then we can spend the afternoon together?'' she whispered.

''Doing what?'' he replied, feigning innocence.

''Anything you like . . .'' she breathed.

Jack was tempted. Ever since that first night together, their passion for each other had grown wilder and more abandoned than he had ever thought possible. In Elizabeth's arms he forgot everything, even Brigid Aherne. But he found he felt no remorse for this. Elizabeth's sophisticated voluptuousness—and his matching desire for her—did not mean he was in love with her. He knew that. Between them was a flame that would burn itself out eventually. Until then he was determined to enjoy the affair in all its fullness. But not that afternoon. He had people to consult before his meeting with Daniel Proudlane: an idea was taking shape in his mind.

Although Jack was not particularly religious—indeed he had not been to Mass since leaving Ireland—he was well aware of the growing influence of the Roman Catholic Church in Boston. As yet it had no resonant voice, but it was spreading its roots deep among the families arriving from Europe, building on its support among the old French families who had lived in America for generations past. Its influence stretched down the eastern seaboard of the United States among all the arrivals from the Old World. Sooner or later, the Church, Jack realized, would have a great say in the law-making process of the new country.

Father O'Flaherty gazed at Jack curiously as he was shown into the priest's small office next door to the Church of the Holy Cross in Franklyn Square.

"Do I know you?" he asked directly.

"I think not, Father," said Jack, standing awkwardly before the priest's desk.

"And yet you're Irish from your voice, my son, and thus I presume a member of the Church. But I cannot recollect you at Mass. Perhaps you're newly arrived, although I'm doubting that from the appearance of your fine clothes."

"Tis a long story, Father, and not one you'd be caring to hear, I'm thinking."

"Sit you down then and jaw, young man."

The priest smiled at him—amused at his visitor's unease—and settled back in his chair. Jack hesitated for a moment, wondering where to begin. He looked at Father O'Flaherty's austere, high-boned features and was reminded of Father O'Sullivan back in Listowel. There was the same twinkle lurking behind the cold, light blue eyes which suggested a man with an understanding of worldly matters which transcended his calling. Haltingly at first, and then with more urgency and fluency, Jack told the priest what had happened to bring him to Boston and all that had occurred since his arrival. He went into detail, omitting only his relationship with Meg Griffiths and Elizabeth Kilfedder. These, he decided to reserve for the confessional.

"A tale fit for a bishop," said the priest when Jack had finished. "Indeed yes, Master Keane. You have supped with a mighty short spoon so you have. And now you want advice on how best to exercise this hold you appear to have over Daniel Proudlane." He looked at Jack with obvious distaste. "Tis a matter for your conscience, such as it is, and I have far weightier matters to consider than easing your problems."

"You don't understand, Father," said Jack desperately. "I intend to have no part of this at all. What I want is advice on how best to help us . . . you . . . Boston town in bringing this corruption to an end."

Father O'Flaherty eased himself back into his chair, an expression of surprise on his face. "So," he grunted reflectively. "Well, the Church has been known to take an interest in such secular matters; Church and State, you realize . . . Church and State."

"Twould be in the Church's plan to rid Boston of Master Proudlane and his gang?"

"Indeed . . ."

"And have selectmen who were beholden to the Church and the Irish," Jack went on eagerly.

The priest pursed his lips and nodded approvingly. "The matter has exercised us, tis true, since so few of our countrymen have the qualifications to vote as yet."

"Then I know what I shall be doing. I'll hand the ammunition to Master Proudlane's opponents on condition that they look well on our interests."

"If you do that, I'm sure they will, Master Keane, but tell me . . . what of your enterprises? Won't they be at an end?"

Jack looked straight at him. "Not with the support of the Church," he said evenly.

Father O'Flaherty started in his chair. "The support of the Church in running a jilt shop, a place of assignation, a house of the divil? Master Keane, I fear you are either mighty naive, a rogue, or insane."

"None of those things, I'm hoping, Father, although you're the second today to suggest I was leaving my senses. When I help Master Proudlane's enemies, the women of the house will be gone and so will the still in the cellar. Mother McCarthy's will become a business where only the best spirits are sold, all properly purchased from Master Felton's distillery, and where the finest foods are served. Twill become an establishment which even yourself, begging your pardon, would be happy to patronize."

Father O'Flaherty shook his head sadly. "A commendable idea, Master Keane, but I fear you would soon be bankrupt. You flourish now in your fine clothes because of your women and your illegal still. Such a new establishment as you envisage, worthy as it may be, would lose you money."

"Not if I had seven such establishments all around the North End and Fort Hill."

"Such schemes, Master Keane . . . an empire so soon . . ." The priest shook his head doubtfully again.

"There are six other groggeries like Mother McCarthy's mentioned in the ledger. I'm thinking their proprietors will be ready to sell up when they hear of the coming change in their circumstances."

A smile, almost beatific, spread over Father O'Flaherty's think features. "Master Keane, I congratulate you." He leaned over his desk to shake Jack's hand. "God and Mammon satisfied. Sir, you have a young body but an old head."

"Then I have your support, Father?"

"Support and blessing. Indeed you have. Perhaps even my occasional custom."

"You'll help me tell Master Proudlane's opponents what we want in exchange for his downfall?"

"Master Keane, tis true what the Lord said about better the sinner who repented," the priest said warmly, moving from his desk to pour two glasses of wine from a decanter on a side table.

The two men silently toasted each other. Father O'Flaherty sat down in a chair by Jack, his earlier reserve and suspicion replaced by interested concern for the young man. He asked Jack about his home and family in Ireland and whether it was his intention to bring his bride back to Boston town.

"Tis in the future, Father, but twill be a difficult decision I'll be having to make, so it will. I want to help Ireland."

"Amen to that . . ." the priest murmured.

"But here I am sensing a future and opportunity. At home, I fear there'll be a mighty long struggle before the English set us free to build our own country as we would want."

"Aye, tis true, young man. Not only in Ireland, though, will there be a struggle, I'm thinking. What happened in France is just the beginning I fear."

The priest leaned forward and gripped Jack's arm. "And that's why it's important to establish the Church firmly here, my son." Father O'Flaherty continued. "Here will come the poor and oppressed from the old world. God knows, the Church has made mistakes in the past—though don't be telling the Bishop I've been saying that—but here is our chance to build again. Perhaps that's why this country attracts us all. It's writing its own history day by day on clean, blank pages, so it is, and that is why the Church must go out into your world if she is to survive and prosper."

The priest insisted on giving Jack a blessing before he left to put his plan into action. He checked the stock of gin to ensure that there was enough for at least a week, then ordered two of his potmen to dismantle the still in the cellar. He would have liked to consult Mother McCarthy but there was no time. He promised himself he would write to her the next day with a full account of what he was planning. His next move was to ask Meg Griffiths to call the girls together in the kitchen, and invite Padraig Costelloe and Homer Penquick to listen to what he was going to tell them.

"Whatever you hear me say don't be surprised, Padraig," he said. "What I'm about to do will be the making of all our fortunes, I'm praying."

But for all his apparent confidence, Jack was at a loss how to begin as he saw the dozen faces looking expectantly at him in the kitchen.

"I have some news for you all," he started. Then he paused. "Hell's teeth, Padraig," he exclaimed. "Pour some drink for everyone else or I'll never get it out." The faces around the table became apprehensive. "Oh, tis nothing terrible," he reassured them. "You're all going to have to change your jobs."

There was silence around the table. One girl began to laugh. Meg rounded on her angrily. "Can't you see Jack's serious? And all you can do is bray like a donkey."

"Tis not that serious, Meg," said Jack, trying to calm her. "It does not mean you'll be without work. In fact, I'm reckoning you'll have to work harder than ever."

Jack explained how and why he was changing the groggery. Dismay crept across the girls' faces as Jack outlined his plans, making it clear that they were no longer to ply their trade with the customers.

"Where are we going to go?" Meg wailed. "You're going to throw us back on the streets."

"No so. Tis not so," Jack replied. "You're still going to serve the men . . . but not as ladies of the town. You're going to be cooks and waitresses."

"Give up the men!" said the girl sitting next to Meg, a defiant tone in her voice. "Never. Give up the men . . . you'll be just as well making us nuns."

"You can still have as many men as you like," said Jack curtly. "But twill be on other premises and in your own time. If you stay here you'll do honest work for honest wages. You can keep your cubicles to live in but you'll not be having men up there."

"There be too many of us just to serve this groggery," sniffed Meg. "Most times you'll be having more waitresses than customers in this hoity-toity establishment of yours."

"That may be true at first," Jack agreed. "But I have ideas of acquiring other groggeries where you can all find work. If you measure well enough, you might be running an establishment of your own before long."

"That's fine talk," complained the girl next to Meg. "But I'm thinking we should stick to the trade that we know best."

"Suit yourself," snapped Meg. "I'm knowing which side of the loaf is crusty."

Jack nodded at her approvingly. "Tis the right attitude, Meg. This way you'll be after building something for the future."

"And what of us?" interrupted Costelloe, gesturing at himself and Homer Penquick. "You won't be needing our fists any more when you become all proper and legal."

"You and Timmy Brehoney can give up your humping on the wharves and join the enterprise, if you want. The same goes for the Penquicks. As for Augustus Hawkins . . . well, I'm reckoning he'll be back to his mountain traps soon enough."

"But we ain't knowing nothing about it, Jack," said Homer Penquick. "They ain't learning us how to be waitresses and cooks down on the plantation." He rolled his eyes. "We ain't nothing but Nigra trash, you be forgetting, Mister White Man."

Jack joined in the general laughter at the sorrowful expression on the big Negro's face. "What you're forgetting, Homer, is your own people will be wanting to use proper eating and drinking houses as well. They'd be mighty easier if one of their own folk was running it for them."

"You mean that?"

"Why not, indeed? Nigra money spends as well as white money, doesn't it? And as for being cooks and waitresses . . . well, you'll learn as quick as I did. There's not much to it." He tried to imitate Homer Penquick rolling his eyes. "Why down in the bogs, they didn't teach us Irish trash much either."

Most of those in the kitchen seemed to approve of Jack's plan. They chattered their way excitedly back into the groggery. Two or three of the girls, though, still wore sullen looks. Jack called Meg to one side.

"Them that don't approve . . . see them off the premises by tonight. Give them five dollars from the monies behind the bar and send them on their way with a square meal inside themselves and a bottle of gin."

"And that'll make this place respectable?" said Meg, sceptically.

"Get a sign made to go on the bottom of the stairway. Something like 'No customers allowed upstairs' should be enough."

"And where be you while all this respectablizing is going on?"

"Well, I reckon I'll be buying some proper liquor from Master Felton and then giving a certain gentleman some mighty disagreeable news. When I return tonight, I want the groggery fit to entertain Bishop Fenwick himself."

Meg pulled a sour face. "It'll be terrible dull and no mistake."

"The duller the better," said Jack cheerfully. "Tomorrow we start painting the house in pretty colors so twill be better if you all get a night's sleep without your usual exertions."

"And yourself?" Meg asked slyly. "Will you be learning how to serve proper ladies up on Beacon Hill tonight?"

"You're above your station, waitress," laughed Jack, slapping her behind playfully.

"And are you sure that you're not, Irisher?" said Meg shrewdly. "I'm remembering the scars on your back and how you got them scarce a year since and here you are all high and mighty with society and political folk. Mind you're not scarred some more."

Meg's warning returned to Jack's mind as he strode towards Daniel Proudlane's house in Salem Street. His business in Felton's distillery had gone well although there had been raised eyebrows at first when he'd said he wanted wines, whisky, gin, and rum delivered to Mother McCarthy's.

"And has the still broken?" Master Felton inquired.

Jack looked at the large, jolly man, well padded with fat, his appearance advertising his wares. "You could say that, sir, and it won't be getting repaired again, I can assure you."

"Then, Master Keane, we can conduct business at a proper discount," the distiller had replied.

Was he indeed rising dangerously above his station in life, Jack wondered? He remembered dancing at the crossroads at Ballybunnion when Brigid Aherne had declared her love so openly. He remembered the silence and space of Kerry, the dew-fresh mornings, the vividly wild sunsets, as he moved through Boston's narrow, busy streets. He listened to the sound of his shoes striking the cobbles and thought of how his parents had used their own footwear so sparingly. A pang of home-sickness wrenched at him. Wouldn't it have been a better life in Ireland despite the poverty and disease and hide-bound class system? Wouldn't he have been happier in a small cabin with Brigid, rather than wearing fine clothes and intriguing against men of high education and low cunning? Jack shook his doubts from him. No, Ireland and all it meant had passed for the moment. It was there to be savored, but in the future. He squared his shoulders as he approached Daniel Proudlane's wooden framed house.

The selectman awaited Jack in his neat front parlor. Two copper bedwarmers hung, gleaming, each side of the wide, empty fireplace. The furniture was dark and well polished, the chairs were deep and upholstered. It was a room which spoke of secure affluence. Jack was impressed.

"Well, Master Keane, I cannot say it is a pleasure to welcome you to my home," said Proudlane sourly after the servant had left them together. "I have been pondering all day on whether to give you to the constables for threatening me as you did at the State House."

"Threatening, Master Proudlane? How so?"

"All this nonsense about funds and kindnesses from Kilfedder. Your tone implied you have a hold on me."

"There is a ledger . . ."

"Showing proper business transactions, no doubt."

"As far as Kilfedder was concerned they were proper," said Jack, somewhat taken aback by Proudlane's confident attack.

"And so they were, young man," Proudlane said, putting an avuncular arm on Jack's shoulder to guide him to a chair. "Kilfedder and myself had a business arrangement, that's true, but it was for the best of motives. He helped finance my elections and my work in the ward."

They sat on opposite sides of the fireplace. Proudlane offered him a churchwarden pipe of tobacco but Jack refused politely.

"Tis not a habit I have."

"Seems to me, though, Master Keane, you have other

habits equally addictive," said Proudlane, smiling tightly. He puffed at the long clay stem of the pipe. "Like the habit of honesty; the habit of curiosity, or call it meddling; and the peculiarly Irish habit of blind naivety."

"Sir?"

"I've explained what it was between Kilfedder and myself and why it was thus. I'm not sure whether you understand yet."

"I do understand. The practice of politics, it seems to me, is merely a way for those with the most money to have the biggest say. If I'm not mistaken, the system you approve of is very much like that at home where the biggest landowner either goes to Parliament as of his right or pays someone else to do his work for him."

"Exactly," purred the selectman, relaxing a little in his chair. "You see most events most clearly, Master Keane."

"Perhaps I do, sir. And that's why I'm concerned at the payments shown in the ledger I'm holding. They're clearly illustrating that the old system of doing things still applies to the Americas. And I'm thinking that that isn't right at all."

Proudlane hunched forward in his chair again. "And, pray, why not, my young Irisher?"

"Because you fought to have it otherwise," Jack replied calmly. "The Yankees who died fighting the English this century and the last died because they wanted a different way. They wanted a say in the running of their lives. They wanted their voting at elections to mean something."

"I don't want to sound a cynic, Master Keane, but there have always been those who want and those who get. Those who want live in a world of dreams. I state that those who get deal in the real world. The true reason we fought the English was because we didn't like paying our taxes to them and then having no say over how they were spent. Talk not of glorious revolutions nor wars of independence. The man in the real world knows that they're only squabbles between those that have money and power and those that don't. Sometimes those without money and power win the squabbles by force of arms, by superior numbers. But, when they do win—and this is the truth, Master Keane, despite the distaste on your face—they quickly make sure to re-establish the old order. They elect themselves leaders to gain power and with that power comes money, and out of money comes power and out of power comes money and so on and so on until the next squabble."

"In your case, Master Proudlane, you had the power and J. P. Kilfedder had the money. Or was it the other way around?"

"It matters not. They're interchangeable."

"But not unchanging, I'm thinking," said Jack quietly. This time the selectman looked puzzled. "I don't . . ."

"Well, it seems that I have the power now. And it appears you don't have enough money. So you're out of your real world, as you put it. You have neither power nor money."

"You are threatening me again, Keane." The politician's voice began to rise in anger.

"No. I'm telling you," said Jack calmly. "Sure and I don't live in your real world because what I'm going to do is give away my power to someone else. I'm going to hand it back to the people who voted for you by opening the ledger to them so they can see your real world and how it operates. Then I won't have the power, nor will you." He leaned forward in his chair, jabbing his finger at Proudlane to emphasize the point. "The people who will have the power will be simple people, ordinary people who should have had it all this time while you and Kilfedder have been running things the way you want."

"Then, sir," Proudlane snapped, "you will be nothing. I

shall show you who has the power. The elections are two months away and by that time you shall have no business."

The selectman stood up, his face white with anger. "I've tried to be reasonable, but you are as ignorant as your background suggests. You Irishers will never succeed in this country until you empty your heads of your dreams. There is only one place for your heaven and it isn't on this earth."

Jack shrugged. "That may be . . ." He rose from his chair and walked towards the door.

"May be . . . may be . . ." Proudlane flung after him. "Even your precious Church knows where the power lies in this life."

After Jack left the house, he stood outside in Salem Street for a moment, breathing deeply. He could understand Proudlane's anger. Jesus, he thought, I must have sounded a proper prig with all that talk about simple, ordinary people. But Jack knew he had reacted to the politician's gross cynicism. He knew that some of what Proudlane had said was probably correct. But the selectman's total contempt for the voters and his naked greed for power had sickened him. Other politicians, he believed, lived in the real world, as Proudlane kept calling it, but still managed to reconcile it with an honest desire to serve their voters. Josiah Longman, he was certain, was such a man.

The next morning, Jack woke early and roused everyone. By the time he'd finished a quick breakfast of bread smeared with pork dripping, the girls had come downstairs and were sitting in various states of undress at the tables around the bar. They looked at him blearily as he repeated his instructions of the previous afternoon. Some of them groaned as he announced that he wanted them to begin painting the establishment that morning.

"The groggery will be closed for two days for the work to be done," he said. "That should be enough time for the customers to realize that Mother McCarthy's is on the change.''

"They realized that last night," Meg complained. "Dozens of them left when we told them there was no service upstairs any more."

"They'll get used to the new ways soon enough," Jack replied with as much confidence as he could muster. In truth, by the light of the new day he was wondering if he had not made a series of grave errors. Had he committed himself too firmly to too many people? He cursed himself inwardly for not leaving himself more room for maneuver. If his plans failed, if he was rejected by Longman, then he knew he had lost the business. And then there was still the problem of unseating Proudlane; perhaps the voters would prefer the morals of a corrupt politician to those of a reformed proprietor of a former jilt shop!

Those doubts persisted as he paced nervously at the foot of the steps leading to the State House. He had decided to waylay Josiah Longman rather than risk another confrontation with Proudlane in the lobby of the State House. The sun was almost directly overhead by the time Jack saw Longman arrive in a carriage.

"Be you back at four o'clock, Joshua," Jack heard Longman instruct the Negro coachman before he turned to hurry up the steps.

"Master Longman," Jack called after him. "Master Longman . . . a moment if you please."

The politician turned and saw Jack. A flicker of recognition crossed his face, followed by a friendly smile.

"When I said yesterday that I hoped we would meet again, young sir, I little realized it would be so soon."

"The truth, Master Longman, is that everything is happening to me sooner than I anticipated."

"I have yet to meet a young man not in a hurry, sir, either

to make his fortune or to fall in love. Of what service can I be to you now? I trust it will be of more pleasant a nature than an introduction to Daniel Proudlane." He placed a hand under Jack's elbow to urge him up the steps.

Jack shook his head. "Twould be better if we talked outside the State House, Master Longman. Too many ears to listen, and that's the truth . . ."

"Well then, where shall we go? A stroll on the Common perhaps? Fresh air would do me more good than all the stale words I'd have to listen to in there." He jabbed his thumb at the State House behind him.

Jack nodded in agreement. "Twould be fine, Master Longman. And then perhaps tis I can offer you a glass of refreshment at a friend's house along Beacon Hill."

"Capital, sir."

As the two men strolled in the summer sunshine through the glades and along the paths of the Common, Jack explained his predicament for the second time in two days. Josiah Longman interrupted him rarely, but from time to time, glanced sideways and upwards at his companion, assessing and weighing his words.

"A pretty tale, indeed," he grunted when Jack had ended his story. He smacked one fist into his other and repeated, "A very pretty tale indeed. 'Pon my word it is."

"You don't seem surprised, Master Longman, at the association between J. P. Kilfedder and some of your colleagues?"

"Surprised? Surprised? Not in the least, sir. There have been rumors for some time that Proudlane and the lesser denizens of his party were not all they seemed. Not that I don't suspect some of my own colleagues of soiling their hands in similar manner. It is a common ailment in politics, sad as that may be."

"But you'll help me, won't you?" Jack asked, slightly

worried at the politician's apparent cynicism over his allegations of corruption.

Josiah Longman stopped for a moment. He looked Jack up and down. "Are you sure you wish to proceed on this course? It's hard enough for a newcomer to survive in this town. If we fight an election using your evidence, you might go under in the storm that will blow."

"The hatches are battened down to weather the storm. You forget my experience at sea."

Longman laughed. He reached up and patted Jack on the shoulder. "Indeed I do. Why, any man who has sailed the Atlantic, outrun the English army, and done as well as you have, must have an instinct for survival. Such an instinct is possibly the most valuable weapon in life's battle. People talk more of heroes than survivors but then heroes tend to be with us for less time. Heroes are useful but not half as useful as survivors. That, my boy, was even the considered opinion of General Washington. Why, I remember . . ."

"Master Longman," Jack interrupted. "You will talk with Father O'Flaherty about choosing a candidate to fight Proudlane?"

"I'm sorry. I was digressing. Of course I shall, sir. I already have someone in mind who is not only totally trustworthy but of Irish descent. He might be an admirable choice to satisfy yourself, the Church, and my colleagues." Again he chuckled. "Pon my word, Proudlane will never stand a chance against such holy opposition. With this ledger of yours . . ."

"Will you be wanting to peruse it?"

"Of course, my boy. As soon as possible. And we must satisfy ourselves that it is in safe keeping."

"Tis not far away, at my friend's house."

Longman patted Jack on the shoulder again. "Lead on." He gazed up at the sky. "Every moment with you in this fresh air is making me feel quite young again. You did a great service in insisting on walking with me."

By the time they had arrived at Elizabeth Kilfedder's house, the two men had slipped quite easily into first name terms.

Jack rapped at the front door. After a short wait it was opened by Naomi, Elizabeth Kilfedder's maid. Her eyes brightened as she saw Jack standing on the step.

"Why, Master Jack, we were expecting you last evening," she said as the two men stepped into the hallway. "Why, Mistress Elizabeth was so worried that she was almost sending me on a message to you."

"Naomi, who is calling?" Elizabeth's voice came from the salon.

"Master Jack," the maid called. "I done tell you there was nothing to . . ."

"Hush your chattering, Naomi," said Elizabeth as she hurried into the hallway. She ran towards Jack, her arms outstretched. Then she noticed Josiah Longman. She dropped her arms, and a blush appeared high on her cheekbones. Longman's twinkling eyes missed nothing. He looked at the beautiful young woman and then glanced at his new friend.

"Elizabeth," said Jack, "may I present Josiah Longman, a friend of mine who is here to help us."

She curtseyed, immediately recognizing Longman's name. "You are most welcome to my home, sir," she said.

"The pleasure is mine, dear lady," Longman replied.

"'Tis Elizabeth Kilfedder, Josiah," Jack explained. "The wife of J. P. Kilfedder who saw fit to desert her."

"My commiserations, madam," said Longman. Then he added slyly, "But how nice to know that Jack here is affording you his protection in your difficulty." He looked sideways at Jack. "Your circle of acquaintances continues to amaze me. It does indeed."

"Naomi," Elizabeth ordered, "let us have some wine."

When the claret had been poured, Jack explained to Elizabeth about his arrangement with Longman. At first she seemed alarmed but gained confidence quickly as she heard of the precautions taken by Jack.

"And now for the famous ledger, dear," said Jack. "Will you fetch it for Josiah?"

The politician put on half-moon spectacles to study the heavy book. Elizabeth explained the index to him in the same way she had done for Jack. Longman's face darkened as he read the pages that indicated the extent of the corruption.

"A public disgrace," he muttered. "These men are nothing but villains, pure and simple." He slammed the ledger shut and handed it to Jack.

"It must be kept safe and its existence must not be revealed to any more people than already are aware of it. Thus, when we do expose its contents nearer the election, its effect will be heightened."

Chapter 11
March, 1826

Paper lamps with candles burning inside them hung from the whitewashed ceiling of Mother McCarthy's. Their light shone blue, red, yellow and green on the faces of the two hundred or so people packed into the bar. They swayed and turned, throwing their colors in every direction, in the currents of warm air rising from the noisy chattering crowd. The lamps danced in time to the reels and jigs and the musicians stamping their feet on the floor. The sounds from the groggery—now officially re-named "Mother McCarthy's House of Refreshment"—reached out into the warm night air of late summer in Bread Street and dragged more and more people inside. Potmen, trays held high above their heads, thrust their way through to deliver bottles and mugs to tables. Six girls, supervised by Meg Griffiths, darted back and forth behind the bar, green silk bows bobbing in their hair, trying to keep pace with the orders. People kept looking expectantly at the long trestle table, covered with a gleaming white linen cloth, which stood empty at the end of the groggery by the stairway. Then, those with sharp enough ears picked out the sound of a drum beating steadily and the cheers of a crowd approaching, closer and closer to the groggery.

"They're here," shouted someone by the door. "They're here!"

People surged to the windows and through the door to watch the procession burst noisily into the narrow, cobbled street. At its head Padraig Costelloe and Homer Penquick held the poles of a long canvas banner proclaiming simply "Vote Finucane." Under the banner a single drummer rapped out the marching pace. A crowd of about one hundred followed, most of them with burning, smoking torches held high. In the middle of this crowd a youngish man swayed uneasily on the broad shoulders of Jack Keane and Timmy Brehoney, waving at the people who leaned from the upper windows of the houses on either side of the street. Their cheers and those from the procession almost drowned the staccato drum beat. The banner was dipped and thrust into the entrance of the groggery, forcing the crowds to move aside and make a pathway. Inside, it was unfurled again and the drummer led it around the bar. Jack Keane leapt up the stairs, becoming visible to all in the room, and signalled with his arms for silence. The hubbub grudgingly subsided.

"Friends," he shouted. "Friends, the vote went as follows . . ." Jack plucked a small piece of paper from his waistcoat pocket and read from it. "Daniel Proudlane . . . one thousand and ten votes."

There was silence now.

"Matthew Finucane . . . one thousand, six hundred, and . . ."

A great cheer erupted, drowning the rest of his words. People hugged each other, jumped up and down, kissed the nearest woman, and hurled their hats into the air. Little Horace Penquick turned a cartwheel of joy on the floor.

Jack allowed the wild celebration to continue for more than a minute and then shouted and gestured for silence again.

"And so I present you with your new selectman . . . Matthew Finucane."

There was another roar as he stepped back and the man who'd been chaired into the groggery jumped up the stairway, hands clasped above his head. He stood alone for a moment and then grabbed Jack's arm and raised it so that both men acknowledged the delirious shouts from the crowd. From the groggery door a chant began, reinforced by the stamping of feet which made the paper lamps dance and sway even more.

"Speech! Speech! Speech!"

The chant and the stamping spread throughout the groggery.

"My friends," Finucane began, shouting against the noise reverberating around the room. "Me mam and dad came to this town nigh on thirty years back from County Clare . . ."

Another roar went up. Finucane waited for it to die away before continuing.

". . . so that makes me as Irish as any of you. But I was born here so I speak to you as one of the first Irish-Americans. What happened tonight is just the beginning. At last you will have a voice in the running of this town; a voice that understands your needs and problems; a voice that will listen to the counsel of our Church. It says a deal for this new country of ours that this should be so. We bring to this land many cultures and legends. Let us not forget them, rather let us treasure them, but we must not forget that we are now Yankees first and Irishers second. There will be many who will resent us coming here; there will be many like my unlamented opponent, Daniel Proudlane, who will try to exploit us; there will be many who will pour scorn on our beliefs and our customs. Let them, because, in time, they will become the strangers in this land; their voices will be the ones crying from the wilderness of ignorance and prejudice and bigotry. Not ours. Ours will be the voices giving thanks for this new land where we can ensure that the wrongs of the old world are not repeated. Friends, I thank you, and particularly I thank my friend, Jack Keane. Bless you all."

For a moment there was silence and then another gust of cheering swept through the groggery. Some of the crowd, moved by Finucane's rhetoric, were crying openly; crying and smiling at the same time.

The politician pushed Jack forward against the banister of the stairway. "Go on. It's your turn now. Say something, Jack," he urged.

"Come on, Jack," came a shout from the front of the crowd. "Let's be hearing you."

Jack raised his hand for silence. "I'm not a man for speechifying," he began, his hands nervously clutching the banister. "And hasn't Matt Finucane said all there is to be said, and that's the truth." He looked desperately around him for inspiration. At the top of the stairway, hidden from the crowd below, he saw Elizabeth Kilfedder, her eyes shining with excitement. At her side was the dumpy figure of Mother McCarthy, who'd insisted on returning for the election party, dressed in a voluminous beige silk gown, her hair neatly combed, a strand of Elizabeth's jewelry around her throat. The effect was only slightly spoiled by the inevitable mug of gin in her gloved hand. Jack smiled at them and then turned back to the crowd that waited expectantly for his next words.

At that moment, Padraig Costelloe thrust a mug through the rails of the stairway. Jack bent down to take it and then raised it, turning to salute the two women at the top of the stairs. "Friends," he called, "the toast is 'The Ladies.' God bless 'em!"

The building shook with the response from the hundreds crammed inside and from those still outside in Bread Street unable to force their way through the door.

"Now that's enough talk," Jack shouted. "Let's have a proper hooley." He bounded up the stairs and hugged Mother McCarthy and Elizabeth Kilfedder in turn.

"Come on down and join the party," he said, slipping his hand into Elizabeth's.

"Am I looking in fashion enough?" asked Mother McCarthy anxiously. "Why, I've never been dressed as such since I wed McCarthy. Not that he noticed with the drink in him . . ."

"You look fine," Jack reassured her. "All the country air has brought color back to your cheeks. If you're not careful you'll be finding yourself in front of a priest again with another man at your side."

Mother McCarthy laughed throatily. "At least the next time I'll be knowing what to do with him on the wedding night."

Jack felt happier that evening than ever in his life. He felt a twinge of guilt at clasping such happiness to him. Images of his parents, his dead brothers, and Brigid Aherne came briefly to his mind but he deliberately pushed them away as he gazed down the table at his guests.

At the head of the table, opposite him, was Matthew Finucane, a man in his early thirties, already becoming successful in his cooperage business. Jack had taken to him immediately, realizing that Longman had chosen the ideal candidate; transparently honest, solidly respectable; in all, the perfect contrast to Daniel Proudlane. If Proudlane and his friends hadn't spent so much money buying votes then

Finucane's victory would have been even more decisive. But then, Jack reflected, Proudlane had been forced to spend money desperately to try and offset the damning evidence in the ledger. Throughout the election, which had been surprisingly free of trouble, the ledger had lain open, available for anyone's inspection, on a table at the groggery in Bread Street. Hundreds had come to see it, not only helping Jack's business, but decisively undermining Proudlane's campaign.

On his right was Matt Finucane's wife, Alice, complementing her husband with her charm and fresh looks. "And what plans are you hatching now, Master Keane, so deep in dreams that you are?" she asked.

Jack started out of his thoughts. "Plans, Mistress Finucane? What plans now?" He glanced at Elizabeth Kilfedder to his left and saw that she was watching his reaction closely. He smiled to himself. Women together, he knew now, would always attempt to harry an unmarried man to the altar. It was as if the state of bachelorhood was a personal affront to them.

"Well, you've achieved so much so quickly that I was thinking you would have further ambitions."

"My ambitions are to enjoy the company of my good friends around this table. And as for achieving what you call so much, so quickly, why, I've had the luck of the Irish, and that's the truth. No. No more ambitions on this side of the ocean except to dance this night away." He turned to Elizabeth. "And will you help me realize that ambition, too?"

"Of course, Master Jack Keane," she smiled brightly. "Yours is to ask and mine to accept."

By midnight, the crowd in Mother McCarthy's had thinned out. Most of Jack's guests had left. Padraig

Costelloe was asleep at the table, head buried in his arms, snoring loudly. Meg Griffiths had helped Mother McCarthy to bed and then returned to the establishment she managed four streets away. Josiah Longman had given Father O'Flaherty a lift in his carriage and the Finucanes had hurried home to their family. Timmy Brehoney and the Penquicks had joined some cronies at another table and were clearly set on drinking and yarning into the small hours.

"Well, Elizabeth," Jack said, holding her at arm's length, "are you going to spend the night here in my room?"

She looked around the groggery, noting the people still present, and shook her head.

"Twould be too public, dear Jack. I have little enough reputation already in the eyes of the town without that. My carriage should have been outside for an hour since. Come back to Beacon Hill."

"Yours is to ask," he said gently, echoing her earlier words. She smiled softly at him and inclined her head.

Jack escorted Elizabeth toward the door.

"Don't be up all night," he called to Timmy Brehoney and the Penquicks.

They waved to him and then, almost as an afterthought, Brehoney hurried to his side. "Here, take this, Jack," he muttered, pulling a shillelagh from under his coat and thrusting it into Jack's hand. "You can't be too careful; not with Proudlane's men around. They're still mighty upset at his defeat."

Jack tried to push it away. "There's no need, Timmy. We're not going on foot."

"Take it, for God's sake, and don't be so foolish, man," urged Brehoney.

"For peace's sake," said Jack, reluctantly putting the thick stick under his coat. "But you're fussing about nothing."

Outside, he helped Elizabeth into her carriage, letting his hands hold her slim waist longer than was strictly necessary.

"What was Timmy giving you that stick for?" she asked as the carriage clattered over the cobblestones.

"The drink had made him fearful," Jack explained lightly. "He thinks Proudlane's men will want to crack my skull."

"And will they?"

"Not at all. Proudlane, whatever he may be, is no fool. He'll be spending his time plotting to get back his position, not chasing Irishers for revenge."

"Are you sure?"

"I'm sure," he said, putting his arm around her shoulders and pulling her closer to him.

The carriage passed hardly anyone on its journey to Beacon Hill.

"There," he said as it pulled up outside her house. "Nothing at all to worry about. Brehoney's worse than an old woman, that he is."

They stood for a moment on the footpath as the carriage moved away toward the stables at the back of the house. Then they turned, arm in arm, to go indoors.

Suddenly, from the darkness behind him, Jack heard footsteps. A voice shouted hoarsely, "At last, you bastard spalpeen!"

Sensing mortal danger, half-recognizing the voice, he pushed Elizabeth away from him, at the same time spinning around in a crouched position. His hand darted toward the shillelagh under his coat. He caught a glimpse of a white, demented face, full bearded, and two flintlock pistols pointed at him. Before he could move any further Jack felt a smashing blow in his chest followed by the flash and roar of a pistol. He staggered and began to fall. Dimly, before he spun into blackness, he heard Elizabeth scream wildly and then another roar from a pistol.

An eternity later, he opened his eyes and groaned. The anxious face of Naomi the maid swam fuzzily into view. He tried to move but groaned again with pain. The left side of his chest felt as if it was on fire. I've been whipped again, he thought weakly. Then the memory of the man with the pistols flooded back to him.

"Kilfedder," he muttered. "J. P. Kilfedder. He came back."

"Hush now, Master Jack," Naomi murmured. "Just you rest. You been injured."

He lifted his head slightly and saw that he was lying on cushions spread on the floor of the salon. His shirt had been removed and white bandages bound tightly around his chest. As Naomi bent solicitously over him he felt spots of water falling on his bare shoulders. He blinked his eyes, making another effort to focus them. He looked into the Negress' face. She was crying silently, tears running down her cheeks. He shook his head slightly and blinked his eyes again.

"Your mistress?" he whispered. "Elizabeth? Where is she?"

Naomi sobbed loudly. She turned her head away and wiped her hand across her eyes. "Don't worry, Master Jack," she said quietly. "Mistress Elizabeth is just fine. Just fine."

"Where is she?" Jack demanded, his voice becoming stronger. He forced himself to sit up, choking back a shout of agony. "Where's Mistress Elizabeth?"

"She's resting, Master Jack," Naomi said gently. "She is in good hands. You just lie back until your men come. I sent the coachman to Bread Street for them near an hour back."

Despite his pain, Jack shivered. From Naomi's tears and words he suddenly knew. "She's dead, isn't she, Naomi?" he said evenly. Then more fiercely. "She's dead, isn't she. Tell me."

Naomi nodded her head and began crying openly. "She done gone with her Maker, Master Jack. She done gone."

"I want to see her," he demanded, his own pain now totally forgotten. It seemed as if his whole body was filling with a clammy emptiness.

"No, Master. You lie and rest. You been hurt bad."

"Pull me up," he shouted. "Pull me up or I'll crawl."

Reluctantly, Naomi helped him to his feet. He put his right arm around her strong shoulders and stumbled into the hallway. He gripped the banister somehow and hauled himself up the stairs, wincing in his agony. Naomi supported him as best she could as he limped towards the closed door of the bedroom where he and Elizabeth had shared so many hours of love. Naomi pushed the door open. Jack leaned against the door jamb and looked inside. A candle burned on each side of the bed. Elizabeth lay there, her blonde hair spread on the pillow, a single sheet covering all but her face. Jack moved to the side of the bed and looked down at her. Her face was pale and in the soft, flickering light, she seemed asleep, her eyes gently closed. Then, with a sudden movement, Jack grasped the edge of the sheet and wrenched it aside. Elizabeth's hands were folded over her naked breasts. Just below her left breast there was a small hole, tinged with a blue-grey bruise. There was no blood. Just that obscene hole. Jack's eyes travelled the length of the perfect, empty body.

"We done cleaned her, Master Jack," Naomi said beside him. "We dress her later to make her proper."

He groaned and tried to speak. But the room began swimming around him. With a low moan he fell forward across Elizabeth, his arms stretching around her.

The next three days for Jack were spent in long periods of unconsciousness and brief spells of lucidity when he was aware of being back in his room at Mother McCarthy's tended by Dillon the physician or being watched over by Meg Griffiths, Padraig Costelloe, or Timmy Brehoney. Their faces would swim out of the blackness. He would hear comforting, murmured words or feel gentle hands soothing him before the room slipped away from him again. On the fourth day he awoke just after dawn. He moved his head on the pillow and saw Meg Griffiths in a chair by the bed. Her head was sunk on to her chest, her breath coming in light snores. Jack stretched out his right hand and plucked at her skirt. She wakened instantly, tossing her head up. He smiled at her weakly.

"Water, for the saints' sake, Meg."

She rose quickly from her chair to pour him a mug from a pitcher set on the floor. She lifted him gently and helped him sip the liquid. He sank back on to the pillow.

"How long?" he whispered.

"Four days," Meg replied quietly.

"And Elizabeth?"

A worried expression crossed Meg's face.

"I remember what happened, Meg. I know she's dead."

Meg took his hand. "She was buried yesterday."

Jack nodded. "It had to end," he murmured. "One day."

Meg lifted his hand, kissed the palm lightly, and then laid it against her cheek.

"'Twas Kilfedder, you know. He came back."

"We know. The coachman glimpsed him running off on to the Common, but it seems he's clear away."

He glanced down at his own body covered by blankets.

"Why not me, Meg? How did he miss?"

"He didn't, dear Jack. The ball hit Timmy's shillelagh under your coat and went around your ribs. Master Dillon said if it hadn't been for the shillelagh it would have pierced your heart for sure."

"Dear God. Saved by Timmy's stick. And there was I after not carrying it."

"Now rest, Jack. No more talking. I'll be making you some gruel soon for your strength."

"You're a fine girl, Meg."

"Hush now. Just rest."

She patted his hand and slipped it back under the blankets. Jack's eyes closed and he fell deeply asleep.

It was another week before he was strong enough to get up. He no longer felt keen pain at Elizabeth's death. There was an emptiness but not deep grief. She had died at her loveliest and happiest knowing that he adored her. Perhaps, he thought, she would have wished it like that, realizing, as he had done, that the affair would eventually have come to nothing. Now, he would never forget her: he would always remember her as warm and vibrant and passionate, as full of life and love.

The first day he was allowed to go out, he walked stiffly, his ribs still bandaged, with Costelloe and Brehoney to the church in Park Street to visit Elizabeth's grave. It was covered with flowers but had no headstone as yet. It looked tiny in the shadow of the church's four-tiered spire pointing thinly into the sky. He stood by the grave for a few minutes thinking of the laughing, sensuous warmth of the four-poster bed. He knelt to place a large spray of red roses at the foot of the grave. He tried to think of a prayer but none came to mind.

"Be happy, mavourneen," he said in a low voice. And then he rose and walked away without a backward glance.

Jack never visited the grave again, but every year he sent one of his friends to place flowers there.

During the months after her murder he drew closer to Matt Finucane and his family, taking comfort from the tranquillity and happiness of their settled home life.

Twice more he helped Finucane in election campaigns and twice more they beat off challenges from Daniel Proudlane. Jack never told Finucane but in the second election he had to resort to Proudlane's tactics of buying votes to ensure that the Irish people's candidate was elected. Indeed, during these elections, a relationship of grudging admiration grew up between Jack and Proudlane. They came to recognize and appreciate each other's cunning.

"Politics makes the strangest of bedfellows," Proudlane observed to him during the second election as they waited for the votes to be counted. "I remember talking to you, Master Keane, about power and money and here you are using my former strengths against me."

"I've never claimed cleverness," Jack said cheerfully. "Only a willingness to learn, Master Proudlane."

"If only we had met under different circumstances. You could well have been my campaign manager."

"But then tis I would have been supporting a loser."

Proudlane shook his head ruefully. "A bad mistake not to realize the dangers in an Irisher's open face, his way of spinning words into dreams, and his totally ruthless cunning. A mistake, I believe, many others will make after me."

"Perhaps so, Master Proudlane. Perhaps so. Better maybe to join us than fight us."

The politician laughed shortly. "How many years, I wonder, before there comes a brood of you Irishers strong enough to be Presidents of the United States, all proudly proclaiming their heritages and all having to use maps to find their ways back to Ireland."

"Twill not be in my lifetime, I fear, Master Proudlane. At present we hang on by our fingernails, so we do."

"And not in my lifetime either, I hope, because another political truth is that men with dreams are the most dangerous of this profession. Realists, pragmatic men, are safer than any dreamer. Take that as another free lesson to be learned, Master Keane."

A year after Elizabeth's death, Mother McCarthy's health began to decline sharply. A winter of early snow and icy winds from the Atlantic brought her to her bed and her friends realized that this was one winter she was unlikely to survive. In the strange way that dying people have, Mother McCarthy herself knew that her time had nearly come. She sent for her lawyer and drew up a will which made Jack her sole beneficiary. She explained this to him as she lay, weak and drawn, in her room during the second month of her illness.

"You'll have everything, Jack Keane, when I've gone," she wheezed.

"Talk not like that. Tis you'll see the spring buds," said Jack, trying to comfort her.

She smiled at him wearily. "Tis you always had a sweet tongue but then I'm hearing McCarthy himself calling me away. I'm terrible tired of this life so I'm not being afeared of the next. You must remember to make provisions yourself for all those that are working for us. As I've tried to watch over you, so you must care for them."

Mother McCarthy died in her sleep two days after the

bells of Boston's churches had rung in the year of 1828. Her funeral was probably the biggest ever seen by the growing Irish community. Her wake beforehand lasted for a full two days, aided by the five hundred dollars left in her will for drink to be given to the customers of the seven establishments. The hearse was drawn from Bread Street by four black horses with plumes of black feathers nodding on their heads, their hooves slipping and sliding on the icy, snow-covered cobbles. A fiddler walked in front playing laments, and behind a crowd of about four hundred proceeded to the Church of the Holy Cross for a funeral Mass conducted by Bishop Fenwick.

Afterwards, Jack invited his closest friends back to Bread Street for food and drink. Ever since Mother McCarthy's death he had been thinking of a scheme to protect them in the event of anything happening to himself. The occasional twinges from the scar tissue along his ribs reminded him how near he had already been to death.

"Tis you're going to become owners of the establishments you've been running," he told them. "Twould have been Mother McCarthy's wish."

"But we can't afford that," said Meg Griffiths, "the money needed is beyond us all."

"Women!" muttered Homer Penquick contemptuously. "Ain't you ever learning just to listen?"

Jack looked at Meg with affection mingled with irritation. "As Homer said, just listen for a moment. I'm going to give you the establishments at values suggested by my banker, Master Dunwoody. If you disagree with the values then Matt Finucane will hold the ring, and I promise I'll accept his decisions."

"There's still money to be found," grumbled Meg. Jack ignored her.

"You'll pay me the values at so much a quarter out of your profits over as long a time as you can afford. That way you won't be noticing it so much. And with the money you give me, I'll be paying off the loans I needed from Master Dunwoody to buy the establishments in the first place."

"As simple as that?" asked Padraig Costelloe.

"Just one condition . . ."

"Ah!" said Meg triumphantly, her suspicion apparently vindicated.

". . . You have to keep your present signs outside. They must all stay as 'Mother McCarthy's.' Tis a fitting memorial to her."

"Is that all?" asked Meg, somewhat disappointed in tone.

"Tis so, you shrew. By the heavens, you be making a fine, grasping businesswoman and that's the truth. I'll be trusting you all to run the establishments as they are now. You'll not be wanting to besmirch Mother McCarthy after a bishop conducted her funeral, I'm sure."

And so it was settled. Jack kept the original establishment in Bread Street, now free of all debts with the help of the bequest from Mother McCarthy. The business continued to prosper, the people of Boston coming to realize that he offered honest food and drink and honest prices. His boast to Father O'Flaherty even came to fruition when Bishop Fenwick and a party of priests set the seal on his new respectability by dining at Bread Street.

But as his standing in Boston grew, so did his loneliness. After Elizabeth, he couldn't bring himself to form another attachment with a woman. There were plenty of opportunities, many of them engineered by Matt Finucane and his wife, but Jack's memories were too powerful to allow him to be deeply interested in any of the young women he escorted to supper parties or formal dances.

"You're really breaking Alice's heart," Matt Finucane remarked to him one day. "One of the most eligible bachelors in all Boston and she can't find a suitable girl for you. You could have your pick, you know, Jack."

"Maybe so, Matt, but I'm finding my heart is turning more and more to Ireland again. With Elizabeth still alive, I might have settled here happily enough with all my resolves about going back. As it is, with her and Mother McCarthy gone it does seem a terrible empty life."

"But you've many friends. Alice and I . . ."

"I know that. Many good friends, and true they are. And all wanting to see me happy, I know. Yet inside me there's a mighty yearning to visit home again."

Jack's homesickness grew with each letter brought to him by his old shipmates, Martin Flannery and Patrick Deane, on their annual visits to Boston. The letters were now written in a different hand. The one that reached him in 1829 informed him that Father O'Sullivan had died and that the writer, Father Jeremiah O'Mahony, was the new parish priest.

"A nice young fellow," Flannery commented. "From Killarney, your mam tells us. Most concerned he was when he learned of how you'd been driven out of the district."

"Said he'd be happy to do all he can to settle the matter with the police and the army," Deane added, filling up the mugs again with Master Felton's best rum.

"Much chance of that," Jack said glumly. "Here I'm sitting with all the money a man could be wanting and not able to visit my home."

"No, Jack. Don't be disheartened," said Flannery, as optimistic as ever. "This new priest's a real spinner of words and no mistake."

"We told him what you'd done here and he was mighty

impressed," Deane continued. "Things haven't been quiet in Kerry over the past year or so, not since that Captain O'Hare got himself elected to Parliament, so Father O'Mahony does reckon his words about you will be listened to."

"Listened to maybe," said Jack. "But acted upon? Tis a very different mare. Jonathan Sandes is still high in the saddle as Watson's agent so what can have changed?"

"What's changed, Jack—don't you realize it?—is that you're now a man to match Sandes. Your clothes are as fine as his; your pockets are just as full; your name's as powerful."

"Maybe here, my friends, but not there."

"Doesn't do to underestimate the word of the Church," said Flannery. "There's word in Kerry that some cleric in Boston has been writing mighty pretty letters about you to the priests back home."

"Tis not as if your mam and dad have kept silent either," Deane broke in. "The word is around the Shannon that the bilge rat of a stowaway we brought to the Americas has become a powerful strong man in this town."

Jack looked at both of them. They wore smiles of smug self-satisfaction as they raised their mugs and clinked them together.

"I'm thinking I don't have to look far to see those people who've made my reputation such," said Jack. "Tis the two of you who've been blathering, I'm not doubting."

"Us, Jack?" said Flannery with an air of hurt innocence. "Us blathering?"

Deane nudged him in the ribs and all three men began laughing.

"Just you be remembering us now you've turned that respectable," said Deane with a wink. "Take us where that

Meg girl works and we'll still be regarding you as a friend and putting the proper word in for you."

As the years passed, the visits of Deane and Flannery became more and more eagerly awaited by Jack. With them, he could reminisce without feeling embarrassed; he could get drunk and forget his deep loneliness; he could breathe through them even for a day and a night the peat-fresh air of Kerry.

The letters they brought from his parents were always cheerful, although the one that came in 1831 contained for the first time no mention of Brigid Aherne. Jack's parents seemed to be coping well and enjoying a few luxuries with the money he had been sending back across the Atlantic. The cabin had glass windows now, and his parents had a proper wooden bed, raised from the floor. Although his mother still insisted on keeping fresh straw underneath the bed in case it might collapse.

In June of 1833, the two seamen again came to Boston and immediately made for Mother McCarthy's in Bread Street. By now, after so many years, Jack had a warning system from his customers on the wharves about the arrival of the *Grannia*, still plying across the Atlantic on the timber trade. A steaming pot of rabbit stew awaited Flannery and Deane as they came through the door in Bread Street together with, by custom, two flagons of the best rum.

But this time Jack noticed they seemed ill at ease after he had greeted them and sat them down at the table.

"A bad voyage, friends?" he inquired. "Captain Higgins driving you harder with the years?"

"Tis not that, Jack," said Flannery, pushing away the plate of stew served by a waitress. He took a long pull at his mug of rum.

Jack looked across the table at Deane and saw that he was equally ill at ease. Jack lowered his head.

"Tis the news, isn't it?" His dealing with people over the years, and his own experiences, had taught him to recognize those bearing bad news which they were reluctant to impart.

"Tis only life, Jack," said Flannery quietly, handing Jack a letter addressed as usual in the spidery hand of Father O'Mahony. Jack opened the letter, smoothed it out on the table, took a gulp of rum, and began to read.

Father O'Mahony regretted to inform him that his father had passed away in the spring of that year, peacefully, after a sudden attack of the chest ailment.

"Twas sudden," said Flannery softly. "Knew nothing of it says the tell."

"A blessed way," echoed Deane.

Jack said nothing. He continued reading. "Your mother took the event well," the letter said, "although it is I must be informing you that there is much opinion that she is ailing herself. Certainly from this writer's observation, it is doubtful how she can sustain the farm during the coming winter. This writer must express concern whether she can plant, let alone gather, the crops necessary for the farm's or her survival."

Jack gazed at his two friends. It was obvious to him from their glum expressions that they knew the import, if not the exact contents of the letter.

"Read on, Jack," said Deane. "Your dad brought a lot of good for you even in his dying."

Jack blinked his eyes, finding it difficult to focus on the writing.

"Your father's untimely death has caused much genuine concern in this district, and happily, I am able to inform you, on a word satisfactory to myself, that your presence at your home to care for your mother would not lead to unusual harassment, attention or action from the authorities."

Jack smoothed the letter again and reread the paragraph. "Tis so?" he asked his friend.

"Aye. Tis so," Flannery replied. "The word is given in the district. You can return."

Chapter 12
July, 1833

The hooves of the dapple-grey horse raised puffs of dust as it eased into a gentle canter along the track leading from Tarbert in North Kerry. Jack Keane looked neither left nor right as he clung grimly to the reins and bumped along in the saddle, gripping the sides of the horse tightly with his knees. The dealer who'd sold him the horse had assured him that it was the mildest of creatures but its rhythm was still strange to its new rider. The two bags of gold sovereigns he'd obtained from Master Dunwoody's bank before his hasty departure from Boston banged comfortably against his thighs, safe in the deep pockets of the heavy brown top coat he was wearing. Two pistols, loaded and primed, nestled in leather holsters slung across the horse in front of the saddle. The rest of the possessions he'd brought were in a chest back in Tarbert awaiting more leisurely delivery by a carter to the family cabin in Drombeg townland.

Master Dunwoody and Matt Finucane could be trusted to wind up his business affairs in Boston and transfer the remainder of the proceeds across the Atlantic to him. He'd wanted the ownership of the establishment in Bread Street to pass jointly to his friends and was surprised when Finucane made a firm offer for it. But after Finucane had explained that it was a natural diversification from his cooperage business, Jack was happy to accept the offer with proper guarantees about the futures of the other businesses. It had happened so quickly, that there had only been time for perfunctory farewells, although everyone had come down to the Long Wharf to wave goodbye as the *Grannia* had slipped her mooring.

During the voyage Jack had many doubts about his decision to leave Boston but as soon as he glimpsed the coast of Ireland, just north of the Shannon Estuary, he knew there had been really no choice. It was inevitable and right that he should return to his home.

The countryside south of Tarbert seemed to have changed little in the nine years he'd been away. Everywhere and everything was the same; the tiny cabins dotted here and there with the occupants working the rough fields around them; the sense of space and permanence under the clouds scudding off the Atlantic, the dampness of autumn in the air changing to a light drizzle as he trotted through Ballylongford, every stride of the horse taking him nearer and nearer to his home, his mother and Brigid Aherne. He thought fondly of his mother, remembering her strength and hoping that she hadn't changed too much, that the years hadn't taken too much of a toll. He imagined Brigid as he had last seen her, fresh, loving, her black hair framing her beautiful face. He wondered why the last letters from his parents had not mentioned her. As soon as possible, he resolved, she would leave the service of Jonathan Sandes and marry him. He would build the best cabin money could buy, not too far away from his mother's, and then purchase a score of cows and pigs so that they would never again have to rely on the fickle harvest.

Along the way, as he turned east towards Listowel, he exchanged greetings with other travellers. There seemed little movement in the countryside but then he remembered that it had always been quiet on market days. He would have to stop comparing everything with the bustle and prosperity of Boston town. Now he remembered just how poor and deserted Kerry was. His memories and reminiscences had blurred the edges of the truth that was all around him.

As he passed the first cabins of Drombeg townland, he looked in vain for familiar faces: the people outside their cabins simply gazed dully back at him. One woman, a shawl on her head, a pipe stub in her mouth, actually curtseyed to him as he went by. He was puzzled and embarrassed until he realized that, of course, any person dressed as he was, riding a horse, displaying pistols, would naturally be taken as someone in authority. He wanted to shout aloud, "I'm only your Jack Keane, back from the Americas. I'm no different from you. No different at all." But he didn't and felt guilty that he didn't. And then, a hundred yards away, there was the cabin where he'd been born and raised.

The only sign of life was a thin trickle of smoke rising from the thatch. There were no animals outside; the fields were untilled; the walls in obvious disrepair, covered with large bare patches where the whitewash had flaked away. He reined in the horse and looked at the cabin with dismay. Suddenly, all the cheerful words from his parents' letters came back to him and he knew they had been a proud sham, a pretense to ease his own worries.

Jack dismounted from the horse, deep shame filling his heart, and then called out. "Mam, are you there? Mam?"

He heard a chair pushed back inside the cabin. A thin voice replied, "Who is it there?"

Jack walked to the rough wooden door and pushed it squeakily open. "Tis me, Mam. Your Jack. Tis your Jack." His eyes peered into the darkness inside.

"Jack?" the voice quavered.

And then he saw her standing by a table in the middle of the cabin, a shawl over her shoulders, grey hair falling over her begrimed face; a bent, old woman.

"Oh, Mam," he muttered quietly. "Oh, Mam, you should have said." He took two paces and gathered her into his arms. She had no weight to her. He could feel her bones through her clothes.

"Tis really you, Jack?"

"Aye, I'm home, Mam."

She pulled away from him and looked up into his face. Her eyes, once so strong and inquiring, were dull and rheumy. But they brightened as they gazed up at him and began misting with tears. Soon her whole body shook with sobs.

"There now, Mam. Tis all right now," he said softly, guiding her back to the chair and helping her sit down. He pulled a second chair around the table and sat close to her, holding both her hands. Her fingers were thin, the nails broken and dirty.

"Oh, Jack," his mother kept repeating between sobs. "Tis really you." After a few minutes, she pulled one hand away from his, picked up a corner of the apron she was wearing, and wiped her eyes. "You must think me a silly old woman, squealing like this," she said, smiling tearfully at him. "Twas the shock of you. Here was I sitting and thinking on you and your brothers—the Lord keep them—and suddenly there you were as if conjured from my dreams."

"I know, Mam."

"And why, haven't you changed, son? You're the build of your dad without his belly yet." She reached out and touched his hair. "And what's all this? Your sailor friends never said you'd white in your head."

"They never said a lot of things, Mam, so I'm thinking," said Jack, at that moment silently cursing Flannery and Deane for keeping the truth about his parents' condition from him.

He looked round the cabin. The chicken coops and pig pens were empty. The earthen floor was littered with dirty straw, the bed in the corner covered with stained sacking. The glass windows were so filthy that light hardly penetrated them. The peat fire was small and giving out little heat.

His mother saw the dismay growing on his face. "Since your dad went, there's been little to live for," she said quietly.

"But what about the money I sent? Didn't that help?"

"Did keep us alive and in the cabin for the last two years. Your dad couldn't work the fields much so we sold the chickens and the pigs gradually to keep going and pay the rent."

"Why, in God's name, didn't you say? Why didn't you ask?"

"Your dad, his pride . . . and fearful proud of you he was until the end."

Jack shook his head in bewilderment. "You should have told me."

"Oh, well, tis over now. You're home and that's the blessing. Now tell me all you've been doing."

"No, Mam, not yet. When did you last eat?"

"The other day or so . . . yesterday, I'm thinking . . . but I'm not feeling the hunger as I used to."

"What food have you?"

"Some lumpers and some bacon fat I was keeping for a wee treat."

"Right then, we'll make a feast of them now. You start

preparing them while I'll be building up the fire. And then when we've tidied a bit and filled our bellies we can jaw . . . but not until then."

By the time they'd finished their meal, the cabin was glowing with heat. The flickering flames and shadows from the fire played around the cabin, investing it with the kind of cosy homeliness he had always remembered. He'd brushed the floor, wiped down the windows, changed the sacking on the bed, taken the straw from under it to spread outside for the horse.

He produced a bottle of Master Felton's rum from the saddlebag, poured himself and his mother a mugful and settled back in his chair.

"Now then, Mam," he said, stretching his legs out toward the fire. "Tis I who'll be asking the most questions I'm reckoning."

"How long are you staying, son?"

"For good, Mam. I've sold up in the Americas. We'll be needing the money to put this farm on its feet again. Tomorrow I'll be taking you to Listowel to buy all the provisions we'll be wanting and a few more besides. We'll be buying some animals and maybe even a good trap so that the horse can be taking you on your calls. And then I'll hire myself a man to help get the fields back from the weeds and then we'll paint . . ."

His mother held up her hands to interrupt him. "So many plans you're having, Jack. You always were the one with plans to change the world, but tis an awful lot of money in one gobful of words."

"Don't be worrying about the money, Mam. There be enough even to make Master Jonathan Sandes pull on his boots with envy."

His mother lowered her eyes when he mentioned Sandes' name.

"And how has the fine land agent to the mighty Sir James Watson been these years past, Mam?" he asked sarcastically.

"He hasn't harmed us. He called after your dad went and was right gracious. He was asking after you and your affairs in the Americas and saying that he'd told Father O'Mahony that the price was off your head."

"How fine of him after so many years!" Jack's tone was bitter. "I'll be paying a call on him soon enough to sort out the rent so I'll be giving him the thanks due, and that's the truth."

"He's no better, no worse than the others," his mother said. The warmth of the fire and the rum was putting the color back into her cheeks. Her voice sounded stronger already.

"And how of Brigid Aherne? Why haven't you been mentioning her to the priest for the letters to me?"

His mother stood up and poked at the fire, sending showers of sparks into the air. "She be in the district," she said noncommittally.

"But how is she?"

"Like all of us, I'm guessing."

"Does she still work for Sandes?"

"No. No more."

"You're not saying she's off and married?" he asked anxiously.

"No. Not married. Not her."

"Thanks be," he said, relief flooding through him. "Then where is she? Why won't you be telling me more?"

"She's at Gortacrossane as always and I'm thinking you should find out yourself how she is."

"I will. I will that. As soon as we've been to Listowel for the provisions."

They talked for hours: Jack telling her about some of his experiences in Boston; she telling him about his father's last years. Eventually, the combined effects of the fire and the rum made them both sleepy. Jack damped down the fire while his mother stumbled into her bed and then settled down on the hard-packed earth. One of his first purchases, he decided, would be another bed.

Jack woke early after a fitful night's sleep. He looked around the cabin in the greying light of dawn and smiled ruefully to himself. So this was the house he'd been dreaming of for so long. He rose and washed in the stingingly cold water in the butt by the front door. The sun was just peeking redly over the hills to the east, lighting the mists on the fields. For the first time since he'd left Ireland, Jack listened to the silence and felt peace; not contentment because he knew a great deal of work lay before him, but peace. This truly was the land of the saints, he thought. Harsh, unremitting, violent, yet with a deep reservoir of peace. He went back into the cabin, and then roused his mother. "Let's away to Listowel. We'll breakfast at the inn before doing our purchasing."

"At the inn?"

"A breakfast you've not seen the likes of. You'll be needing flesh on your bones for all the work we've to be doing."

Before they left the cabin, Jack hung up the wooden crucifix he'd taken with him to Boston, and beneath it he tucked the dried and brittle sprig of hawthorn he'd carried on his journey those many years before.

"Now doesn't that look like home again?" he said,

standing back to admire his handiwork. "They'll be in the family forever, and that's a promise."

They arrived in Listowel as it was beginning to come to life. People looked strangely at them, the old lady high on the horse, the handsome, well-dressed man at her side. A couple of women outside a shop in Tay Lane muttered to themselves, seemingly recognizing Mary Keane and wondering about her sudden change of fortune.

At the coaching inn in the market square, Jack helped his mother down and instructed a boy to take the horse to the stables at the rear. The potman inside looked at him deferentially and then more curiously as he seated his mother at a table. She was clearly a poor woman and yet was being treated courteously by a man of means and quality.

"You have some eggs and meat?" Jack demanded.

"'Tis the very finest beef, your honor, and sure aren't the eggs just dropped from the hen," said the potman.

"Well then, we shall be having two best cuts of your beef, six eggs to lay alongside them, a loaf, and some butter," ordered Jack. "And a bottle or two of your best claret to wash them down."

"Indeed, sir. Oh, indeed, sir. As quick as the cook can prepare them."

"'Tis a lively man you are." Jack took a sovereign from his pocket and placed it on the counter. "And be taking the care of my horse out back from the change."

The potman sprang into action around Jack like a moth near a flame. "And have you been coming far, your honor?"

Jack smiled into his face. "Me mam and I have just

ridden in from our cabin at Drombeg and mortal hungry we are.''

The potman's face fell. "From Drombeg, sir? Tis I was thinking I was knowing most people hereabouts, but I cannot be recalling serving you before.''

"You might have a way back but I'm thinking you would have known me dad, Joe Keane.''

"Joe Keane, the fighting man who went this springtime, God rest him?''

"The very same.''

"Well, bless me, sir, then you must be Jack Keane from the Americas.''

"Fresh back yesterday.''

The potman almost danced with delight. "And isn't that the news then? Isn't that just the news? The town will really be on its ear about this, and that's the truth.''

After the meal, Jack escorted his mother around the shops to order provisions and the materials he would need to transform the cabin: timber and nails, whitewash and brushes. He haggled with some drovers who had brought cows, pigs and chickens into the market square on the chance of a sale and eventually selected the livestock he wanted. The drovers were only too happy to promise to bring the animals to Drombeg when they realized he was ready to pay hard cash. Everywhere Jack and his mother went, they received curious glances and whenever he turned there seemed to be a crowd of people watching him, virtually following from shop to shop. But their innate sense of courtesy prevented them from approaching and asking all the questions they were bursting to put. Indeed, so intense was the scrutiny that Jack was glad to finish his buying and return to the coaching inn to collect the horse for the journey home.

"And is it really yourself, Jack Keane?" a voice called from outside the inn as he led the horse from the stables and into the bustle of the market square. He instantly recognized the barrel-chested man advancing towards him. There could be no mistaking the scars on his face.

"Quillinan! Paddy Quillinan!" Jack shouted.

"Aye, tis so, but the truth is I wouldn't be recognizing you, Jack, if it hadn't been for the prattling potman in the inn here."

The two men embraced, slapping each other on the back, and then stood apart, delight on their faces.

"You're back for good?"

"Aye."

"Then we must talk. There's much to tell . . ."

"You're right, Paddy, but not now. Me mam . . ." Jack gestured up at his mother who was holding tightly on to the pommel of the saddle at the same time as balancing two sacks full of provisions.

"And wasn't I forgetting?" said Quillinan. "You must be a mighty happy woman this day, Mistress Keane."

"That I am, Master Quillinan. That I am."

"Let me walk with you, Jack. Give me down those sacks, mistress. Does seem you're having enough to do staying on this fine animal."

"But tis out of your way, Paddy," Jack protested.

"Sure and I'd be walking home through Galway today just to have a jaw with you. You cannot be imagining how glad I am to see you. The Keanes have been weighing mighty heavy on my mind these last years."

As they made their way out of Listowel, Quillinan chattered excitedly away. "And sure you should have returned years back," he said. "The Whiteboys have all but disbanded. Things are awful quiet in these parts nowadays. Isn't that so, Mistress?"

"Father O'Sullivan, the saints preserve him, saw to that, Master Quillinan."

"He did that, mistress. He did us more harm than any of the soldier boys."

"More harm, Paddy?"

"Aye, Jack. After your John died and you left for the Americas, he preached stronger than ever against us and raised petitions all over the district. The people were awful hurt by what happened to your brothers. And to tell the truth, the association lost a deal of its heart for the fight what with the people turning against us."

"So Sandes and his like won again, Paddy," said Jack bitterly. "Michael and John died for nothing, eh?"

"Oh, no, Jack," Quillinan tried to reassure him. "The days of the bad landlords are numbered what with Daniel O'Connell winning support everywhere for the repeal of the Union. Your brothers were martyrs to the cause, so they were."

"O'Connell? I heard some tell of him in Boston town."

"He's the man we follow now. Didn't we give him a powerful welcome when he came to Listowel a few years back. He'll be getting us our rights through the Parliament, just you see."

"'Tis true, Jack," his mother interrupted. "As the Father said before he was taken, your brothers and the other martyrs before them had to die to get the politicians talking. Master O'Connell will be getting us our dues."

"We'll see, Mam. I'm just hoping your man O'Connell isn't just all words. Spinners of words and dreamers is what this politician in Boston thought of us Irishers. We fight one minute and talk the next as though no blood had been spilt. Talking and fighting and dreaming, that's us. Now isn't that the truth of it?"

"And is that bad?" Quillinan said, recognizing the cynicism in Jack's words. "Isn't that the way it has always been?"

"And will always be, eh, Paddy?" said Jack. Before he'd fled the district he'd always reckoned Quillinan as the fount of all wisdom. Now he saw him as a man of simple beliefs, ready to fight or not to fight, ready to listen or not to listen, according to what the people around him believed. He remembered Daniel Proudlane's strictures about those who shaped the world and those who were shaped. Quillinan was undoubtedly not a shaper. And as he realized that, Jack felt guilty about his patronizing re-assessment. He gripped Quillinan's shoulder and smiled at him. "Daniel O'Connell is sure to succeed with men like you behind him, Paddy."

"Aye, tis true, Jack," said Quillinan, visibly brightening. "We'll be ruling ourselves and worshipping how we chose without any interference from the English, when O'Connell has his way."

"But until then, Paddy, tis a powerful amount of work I've to do to set the cabin and the fields properly as they should be . . ."

"I'll help, so I will, Jack. And so will the rest of the boys."

"That's what I was wanting to hear."

Jack pointed to the family cabin as they approached it. "Me mam's cabin needs a new thatch, some paint, the walls want rebuilding . . . and won't I be paying a fair wage for the labor as well?"

"There's no need for that, Jack."

"No, Paddy. I can't ask you to neglect your own fields without payment. And twill be a way of sharing my good fortune with my old friends. And then there'll be the building of my own cabin for Brigid and . . ."

"Brigid?"

"Brigid Aherne. Don't you remember her, Paddy? Now I've my fortune and she's stopped working for Sandes, we'll marry."

He noticed Quillinan look quizzically up at his mother. She shook her head slightly.

"What's this between you?" he asked. "Me mam's close-mouthed about her and here's you seeming to have forgotten her."

"Tis nothing, Jack," said Quillinan hastily. "Have you seen her since coming back?"

"No, not yet. When we've stowed the provisions at the cabin I'll be riding over to Gortacrossane to pay a call."

"Things change, Jack," said Quillinan quietly. "Now let's be setting these provisions down. Where will you be wanting them?"

After Quillinan had left, Jack built up the fire before telling his mother he was leaving for Gortacrossane.

"So be it, son," she sighed wearily. "I'll be waiting for your return."

If anything, Gortacrossane looked more miserable and poverty-stricken than Drombeg. Most of the cabins had gaping holes in their thatches. A few people were working in the fields but many more were simply sitting, shoulder hunched outside their cabins, smoking stubs of pipes and gossiping. Their clothes were ragged—their faces smeared with dirt, their expressions sullen and uncaring. There was an air of despondency; a feeling everywhere of listlessness and acceptance of defeat. Jack dismounted outside the Aherne cabin and called inside.

"Is anyone there?"

He heard the chatter of children and then a man he didn't recognize came to the cabin entrance. He looked at Jack's clothes, his boots and then at the horse.

"If you're from Master Sandes, you can be telling him there's no more rent to be squeezed from here," the man said defiantly. Jack judged him to be in his early thirties but he was bent and thin; older, much older than his years.

"Rent? Master Sandes?" Jack replied, a sinking feeling beginning to grip his heart. "Why say you this?"

"You're from Sandes, aren't you? And wasn't I telling that divil Finn Bowler he'll have to be waiting for the money or else be putting us in the ditch along with five wee ones."

"No, not from Sandes or his man Bowler . . ."

"Well, what do you be wanting?"

"Brigid Aherne. This is the Aherne cabin?"

"Was . . . was their cabin until the typhoid took them nigh on six years ago. Now it's mine for all the good it does."

"But I was told Brigid Aherne lived in the townland."

"That she does, your honor, but not here. The cabin on the outskirts is hers." He pointed in the direction of Listowel. "Just keep heading that way and tis the last cabin before the fields."

Jack felt in his pocket for a coin.

"Here. Take this for your trouble," he said, handing the man a shilling piece.

The man held the coin up before his eyes as if

disbelieving his fortune. Then he bent in mockery of a bow. His thin features twisted into an obsequious smile. He put a knuckle to his forehead. "Bless you, your honor, for your charity," he muttered.

The cabin to which he was directed was simply four stone walls with a small amount of thatching over one corner to protect its interior from the weather. Jack felt as if he was living in a nightmare. Surely no one could live here? Surely not his Brigid?

"Brigid," he called. "Brigid Aherne. Is it you there?"

A woman's muffled voice came from beneath the thatch.

"Who be wanting her?"

"Jack Keane. Your friend Jack."

"Jack Keane? Is it you there?"

"Brigid?"

"Wait a moment," said the voice, excited now. Jack heard sounds of movement before a shawled head peered around the doorway.

"Jack?"

He looked into the face, framed by the dark red shawl. The skin was stretched tight over high cheekbones, the green eyes seemed hugely luminous, ringed with dark lines of fatigue. Jack jumped down from the horse and walked slowly up to her as she moved fully into the doorway. He saw that her brown skirt was torn and ragged and stained; her feet bare and dirty. He gazed into her eyes so deeply green, and knew that he had found her.

"Brigid," he said softly, holding open his arms. "Oh, Brigid."

She hesitated for a moment and then ran towards him. She threw her arms around his neck. He lifted her up, feeling how light she was, and whirled her around before putting her carefully to the ground again.

"'Tis you, Brigid."

"Aye, 'tis me, Jack Keane."

He held her at arm's length. "And how, in God's name, did you come to this?"

She moved close to him, burying her head in his chest. "You were away a long time, Jack," she whispered. "An awful long time."

He looked over her shoulders and saw a small child, no more than three years old, standing in the doorway. The child, a boy, by the cut of his jet black hair, sucked his thumb as he looked curiously at them. He was dressed in sacking with a piece of string pulling in the waist. Jack watched the child toddle forward on thin, stick-like legs and tug at Brigid's skirt.

"Mam," the child sniffled. "Mam, I'm cold."

Brigid bent down and picked him up, tucking his head under her shawl. "Hush, babbie," she murmured. "Hush, avourneen."

She kept her eyes averted from Jack as she comforted the child. Then she stared directly into his face.

Jack nodded at the child snuggling against her for warmth. She shrugged her shoulders and smiled ruefully.

"You can't keep a babbie secret, Jack Keane. 'Tis mine. You're right, 'tis mine."

He began to speak but she interrupted him fiercely. "He's mine and no one else's. One day perhaps you'll be knowing more but not now . . . not now, Jack. Please."

"His name, Brigid?" asked Jack softly, reaching out to brush the child's soft cheek.

"Matt. Matt Aherne. That's all."

"A fine boy."

"He is that. Aren't you then?" She smiled down at the child in her arms. "They say he has my looks."

"Your family? The girls? Your mother?" Jack said, still speaking softly, standing close to Brigid.

"Gone. Dead."

"All of them from the typhoid?"

"Aye. You heard tell then?"

"Just now . . . from a man at the old cabin."

"And was he telling you else about me?" she asked slyly.

"No. That's all."

Brigid sighed. "Well then, you're knowing most of what you should know."

"How, Brigid?"

"I said not now, Jack."

"No, not that. I meant how do you manage, the two of you in this place?"

"We have a small fire and each other to keep the other warm."

"But food?"

"What the Cooleens give me . . . what I scratch from the fields when no one is watching."

"But why didn't you go to my people?"

"With you away and them Mulvihills? The Cooleen men wouldn't have helped me then."

Jack raised his arms and looked to the sky in a hopeless gesture. "Cooleens . . . Mulvihills . . . and you near starving with a child in this . . . this . . . this hovel. Tis true, we're a race of madmen."

"Jack?"

"Oh, it matters not now. The main thing is to get you away to warmth and shelter."

"And where might that be? I heard tell of your fortune in the Americas but are you a magician as well?"

"Gather whatever you have. Matt and you are coming home with me."

"But . . ."

"But nothing. There's me mam to care for and now you two. You can all be putting flesh on your bones and some warmth in your bellies together."

Brigid looked up at the low, grey sky, sniffing the approaching bitterness of winter in the air, and shook her head reluctantly.

"I'm not sure you know what you are asking, Jack. The Cooleen men have been good in their way to me. They won't be liking me taking Mulvihill protection."

"Think on the child here. He's as skinny faced as a gombeen man when his money's due. And, anyway, weren't you spoken for before I had to flee to Boston town? You have no one to care for you but me. Can't you be seeing that?"

She hugged the child closer to her. Jack could see that beneath the shawl she wore a rough blouse made of the same sort of sacking that covered the toddler. He remembered suddenly the bright-colored blouses that Brigid used to wear. He put his hand on her shoulder, thinking that she was still beautiful, even as thin and worn as she was now.

Brigid bent her head. "For the babbie, then, Jack. I'll come with you; not for meself but for the babbie. You hold him while I gather a bundle together."

"I'll help."

"No. You stay out here and mind the babbie," Brigid said firmly, pushing Matt into his arms. He unbuttoned his top coat and wrapped it around the child to give him some warmth. Matt Aherne had his mother's green eyes.

In a few minutes, Brigid came out of the cabin dragging a sack behind her.

"You ride on the horse with Matt," said Jack. "I'll carry

the sack." He lifted her into the saddle and handed the child up to her. Brigid smiled down at him.

"Not what you were expecting, eh?" she said quietly.

Jack shook his head. "Twould have been better if someone had warned me. But what's done is done."

"And that's the truth, dear Jack."

"Me mam'll have a shock, so I'm thinking."

"I doubt that if you're meaning the babbie. The district's fallen woman, that I am, and well known for being so. But I've prayed to the Virgin and can find little shame in my heart for what happened."

Brigid began protesting when she realized Jack was leading the horse back through Gortacrossane.

"For pity's sake, don't be passing the cabins. They'll be anger enough when it's discovered I've gone with you. Don't be flaunting it in the Cooleen faces."

Jack shrugged. "So be it, woman. We'll take the long way round the townland though I'm thinking the sooner everyone knows the matter, the sooner we can settle it."

"Time enough then, I say."

"As you like, woman."

"You've changed in the years, Jack," Brigid remarked as they skirted the cabins and headed for Drombeg.

"Changed? And haven't we all?"

"Not the lines on my face or your white hairs, silly . . ."

". . . lummock, you used to say," Jack interrupted. "Remember?"

"Only too well. But I cannot be calling you that now. The years have made you a fine man, that they have."

"There have been many things to forget in those years," Jack replied, looking back at her over his shoulder as he plodded along in front of the horse.

"For both of us, I'm thinking. But when I wanted to forget, I always thought on us in that summer we had."

"We'll have others, Brigid."

"Perhaps so. Perhaps not. You can't go back in time, though. If me mam hadn't forced me into service . . . if you hadn't gone with the Whiteboys . . ."

Jack stopped the horse. "You're talking with melancholy, Brigid Aherne," he said sternly. "Be forgetting the things that have hurt us both. There's a deal in the past that was fine and warm and worth thinking on, and there's more in the future that'll be the same. Think on that."

Brigid paused for a moment before replying. "Pray it be so," she said quietly. "Pray that it be so, Jack, but in the Americas you made your future in a place which had one. You forget that here there's none for the likes of me, or for the likes of you as you were."

"Well, I changed my future, then," Jack grunted. "And I'll be changing yours if you stop being so gloomy."

"And sure and divil you will," Brigid laughed. "Jack Keane, you always had your dreams."

They travelled on in silence, both locked in their own thoughts, until the cabin at Drombeg came into sight. By now the light was leaving the sky with early evening settling over the fields, painting them and everything around them with greyness.

"Oh, Jack," Brigid cried suddenly when they were less than fifty yards from the cabin. "I'm scared, Jack. Take me back for God's sake."

"Don't be so silly," he said shortly. "You can't be going back ever again."

"But your mam, Jack . . . what'll she say?"

"A mighty lot if I'm knowing her. But nothing that should be worrying you."

He tied the horse outside the cabin and lifted Brigid and her child down from the saddle. The cabin door squeaked open and his mother stood watching them, framed in candlelight and the rosiness of the peat fire. Brigid hung back until Jack put his arm around her shoulders. They walked forward towards his mother. She didn't move from the doorway. Her face was without expression.

"Mam," Jack said in a quiet, firm voice. "We're back."

His mother looked at Brigid for a moment and then her mouth softened. She smiled as she saw Matt's head peeping out from under the shawl. "'Twill be good to have a child in the cabin again," she murmured. She stood aside to let them enter the warmth. As Brigid passed her, her eyes fixed firmly on the floor, Jack's mother leaned forward and kissed her on the cheek. "Welcome, again, Brigid Aherne," she whispered.

"We're cold and we're hungry, Mam," Jack said, suddenly embarrassed, not quite knowing how to fend off what he thought would be the inevitable questions.

"Well, be warming yourselves. There's lumpers and bacon for your meal. Plenty for all, I'm thinking," said his mother.

"I'm sorry, Mistress Keane . . ." Brigid began.

"Hush, girl. And wasn't I expecting you all along? I knew Jack would be bringing you. My son wouldn't be leaving you where you were. And no more of this Mistress Keane, if you please, Brigid Aherne. In this cabin, I'm mam and that's all. And let's be looking at the babbie then."

Brigid handed Matt to her. Jack's mother felt his bare legs as she pressed him close.

"So thin and cold, you wee man. But we'll be feeding you up now, just you see. You'll be as big as your dad in no time." Then she realized what she'd said. "I'm sorry, Brigid. Sorry . . ." she stumbled. "An old woman's tongue . . ."

Brigid smiled gently. "No need to be sorry, Mam. In time he'll know his dad and so will you all. But as I said to Jack . . . not now, please."

"In the district there's tell . . ."

"I know," Brigid said wearily. "There's tell . . . if you're believing all the tell then every man's his dad, particularly every Cooleen man."

She sat down heavily in one of the chairs at the table and sunk her head into her arms. Her back began heaving with sobs.

"Hush, child," said Jack's mother. "I said I was sorry. I'll not be mentioning . . ."

Brigid raised her tear-stained face. "Tis not that, Mam. Not that. Tis not that. Tis Jack. Why didn't you tell him I was the Cooleen woman?"

"I knew you were Cooleen . . ." Jack broke in.

"Yes, you knew that," Brigid said bitterly. "But you didn't know how they took payment for all their kindness to me, did you?" Her voice rose shrilly. "I'm the Cooleen whore. That's what. When they want a woman they come to me. Any Cooleen. Any time. Just for a penny, or a lumper. Anything. Didn't matter. Anything to keep alive." She looked pleadingly at him. "Don't you understand. There was nothing else to give. That's why you should have left me where I was. Don't you see?"

Jack sat down in the chair next to her. He put out his hand and cupped her wet cheek, smoothing the tears away with his thumb. His whirling thoughts went back to Meg Griffiths and all the girls he'd known in Boston; all the girls who'd nothing to sell but themselves. He remembered their compassion and how much he owed them.

"Brigid," he started. "Brigid, I understand. I do, truly. As I said before, be forgetting the past. Think on the future."

He heard his mother sniff and stifle a sob behind him. "Now look on this," he said. "All the women sobbing away and I'm back only a day."

Brigid smiled at him through her tears.

"That's right, mavourneen. Smile. You're here and that's all that matters. You're to stay here for as long as you like. Perhaps for always. But that's to be your choice. Not mine. I've made mine."

Chapter 13
June, 1834

Hundreds of small fires built from driftwood spattered and crackled their glowing sparks into the warm summer night among the dunes. At both ends of the wide beach at Ballyeagh, a few miles south of Ballybunnion on the coast of Kerry, the fires danced their reflections and shadows on to the faces of more than two thousand people who had built makeshift shelters along the beach to protect themselves from the chill that would come in the night. Here and there, the tune from a fiddle rose above the sibilant slapping of water on the sands. A shriek of laughter punctuated the low murmur of conversation, climbing into the clear sky pricked with stars. Occasionally, people camped at one end of the beach would glance at the fires burning at the other end, make a remark to their companions and another burst of ribald laughter would be heard. But there was little hilarity in the buzz of talk along the beach, a definite tension reached into the darkness dividing the two camps.

"And aren't you feeling honored, mavourneen, that all these people have come here because of you?" Jack Keane asked Brigid Aherne jokingly as they lay in the soft sand and looked across the beach.

"Honored? More like mortal scared . . . so many of them. Where have they all come from?" said Brigid, leaning up on one elbow and trying to count the number of fires. "Oh, they're too many even to guess at."

"Well, this had been a long time arranging so I'm thinking the word reached out to every faction man in the west."

Brigid touched his hand. "Couldn't we just be stealing away now, the two of us?"

Jack laughed, reaching out to ruffle her shining hair. "Tis a bit late for that. You were the one saying we should try to make everything proper. And didn't I do just that? Didn't I jaw with your Cooleens till me teeth near dropped out? And now you're mortal scared . . . women!"

The first approach from the Cooleens had come only two weeks after Brigid and Matt Aherne had moved into the cabin at Drombeg. Jack and Paddy Quillinan had been working in the fields, restoring the dry-stone walls, when they had been hailed from the nearby track by a man seated on a donkey.

"Is Jack Keane there?" the man shouted.

Jack waved and walked over to him. Paddy followed on a few yards behind.

"You're calling my name?"

"A fine day, Master Keane, is it not, thanks be to God."

"It is that," Jack replied, wiping his forearm across the sweat on his brow. "And who might be calling here?"

"Flaherty's the name. Sean Flaherty . . ."

"Well, welcome . . ."

". . . from Gortacrossane, and from the Cooleen men."

Quillinan advanced menacingly on the man. "I'll crack him one, Jack, and send him back asleep on the donkey."

The man began pulling the animal's head around, ready to try to make his escape.

"Whoa there, Sean Flaherty. No need to be hurrying off. Leave him be, Paddy. I expected a call from the Cooleen men sooner or later."

Flaherty smiled with relief. He dismounted from the donkey and led it up to the wall. He was a tall man, as big as Jack, with curly hair flapping from under a battered felt hat.

"You're a wise man, Master Keane. There be no need for unpleasantness between us," he said with a grin that displayed a mouthful of broken, black teeth. "There's talk we must have about Brigid Aherne."

Jack heaved a sigh.

"The Cooleen men have sent me here in great respect," said Flaherty. "They knew your dad well, Jack Keane, many of them to their personal cost." He laughed shortly. "And haven't I felt the weight of his stick meself? A fighting man so he was, a credit to any faction. And we be knowing of your history as well how you suffered under the soldier boys; how you made your fortune in the Americas and then returned here to care for your mam. Tis a fine man you are, Master Keane, but the Cooleen men are thinking you're forgetting the ways of the factions during your travels."

"I did that, thanks be," Jack grunted. "Go on."

"Well, the Cooleens cared for Brigid Aherne out of memory for her dad when she was alone and with child. Without our protection, she and the babbie would have been frozen in a ditch these winters past."

"You call it protection to keep her in a hovel and treat her as your whore?" Jack said bitterly. "Is that your protection?"

"Twas more than the Mulvihills offered. Twas more than you could offer, Master Keane," Flaherty replied with a disarming smile. "Now isn't that the truth of the matter?"

"That's not fair," Quillinan protested. "Jack was away . . ."

"Fair or not," Flaherty continued, "tis a fact that only the Cooleens helped. We're as poor as anyone else in the district. We couldn't be offering much but the fact is they survived in their fashion, so they did. And then Master Keane here comes tripping back from the Americas, ordering banquets at the inn, buying animals from every drover in sight and, without a by your leave, takes it upon himself to carry this Cooleen woman away. Can't you be imagining how the men feel? To tell the truth, they're mighty angry with you, Master Keane. They're wanting some satisfaction."

"Satisfaction, Flaherty?" asked Jack. "What sort of satisfaction?"

"Tis the Cooleen men are wanting her back," said Flaherty quietly. "And they're demanding an acknowledgment from you that you did them wrong. That's the message I'm bringing, so I am."

Jack stared at him for a moment. Truly, he thought, I've forgotten the ways of Ireland where men barter over a woman as if she was prize livestock.

"Sean Flaherty," he said in an icy voice, "I'll talk to you if it's a matter of paying you money for all the troubles you've taken over Brigid and I'll talk to you in the proper old way about arranging a marriage but you can go to the divil if you ever expect me to return her to being your whore."

Flaherty tried to deflect Jack's obvious anger. "Master Keane, your views come as no surprise to me, no surprise at all," he said in a conciliatory tone. "I'm only the message boy but I can be telling you the Cooleens, out of respect for you and your family, are willing to talk to your man about any arrangements you may be offering. Tis the custom after all and the Cooleens are not denying that."

"Quillinan here will talk for me," said Jack. "You be telling him where and when and he'll do the talking."

"Twill be as you say, Master Keane," Flaherty replied,

rising to his feet. "I'll bid you good day and thank you. But may I be reminding you that under the custom you should tell Brigid Aherne of what's being proposed."

"Aye," Jack agreed. "Tis the custom and she's the right to know."

That night after they'd finished their supper Jack told Brigid and his mother of his talk with the Cooleen messenger. Neither of them expressed the slightest surprise at the news.

"I told you there'd be trouble, Jack," said Brigid. "Wasn't I telling Mam the very same only this day?"

"Why trouble, mavourneen? They simply want to talk. I'll pay them some money for their trouble, call it a wedding dowry if you must, and that'll be the end of the matter."

"I doubt that," his mother said, now almost her bustling self again after a fortnight of proper food and warmth. "Your dad always said the Cooleens needed little enough excuse to call for a fight and here they are thinking they've every reason in the world now."

"You're right, Mam," Brigid echoed. "That's just what they'll be wanting . . . a fight. They've had little enough cause for years past so they're losing a deal of support whenever they've sent out the word for their men to be joining in some head-whacking."

"You women are always seeing the dark side of the moon," Jack laughed. "We'll go through the old customs about a marriage, sweeten them with a handful of gold, and that'll be that, so it will. It'll all seem different in the morning," he continued as he got up from his chair and began setting up a curtain of sacking to divide the cabin. "Young Matt there's got the proper notion, bless him," he said, gesturing at the child asleep in Brigid's arms. She rose slowly and carried Matt over to Jack's sea chest, which now doubled as his cot.

From her first night at the cabin, Brigid had shared the bed with Jack's mother while he had to content himself with a pile of straw as a resting place. But, within a few days, the bed he'd ordered in Listowel had arrived and been placed in the further corner. As he'd lain back comfortably during his first night for weeks in a bed, the sacking had whispered apart and Brigid had slipped into his half of the cabin. She stood by the side of his bed for a moment, looking down at him, her black hair, grown long, hanging down over a well-patched shift she'd been given by Jack's mother. He smiled up at her and lifted the covers as he moved over in the bed. Brigid put a finger to her lips as she clambered in beside him.

"No noise," she whispered. "Mam's fast asleep and we wouldn't be wanting to wake her." He felt her breath against his cheek. They snuggled against each other. Jack could feel every outline of her body against him through the thin material of the shift. He shivered as an overwhelming tenderness flooded through him.

"Are we cold?" Brigid murmured, a giggle in her voice. "Well, I'll warm you but no more till the priest has said his words. It must be proper between us, don't you see that?"

"Aye, mavourneen," Jack replied, disappointed and pleased at the same time. "I want you awful bad but let it be in the marriage bed. Then we can truly make a fresh start, both of us."

"Not that fresh," Brigid said softly. "I want to know what sort of man I'm getting, and isn't that my proper due?" Her hand slipped under his long shirt and began caressing his strong body. They lingered, wondering, over the scars on his back and along his ribs and then moved lower to stroke and grasp his stiffening nakedness. He twitched as she touched him and they smiled broadly at each other in the darkness. There was a confidence between them now that the pact had been sealed, a confidence born out of experience and their mutual desire to give pleasure to each other. His hands caressed the smoothness of her back and played around her buttocks. They kissed deeply and soon the silence of the cabin was broken by their low sighs and moans.

Suddenly, Brigid pushed her hands flat against his chest. "No more, Jack. No more, avourneen," she panted against his mouth. "Else our resolutions will have vanished as soon as we are making them." She kissed him once more before she returned to the other bed behind the sacking.

She came to him most nights but now they knew how far to allow their love-making to go. They joked sometimes with each other about their frustrations when his mother was out of earshot, but both agreed that the final consummation of their love should wait until all the obstacles to marriage had been removed.

In the meantime, Quillinan had a series of meetings with the Cooleen leaders. He put to them Jack's proposals but they remained adamant that Jack should acknowledge publicly that he'd offended against the unwritten code of the factions.

"I won't do it," Jack declared. "They won't be getting that humbling from me, and that's my final word, Paddy. They know I did no wrong except to show everyone their shame at the way they'd been treating Brigid. That's what hurts them, and so it should."

The negotiations were virtually suspended for the winter since neither party was willing to travel far in the biting weather. Jack spent the months transforming the cabin at Drombeg into one of the cosiest and neatest for miles around. He built a small, thatched stable on to the side where all the livestock wintered together, and employed a carpenter to lay a wooden floor in the cabin. The women, now restored to full health and vigor, busied themselves making pretty curtains and colorful bedspreads and soon the cabin's interior was as bright and attractive as the outside. When the warmth of an early spring came to the district, the Cooleens agreed reluctantly to a formal meeting where a marriage contract could be considered.

Brigid dressed herself in the new clothes Jack had bought her for the meeting at the cabin of one of the Cooleen leaders, Thomas Sheehan.

"Tis not too dazzling for them?" she asked nervously as she twirled around in front of Jack and his mother to show off the deep red skirt and the lace-edged white petticoat underneath.

"Oh, tis lovely, sweet one," breathed Jack's mother.

"They'll think you a princess from the little people, so they will," Jack smiled. "They won't be daring to refuse you anything."

"Would that my head told me what my heart was wanting to hear," Brigid replied with a wry grin.

Some of her fears vanished when Jack, Quillinan, and herself arrived at the Sheehan cabin. They were greeted outside with solemn courtesy and respect by Sean Flaherty. He, too, was clearly dressed in his best clothes. His eyes widened as he saw Jack help Brigid down from the horse. Her skin shone with health. Her eyes were bright and clear. Her round face was framed by gleaming black hair. Flaherty could hardly recognize the bedraggled, half-starved woman he'd known only a few months before.

Inside the cabin, they were met by three other Cooleen leaders who offered them each a mug of poteen. After the introductions, Sheehan, a small, wizened man past middle age, invited Quillinan and Jack to sit at the table.

"As is the custom, the woman being the subject of the meeting will wait outside with those who are not the principals," he announced firmly. "The door will be left open so she can hear the matters discussed but she is not to be present."

Jack glanced at Quillinan. "Paddy will wait outside with you, Brigid," he said.

"Suspicious, Master Keane?" asked Sheehan. "Fearing a trick, are you?"

"No, Master Sheehan. The poor girl's nervous as it is. Can't you be seeing that? She'll be happier with Paddy here to keep her company." Jack lied with little conviction. The fact was that he feared the Cooleens might try to abduct Brigid if the negotiations proved unsuccessful.

When the cabin had been cleared, Jack sat down at the table opposite Sheehan and Flaherty.

"Well, let's be beginning this custom of yours," he said curtly.

"Tis your custom as well, Master Keane. Be remembering that," Sheehan replied.

"Was my custom, perhaps. But I find it distasteful now, mighty distasteful."

"The tell is you're finding many things distasteful about the old customs since your returning from the Americas," Flaherty said.

"You know my feelings well enough, but still I'm here at this meeting to discuss the marriage, aren't I?"

"Not only a marriage," Sheehan broke in. "There's also the matter of stealing this Cooleen woman away from her people who'd been giving her their best protection . . ."

"Protection!" Jack snorted.

"Protection," Sheehan repeated. "The best that could be afforded. So before any marriage contract can be arranged, there has to be an acknowledgment of the wrong else the Cooleens will have lost a deal of face."

"That cannot be," said Jack, crossing his arms across his

chest and leaning back in the chair. "I'll recompense the Cooleens . . ."

"How much?" Flaherty asked eagerly.

"Twenty sovereigns."

Sheehan's eyes narrowed. "An awful amount of money, Master Keane," he muttered. "An awful amount . . ."

"Tis on the table if you're wanting it."

"We could be saying it was payment for the wrong caused?" Flaherty asked tentatively.

"You can call it what you want but I'm calling it a repayment for the protection you say you gave to Brigid. Twill settle all debts."

"And an acknowledgment of the wrong to the Cooleens?" Sheehan pressed, mistakenly believing that Jack was weakening.

"To the divil with an acknowledgment," Jack said fiercely. "I made that clear to Flaherty. There'll be no acknowledgment from me and each time you be mentioning it I'm thinking I'll reduce my offer by one sovereign."

"You're a hard man," said Flaherty, loath to lose the offer of such money. "A hard man, just like your dad."

"And as pig-headed as him as well," Sheehan added angrily. "You have little rights in this matter at all. Brigid Aherne is Cooleen and is beholden to us. After Tom Aherne died tis we helped the family; when her mother and sisters were taken, we paid for their burial; when Brigid was with child, our women delivered her; when she was starving, we gave her the means of surviving; when she was shunned by all the district for having a babbie with no husband, we gave her companionship . . ."

"Companionship?" Jack's anger was showing on his face now. "You used her as a whore."

"She didn't have to accept the men who called. There was no force, believe me Keane, and . . ."

"And no choice either. You sicken me. She's a grown woman. She belongs to no one but herself. Not to me and certainly not to the Cooleens. She is herself, not the chattel of one faction or the other."

Sheehan jumped to his feet, sending his chair clattering to the floor. "By the saints, tis enough," he shouted, almost hopping with rage. "You're piling insult upon insult, Keane. There'll be no marriage here blessed by the Cooleens, and that's my word. You've wronged us; you've tried to buy off our rightful grievance with your American gold; and now you abuse us. Tis enough, I say."

"But the money, Mick . . . the money," Flaherty interrupted.

"To the divil with the money, Sean. We'll be taking our satisfaction in a fight, so we will."

Jack began to laugh as he realized that Brigid and his mother had been correct all the time. The formal meeting, short as it had been, was nothing more than a sham. The Cooleens had never had any intention of settling the matter peaceably.

His amusement enraged the Cooleen leader even more. Sheehan banged the table with his hand. "In my cabin, he insults us . . ." he sputtered. He leaned across the table, fists raised, face distorted with anger. Jack pushed out his arm and shoved Sheehan gently, almost lazily, away from the table. The small man stumbled back, caught his legs in the upturned chair behind him, and, with a howl of surprised rage, fell heavily on the floor. As Flaherty went to help his leader, Jack rose from the table and was at the door in three strides.

Quillinan, already alerted by the shouting and clattering, had pulled Brigid away from the two Cooleens who were now peering anxiously into the cabin. Jack shouldered his way past them, quickly lifted Brigid up on to the horse and began leading it away at a jog.

"You watch the rear, Paddy," he called. "They're awful upset, those Cooleens. They might be wanting to start the fight here and now."

He glanced up at Brigid. "And don't you be saying you told me so, mavourneen."

"There'll be a fight?" she asked.

"I'm guessing so."

Angry shouts pursued them until they were about a hundred yards away but the Cooleens made no attempt to follow. Jack slowed the horse down to a walk and turned towards Drombeg.

"What happens now, Paddy?"

"A proper challenge to the Mulvihills," Quillinan replied shortly. He was still slightly puffed by their hasty retreat.

"How long?"

"Oh, it'll be taking some weeks to arrange. All the factions will have to be told. They won't be waiting for the Tralee Fair so I'm thinking they'll want it to be at the Ballyeagh Races."

"And will we be having enough people?"

"What with the boys from the association who'll be supporting you, I'd say more than a thousand."

Jack whistled through his teeth. "A thousand? That's a terrible lot, Paddy, just for a cudgel fight."

"Not with the Cooleens as angry as they are. They'll muster all they can and that'll be not much less than a thousand, perhaps even more. Tis an important matter of face this."

"As everyone keeps saying . . ."

"What'll be the outcome of it all?" Brigid said, anxiety clearly in her voice.

"The Mulvihills will pulp them as usual," Jack said

confidently. "And that'll be the last we'll be hearing from the Cooleens about you."

"But what if they win?"

"Don't be worrying your pretty head, mavourneen. In the case of that miracle, we'll still be together even if I have to be taking the pistols out of their holsters for a while to show I really mean to keep you. The fight is all about face, as Paddy says. Tis ridiculous, but then wasn't it ever so?"

He had no reason to change that opinion, Jack reflected, as he looked down on the gathering of the factions at Ballyeagh. All these people, he thought, had travelled miles from all over Kerry to hammer at each other with shillelaghs. At least three quarters of them, he reckoned, would not know the fine points of the dispute that had brought them there to huddle around their camp fires. They had simply answered their traditional rallying call like so many sheep.

Jack lay back on the sand, hands behind his head, and gazed up at the stars. Brigid leaned over and kissed him softly on the lips. "Tis I remember, mavourneen, a time when I looked at the stars long ago and a sailor friend of mine said he wondered if there were people up there looking back down at us. Twas long ago but I've never forgotten that."

"And what would they be thinking, those wee people up in the stars?"

"I'm thinking they'd be mighty puzzled."

Brigid kissed him again, more deeply, her tongue slipping between his lips.

"Does make me feel embarrassed thinking they might be watching us," she whispered against his ear. "But at least tonight we won't be having to worry about mam hearing us."

He reached up and gripped her shoulders.

"And what would you be saying?" he grinned. "Don't be forgetting our pact, you hussy."

"I will if you will, avourneen," she murmured. "You've said that whatever happens tomorrow we'll be wed soon. It's an awful wasting of time."

They stared at each other for a long moment, smiling gently. Without a word, they crawled into the small tent rigged by Jack with blankets and wooden poles carried from Drombeg. He closed the entrance carefully and looked around at Brigid as she lay on the blanket on the sand. Brigid unbuttoned her blouse, slowly, tantalizingly, and shrugged it from her shoulders. Next, she unfastened her skirt and kicked it from her. He experienced a feeling of sudden loving, lusting wonder as he gazed on her perfect nakedness.

He lay down beside her, kissing her smooth throat, moving his hands slowly over her body. She opened his shirt deftly, her breath fast against his skin, and helped him wriggle out of his breeches. They hugged against each other, caressing and kissing, until, at last, he moved over her. Jack gasped as he slid into her. He paused and looked down at her. Her face was turned to one side on the blanket, her eyes closed, a smile playing around her lips. He moved gently at first, in rhythm with the water breaking on the sands below them, and then more fiercely as her calves and ankles tightened around his thighs, urging him closer and deeper.

"Dearest, oh, dearest," she moaned as she moved her hips under him in unison with his quickening thrusts. Her hands moved urgently on his buttocks, the nails pressing into his skin, and finally tightened and clutched convulsively as she felt him shuddering inside her, matching her own climax. He lay panting on her for a few moments before pulling slowly away. They kissed staring closely into each other's eyes.

"Mavourneen," he whispered. "Oh, Brigid, you're really mine."

"I always was from that first day at Ballybunnion. No one has ever meant anything to me except yourself. I've never felt a man's loving before until you. Nothing has ever counted until now."

"I love you, Brigid."

"And I you, dearest, dearest Jack."

They held each other close throughout the night, laying contentedly together, caressing and kissing, languorously, idly, or locked together in overwhelming passion. At times they dozed but then one would wake the other and the loving would start again. As the dawn light began to sneak into the tent, they dressed and embraced kneeling on the blanket.

"We'll never forget this night, Brigid."

"No, not ever. It was ours, only ours, so it was."

Jack pulled aside the blanket and peered outside. A sea fret was covering the beach with misty dampness—a sign that the day would be fine and warm. He could only see for twenty or thirty yards as he went searching for some wood to rekindle the fire. As he moved among the dunes, he greeted the other early risers who were crawling from their shelters and tents to yawn and stretch the sleep from them.

"A good night, Jack?" called Quillinan from his tent about ten yards away.

"'Twas so, Paddy, thanks be to God," Jack answered cheerfully. "Does promise to be a fair day for the fight. Let's be meeting in an hour or so to talk some tactics."

He lit the fire again with some difficulty and thrust four lumpers into the burning wood to cook for breakfast. Brigid emerged from the tent almost shyly to sit beside him. Hands clasped they looked into the flames, both thinking about the night that had just passed. Jack gazed at her profile and felt a surge of possessive pride.

"Tonight, avourneen, tis I'll be telling you all you should know about Matt and what went on while you were away," Brigid said quietly, talking into the darting flames. "There can be no secrets between us now."

"You're wanting confessions, woman?" Jack smiled, putting an arm around her shoulders and drawing her close. "Well tis I have a few to tell and no mistake."

Jack knew that the exchanging of confidences would be the final link in the chain binding Brigid and himself. He would never tell her that his own discreet inquiries had already satisfied him about the identity of Matt Aherne's father. The final confirmation, he knew, would have to come from Brigid herself and at a time of her own choosing.

The sea fret was already lifting from the beach by the time they'd finished breakfast, juggling the hot potatoes in their hands to bite into the succulent flesh. Paddy Quillinan wandered over to join them and together they studied the layout of the beach. The mouth of the Shannon was to the west and the waters that washed Ballyeagh strand were those of the River Chasen, a hundred yards and more wide at this point with fast, treacherous currents. The river, leading off the Atlantic and the mouth of the Shannon, divided further inland into the rivers Feale, Brick and Galey. The Mulvihills were gathered at the west end of the beach, nearest the Atlantic, with the Cooleens to the east, near to the landing point for the boats which ferried people from the south bank of the Cashen. Already the boats were busy carrying people over to Ballyeagh.

"Bound to be Cooleens," Quillinan observed. "There's a deal of them south of the river."

"Tis right you are, Paddy," said Jack. "And look

there . . . by the fill of the pockets and sacks they're bringing over their ammunition with them."

"So they're planning to be hurling stones," Quillinan muttered.

"Seems so. Let's be watching where they store them."

"I'll be sending one of the boys to travel the ferry. He'll be finding out."

They discussed other tactics before Jack sent Quillinan hurrying around the Mulvihill supporters with their instructions. For the next couple of hours, he strolled with Brigid among the dunes as preparations were made for the race meeting to begin when the tide was out, about midday. Dozens of tinkers were setting up stalls selling everything from pots and pans to straw hats to keep the sun off the women's faces; from hot lumpers stuffed with bacon fat to bottles of poteen and cheap whiskey. Music from the fiddlers drifted along the sands to mingle with the sounds of a fife and a bodhran, a large tambourine, being played by two old soldiers, with a felt hat before them to collect any offerings. Everywhere there was color and noise and music; mothers shrieked at their children as they dashed into the wavelets for a swift paddle; men, already in drink, called bets to each other about the forthcoming races; officers and soldiers of the 69th Regiment in their tall black caps and red, white and yellow uniforms shouted at the crowd, ordering them behind the rope to keep them off the sands when the races started; a dozen or so constables wandered among the throng watching for any pickpockets; the "quality"—the nobility, their land agents, doctors and lawyers—sat in their carriages with their ladies, picnicking on cold chicken and hams washed down with claret.

A great roar went up from the crowd as five stewards walked out on to the glistening sands to set out the poles which would mark the course for the riders. It would run from the west end of the beach to a pole half-a-mile away. The riders would go around the course twice, a total distance of two miles. But above the mounting excitement and joy and fun of that St. John's Day meet at Ballyeagh in 1834, there was the brooding presence of the two factions at either end of the beach, gathered beyond the furthest poles of the racecourse. They sneered at the soldiers who'd been detailed to stand in front of them. To most of the crowd it looked a vain hope that no more than sixty soldiers would be able to contain upwards of two thousand men intent on cracking one another's skulls.

There was a great roar from the watching crowd as the stewards flagged away the first seven riders, colored scarves tied to their arms for identification. Clods of still-wet sand flew into the air as the horses thundered along the flat beach, their manes flying in the breeze. One horse charged through the surf, sending sprays of water over its jockey. The horses were hunched close together at the first turn but a rider wearing a yellow scarf just managed to reach the pole first. The speed of his horse meant that he had to round the pole in a wide sweep but he escaped the bumping and boring which went on among the riders and horses a few yards behind him. One rider pulled his horse around too violently, and his mount slipped in the sand. In falling, it took the legs away from another horse. They tumbled on to the sand whinnying and kicking. One jockey rolled away from his mount in time but the other received a flailing hoof in the small of his back. He tried to rise but fell back with a loud groan. Two constables dashed forward from the ropes and pulled him clear. The five horses still in the race were at full stretch as they approached the starting line again but the rider with the yellow scarf retained a narrow lead. On the second lap he was overhauled by a big grey horse whose rider sported green favors. These two rounded the far pole together but the grey made a smaller turn and was a head in front as the two horses pounded towards the finishing line. Both jockeys were now using whips on their horses, occasionally slashing at each other. The noise from the thousands watching was at a crescendo as the two animals strained for the line, ears flattened, nostrils flaring, hardly an inch between them. With a dozen or so strides to go, the jockey on the grey caught his opponent across the face with a particularly vicious swipe of his whip. The rider lost his grip momentarily and the grey swept past the finishing line a clear head in front. From the wild applause of the crowd, he was a popular winner.

Quillinan, who'd watched the race with Brigid and Jack, was beside himself with delight. "Well, the rent money's safe," he roared before pushing through the crowd to find the man with whom he'd struck his bet.

"Paddy doesn't seem to be worrying about the Cooleens," Brigid laughed, her face glowing with excitement.

"Not he," said Jack. "To Paddy, a horse race and a fight are all part of a day's enjoyment. Are you wanting to strike a bet on the next race?"

"No, I'm preferring just to watch with you." She clasped his arm tightly. "When is it the fighting will start?" she asked anxiously.

"Mighty soon, I'm thinking," Jack replied. "Look at those Cooleens. They're so much in drink they're scuffling amongst themselves already."

He pointed towards the further end of the beach. Brigid stood on tiptoe and saw a swirling movement in the men penned behind the rank of soldiers. Four Cooleens were struggling together on the sand, punching each other around the body.

"'Tis someone not paying a bet, I'm guessing," Jack

grunted. "Let them be wasting their energy on themselves, the animals."

Six more horses cantered on to the sands, their jockeys standing high in their stirrups, and the crowd settled down to watch the next race. But, suddenly, as the horses lined up at the start, there were screams of alarm from the women in the crowd nearest to the Cooleens. In an instant Jack saw what had happened. The small fight had been merely a diversion. The soldiers had been lured into the Cooleen crowd to drag the four men apart and as soon as a gap appeared in the soldiers' ranks the Cooleens had burst through. Now hundreds of them were running across the sands towards the horses and the Mulvihills. As they advanced, they pulled shillelaghs from under their coats and shirts and began fastening green ribbons around them.

"Coolee . . . coolee . . . coolee . . . coo-leeee . . ."

Their chant swelled and grew to blot out all other noise along the beach. The crowd began scattering back from their positions along the rope towards the safety of the dunes. Six constables, arms linked, tried to form a line to stop the advancing mob but were brushed aside and swallowed in the crowd.

Quillinan ran towards Jack, pushing his way through the families who were struggling in panic to leave the beach.

"Get the men on the strand as we planned, Paddy. I'll lead the others."

"Good luck," Quillinan cried as he raced through the dunes, urging the Mulvihills to follow him. As they ran they fixed white ribbons to their sticks and began their own chant.

"Mmulvi . . . mmulvi . . . mmulvi . . . mmulvi . . ."

Jack turned to the hundred or so men who had stayed behind according to plan.

"Hide yourself in the dunes," he ordered. "We'll be biding our time." The men fell on their stomachs, keeping their shillelaghs close by them. Jack pushed Brigid down beside him.

"Now when we move, you stay here, mavourneen, and keep out of sight. I'm afeared the Cooleens may be looking for you." He gave her a quick kiss. "And don't be worrying yourself. Paddy and I have a fine plan."

"Oh, I'm so scared for you, Jack," Brigid cried, trying to put her arms around his neck. He pushed them away and smiled reassuringly at her.

"In less than an hour, it'll be all over, and we'll be together for always." He kissed her again and then peeked over the dunes to watch the battle beginning on the sands below.

The first Mulvihills to reach the beach were already engaged in running battles with the Cooleens, swinging their sticks and hitting empty air more often than not, as the main body of Mulvihills took up their positions.

Instead of meeting the Cooleens head on, the Mulvihills formed themselves quickly into a square. At first, the result was total confusion as the Cooleens, advancing in disordered ranks, found no one to fight except the close-knit Mulvihill formation. The Cooleens swirled around the square not knowing where to press their attack. The Mulvihills stood firm in their square, not moving out of position until a Cooleen came into easy range.

"Tis working," Jack cried excitedly as he watched the uncertainty in the Cooleen ranks. Instead of the individual combat they had expected, the Cooleens were faced with a solid phalanx of opponents standing their ground and responding only to the most suicidal of attacks. But soon the Mulvihill square was surrounded by Cooleens pressing in from all sides and the combat became sterner. Curses and groans mingled with the sharp cracking sound of shillelaghs striking bones as the factions closed together. And then, on a shouted order, the Cooleens withdrew a few yards as the men behind them lobbed a hail of stones into the Mulvihill ranks. The first barrage caused many injuries; Mulvihills in the middle of the square staggered and fell; scalps were split apart by the stones. Then Quillinan's shouted orders began to be obeyed. The Mulvihills inside the square knelt as the stones rained down and warded them off by spreading their coats and shirts tautly above their heads. The flying stones continued to take their toll but most of them bounced harmlessly off the improvised Mulvihill shields.

The factions closed together again as the Cooleens' supply of stones ran low. Jack watched as the men joined in combat, punching, kicking, hitting out with their cudgels. Only the keen eye could see that the square of men with white ribbons on their shillelaghs was standing firm.

By now, thousands who had come to watch the Ballyeagh races were spectators to another event, taking the best vantage points overlooking the beach to watch the faction fight. One or two of the braver tinkers were still trying to rescue their wares but, in the main, the beach had been given over to the men with ribbons on their sticks.

The battle went on for more than half an hour before Jack was satisfied that the Cooleens had committed all their forces. The casualties from both sides were crawling away from the fighting, trying to find any refuge from the flailing sticks, staunching bleeding wounds with anything they could find. But still the battle was even. The Cooleens had not managed to break into the Mulvihills' ranks. It was clearly a stalemate.

Jack motioned to the men lying in the dunes around him.

"Keep down," he shouted. "We'll keep low till we're on them."

Jack crouched, waving his arm in the direction he wanted the remaining Mulvihills to follow. Before he started moving, he ran his hand gently down Brigid's back.

"Stay here, mavourneen," he said. "Be out of sight."

Brigid nodded, her eyes wide with fear from the sounds and sights of the battle. She said nothing, only mouthed the words, "Take care, avourneen."

For nearly half a mile, Jack crept away through the dunes with the rest of the Mulvihills. His legs and back ached from the crouching position they had adopted. They had almost reached the end of their cover in the dunes before they came across the cache of stones that Quillinan's spy had found earlier. Young Cooleen men were filling wicker baskets from the pile and carrying them two hundred yards to their elders to hurl into the hard-pressed Mulvihill formation. For a few minutes, Jack watched them before signalling his men forward. The Mulvihills rushed from their hiding places in the dunes and clubbed the Cooleen youngsters unconscious with hardly a sound except that of wood meeting bone.

The Mulvihills stuffed their pockets and shirts and coats from the pile of stones and on Jack's command moved forward towards the fighting. As they reached the Cooleens, now pressing closer than ever against the sorely-tried Mulvihill square, they were greeted with smiles and shouts of encouragement. To the Cooleens there was no way of distinguishing their enemies since Jack's contingent of Mulvihill reinforcements wore no ribbons. But, suddenly, awfully, the Cooleens realized their mistake, as stone upon stone ripped into their backs, slashing open legs, arms, and heads. Jack concentrated his attack on one section of the Cooleens and as they fell away, confused and hurt, the Mulvihill ranks opposite them advanced. In a few minutes, the battle of Ballyeagh sands was transformed as the

Mulvihills switched their formation from a square to a wedge, splitting the Cooleen ranks and cutting them off from any retreat into the dunes. The effect was dramatic. At one moment the Cooleens were surrounding and seemingly pounding the Mulvihills, the next they were split into small groups fleeing for their safety under a hail of stones they themselves had brought to the battle. Jack directed his men but so sudden was the collapse of the Cooleens that he hardly had time to strike out at any individual. The beach was filled with men running wildly through an avenue of cracking shillelaghs, trying desperately to reach the rowing boats which would take them out of range across the river Cashen. But even those who were in the boats suffered under the barrage of stones.

Paddy Quillinan, a small cut on his forehead, shouted his men on as he came towards Jack. "Tis a rout," he exclaimed. "Just as you said, Jack. Them Cooleens will fall for any trick."

Jack threw his arms around his friend. "And wasn't that just a fight, Paddy. I thought you were nearly done for till we crept up behind them."

Quillinan's battered features split into a huge grin. "A fight? Twas a massacre so it was . . . and with their own stones they'd carted all the way across the river."

"How was it though, Paddy?" Jack asked, his voice quiet and serious.

Quillinan's reply was in an equally serious tone. "To tell the truth, Jack, we couldn't have held out much longer. They'd nearly broken a side of the square and that would have been that."

"No fear, Paddy. They didn't and that's what matters. Just see them running now."

The two men looked over the beach as the Cooleens scattered in all directions, pursued by Mulvihills. Many of the Cooleens had taken to the boats and were frantically trying to row across the river. Jack watched, laughing, as the Mulvihills stood on the shore hurling stones at the boats, seeing the splashes as the missiles fell near or the Cooleens clutch at their bodies as a stone hit them.

"Oh, Jesus, Paddy," he suddenly cried as he caught a glimpse of a woman in a red skirt in one of the boats crossing the river. "Tis Brigid. They took Brigid. She's out there."

Quillinan followed his pointing finger. "You're right, Jack. But where . . . ?"

"I told her to stay down. They must have been after taking her all the time."

Jack could see her more clearly now. She was in a boat being rowed by Sean Flaherty. On either side of her were two Cooleens holding her arms. She was struggling wildly to escape but to no avail.

Flaherty was bent over the oars, pulling strongly for the far side of the river, when a fusillade of stones smashed down on him from Mulvihills who'd waded knee-deep into the river. For a moment, it seemed as if they'd all missed him but suddenly he clutched the back of his head, half stood up in the boat, and then tumbled overboard. As he went into the water, the boat capsized, throwing everyone into the river.

"For God's sake, stop them," Jack screamed as he saw more and more stones splashing into the water around the upturned boat. He began running towards the water's edge, tearing off his shirt as he went. Quillinan began shouting orders at the Mulvihills who were standing in the surf throwing stones.

Jack saw Brigid struggling in the water, breaking free from the men around her and striking for the shore. And then, as in a nightmare, a slow dream, a ghastly dream, he saw a stone smash her forehead. Her hands reached up for the wound, her head vanished under the water, a hand surfaced briefly, and she was gone.

Jack swam thirty yards into the river and trod water frantically as he looked for her. Despite Quillinan's orders, stones were still raining down on the Cooleens in the river. One of them struck Jack on the shoulder but he scarcely felt the blow. All around him were the screams and groans and cries of drowning people but nowhere could he spot Brigid. And then he saw her. She was floating face downwards twenty yards from him, moving away with the tide, her red skirt billowing voluminously on the surface. Jack's arms clawed at the water as he surged towards her. He reached her and turned her face upwards, dragging her by the shoulders back towards the beach. But as he looked into her face, eyes glazed open, jaw sagging wide, hair straggling over the gaping wound, he knew it was too late. He pulled her into the shallows, callously pushing aside the bodies of drowned Cooleens, and picked her up in his arms. Her green eyes, reddened by the water, stared sightlessly at the sky.

He carried her over to Paddy Quillinan and lowered her gently on to the sand before him. Quillinan was crying openly.

"Call them off, Paddy," said Jack quietly. "There's nothing to fight over any more." He looked down at Brigid's body at his feet. "We won, Paddy, didn't we?" he asked. And then in a voice that carried across the beach, "Oh, Jesus, we won, didn't we?"

The report of the official government inquiry into the Battle of Ballyeagh reached its inconclusive findings and the people of Kerry read of them in their rudely-printed newspaper, Master Chute's *Western Herald*.

Who was to blame, had asked the lawyers, for the deaths of perhaps twenty people? The final toll was never known. Everyone and no one, the inquiry decided. It was just faction fighting and that, all agreed, had to be stopped. And so it was on any large scale. There were spats between the factions but only involving two or three dozen men and then infrequently and well away from the eyes of the authorities.

Thin blades of grass soon began to grow on Brigid Aherne's grave next to those of Joe and John Keane at the bottom of the far field near the cabin at Drombeg. Each Sunday, whatever the weather, Jack and Matt Aherne walked hand in hand to Brigid's grave to replace the sprigs of hawthorn or sprays of wild roses.

Matt, now a sturdy-growing little boy, knew for certain that his mother was with the angels, because Father O'Mahony had said so and for sure she wasn't around any more to comfort him when he fell over or was pecked by a chicken. Sometimes Matt remembered his mother vividly, her smell, her eyes, her black hair, but he was well content in the arms of the grey-haired old woman he knew as Mam Keane. Gradually, the memories of his mother faded although, for some reason, he always told people otherwise. It was clearly what they wanted to hear, because he was invariably rewarded with a pat on the head or a hug.

But he did remember—or later told his children that he did—a day, not long after his mother died, when a tall man on a big horse rode up to the cabin. The person he always called Jack-Da lifted him up to the man on his horse. The man held him at arm's length, examining his features closely, then hugged him before pressing a shiny gold sovereign into his tiny palm and handing him back.

"This won't be forgotten, Master Keane," the man on the horse said.

"And that's the truth," Jack-Da said shortly.

"You have truly shamed me."

"Tis your shame."

"But don't you understand?" the man on the horse added, almost a begging note in his voice. "My position . . . in my position it was impossible to do anything . . . to acknowledge this."

"No man would want to be ignoring his own son," Jack-Da replied.

"I offered money but she refused."

"Aye, she would be doing that, I'm thinking. She had a pride too full to be taking your money."

"We both loved her you know," the man on the horse pleaded.

"Aye, to our likes," Jack-Da said contemptuously, glancing over his shoulder as he led the small boy back into the cabin. "To our very different likes, Master Sandes."

BOOK
TWO

Chapter 1
July, 1845

It was a warm, lazy summer day. The earth threw up a fecund smell of contentment. The crops of corn and wheat moved gently, serenely, in the soft breezes whispering over the North Kerry plain from the Atlantic. The black dairy cattle sought what shade there was between yielding pails of rich, frothing milk. The pigs in their sties fattened steadily, nosing somnolently into their feeds of maize. The chickens, almost stunned by the heat, stayed out of the midday sun, saving their clucking energies for early morning and late afternoon. Even the flies, inevitably gathered around the dung pit at the rear of the cabin, swarmed only in the coolness of sunset, seeming to ignore humans and animals alike during the day.

By any standards, June and early July that year had been particularly dry and hot in the west of Ireland. The fields were still green from the water stored during the wet season but on the mountains east of Listowel the heather was becoming parched.

Despite the heat, Jack Keane and Matt Aherne worked steadily alongside their five laborers in the neat fields surrounding their cabin at Drombeg townland.

Ever since he had returned from Boston twelve years since, Jack had worked to expand the farm until it had become one of the most prosperous in the district. As adjoining fields had become vacant through eviction, death or emigration, he had systematically acquired them, paying rent in advance to Sir James Watson through his agent, Jonathan Sandes. At first, Jack had had to dip into the reserve of money he'd brought back from America but by the time his mother had died in 1837 the farm was making enough to pay the annual rent of £12 an acre, on all its eighty acres.

Sandes made numerous gestures in an attempt to curry favor, but Jack had only to look at Matt Aherne for his heart to harden once more against the land agent. The young man grew to resemble his mother more during each passing year. He had her green eyes, shaded with brown, her oval face, her jet-black hair. From his father, Jonathan Sandes, he had acquired only a tall, wiry build, unlike his guardian's which had thickened with years of good eating and drinking despite all the hard work. By the time he was fifteen years old, this hot summer, Matt Aherne stood a head above his guardian. He still called him Jack-Da, although he knew who his actual father was.

Jack had agonized for years about when—indeed whether—to tell the youngster of all that had gone before. Finally, he had decided the boy should know the truth, if only to protect him from any vicious, childish gossip he might hear during his years at the ditch school set along the main track between Listowel and Ballybunnion.

Matt had listened intently, wide-eyed, as Jack told him the story surrounding Brigid Aherne's life.

"So there you are, Matt," Jack finished. "Your real father is the land agent Sandes. I'm thinking he'll not want you with him but I'm sure he'd give you a preferment in Sir James' service if you want to leave here."

"Do you want me to, Jack-Da?" Matt asked, a suspicion of a tear trembling in the corner of one eye.

"Want you to leave? Never, Matt. This farm is your home and your birthright if you wish it."

This July day they worked the fields as father and son. With the sun at its fullest, they slumped gratefully into the shade of a wall to share a snack of lumpers and milk.

"Has it ever been so hot a day, Jack-Da?" Matt asked, wiping his shining brow with the tail of the shirt tied round his waist.

"Be not complaining, lad," Jack grunted. "Tis the weather for farmers like you and me and, pray God, it stays till September. Rain then and we'll be lifting the tatties from soft enough soil."

"When you look at the other folk in the district, you don't know how they survive." It was more of a question than a statement from the youngster.

"Aye, that's true. There be too many people and not enough land to work. But tis the tradition to divide the land among the children. Over the years, it has been cut up so much there are families trying to find a living from half an acre. This'll be a good year for them though, and the hanging gales are likely to be paid."

"The rents?"

"They're near twice as high as in England because of too many people sharing too little land. They take a field, build a cabin on it, and then pray mightily for a good first harvest. The landlord's agent is forced to let the rent hang over until the harvest to collect his money, unless the farmer goes borrowing against his crops from the gombeen man."

"And if it's a bad harvest?"

"Evictions like you've seen, lad, and someone else takes the land."

"Tisn't fair."

"Fair? You want fairness from landlords? Know this . . . if I failed with my rent I'd be thrown off these fields without one penny compensation, not even for all we've been building to the cabin or how we've improved and cleared the farm. Up in Ulster, they'd be getting some compensation but nowhere else in this country."

Jack took another swig from the tin can filled with milk, held out to him by Matt.

"You won't be remembering the monster meetings held by Daniel O'Connell and his Repealers but you've seen his lawyer man, Mahony, who's living on the Feale at Kilmorna. Until the Repealers get a parliament again in Dubin, Ireland run by Irishmen, then the landlords will be riding high over us."

"But the Repealers are a force in the English parliament, aren't they?"

Jack snorted contemptuously. "Anything they be getting through that Parliament is soon stamped on by the lords above them and they're the parasites who live off our backs. God forgive them, many of them were born in Ireland themselves, not that they speak our language or worship at our Church. But Irish they are. Now think on that, lad. Irish against Irish. Be thinking on that while we get back to the fields."

Jack Keane had resisted considerable temptation to take part in politics.

On many occasions he'd met Daniel O'Connell's lawyer, Pierce Mahony, at Listowel market. They'd drunk wine together at the Listowel Arms while Mahony had urged Jack to fight for a parliament in Dublin, once even suggesting he stand for election in Cork. The slight, thin-faced lawyer was full of assurances that Jack could become a member of parliament if he wanted to. His forceful arguments led Jack to promise he would consider the matter seriously. He talked for many hours with Father O'Mahony, now his trusted confidant, and even travelled with the priest to

Limerick, spanning the Shannon, to attend one of O'Connell's self-proclaimed "monster meetings." He'd been impressed by the oratory of the fat, balding politician but the open adulation of the huge crowd had disturbed him. The banners fluttering everywhere acclaimed O'Connell as "The Liberator" or "The Great Liberator" or "England's Scourge" yet the politician still spoke of a parliament in Dublin giving loyalty to the British monarchy.

"Tis strange that, Father," Jack remarked to the priest as they journeyed back together to Listowel. "The mob call him Liberator yet he would still tie us to the English."

The priest smiled gently. "A good politician—and O'Connell is certainly that—is akin to a parish priest, Jack. Haven't I drunks enough come to confession? Now how would it be if I told them they'd find eternal damnation if they kept on with the bottle. They'd think me a fool; they'd not cease the drink; and, likely as not, they'd not be confessing again . . ."

"So . . . ?" Jack interrupted, rather impatiently.

"So, my friend, I chide them gently, remind them that money spent on drink doesn't fill the bellies of their children, and pray to God that their natural goodness—and don't all men have that?—will bring them moderation."

"With respect, what's that to do with O'Connell?"

"Don't you see, Jack. Like me, he's only interested in the possible. Why, he knows that the English will never let Ireland go while memories are still fresh of the '98 rising and the offers of Ireland to Bonaparte as a base to fight, even to invade, England. So O'Connell tells the English—you find us so troublesome to govern, why not let us govern ourselves under your control?"

"O'Connell promises the mobs what he can't give them, then?"

"Oh, no. He tells them the truth, but so that they believe he is promising more than he is. Tis politics, old friend."

"Tis cynical," Jack retorted, recalling another conversation in another country when a politician had attempted to explain what he regarded as the realities of the world. In that moment he decided against accepting the offer of a safe entry into politics.

"Politics should be about beliefs, Father," he explained later when he told the priest that he was going to remain a farmer. "Tis my belief that if the people of Ireland want freedom, then they should grasp it, wrest it from the English, die for it if necessary. The Yanks did it. Why can't we if we crave it so much?"

"But you're forgetting that there's no Atlantic Ocean between us and the English," Father O'Mahony said quietly. "We're in each other's pockets, so we are."

"No, you're wrong," Jack insisted. "The poorness of land, our poverty of belief in ourselves, make it so. Nothing else."

And so Jack Keane was pleased this fine summer to work his farm with Matt Aherne, certain of his skills, sure in his political beliefs, settled in his mind. He sat the nights in the comfortable cabin at Drombeg, talked with Matt until the lad went to bed, then thought his thoughts alone, taking occasional mugs of rum.

He had toyed with the idea of marriage, thinking that Matt would need a woman's help and influence, particularly after Jack's own mother died. He'd discussed the matter at length with Father O'Mahony and the priest had agreed that a woman's presence in the cabin might help Matt during his formative years. He'd even gone as far as introducing Jack to eligible young women. A couple of girls had been pretty and intelligent enough to send a stir of longing through Jack Keane. But as he continued his acquaintanceships with

them, subtly pressed on all sides to begin a formal
courtship, fierce memories of Brigid Aherne, fond thoughts
of Meg Griffiths, dark remembrances of Elizabeth Kilfedder, continued to haunt him. He measured the local girls
against the previous women in his life and found them
wanting. The memories kept him from loneliness. They
were always fresh in his mind. Sometimes, as he sat by
candlelight, he wondered if he was living too much in the
past. Then he would think of Matt and realize he was living
for the youngster's future. He was content in his small
world, perhaps even a trifle smug, that glorious summer of
1845.

But one morning towards the end of July, Jack awoke, the
light in the cabin still grey, feeling cold. He'd been sleeping
uncovered during the past weeks of summer heat. Now he
was shivering with cold. He tiptoed to the window, and
rubbed away the condensation on the glass. There was
nothing outside but the clinging, grey cottonwool of fog. In
July, he thought. Fog?

"What is it, Jack-Da?" Matt was standing by his
shoulder, his white shirt reaching to mid-thigh.

"Fog, lad. Tis fog."

"Now?"

"Aye, in July."

"But it was steaming yesterday."

"So it was. A real burner but now tis fog. And cold it is,
as well."

"Shall I be getting the rugs from the chest?" Matt said.

"No, lad. Tis nearly dawn or past it. We'll dress and take
a meal."

The two of them struggled into their breeches and tucked
in their shirts. "We'll be tending the animals before getting
to the fields when this murk clears," said Jack.

Sudden mists and fogs were not uncommon in a Kerry

summer as layers of cold air met warmer vapor from the night sea.

But Jack and Matt couldn't work the fields that day, nor for the next three weeks, as the appalling weather continued. It was as if the North Kerry plain had been robbed of all natural light during those long days. The nights merged into dusk-like, chill days when there should have been bright sunshine and lively breezes. The fog and rain hovered, unmoving, over the entire country and, from newspaper reports, over many neighboring counties. The initial sullen acceptance of the weather began to change into panic by the middle of the second week. A few more days and the farmers were despairing of their crops.

At Listowel market that third week, the farmers stood around in small groups openly forecasting their own and everyone else's ruin. Jack, with Matt at his side, moved from group to group, commiserating, listening.

"Tis fine for you, Jack," one of the neighbors told him. "You've the animals to tide you through."

"And what to feed them on if nothing grows?"

"At least you'll be eating them . . . me? . . . well, you know I've scarce two acres of lumpers with a woman and four wee ones to feed. What if that crop dies? What then?"

Jack realized that it was precisely that question which was causing so much worry. All the farmers knew that there'd been at least a dozen failures of the potato crop in various parts of Ireland during the last fifty years or so.

"This time it's our turn," they moaned. "Tis Kerry's turn now."

Jack, in a position of comparative safety with his spread of crops and livestock, tried to cheer them up. He'd gesture toward the stalls lining the gentle slope of the market square.

"Be seeing the bags of new tatties for sale alongside the old lumpers. There's plenty for all still."

"And what of those in the trenches, Jack?"

"They're looking well enough if you can see them in the fog and I'm reading in the newspaper from Dublin how the tattie crop has never been so large or abundant."

By the middle of August the farmers' depression and panic dispersed along with the fog.

In September, Jack took a good harvest of wheat from his fields, milled it in Listowel, and stored the bags of flour in one of the three outhouses he'd added to the cabin. He planned to use these along with turnips lifted from one field to help feed the livestock through the winter, make the rough, unleaven bread he and Matt liked so much, and then sell the remainder at market the next year when the prices should have risen. The last job of the season, before the late autumn ploughing, would be to lift the potato crop from the five fields. By common agreement, he and his neighbors decided that the second week in October provided the ideal weather, the soil damp but not clinging, the skies cloudy but not threatening. Any lingering doubts they had vanished as they dug the tubers from the ground. The potatoes were firm, large and unmarked, as they were laid on straw by their trenches to dry off for a couple of days.

"We'll be eating well this winter, young Matt," Jack said, open delight on his face. "The lumpers are better than some years past, the flour's bagged, the pigs are fattened . . ."

". . . the hens are laying, the cows are milking," Matt chimed in, mischievously.

Jack laughed, recognizing his own self-satisfied pomposity. "You gosseen! Don't be checking your elders and betters," he roared in mock anger. "Run to our neighbors and find how their lumpers are. Be off with you."

Matt raced off across the fields, black hair streaming, hurdling the stone walls without effort. Jack knew that at each cabin Matt visited, he would be pressed to eat a little something, perhaps a scone cake fresh from the griddle, and then given a mug to drink. One or two of the farmers would delight in slipping the youngster a nip of poteen to send him light-headed on his way. Jack would do the same to their sons who'd soon be calling out of breath at his cabin. It was a ritual, this swapping of news about the most important crop of the year. As he sat at the table in his cabin, waiting for the first caller, Jack uncorked a bottle of rum, poured himself a generous measure, and buttered slices of new-made bread. He reflected that, if there was a luckier or more content man in the west of Ireland, then Jack Keane didn't know him.

Jonathan Sandes moved uncomfortably in the chair by the front window of his drawing room as a spasm of rheumatism stabbed his right hip.

Always in October, he thought bitterly. Cursed weather.

He was getting old. His body told him so every day. His stomach revolted at large meals. His liver complained at an excess of wine. His legs trembled in protest at too long a walk. The knowledge hurt him every bit as much as the symptoms of his physical decline.

The land agent looked out on the milling crowds in Listowel market square. He'd heard as soon as anyone that the potato crop lifted in the last two days was good. That meant rents would be paid, yet Sandes was still unhappy.

"God, they all look as if they've found the crock," he muttered to himself. He scanned the crowd, trying to see his wife, who was out among the stalls with their son, George, the child who'd arrived when he and his wife had virtually abandoned all hope of having a fruitful marriage. The boy was now ten years old, nearly eleven, and much loved. "The apple of my eye," Sandes told his friends when he was feeling expansive in company, which was very rare these days.

"Tis the crab apple of his eye," the people of Listowel joked to themselves, noting that Master Sandes showed most of the traits of a spoiled, indulged child, and promised to be as unlovable as his father.

It was not a good day to have rheumatism, to feel old, to gaze through a window at such a happy throng.

Sandes craned forward and peered at the smiling, guffawing, crowd outside the inn. Just like cattle, he thought grumpily. Feed 'em, milk 'em, slaughter 'em. They'd still be happy.

Anyway, there was some consolation. The agent's commissions from Sir James Watson for collecting the landowner's rents would be assured.

Jonathan Sandes decided to risk a glass of sherry before lunch. It might help to ease the pain.

He rang the tiny silver bell on the table beside him to summon his new maid.

As she entered the room and curtseyed before him, young breasts thrusting against her dress, another twinge of pain shot through Sandes. He clenched his teeth in a vain attempt to keep a groan from escaping.

The girl rose, began to move to his side, concern in her soft eyes.

"Sherry," snapped Sandes, trying to control the pain with his mind. "The sherry, Brigid."

The girl paused, then turned hesitantly and went to the door.

"Sir," she said quietly.

"Sherry. Bring the sherry!"

"Sir, I'm Bernadette. Not Brigid."

Another spasm of rheumatism surged through Jonathan Sandes. He looked determinedly through the window but his eyes saw nothing.

The smell, rank and clinging, spread over the townlands around Listowel during the next two days. It crept through windows and under doors, clung to clothes, assailed the nostrils of animals and people alike, and poisoned the air and soul of North Kerry.

Jack Keane stood in the middle of his largest potato field, a wet cloth pressed to his nose and mouth, and looked slowly along the long rows of potatoes lying on straw. He bent to pick one up. Its skin was slippery. The flesh inside felt soft and mushy. Its putrid smell sank deep into Jack's lungs. He began to cough and, as he did so, tears started to run down his cheeks.

"Oh, Mary, Holy Mother of Jesus," he choked. "Oh, Holy God. The whole field . . . all of them . . . they're done for . . . they're rotten."

His streaming eyes looked over his fields and the fields beyond. He turned slowly around to take in every part of the landscape. A watery October sun played among the fast-moving clouds. Everywhere seemed bleak, forbidding, and harsh.

Jack walked down each row of potatoes, stooping now and again to pick one up. They were all the same, rotten or rotting.

"Matt!" he shouted. "Anything there?"

The youngster threw a lumper away from himself, wiped his hands disgustedly, shook his head.

"Nothing, Jack-Da," he called. "They're all lost. A stinking mess."

"Holy Mother, what's to be done with us now?" Jack

whispered. "Without the lumpers, we're done for. Holy God!"

The extent of the disaster became clear as farmer after farmer came to call at Jack Keane's cabin seeking to share their misery, their hopelessness. The potato crop of 1845 was a total failure throughout the area, and, from reading Mr. Chute's journal, throughout Ireland, it seemed.

"Why have we been visited so?" the farmers would ask.

Jack would shake his head, run his fingers through his streak of white hair, and shake his head again.

"They were good when they were lifted, weren't they? Now they're nothing but pulp!"

"Tis that stuff they're calling electricity from all that smoke and steam of those new locomotive things," one farmer would say.

"No, tis the vapors of the volcanoes under the earth," another would contradict. "Sure and wasn't Ireland thrown up from the sea by a volcano? Tis those vapors."

Everything was to blame, and, indeed, was blamed. Confusion, panic and doubt were rife. And when all had been said in those first awful days of the crop's failure, a dullness spread through the townland as it was finally accepted that many faced ruin and hunger, perhaps even starvation and death.

Suddenly, though, leaping hopes were raised by the government's scientific commissioners who published in every newspaper in the land their solution for saving the precious potatoes.

Jack Keane shook his head in disbelief as he read it aloud to Matt while they sat by candlelight in the cabin. "Tis what they're saying so we'll be trying it, lad, but tis mighty strange. Listen to this . . . first, dry the potatoes in the sun, then mark out on the ground a space six feet wide and as long as you please. Dig a shallow trench two feet wide all around, and throw the molding potatoes upon the space then level it and cover it with a floor of turf sods set on their edges. Sift on to this packing stuff comprising of materials made by mixing a barrel of freshly burnt unslaked lime . . ."

"What?" Matt interrupted.

". . . unslaked lime, it says here. Now don't be interrupting." Jack peered again at the small, uneven print in Chute's *Western Herald*. ". . . unslaked lime, broken into pieces as large as marbles, with two barrels of sand or earth, or by mixing equal parts of burnt turf and dry sawdust."

He put down the newspaper and rubbed his eyes wearily.

"Tis all, Jack-Da?"

"Well, them scientists are saying that if we're not understanding it, then we should be asking the landlord or the clergyman to explain its meaning, but tis my opinion that Father O'Mahony nor Sir James Watson won't be helping much."

But, dubious as they were, Jack and Matt, like many of their neighbors, followed the scientists' advice to the letter. It offered hope and raised them from apathy as they worked in the fields again.

At the end of the month, they lifted the potatoes from the specially-prepared pits but, if anything, they were more rotten than before.

But the scientists published more advice and the constables pasted it to walls throughout North Kerry. They admitted defeat in saving the crops but tried to salvage something from the disaster.

For two days, Jack followed the learned advice and transformed the cabin into a smelly, steaming kitchen. First, he grated the rotten potatoes with a jagged piece of metal so that the slimy flakes filled the large tub normally used for collecting rainwater. He washed the resulting pulp, strained it through a muslin cloth, washed it again, and then dried it on the griddle warmed by a low fire. When it was dried through, the substance set like a rough lump of grey stone.

Jack scratched his head in bewilderment. "What in God's name do we do with this?" he wondered aloud.

"Try it on the pigs?" suggested Matt.

"Are you sure? Those scientists say we can be eating it."

"Not me, Jack-Da."

"Well, they say what's left in the tub should be starch which'll make bread when it's mixed with this dried stuff."

They both peered over the edge of the tub at the sticky, noxious liquid inside. They glanced at each other, noted their similar expression of pained disgust, and broke into laughter.

"Tis pure nonsense, so help me," spluttered Jack, as they rushed outside to breathe some fresh air. "We'll be losing even our pigs if we feed them it."

"So, Jack-Da?"

"So, my lad, let's get the whole mess out of the cabin and into the dung pit else we'll be suffocating ourselves with the smell."

Some of Jack's neighbors without his reserves of turnips, maize and flour as animal feedstuff were forced to use the rotten potatoes, however. They boiled them into a mash, mixed in bran and salt and fed their pigs and cattle. The livestock survived on this feed long enough to be sold at market to raise rents or to be slaughtered to provide food for families deprived of their normal diet of potatoes and milk.

As the smaller farmers began to kill the animals, they were left without any means to pay their long overdue rents. The inevitable happened. Eviction notices began being pinned to cabin doors through North Kerry. Most families gave in meekly, standing dumbly by as the bailiffs, accompanied by constables and soldiers, pulled down the thatches and smashed the cabin walls. Their hunger and despair robbed them of any defiance. Once the eviction party had left, some returned to the ruins of their homes and tried to rig up temporary shelter to help them through the winter. Others dug holes in the side of ditches, covered them with tree branches layered with sods of turf, and called this "scalp" their new home.

A few summoned anger from their anguish and resisted the bailiffs. They barricaded their windows and doors against the expected onslaught. Crowds, sullen, jeering, gathered around the cabin to try to obstruct the bailiff's small army of paid thugs. But it was to no avail. A magistrate was quickly summoned. The troops fixed bayonets, the constables drew truncheons and the crowds were moved away from the cabin to allow the bailiff's men into action. With practiced ease, they rigged a battering ram. Even under a hail of stones from the family inside the cabin, sometimes dodging tubfuls of boiling water, the bailiff's men needed only a few swings of the ram to smash aside the flimsy defenses and shatter the mud and stone walls. Then personal scores would be settled while the troops and police held back the crowds. The men of the family who had resisted, including the youngsters, were pummelled and thwacked with clubs. Then the troops and police would leave followed by the crowd, angered yet guilty at its own inability to help. The family, with perhaps five or six children, were left standing amid the ruins in their ragged, inadequate clothing, wailing and weeping, nothing between themselves and the fast-approaching winter. The grim workhouse at Listowel might take the mother and the younger children, but there was no hope for the father and his elder sons or daughters.

As the number of evictions increased, a group of farmers,

threatened with the same fate, approached Jack Keane to ask him to intercede with Jonathan Sandes on their behalf.

It was a difficult meeting between the two men that morning in mid-November 1845. They sat on opposite sides of the drawing room looking out on to Listowel market square. Jack was dressed in his newest chocolate brown coat and breeches, and a white silk stock. Sandes, visibly ailing, wore a long, heavily brocaded dressing gown. Jack declined the land agent's offer of wine, nervously clearing his throat as he tried to find the right weight of words with which to begin the conversation. During his ride to Listowel, he had determined to ask the favors with all the force at his command but he was equally determined not to beg.

"Sad days, are they not, Mr. Keane?" Sandes interrupted his thoughts. "A few days ago, all seemed well but now . . ." He spread his hands and raised his eyes as if appealing to Heaven.

"Now, tis disaster, Mr. Sandes."

"Quite so. A disaster for many. But I trust not for you."

"Not quite. Matt and I shall be surviving since we're not dependent on the potato. You shall be having your rent, have no fear."

"My dear Keane," Sandes said effusively, "I had no concern on that matter. None at all. You are a man of substance, not like those feckless peasants I normally have business with. Your progress has pleased me, as has the way in which you have cared for that young man . . ." Sandes paused, unable for a moment to find the correct phrase.

"Of Brigid Aherne's," Jack broke in, harshness in his voice.

Sandes coughed nervously. "Quite so," he added hurriedly. "Quite so, but I'm sure you've not come to talk of such matters."

"No, tis the plight of some of my neighbors that concerns me . . . the Deanes, the Stacks, the . . ."

The land agent held up his hand. "The names are known to me, Master Keane. All that you may care to mention. Their troubles are known to me. They exercise me. They exercise us all."

"Can't you be holding over their rents? They have nothing."

Sandes smiled wearily. "Would that I could, but Sir James has heavy financial responsibilities to bear in England. He needs the rents."

"But they have nothing to pay with," Jack persisted. "Cannot you be reducing the rents at least so they have a chance to pay? Next harvest will be better. Plenty always follows scarcity, Mr. Sandes. You know that adage."

"Indeed, Mr. Keane. But the people you speak of fail to think of the bad times. When they have money, they pour it down their throats. When they have none, they expect charity."

"Can you be reducing the rents, though?" Jack's voice was beginning to rise in anger at Sandes' unfeeling stubbornness.

"Sir James has been asked—I anticipated such requests, you realize—but he is firm in his intentions. If rents cannot be met, then evictions must follow. Those are his instructions. Lord Listowel has given similar orders, I am told."

"Have they no mercy?" Jack cried. "These people will starve."

Sandes leaned forward in his chair. "Oh, I think not," he said, trying to calm the atmosphere. "Relief is on the way, you know."

"Relief!" Jack snorted.

"The Prime Minister has authorized £100,000 to be spent on buying Indian corn from the Americas."

"I read of that. A generous man that Peel," Jack went on, sarcasm heavy in his voice.

"Some will be stored in Limerick for distribution here," Sandes said quickly. "And there'll be local people on the Relief Committees to ensure that the needy will be helped."

"Like who?"

"Well, two of them will be Dr. Church and myself."

"Land agents both. Landlords' men," Jack said disgustedly.

"Who better to know those in true need?"

"So you and Church will put these people in the ditch, in the scalp, and then hand out someone else's charity. Tis roguery of the worst kind!" Jack pushed his chair back, walked over to Sandes and stood menacingly above him.

"People like you are the curse of the Irish." The farmer spoke slowly and deliberately. "And the time will come . . ."

"Threats change nothing, Keane." The land agent flicked his eyes away, avoiding Jack's challenging stare. "You are safe and will be safe because of my word years back. Be thankful for that. And now I think we've spoken enough."

"We shall never say enough, Sandes," Jack replied. "Tis what is in my heart will make that so. Your kind and mine will speak words again until the time comes when your words are seen for what they are. And then no one will listen again. God, may I live to that day!"

Unknown to both men that day, one of the greatest of the Catholic peers in the House of Lords had just had an inspiration for helping the stricken farmers of Ireland. As Jack Keane broke the bad news to his neighbors in the bar of the Listowel Arms and Jonathan Sandes thought darkly on the future, the Duke of Norfolk was rising to expound his new idea to his peers at Westminster.

"If the Irish cannot eat the potato because of the murrain," the Duke intoned, "then let them eat curry powder mixed with water. It is cheap and plentiful and undoubtedly sustains the millions in India."

The Duke sat down again to a few murmured calls of "Hear, hear." He smiled to himself with a properly modest sense of self-satisfaction.

Chapter 2
November, 1846

"Pon my soul, there are thousands of the creatures," remarked Lieutenant Peter Markison of the 5th Regiment of Foot, a distinct note of worry in his thoroughly English voice. He stood at a second-floor window of Listowel workhouse, looking down at the mob converging on the building from three sides. "Sergeant," he called. "Position twenty men outside, bayonets fixed, muskets loaded with ball. But on no account are they to open fire without a direct order from myself."

The sergeant saluted then hitched his pack more comfortably around his shoulders before hurrying off to execute the order.

"What do you make of it all?" the British officer asked, turning to the older man beside him.

"A rabble, Lieutenant. Just a rabble," snapped Jonathan Sandes, hunched over a thick cane. "A few constables could deal with them, let alone a platoon of the British Army."

"They're chanting something, sir. Shall I open the window?"

Without waiting for an answer, the officer pushed up the sash window. The land agent stepped unsteadily backwards as a blast of icy November air enveloped him.

Through the open window, carried by the wind, came a

319

roaring sound, indistinct at first in its cacophony, but soon clearer as the chanting mob approached.

"Bread or blood . . . bread or blood . . . bread or blood . . . bread or blood . . ."

Sandes permitted himself a half smile. "There's no bread here but there might be a deal of blood, eh, Lieutenant?"

"But, sir," the officer protested, "we've more than ten score sacks of Indian meal here and a similar amount in the store near the castle."

Their chant continued. "Bread or blood . . . bread or blood . . . bread or blood . . ."

Sandes was forced to raise his voice in order to be heard. "If you allow even one sack out, those peasants will tear down these walls to steal the rest."

"But, sir . . ." Lieutenant Markison began.

"Anyway, my gallant young officer of the line," Sandes continued, brushing aside the interruption. "We have firm instructions from Charles Trevelyan at the Treasury in London not to give away any relief supplied. They have to be sold. Market conditions must prevail. Those are Trevelyan's firm instructions. Sell the corn at market prices and let the charity people, like the Society of Friends, give anything away free they wish. But not us. Not us."

"If that is the situation, sir," the lieutenant replied heavily, "I think I should join my men outside. With your permission, of course, Mr. Sandes."

"I fear you're doing little good here, young man, with your ill-informed prattling." Sandes made little, if any, attempt these days to mask his impatience with the methods used to alleviate the disaster which had befallen Ireland in the past year.

As he had prophesied, the Irish farmer had just survived the winter of 1845 after the failure of the potato crop. The government had set up public works, mainly road building, and paid the farmers who turned laborers between sixpence and tuppence a day to work on them. A man might have to walk seven miles to work and back in a day but his wages enabled him to keep his family from total starvation, with perhaps, a meal of turnips one day, a portion of oatmeal the next. Some of the more foolish and desperate, Sandes reflected, had even eaten seed potatoes, seed corn and seed oats, but nevertheless the weather in May and June of 1846 had been good, raising hopes of plentiful and early crops. In August, the potato fields had been in full bloom but by the end of the month, as mysteriously as before to the farmers, the leaves were scorched black and the stench of diseased tubers covered the townlands once more.

Even Jonathan Sandes had been shocked by this second total failure of the main crop. There was little he could do for his most important patron, Sir James Watson. He realized the small farmers had no money. There was little point in evicting any more families because no one wanted to work the blighted land. The people were starving. He told London so in dispatches in his capacity as a Relief Commissioner. But the unwavering reply that came from Charles Trevelyan, the Assistant Secretary at the Treasury, was that market conditions must prevail. It wasn't as if there was no food in Ireland. The wealthier farmers still grew corn and maize, continued to raise cattle and pigs, but no one could afford to buy them at local markets and they were forced to export to England. The troops and constables had been kept busy as the starving peasants tried to ambush the convoys of food and livestock on the way to the docks.

Now it had come to this, Sandes thought, as he surveyed the milling throng outside the workhouse door. The public works program had ground virtually to a halt. The relief inspectors, hidebound by the rigid rules, were unable to pay even those with employment tickets allowing them to work on the existing projects. And when they were paid they could only afford to buy small amounts of Indian corn because of the high prices of vegetables like peas and cabbages.

Beggars lined every corner of Listowel. But few had money to spare for them. The people had started eating grass, weeds, and nettles. The march on the workhouse had been inevitable. Jonathan Sandes, aching with cold and rheumatism, was surprised that it had come later rather than sooner.

At close quarters, the sight of the mob filled Lieutenant Markison, late of Rugby School and his father's gentle estates in Gloucestershire, with overwhelming horror. He had arrived that July for service in Ireland with his regiment. Since then, everything had been a cameo to be thrust into the recesses of his mind, hopefully forgotten except in moments of half-sleep. Before him now was a gigantic canvas filled with the suffering of the people of the North Kerry plain—of all Ireland.

Families huddled together for protection from the shrivelling wind. Around the men's heads were hats fashioned of old sacking: some completely covered the head except for jagged holes for the eyes. All the faces which Lieutenant Markison could distinguish were pinched, almost opaque, skin stretched tight over cheekbones, the eyes dull with dark rings, sunk deep into their sockets. Women were swathed in shawls, sacks, cast-off petticoats; their feet wrapped in the ubiquitous sacking; their legs protected with old newspapers stuffed with straw. Children leeched on to their parents for any warmth, faces lined and gaunt from hunger. Their constant condition of near starvation had caused clumps of hair to fall from their scalps—some were totally bald—but, strangely, horrifyingly, downy hair grew on their foreheads and their cheeks. Many resembled wizened monkeys. In every hand was a mug or a bowl thrust towards the soldiers. One young soldier was crying at the sight before him, tears running silently down his face, but still his musket and gleaming bayonet were steady, pointing upwards and outwards towards the encircling wraiths.

A low murmur ran through the crowd as the impressive figure of Lieutenant Markison came into view. A hum of expectant conversation swept through the waiting thousands until a group towards the back took up the chant again.

"Bread or blood . . . bread or blood . . . bread or blood . . ."

The sound beat round Lieutenant Markison. Instinctively, he surveyed the tactical position of his men and himself. There was no doubt his platoon was trapped. The only possible help would be from the dozen constables half a mile away at their barracks. The nearest regular troops were at Tralee, nearly a day's march away. At that moment, the lieutenant was certain bloodshed was inevitable. His men might be able to loose two rounds of fire before retreating into the workhouse to defend it. But he also knew that their ammunition stocks were inadequate to hold off such a large mob. Men, women and children would die before the mob broke through the defenses but when that happened the lieutenant knew there would be no mercy. Already, he had noticed men, dotted here and there in the crowd, holding shillelaghs with nails driven through the clubs' heads.

Lieutenant Markison looked quickly up at the window where he had been standing, hoping for some sign of guidance from Jonathan Sandes, but the land agent had retreated to a safer position.

The officer raised his arms. "Quiet. Quiet," he shouted against the throbbing tide of the chant. "Quiet! Listen to me!" And then in a quieter voice to his men, "Keep steady, lads. Show 'em no fear or we're done for. Steady."

"Quiet," he roared again. "Be silent or listen!"

"Bread or blood . . . bread or blood . . . bread or blood . . ."

The chant drowned his words. The mob started slowly to press forward. The men at the front looked dully, rather than fearfully, at the bayonets bristling in front of them, as they were thrust nearer and nearer the sharp steel by the pressure of the throng. They began pushing their women and children behind them, as if accepting that their fate was to die first. There was no terror in their faces, Markison realized, rather expressions of relief as if it were better to die quickly than to continue in their present sufferings.

There was little choice left to him. He lowered his arms and began moving his hands gingerly towards his pistols. He thought of his father, gruff pride in his voice, presenting him with the finely-chased guns on the day he'd obtained his officer's commission. Such weapons, the lieutenant thought, were not made to be used against the pathetic targets which faced him now. Sadly, there seemed no alternative.

Suddenly he noticed a movement towards the front of the crowd as it parted reluctantly, grudgingly, to allow a tall man through its ranks. At first, Markison could only see that the man had a shock of grey hair and was enveloped in a thick black cloak which swirled about him. Some of the crowd, particularly the women, crossed themselves and bent to their knees in half-curtseys as the man brushed by them. As he came to the front of the crowd, the officer saw he carried a large Bible thrust out in front of him. Lieutenant Markison, although not recognizing him, realized immediately that the man must be the parish priest, Father O'Mahony. His hands moved away from the pistol holsters. He raised his arms again and shouted for quiet.

The young officer knew that the next best thing to a troop of dragoons had come to his aid.

The priest walked forward from the front of the crowd until the ring of steel around Lieutenant Markison was only inches from his chest. His face was grim but his deep-set blue eyes looked calmly at the British officer.

"Let the priest through," Lieutenant Markison ordered. The bayonets lowered, parted, and Father O'Mahony stepped into the protective semicircle.

"You have a wise head, sir, on such young shoulders," he said in a surprisingly resonant voice. "One shot and this would be a massacre. In the madness, I doubt that even I would be spared." The priest smiled.

"But what can I do, Father? My clear orders are to stop these . . . these . . ."

"Human beings," Father O'Mahony interrupted gently.

". . . these people from entering the workhouse."

"That is clear from your demeanor, Lieutenant, and I'm sure that you would carry out your orders to the letter. This is not of your making, nor mine, nor of these poor wretches." The priest gestured towards the crowd which had been silent as it watched the priest and the officer talking but had now begun to chant again.

"Bread or blood . . . bread or blood . . . bread or blood . . ."

The priest leaned close to Lieutenant Markison. "Have you any bread in the workhouse, sir?" he shouted above the din.

"No, Father. No bread. There is . . ."

"Hush, sir. Tell me no more. If you have no bread, then that is all I need to know. I shall not, nor ever will, lie to my people. Now, if you will, please move your men aside so that the crowd can see that I am unmolested. Let us discover together, Lieutenant, the power of the Church and pray that it possesses enough."

Lieutenant Markison hesitated for a moment, then nodded. "Part the ranks, Sergeant," he ordered. "Move back into the workhouse."

A great cheer broke from the crowd as the troops shouldered their muskets before filing back into the building, a few of them looking fearfully over their shoulders as they passed through the doors. The mob surged forward expectantly towards the priest and the young officer, now standing side by side on the workhouse step.

The priest spread his arms, the cloak unfolding like a raven's wing, holding the Bible aloft, allowing all in the crowd to see his cleric's collar and the cross dangling on his chest.

"My people, my poor people," he began. The chant died away gradually. The crowd stopped and strained to hear the priest.

"You know me. You all know me. Father Darby. Your Father Darby who's received you into the Church, who's danced at your weddings, who's keened at your wakes, who's heard your confessions and eased your mortal souls, who's taken a jar or two more than he should with many of you when times were better . . ."

There was laughter from some in the crowd. Father Jeremiah "Darby" O'Mahony was known and loved as a man who liked his jar or two as much as he liked collecting rare books.

The priest seized on the laughter. "And who's confessing now? And to the biggest congregation of his life? Why, anyone could be telling the lord bishop, so I'm thinking I should be asking this young bucko of an officer to be taking round his hat for my last collection!"

He pointed at Lieutenant Markison's tall uniform helmet, an exaggerated expression of pleading on his face.

The crowd broke into general laughter. "Twould make a mighty fine piss-pot, Father Darby," someone shouted amid the growing laughter. "That's all that'd be collected here and that's the truth."

"And don't I just know that, friends?" the priest shouted. His tone became serious. "Sure and I'm knowing you have no money and little enough food for your wee ones let alone yourselves." He shook the Bible in the air. "Oh, that Lord Jesus was here himself to perform the miracle of the fishes and the loaves, for you cannot be expecting any miracles from your Father Darby. Sure and I pray for one every waking moment, but so many miracles are being asked of Our Lord from this poor land that I'm fearing He hasn't one to spare for us. But twill do no harm, no harm at all, if all of us here joined in prayer now."

"What about the bread, Father?" a voice cried from the back of the crowd.

"There is none, my friend. I have the word of this young officer beside me that there is no bread in the workhouse. And he wouldn't be lying to me and then standing by men now, defenseless, away from his soldier boys, if that wasn't the truth, now would he?"

Many of the crowd nodded in agreement.

"No, there is no bread here, my people," Father O'Mahony hurried on, his voice rising as he tried to retain his momentary control over the thousands. "But let us join in prayer that soon there shall be bread—not only for you, but for the poor wretches lying, starving, inside this workhouse itself. We'll be having no bread by spilling blood this day. Let us pray instead." He fell to his knees, the Bible clasped between his hands. Lieutenant Markison stood awkwardly above him. "Get down, sir," Father

O'Mahony muttered from the side of his mouth. "You've been wanting a miracle to save you and your men, so give thanks you might be having one." The officer slipped off his black chin-strap, pulled off his helmet, and knelt quickly by the older man. Lieutenant Markison's blond hair ruffled in the biting wind.

"Oh, Lord Jesus, who knows all things . . ." the priest began. The people in the front of the mob dropped to their knees as they heard the start of a prayer. The remainder quickly joined them. "Oh, Lord Jesus, who knows all things," the priest repeated. "Look into the hearts of these your people this day and know their love for You who were born of Holy Mary. As You suffered on the Cross, Jesus, look down on our mortal sufferings with mercy. Let not your people's sufferings cause anger in their hearts, Lord, rather let their weakness and hunger bring them closer to You who knew the same weakness and hunger. Oh, Lord Jesus, if You cannot comfort their bodies, then give them the strength to endure, just as you endured the nails and the thrust of the spear."

Father O'Mahony lifted his face to the sky. A shaft of sunlight daggered through the clouds and lit his features. "Oh, Lord Jesus, give us the strength to endure for truly Thine is the power and the glory. Amen. Thine is the power and the glory. Amen."

A rumbling "Amen" rolled from the crowd. The priest lifted the cross on the chain around his neck and pressed it to his lips. He stood up, watching the people—his people— in their thousands cross themselves before scrambling to their feet again.

"Go to your homes, my friends, and God be with you," he roared. "Go to your homes." The people began dispersing slowly, talking quietly among themselves.

Then the priest realized the young officer was still on his

knees by his side, eyes screwed shut, lips moving silently. He put a hand on the gold epaulette on his shoulder. "Your prayer has been answered, my son," the priest said softly. "They are going now. There'll be no bloodshed."

Lieutenant Markison stood up, brushed the dust from his trousers, and watched the departing thousands, backs bent in weary resignation. "My prayers might have been heard, Father," he muttered. "But what of theirs?"

"God knows, Lieutenant. Only God knows."

Suddenly a small boy ran up sobbing, past tears streaking his face.

"Come quickly, Father. They've eaten the weed."

"What weed, boy? Quickly now."

"Someone said tis called praiseach."

"Oh, Lord," the priest cried. "Show me, boy. Fast now. Show me."

The priest pushed through the crowd, followed by the British officer.

"Oh, Lord," he repeated. On the ground by the hedge-row lay nine men, seven women and eleven children.

They were writhing in the dirt, legs kicking, backs arching, frothing at the mouth, screaming in agony, hands clutching first at their throats then at their stomachs.

"What is it, Father?" shouted Lieutenant Markison above the awful cries of pain.

The priest said nothing. He just pointed at a luxuriantly green bunch of weeds growing under the hedge. Then he began to administer the last rites of the Church to the people in their death agonies around him.

"What is it?" the lieutenant asked the people in the crowd, bewilderment in his voice.

"Tis praiseach. Poison weed," one man replied, his eyes transfixed by the scene before him. "They were so hungry, they ate the weed. Just plucked it and thrust it down their throats. There was no bread so they ate the weed."

A harsh light filtered through the high arched windows of the Faneuil Hall in Boston. The market on the ground floor had long since ended its day's business leaving the building to fulfill its natural role as the town's public focus. Outside, a fine sleet was falling this February day in 1847, making the cobbles slippery for horses and carriages, yet hundreds had packed into the hall to discuss the plight of the Irish. Already, hundreds of thousands of dollars had been raised by the town's Catholics and by merchants of all denominations to buy cornmeal to send to the starving millions across the Atlantic. From one church collection alone, Bishop Fitzpatrick had sent provisions worth more than one hundred thousand dollars.

Boston hardly needed reminding by Thomas D'Arcy McGee, the editor of the *Boston Pilot*, that the Irish should not be regarded as foreigners but as an indispensable factor in the growth of the young nation. In an impassioned editorial McGee told Boston "that Ireland did supply the hands which led Lake Erie to the sea and wedded the strong Chesapeake to the gentle Delaware, and carried the roads of the East to the farthest outposts of the West."

Alderman Matt Finucane, still the elected representative for the town's Ward 8 district where many of the emigrants had settled, was rightly proud of what had been done. Indeed, much of the support had been at his instigation.

"The conscience of Boston can be clear," he told the gathering of merchants and their ladies from the podium in Faneuil Hall. "But something more should be done, must be done. Something that will show the world that not only Boston but all of America extends its generosity, its pity, to those starving nigh unto death."

A murmur of assent ran through the hall followed by a ripple of applause. Matt Finucane, grey haired and respectably portly as befitted a substantial man of business, waited for the noise to subside. He glanced sideways at his wife, Alice, and his youngest daughter, Mary, sitting on the platform behind the podium, and smiled. He had rightly judged the mood of the meeting.

"The English government might be excused of tardiness in helping our brothers but then think of the enormity of the task," he went on. "It is true that that government has given millions but it is also true that some of the high and mighty of England have shamed themselves by their utterances . . ."

"The Duke of Cambridge," someone shouted from the body of the hall. There was an angry stir mingled with contemptuous laughter.

"Yes, friends, people like the great Duke of Cambridge. Do you remember what he said? That everyone knew Irishmen could live upon anything and that there was plenty of grass in the fields. Yes, that's how the mighty duke will be remembered wherever this sorry episode is told and retold but . . ."

Finucane paused for effect. He jabbed a finger at the audience.

". . . but be remembering this also. The ordinary citizens of England have not forgotten the starving ones. They have dug deep into their purses and sent even more charity to Ireland than we have. So today let us decide upon a gesture which will not only help the poor and weak in Ireland but will show them also that their suffering is our suffering."

The alderman scanned the hall and the sea of high-crowned hats and bonnets in front of him.

"In this town's harbor, under our very noses lies

America's messenger to poor Ireland—the sloop of war, *Jamestown*. She lies there, swinging at anchor. Let her be provisioned and sent across the ocean in order that the Stars and Stripes should be seen fluttering off Ireland's coast, thus demonstrating that she is deep in our thoughts and hearts at this time of her awful travail.''

There was silence in Faneuil Hall for a moment before the merchants, politicians, and ordinary Bostonians began cheering, applauding, even stamping their feet in approval.

Within weeks, the United States Congress had granted Boston's petition and the sloop *Jamestown* was heading for landfall at Cobh with forty thousand dollars' worth of grain, meal and clothing in her holds.

A few days after her arrival, a dying man caught the eye of the bewigged Speaker in "the mother of parliaments" by the River Thames, and hobbled painfully the dozen steps towards the large ornate table in the center of the House of Commons. He paused for a moment, catching his breath, and looked around the debating chamber at his fellow members of Parliament. They were chattering away among themselves, virtually ignoring him, where once they would have been silent, attentively listening to his every word.

Daniel O'Connell, "the Liberator," gathered his remaining strength and began to speak in a low, halting voice. At times his speech was delivered in a whisper. Even the official reporters were unsure of what he was saying for much of the time as O'Connell criticized the government for not doing enough to help Ireland.

The politicians who were near him shrugged their shoulders as O'Connell rambled on. Hadn't the government spent eight million pounds on aid, they asked themselves? Hadn't the young Queen Victoria personally given £2,000 from her own fortune? What more did the old man want?

O'Connell heard the deprecating comments all around him. He made one more effort to be heard amid the growing chorus of disinterest.

"Ireland is in your hands, in your power," he tried to declaim with all his former power but his voice hardly rose above a mutter. "If you do not save Ireland, she cannot save herself."

He moved slowly back to his seat as another member of Parliament caught the Speaker's eye and raised a point of order.

Daniel O'Connell's final illness had struck when Ireland needed him most. He gazed around the dark panelled chamber for a few minutes before nodding his respects toward the Speaker and leaving the House of Commons for the last time.

Hunger and disease had killed about a million people by the spring of 1847. Jack Keane didn't know whether he and Matt really were lucky to be alive in the middle of such desolation. The agony of living among wholesale suffering was made worse by the knowledge that there was little he could do to help. He was virtually bankrupt, both emotionally and materially. He had worked unceasingly to help his poorer neighbors and his own laborers only to see them disappear one by one, either dying from starvation and disease or joining the ragged thousands in their agonizing march to a new life in the English slums, the industrial cities of North America, even to far-off Australia.

Jack couldn't remember how many times he'd stood at the side of a newly dug mass grave at Teampáillin Bán by the track from Listowel to Ballybunnion as his friends had been buried, family by family. Most of the available wood in Listowel had been burned as firewood. There was none left over for coffins. The dead were taken to the grave in a trap coffin and dropped into the earth through its hinged bottom, sometimes two at a time.

He'd sold or slaughtered his livestock to provide fares and provisions for those who chose emigration. Now there was little left. Without help, Jack and Matt found it impossible to work all the farm's eighty acres. The last quarter's rent had been paid only thanks to an unsolicited gift from Alderman Finucane in Boston which had arrived with a letter from his old friend urging him to return to Massachusetts. At first, Jack had dismissed the idea but lately he had given it more and more consideration.

"I can't be seeing a future here anymore for yourself," he'd told Matt when his mind was finally made up. "Twill be years before Ireland recovers—if she ever does. And here, in the west, twill be even worse. We were poor to begin with. Now we have less than nothing. Half the people have died or gone across the sea."

"But if we leave, we'll be giving up all we've worked for," Matt said defiantly.

Jack smiled. He was pleased to see spirit still in the youngster after everything he'd seen and endured. "Twice I've started from scratch, lad. They say tis easier the third time. If we go to Boston town, I'm reckoning my old friends will give us a helping hand."

"But couldn't we survive here, Jack-Da?"

"After a fashion, perhaps, but I'm thinking of opportunities for you. There's nothing here," Jack insisted. "And also there's tell of rebellion in the air. They say the Young Irelanders are planning something but I'm guessing twill come to naught as usual. But when it's all done, why the English will have even less reason or desire to help us. Times will be harder, you mark."

"And in Boston?"

"The world, lad. The whole world," Jack replied,

slapping the table in the cabin for emphasis. "Tis a young country, what they've explored of it. Half of it isn't yet on the map. Tis not tired like Ireland. There's little past there, just the future."

Matt was not completely convinced. "You once said this farm was my birthright. Me mam's here, so are all your folks. Do we just leave them like that? Does someone else take the farm?"

"I'm praying not, Matt. The Keanes have lived in this townland for five generations or more. The family split their nails and cracked their fingers making the farm worthy. That I'll not lose, nor the graves of our own people. You're right to remind me of that and, sure, there's a deal to be struck with Mr. Sandes before we'll be making any more plans."

The next day, Jack rode to Listowel to see the land agent. All along the track half-naked families were crouched in their rude shelters in the ditch and hedgerows, dirty, long haired, grunting to themselves as if they'd become animals of the forest. By the workhouse, more than a hundred women and children were queueing for their free soup. Jack knew that the gruel would pass straight through most of them without providing any nourishment. What was the cost? Less than one penny for four gallons if the soup was made according to the official instructions. An oxhead without the tongue, 28 lbs. of turnips, 3 lbs. of onions, 7 lbs. of carrots, 21 lbs. of peameal, 14 lbs. of Indian corn meal, all mixed together with 30 gallons of water. The stingiest citizen couldn't object to an increased local rate being levied to make such an economic mixture, yet the bigger landowners had found it cheaper to encourage their tenants to emigrate than to subsidize aid and work for them. Perhaps, Jack wondered, Jonathan Sandes would prefer Matt and himself to go to America rather than staying to become charges of the parish. Surprisingly, the land agent took the opposite view.

"This is the right time to be staying on the land, Keane, not to be leaving," he said as he slumped wearily into the recesses of the high-backed chair in his study. "There are so many acres going begging which you could rent for peppercorns. As you've impressed upon me before, plenty follows scarcity. Well then, now is the time to invest your time."

"My mind is certain, Mr. Sandes. I'm not looking to my future, God knows, but to the youngster's. All I'm wishing to retain of the farm are the fields containing the cabin and the family graves. The remainder can be turned over to a new tenant, if you can find one," Jack declared.

"A new tenant, eh? It'll be difficult finding one. Are you sure you won't stay?"

"I'm certain."

"Then, as you like, Keane. As you like," Sandes muttered almost apathetically. His grey appearance and apparent disinterest bore the hallmarks of a man who knew he had little time left.

"Tis Matt I'm thinking of. That's all."

Sandes leaned forward. He coughed wheezily. "The young man has been told of his relationship to me?"

"Aye. Some years past."

"And he has the preference to be going with you rather than relying on this relationship for an advantage hereabouts?"

"That he does."

"Spirited, is he?" Sandes interrupted.

"As his mother," Jack replied shortly.

The land agent smiled wanly, acknowledging the implied rebuke.

"Twas the boy who wanted to keep a hold on the cabin

and the graves," Jack continued. "So I'm thinking he might be returning one day. The rent will be sent from America to keep those two fields."

"Fear not, Keane. I shall give instructions that the young man shall have first call on that land."

"Then, tis a final farewell I'll bid you, Mr. Sandes. Whatever happens, I'm sure I'll be spending the years which remain to me in America. Three crossings are enough for one lifetime."

"As you say, Keane, a final farewell. Even if you return, I shall be in a better place than this benighted land."

Jonathan Sandes held out his right hand. "Once, at least, Keane. Just once," he said quietly.

Jack hesitated for a moment then shook the proffered hand. "It changes nothing," he muttered.

"I know. I know," Sandes replied wearily. "But then it doesn't matter, does it? At the end nothing matters really except the end itself."

Two weeks later, Jack and Matt played hosts at a farewell ceilidh. The drinking and dancing went on into the early hours while they entertained the twenty or so friends and neighbors they were leaving behind. During the evening they divided among their guests the cabin's furniture, the four remaining chickens in the run, and the sacks of maize and turnips still stored in the outhouse.

After a few hours sleep, Jack Keane and Matt Aherne woke and washed, before kneeling in silent prayer before the cross and the tattered picture of the Virgin Mary set into the cabin wall.

"Lord, let this be the right way for us," Jack prayed. "Let us journey in safety."

"Lord, let me return one day," Matt asked.

When the prayers were finished, Jack stowed the cross

and the Virgin's picture in the bundle of clothes and rugs
which were strapped to his horse for the journey to Tarbert
where he hoped to find a ship.

"The graves, Jack-Da?" Matt asked as he closed the
cabin door behind him.

"Aye, lad, for a moment. Then we must be away."

The two of them stood in front of the headstones for a few
minutes. Jack stooped to snap a sprig of the fresh bunch of
hawthorn lying on Brigid Aherne's grave. He handed it to
Matt.

"Here . . . carry this with you always, then you can be
sure of returning one day if you want."

Matt nodded, too full of emotion to risk speaking.

"A long time ago," Jack said gently, "I was told never to
look back. Tis good advice. Carry your memories in your
heart, but never look back, lad."

Matt Aherne smiled gratefully at his guardian, then
looked away. He had never seen a grown man crying
before.

Chapter 3
April, 1847

Captain Josiah Swain had converted the *Egypt* to carry passengers only when he had realized the size of the lucrative trade to be had from the Irish who were fleeing from famine and disease. His instructions to the ship converters at Liverpool had been precise: as many bunks as could be fitted into the main hold with a long table and benches down the center of the deck. Nothing more, nothing less. What could people expect for a £5 passage between the Shannon and Boston, the comfort and speed of Brunel's new iron steamship *Great Britain*? Captain Swain's conscience was untroubled as his passengers—men, women and children—continued to suffer during the fifth day since the *Egypt* with its 258 passengers had left the shelter of the Shannon.

Another spasm of seasickness gripped Matt Aherne as the ship wallowed in the heavy Atlantic swell. He groaned and pressed his face into the foul-smelling lump of cloth stuffed with straw which served as a pillow.

The air in the passengers' hold was rank and fetid. The planks of the deck were slippery with vomit and human waste. Babies howled continuously in their distress and fear in the enclosed world between decks. The creaking timbers, vile smells, swinging oil lamps and heaving decks were terrifying to youngsters used to green fields and fast-running skies.

339

The few passengers who, like Jack Keane, had some familiarity with the sea tried to ease the general suffering.

"Am I dying, Jack-Da?" Matt mumbled, colorless bile dribbling down his chin.

Jack knelt by the bunk and wiped it away. He was confident that Matt would recover shortly but he feared for some of the undernourished babies and young children. The worst affected lay supine in their bunks, hardly ever crying, their eyes bright and feverish, fixed and staring.

"Have you no medicines aboard?" Jack demanded of one of the crew when he was stumping around with that day's water ration.

"Medicine, mate? This is a blurry sailing ship—not a lying-in hospital. There's no medicine in Cap'n Swain's ships 'cept maybe some rum."

"'Tis for the children," said Jack. "Can you not be seeing that the wee ones are dying? They're needing something to help them take nourishment."

"Is that the truth then?" the seaman replied sarcastically. He dropped his pail heavily by Jack. Some of the water splashed over Matt, who tried to sit up.

Jack rose to his feet, glaring at the seaman. "'Tis your manners need improving, I'm thinking, sailor."

The seaman, sharp faced and skinny, slid a hand towards the knife sheathed on his belt. Jack stepped forward and lashed out with a roundhouse punch. The seaman staggered back, and slipped on the wet planks. His arms flailed wildly as he crashed backwards and the back of his head struck the edge of a bunk with a sharp crack.

Jesus, Jack thought, your man's cracked his skull open. He bent over the seaman, looking for signs of life. There was still a strong pulse in his wrist. Jack heaved a sigh of relief, picked up the pail of water and emptied it over the prone man.

The seaman's eyes flickered open. "I'll kill the bastard. I'll kill him."

"You're lucky, sailor. You've had a bad knock."

The seaman wrenched himself away from Jack's grasp. His eyes showed his fury as he looked his assailant up and down. They softened slightly when they took in Jack's girth and obvious strength.

"Are you recovered then?" Jack asked, genuine concern in his voice.

The seaman glowered. "Like a footpad that was. Struck when I wasn't looking," he declared indignantly to anyone in hearing. The incident, in fact, had happened so quickly that few passengers had noticed it. "Cap'n Swain'll know of this. Attacking the crew."

He swayed toward the ladder and began climbing upwards. When he was within a few steps of the main deck, he turned his head. "Blurry Irish, the lot of you. Best if your brats do die."

Jack stooped over Matt again when the seaman had vanished from sight. "Thanks be to God, lad," he muttered as he bathed his brow. " I thought that was the second man I'd killed."

But Jack's relief lasted only a few minutes. He heard heavy sea boots clumping on the deck above him and then begin descending the ladder toward the passengers' quarters.

"That's him," cried a voice from the top of the ladder. "There's the rat who attacked me."

"Stay still or it'll be the worse for you," another stronger voice commanded. Jack, peering up into the light, could make out three men on the ladder. One of them, burly and dark-bearded, carried what appeared to be a blunderbuss. It glinted darkly as it pointed down at Jack.

"Right then. Come up here. Up the ladder and quick

about it," ordered the man with the blunderbuss. Jack presumed this must be Captain Swain, and reluctantly began to clamber up the ladder. The three men retreated before him, but although the captain walked backwards, the blunderbuss never wavered in its aim.

Jack blinked against the strong daylight as he stepped on to the open deck.

"Yes, that's him, Cap'n. Definite."

"You know who I am?" the man in the cap asked.

"Captain Swain, the master?"

"That's right. And you are . . . ?"

"Keane. Jack Keane from Drombeg in Kerry."

"Then, Jack Keane, why did you attack one of my crew?"

In a few terse sentences Jack told him what had happened below.

"True, Sims?" the captain barked. "Did you spill water over him? Did you reach for your knife?"

"Defending myself I was, Cap'n."

Captain Swain lowered the blunderbuss and let it hang by his side. But his finger stayed on the trigger guard. "Riled you, did he, Keane?"

"He didn't seem to care for the suffering creatures below, Captain."

"And should he? They've only the seasickness. They'll recover."

"But the wee ones are in a mortal state, Captain."

"The law says they're to have seven pounds of provisions each week and that's what they're getting."

"They can't eat, Captain. And what they drink, they can't hold down."

Captain Swain looked quizzically across at the man wearing the leather jerkin. "Is that true, Master Mate?"

"No one's told me, Cap'n."

"Haven't you inspected the passengers?"

"Gone below?" the mate said incredulously. "Not since we slipped Tarbert Island, Cap'n. They're having the food and water, I know that."

Captain Swain scowled at his mate. "And what if they're dying on us? Pretty name that'll give this ship." He heaved a sigh. "I suppose I'll have to look for myself," he said, and handed the blunderbuss to the mate. "Stay here but come running if you hear my shout. And don't be afeared of using the weapon." He turned to Jack. "You first . . . and no trouble or your friends will be scraping bits of you from the deck."

Jack started down the ladder with the captain close behind him. After breathing fresh salt air on the deck, the stench of the passengers' quarters was even more oppressive.

Captain Swain coughed and gagged. He pressed a large red handkerchief to his mouth and nostrils.

"Tis your ship, Captain," Jack said sarcastically. "Not a pretty smell, is it?"

The captain waved him on. Jack led him round the bunks, pointing to those in most suffering. At one bunk, he stopped to pick up a baby which was scarcely a year old. He held the child out to the captain. The baby's head dropped sideways because of its lack of strength. The wrapping shawl was stained and stiff with dried vomit. Captain Swain pushed Jack aside and hurried back to the ladder leading upwards. Jack placed the baby gently back in the bunk and murmured some comforting words before following him.

"Well, Captain?" he asked. The captain didn't answer for a moment as he gulped in deep breaths of fresh air.

"It's bad, Keane. I'll give you that. And I should have been told earlier."

"What are you going to do? You cannot just let them die in their own filth like that."

Captain Swain gestured helplessly. "There are no physicians out here, Keane, and my crew are no nurses. The provisions and water they've been having are all that we've aboard. They're in God's hands."

"Have you any opiates?" Jack asked, an idea forming in his mind.

"Opiates?"

"For when any of your crew is hurt . . ."

"Rum?"

"Anything else?"

"Oh, come to reckon it now, my wife did buy some laudanum to ease any ache aboard."

Jack smiled. "Tis not much, Captain, but I've heard tell that such an opiate does settle the stomach. What if we made porridge from the oats in the provisions and then laced it with your laudanum? Such a stirabout would help them, I'm thinking."

"Anything, Keane. Anything," Captain Swain replied quickly. "The crew will help but you'll have to feed the sick ones yourself. Seamen don't like being near such people. They know disease and illness can spread on ships. They're mortal frightened of that."

That afternoon, Jack and the few other passengers who'd found their sea legs began dosing the sick with the mixture of porridge and laudanum. They waited anxiously to see if they could hold down the food and were pleased when most did. The feeding was repeated every three hours and before long most of those who had been sick were able to leave their bunks and get up on deck for fresh air. Inevitably, some of the babies were too ill to respond.

Nine days out of the Shannon, the crew and passengers of the *Egypt* stood bareheaded on the main deck as Captain

Swain intoned a prayer over eleven small canvas bundles. The mothers of the dead children sobbed quietly during the brief, makeshift burial service, then began shrieking hysterically as, at a signal from the captain, the pathetic little bundles were sent splashing into the Atlantic. The suddenness of the burial, its harsh irrevocability, stunned most of the passengers.

"Poor wee mites," murmured Matt Aherne as he stood alongside Jack Keane. "They survived all the death at home only to die on their way to their new life."

Jack looked at the youngster closely. He was still weak from his prolonged bout of seasickness but the color was beginning to return to his cheeks. Jack rubbed at the dark rings of tiredness under his eyes. "We've a deal of ocean to travel yet in this old ship before we reach Boston town. Think not so much on them who've gone to their Maker. They might be the lucky ones. Think more on us surviving the voyage."

"You've a seaman's philosophy, Keane," Captain Swain interrupted as he strode over toward them. "You've travelled the ocean before?"

"Crossed the Atlantic twice, so I have."

"Then, Keane," the captain said, "I shall be wanting help from you. You can be the go-between between myself and the passengers. I'm sure they'll be happier to be told what's going on by one of their own."

"If twill help . . . The coffin ships are in their minds all the time. Everyone knows of the ship which left Westport and then sank in sight of land with all the relatives still watching from the shore."

Captain Swain gave him a sharp look. "The *Egypt* will carry you to the Americas, that she will. With these winds I'm reckoning on another thirty days or so."

For the next three weeks, the old sailing ship bucketed

and wallowed her way steadily westwards. The passengers became accustomed to shipboard life, even organizing ceilidhs to keep their spirits high. Some of the young children continued to suffer from diarrhea but the general health of the emigrants remained fairly high. Then one day in the middle of the fifth week of the voyage with landfall not another seven days away, Matt was strolling on the main deck with Jack when he pointed to a man sitting alone on the opposite side of the deck.

"Has he the toothache, Jack-Da?" he asked. "His face is awful swollen, so it is."

"Aye, lad, it is that. Are you knowing who he is?"

"Murphy, I think. Willie Murphy from Foynes."

Jack sauntered casually across the deck toward the man. A few feet from him, he stopped and took a closer look at Murphy's face. Not only was it swollen, but the complexion was dark and congested, almost blue in color.

"How's it going then, Willie?" he asked, still keeping his distance.

"Not too good, friend," Murphy replied through swollen lips. "All of a sudden I've this bloated feeling all over me. Strange it is. Like I'm swelling up."

There was a definite smell coming from Murphy. It reminded Jack of rotting vegetables. Immediately he knew where he had smelt it before. It had been in a cabin at Gortacrossane where an entire family had died from the black fever, typhus.

"Oh, Lord," Jack murmured under his breath. And then aloud as casually as he could, "How's the family, then, Willie?"

"Just fine now they've their sealegs."

"I'm thinking you should be staying away from them for a bit, Willie," he said quietly, almost apologetically.

Murphy grasped the ship's rail and pulled himself to his

feet. "What are you saying, Mr. Keane?" he demanded, concern mounting in his voice.

"Just that, Willie. It might be nothing but from the look of you, you could have caught what's called a spreading illness."

"Like the black fever?" Murphy was now thoroughly alarmed.

"Aye, like the fever. But that's not saying you've got it. Why, Captain Swain'll probably find you a cabin all to yourself. Just you stay here, breathing all this fine air, and I'll be fixing you up. Don't you be worrying yourself."

"And the woman and the four wee ones below?"

"Leave them to me, Willie. Sure and I'll be telling them enough to soothe them and yet not enough to frighten them."

Jack hurried below to Captain Swain's sparse cabin.

"Come to see the latest position, Keane?" the captain asked with a smile. He pointed to a cross on the map. "There we are. With these southeasterlies as they are, you should be seeing Boston again in four days or so. Ahead of time for once. I told you she was a good old . . ."

"Would that it was tomorrow, Captain," Jack said.

"Eh? Impatient aren't you?"

"Tis not that. If I'm right then we've real trouble aboard. I'm reckoning one of the passengers is sickening with black fever."

"Black fever?"

"That's how tis known in Ireland. Typhus is the . . ."

Captain Swain jumped to his feet, knocking his chair over in alarm.

"Typhus! Merciful Christ, not that. We'll all be dead." He paused and tugged at his beard. "How many are down?"

"Only one that I know. He's on deck at present. I'm

thinking the sooner we put him somewhere on his own the better chance we'll all have."

"Are you sure, man?"

"Have I not seen enough cases of black fever in the last year?"

"I remember one ship I was in as first mate. Near three-quarters of the crew died, they did. We'll get him below into the mate's cabin and lock him in."

"I'll check the other passengers."

"Right. But be careful." Captain Swain beat his fist against his forehead. "Oh, Christ, this would happen. Only a few more days . . . only a few . . ."

"There'll be help in Boston, I'm thinking, Captain."

"If we ever reach there. Pray that the fever doesn't strike the crew or we're all done for."

Half an hour later, Jack escorted the sick man down to the mate's cabin, ensured that adequate provisions and fresh water had been placed there for him, and then locked him in. He tried to turn the key as quietly as he could but still Willie Murphy heard the click.

"What's this you're doing?" he shouted through the door, pounding on the wood. "Don't be leaving me here alone, for God's sake."

"Tis for everyone's good, Willie," Jack shouted back. "We're not wanting a person to wander into the cabin by mistake."

"So tis the fever I've got then," Murphy half-sobbed. "Oh, Jesus have mercy on me."

"Hush there, Willie. Tis just a precaution as I said." Jack hated himself at that moment.

Murphy began hammering on the door again, crying in rage and fear. "Have pity, for mercy's sake," he screamed. "Don't lock me away like an animal. My woman. The wee ones. Oh, Jesus, you cannot be doing this . . ."

Willie Murphy's screams stayed in Jack's ears even when he was out of hearing. On deck, he explained to Matt what had happened.

"We'll be sleeping topside till we reach Boston, lad, and keeping ourselves to ourselves. Tis our only hope and I'm thinking you'd be better by staying away from me as well." Jack took a step away from the youngster. "But don't be worrying," he said reassuringly. "I've not survived all these years to be letting the fever get me."

Matt smiled at his bravado.

Willie Murphy's wife, Mary, was stunned by the news that he had been isolated in the mate's cabin. Her four children, the eldest only eight years old, failed to understand what Jack told them.

"When will we be seeing our da then?" one of them asked.

"Don't be fretting yourself, little one," Jack answered. "I'll be looking after you while your da's getting better."

"Getting better, Mr. Keane?" their mother said bitterly, an accusing look on her face. "Getting better, did you say?"

Jack felt wretched. He could only nod as he moved away from the family whose world had just been destroyed.

"And will we be getting better too?" the woman's shrill voice, edged with hysteria, followed him. "Or will we be hearing some more of your fine words when you'll be putting us all away?"

The first inspection of the passengers failed to find anyone else with noticeable fever symptoms, but the inspection itself, coupled with rumors about Willie Murphy, spread fear and despondency throughout the *Egypt*. That Willie Murphy had typhus was clear by the evening of that day.

Jack and Captain Swain went to the mate's cabin after

supper. They approached the door quietly. Jack slipped the key into the lock and softly turned it. There was little need to enter the cabin to realize that Murphy's condition had deteriorated. The smell was almost intolerable and from inside came the sound of the diseased man's delirious ravings.

Within the next forty-eight hours, as the *Egypt* drew nearer and nearer Boston, the symptoms of typhus appeared in another fourteen passengers, most of them women and children, including the entire Murphy family. There was nowhere else to isolate them so they were kept below in their quarters while the remaining passengers rigged what shelter they could on the main deck. Captain Swain posted an armed guard above the passengers' quarters to ensure the infected ones stayed below. The guard had to be changed hourly because the seamen became upset by the stench and horrendous noises reaching them.

Captain Swain set every square foot of canvas that could be safely carried on the masts of his old ship to urge her toward a quicker landfall. About mid-morning on the 38th day of the voyage, a great cheer swept into the wind as the look-out spied the first grey smudge on the horizon. A few more hours and it became clear that the captain's navigation had been immaculate as the *Egypt* beat her way along the coast of Cape Cod before heading into Massachusetts Bay.

"We'll lay off for the night," the delighted captain told Jack. "And then it's Boston Harbor in the morning. I don't think I've ever been so pleased to reach port in my life."

"Not before time, Captain. Not before time. Another few days and I'm guessing we'd all have contracted the fever."

At dawn the next day, the *Egypt* started to move up the bay toward Boston but when she was still some fifteen miles out the man in the crow's nest sang out, "Sail three points on the starboard bow."

Captain Swain peered through his telescope. He could make out the sleek lines of a small cutter flying the Stars and Stripes.

"What course do you make, Cap'n? She's making a signal now."

The captain steadied his telescope on the rail to read the fluttering, colored message flags in the cutter's rigging. "Heave to. Boarding party alongside," he deciphered.

The captain shouted the orders to reduce sail. The *Egypt* slowed in the water. The passengers crowded the rails as the cutter slipped under the stern of the larger ship into a parallel course fifty yards astern.

A voice came faintly across the water between the vessels. "Who are you? Identify yourself."

Captain Swain pressed his hailing trumpet to his mouth. "The *Egypt*, 39 days out of the Shannon, bound for Boston. We've more than 200 passengers aboard. Who are you?"

"The *Lexington* carrying the Boston port physician. Have you any sickness aboard, *Egypt*?"

Captain Swain grimaced at Jack. "So that's it," he said. "A sick inspection, is it?" Then he shouted his reply to the cutter, "A few cases of ship's fever, *Lexington*."

"Heave to, *Egypt*. The physician will board you."

The captain bellowed orders for all but a small mizzen sail to be reefed in. The *Egypt* came to a virtual stop, only maintaining steerage way, pitching and rolling in the swell, the sea slapping against her hull.

"What'll be happening now?" Jack asked anxiously as he watched a rowing boat being lowered from the cutter.

"I'm not rightly knowing," Captain Swain replied, scratching his cheek nervously. "Could be the physician will take the sick ones off us before we enter harbor. It'd be a blessing, that would."

The rowing boat, with two seamen at the oars and two

passengers in the stern, pulled quickly alongside the *Egypt*.
The passengers—one in a frock coat and carrying a small
leather bag, the other wearing a blue naval uniform—
clambered agilely on to the main deck using the nets and
ladders heaved over the side for them. A crewman directed
them toward Captain Swain who stood by the wheelhouse,
an apprehensive Jack Keane beside him. As far as they both
knew, no restrictions had been placed on the entry of Irish
immigrants into the United States but they realized that
carrying typhus victims might be another matter.

"Good morning, Captain," the man in the naval uniform
called cheerily as he mounted the ladder to the wheelhouse
deck. "A good voyage, I'm trusting."

"Fair winds, sir. Fair winds."

"I'm Captain Tucker, sir, from the port cutter *Lexington*." He turned to his middle-aged companion. "And this
is Doctor Emmanuel Smithers, the official physician for the
port of Boston. He'll be wanting to examine your passengers, Captain . . . Captain?"

"Swain, sir. Josiah Swain." In turn he introduced Jack
and all four men shook hands.

"Some fever aboard, I understand," said Dr. Smithers.

"They're isolated below, sir, after taking sick not three
days ago."

"If I may see them, Captain." The request was polite but
carried the clear note of authority.

"As you wish."

The four men stood to one side as the hatch to the
passengers' quarters was opened. A cloud of foul air rolled
upwards and engulfed the inspection party. The doctor
looked severely at Captain Swain.

"Ship's fever you said, Captain?"

"Well . . . I'm no physician, sir," he replied, hesitantly. "That's what we were thinking . . ." His explanation tailed off lamely.

"The smell, Captain, hardly makes an inspection necessary but I shall go below." The physician pulled out a large silk handkerchief and knotted it around his nose and mouth before clambering down the ladder. Less than a minute later, he returned to the open deck.

"As I thought, gentlemen," he reported grimly as he pulled the handkerchief from his mouth. "Typhus fever and well advanced at that. I counted fourteen sick, Captain. Are there any more?"

"One, sir. The first to be affected. We placed him in a cabin aft and have kept a close watch on him. I fear he has little hope."

"Gangrene already," Jack interrupted.

Dr. Smithers shook his head. "This'll mean quarantine at the very least."

"Quarantine?" echoed Jack and Captain Swain.

"At Deer Island, some five miles from our present position," said Captain Tucker. "Because of the condition of some of the passengers from Ireland, Boston has found it necessary to set up a quarantine station on the island. New York has taken similar precautions."

"After all, many of your passengers may be carrying the fever," Dr. Smithers added. He looked round the emigrants gathered on the deck. "And I see you've some old folk aboard as well. That'll mean bonds being posted if they're to land at Boston after quarantine."

"A thousand dollars for each old 'un," explained Captain Tucker. "Your owners have the money?"

"I'm the owner, sir," Captain Swain bristled. "And I've not a sufficiency of funds for . . ."

"When did all this come about?" Jack demanded. "I know Boston and us Irish have always been welcome. Alderman Finucane wrote only months ago saying that."

"Finucane? You know Matt Finucane then?" the doctor asked curiously.

"Indeed I know him. Twas I who helped his first election nearly twenty years back. He held his victory party at my groggery, so he did."

"So you're that Keane, are you?" the doctor said, rubbing his chin thoughtfully. "To this day, Mr. Keane, your name is well known among the Irishers in Boston. I've often had cause to minister to your countrymen who work the docks and wharves."

"So then, Doctor, what's this quarantine and bonding?"

"The regulations are only a month old. So many sick and old are arriving from Ireland that the town council fears Boston will be swamped by them. There's fear of an epidemic and too heavy a charge on the community in caring for the elderly."

The doctor shook his head. "Unfortunate, Mr. Keane, but that is the plain truth of the matter. This ship'll have to lie off Deer Island for at least fourteen days and then, if the fever is cleared, there'll still be bonds to be posted for the elderly."

"We're done for, that's what," Captain Swain exclaimed, open despair in his voice. "I've no money for the bonds even if we survive the quarantine and I'm sure neither have the passengers."

He looked helplessly at Captain Tucker. "What can I do? We surely can't be the first ship here since your new regulations."

"Indeed not," Captain Tucker replied. He gazed down at the deck as he tried to conceal his feeling of embarrassment and shame. "Since you're sailing under English colors, I suggest you make for the colonies in Canada."

"That's the advice we're giving all British ships which cannot satisfy the port regulations," Dr. Smithers continued quickly. "It's not we're against helping the Irish but we must protect the citizens of Boston. Their welfare is the paramount responsibility. Surely you can recognize that?"

Jack sniffed contemptuously. The doctor grasped him by the elbow and led him to the rail. "You of all people, Mr. Keane, should understand our concern. But if you'll come ashore in the cutter I'm sure we can waive any regulations in your case. After all, sir, you're almost as much a Bostonian as . . ."

Jack pulled angrily away from his grip. "I'll not be wanting any favors. I've been travelling with these wretches and I'll not be leaving them now."

"But . . ."

"There are no buts, Doctor. Just be telling Matt Finucane what's happened. That's all I'll be asking of you," Jack said bitterly. "Just be reminding him of what he said once about people of all races being welcome in Boston."

Dr. Smithers reddened. "As you choose," he said stiffly.

"And before you return to the safety of your hospitable town, perhaps you'll be looking at the poor soul locked in the mate's cabin aft."

The doctor bowed slightly from the waist. Jack led him below decks, leaving the two sea captains to commiserate with each other.

"Now be careful here, Doctor," Jack warned as he slid the key into the cabin door. "Poor Willie's been raving and thrashing around for two days now."

"You have already made clear your opinion of myself

and my position," the doctor said coldly. "I'd be obliged if you would not question my medical training. Remain outside while I examine the patient."

Dr. Smithers entered the silent cabin as Jack stood outside, trying to avoid inhaling the awful smell. There was a murmuring inside before the doctor returned to the cabin door. His face was ashen. He held a hand over his mouth as if attempting to stop himself being sick.

"Any hope?" Jack asked.

The doctor shook his head. Then, as he stood with his back to the cabin, there was a terrible yell from inside and Willie Murphy burst out of the doorway. His charge hurled Dr. Smithers into Jack, knocking the breath out of both of them. By the time they'd recovered, Willie was halfway up the ladder leading to the main deck. Jack leapt after him but was unable to stop him reaching the open air.

Passengers screamed with horror and revulsion as Willie Murphy burst through the hatchway. His naked body was virtually black in color. His limbs were bloated to almost twice their normal width. Blood dripped from his fingers and toes and from the stumps of the teeth still in his mouth. He was roaring with pain and delirium as he ran towards a group of passengers by the rail. They drew back, terrified and hysterical, as Willie Murphy approached them.

Still screaming, he ran straight through them, bowling aside two children, hit the rail and toppled over the ship's side with a last shriek.

Jack and the doctor ran to the rail and looked down. Willie surfaced for a moment, face convulsed, arms splashing, before he sank again. There were a few ripples, a lungful of bubbles, and then nothing as he disappeared finally beneath the waters of Massachusetts Bay.

"The Lord's mercy upon him," muttered Dr. Smithers.

"You shouldn't be wasting your prayers on Willie, Doctor," said Jack, suddenly feeling very weary and drained. "He's the lucky one. He's finished his journey to the promised land."

Chapter 4
May, 1847

The small island looked enchanting from the St. Lawrence River. Trees and shrubs ambled down to the very edge of the lapping water. Long, low white sheds could be glimpsed through the vegetation. On a grassy knoll covered with wild flowers, a small wooden church poked its white spire into the blue sky. To those in the long line of ships standing off Grosse Island, thirty miles downstream from Quebec, it seemed the unlikeliest of places for the Canadian authorities to have established their official quarantine station.

At least twenty ships filled with emigrants had ventured up the St. Lawrence since the winter ice had cleared reluctantly from the river barely a fortnight before. More arrived each day. The passengers from continental Europe, particularly the Germans, were free from disease and, almost without exception, were allowed to proceed upriver in the two steamers, the *Queen* and the *John Nunn*, which made the three-day voyage to Montreal. As they sailed past Grosse Island, fiddlers playing tunes on the steamers' decks, the smiling, healthy passengers looked curiously at the rowing boats and longboats clustered round the island.

Jack Keane and Matt Aherne panted under their masks as they maneuvered a stretcher up from the passengers' quarters and onto the ship's main deck. They tried to avoid looking down at the patient strapped to the stretcher, at his grotesquely swollen limbs jerking against the binding ropes

359

in a typhus delirium. They carried the stretcher to the rail before lowering it, as gently as they could, over the side and into a longboat. Jack counted eight typhus victims already aboard, packed tightly into the well of the longboat. After pushing and pulling their diseased bodies enough room was made for the new arrival. The longboats sank lower in the water.

"Watch how you move, Irisher, else you'll capsize us," the boatman, a grizzled man of about sixty, called to Jack.

"How are you managing?" Jack asked, pulling down his handkerchief mask and wiping his brow.

"All I can do is take them to the shallow water. That's all. After that they make their own way ashore best they can," the boatman replied. "The island's got no landing pier," he added in explanation.

"But this is the third boatload from the *Egypt*," Jack protested. "Have they all been dumped ashore like that?"

"And the rest of them from the fever ships. Near on a thousand of 'em so far."

"Jesus," exclaimed Jack. He looked up at Matt who was peering over the rail. "Stay there, lad, and help all you can," he shouted. "I'm going ashore with this boat."

"Your choice, matey." The boatman shrugged his wide shoulders as if disclaiming all responsibility for Jack's decision. He picked up an oar and began sculling the longboat the few hundred yards to shore.

"Take care, Jack-Da," Matt hailed.

Jack waved back before wedging himself into the bow of the boat. "Are any recovering on the island?" he asked.

The boatman spat into the water. "In a hospital built for one hundred and fifty? Now they're putting 'em in the church, there're so many of 'em."

"'Tis really that bad?"

The boatman nodded. "Look behind you, matey. Just clap your eyes on the river."

Jack craned his neck round and saw that the longboat, only about fifty feet from Grosse Island, was nosing its way through lumps of bloodied straw gummed together with excrement, through lengths of stained bandage, through foul-smelling and discolored mattress covers, through bobbing barrels which leaked yellow pus and vomit.

The longboat scraped bottom twenty feet from dry land.

"Far as we go, matey," the boatman called, shipping his oar. He bent down over one of the typhus victims and began lifting him unceremoniously out of the boat and into the water.

"Hold fast. I'll help," Jack said as he jumped into the knee-deep water. He grasped the sick man around the waist and supported him while he floundered ashore. He turned in time to see the boatman heaving another typhus victim into the cold water.

"Can't you be waiting?" he cried.

"No time," the boatman repeated. "Hundreds more of 'em waiting in the ships to come ashore. Hundreds of 'em. Are you coming back with me?"

"I can't be leaving these in the water," Jack shouted.

"Suit yourself, matey. I'll be back later anyhow."

Jack looked around helplessly as the sick people flopped and flapped in the muddied shallows like a shoal of exhausted fish. Then two middle-aged priests, shirtsleeves rolled up, ran out of the trees and began carrying them onto firm ground.

"Holy Mother of God," one kept murmuring.

"There are scores more," Jack volunteered as he carried an elderly woman into the shade of the island's trees.

"'Tis a miracle they've reached here at all," the priest

grunted. "I'm Father Moylan and him over there is Father McQuirk," he added, gesturing at his colleague.

"Where do we take the sick anyway?" Jack asked. "They can't be staying in the open."

"The hospital's overflowing. The church is full. The sheds we put up not a week ago are packed. They've sent some tents from Montreal so we'll be using those but we haven't had time yet to bang in one peg," Father McQuirk said.

"Four doctors who volunteered are already down with typhus, God help them. No nurses will come anywhere near this island so there's only us, Father O'Reilly, and the medical officer, Dr. Douglas, to look after more than a thousand mortal-stricken people," sighed Father Moylan.

Jack shook his head in disbelief. "I've never seen anything like it. Not in all the suffering back home. Jesus, tis not a question of if I can be helping, but where."

"You're not afeared of the typhus?" Father McQuirk asked curiously.

"I've lived cheek by jowl with it for two weeks or more," Jack said, banging his chest with his fist. "See . . . still fit as any bog-trotter so I am."

Father Moylan laughed and clapped him on the shoulder. "Then, Master Jack Bog-Trotter, let's be showing you what's to be done before you change your mind."

Jack spent most of the day pitching the tents and moving the sick into them. When he'd finished he went off in search of some water and nourishment for the sick. The stench of disease and waste increased with every step he took toward the church and the hospital sheds set in the large clearing in the center of the island.

Jack peeked through the open doors of the pretty little church. Every pew bench and aisle was filled with the sick. A woman lay sprawled across the single step in front of the altar as if in prostrate prayer. The single cross on the altar cast its shadow over her back.

Jack walked down the knoll toward the largest hospital shed, a room of about a hundred and fifty feet by twenty feet filled with more than six hundred fever victims of all ages and both sexes. Father McQuirk stepped gingerly between them, offering ladles of water here and there to those who were strong enough to drink. Those who were too weak had a little water dribbled between their swollen lips.

"It's like we're treating the suffering of the entire world," Father McQuirk said wearily.

Jack shrugged his shoulders. "Those who can, help. Or rather those who can and who want to."

"The people of Boston who turned your ship away?"

"The people would help. Left to themselves, people of any country will help each other. But when the politicians have their say, it all happens different, doesn't it?"

The priest looked Jack straight in the eye and asked, "Will you be staying to help ease them, Jack? We've awful need of able-bodied men like you."

"What can I be doing, Father? They're all most likely to die, help or no help."

"Truly so. But even the smallest comfort will be a blessing for them. Anything that reminds them of their dignity as human beings. It's important to face your Maker as a human being not like pigs in a sty full of swinefever or cattle in a slaughterhouse." Father McQuirk turned and gazed back into the hospital shed. "This may be a charnel house," he said quietly, "but the love of God can be brought to it, the love of being for being."

Jack sighed. "I'll stay, Father. How could I be leaving after seeing all this? But before I buckle down a boatman has to take a message for my youngster."

Four times a day, boats brought the dead from the

emigrant ships continuing to arrive off the quarantine station. By the end of May, forty vessels waited in a line two miles long for clearance to unload their passengers on to the river steamers. Their dead came ashore wrapped simply in canvas or rudely boxed in coffins made from bunks.

Jack watched one lad, scarcely older than Matt, walk ashore, and slump down with his back against a tree. Jack went over to offer a ladle of water. The youngster, his clothes tattered and dirty, shook his head weakly so Jack left him alone. Twenty minutes later he walked back past the same tree. Father Moylan was kneeling beside him, administering the last rites.

"When I came by I thought he was asleep in the sun," the priest said when he had finished. "But when I looked closer I could see he had gone from us."

"He's only a youngster like Matt, so he is."

"I think he was simply too weak to manage. He's probably had no proper food nor rest for weeks. He just gave up the ghost."

Jack swayed slightly as a wave of dizziness passed over him.

"Are you unwell, son?" asked the priest, jumping to his feet in concern.

Jack waved him away. "Tired, Father. Tis tired I am. Just that." He steadied himself by holding on to the tree trunk. "I'm thinking of Matt. If this poor lad can keel over and die like that, then how's my youngster going on?"

"Are you wanting to go back to your ship then?"

"I reckon I must, Father. Tis about time we were free from quarantine and heading upriver."

A boatman rowed Jack back to the *Egypt*, swinging serenely at anchor in the wide river. He wondered how many tens of thousands of Irish people had perished in their attempts to reach America and how many more were waiting to risk the crossing. If only he had known the truth, Jack thought, he would have taken the shorter route to the English slums in Liverpool, Birmingham or London. Matt and he might not have had such opportunities in front of them but at least they would not have faced death at such close quarters.

A shout of welcome pulled him out of his morbid thoughts. He looked up and saw Matt's face grinning down at him as the rowing boat slipped into the shadow of the *Egypt*. Jack jumped for the ladder. Suddenly, his strength left him. He rested for a good minute before he started climbing slowly upwards. When he was nearly at the top, panting with exertion, Matt clambered over the rail to pull him up the last few feet.

Jack staggered when his feet hit the main deck. The familiar faces of Matt and the captain whirled in front of him and he fell into blackness. Matt's voice, anxious, pleading, came from a long way off as he slid back into consciousness. He came around sitting under the ship's rail. He blinked to focus his eyes.

"You scared us, Jack-Da," Matt said, holding out a mug.

Jack took a sip and spluttered. The rum brought him fully to his senses.

"How are you, lad?" he asked, smiling up at Matt.

"He's fine, Keane. Fit as a flea," Captain Swain said cheerfully. "More to the point, how are you? Falling aboard like that. You're sure you're well, Keane?"

"Aye, Captain. Just hand me to my feet and give me another sip of rum." Jack gripped on to the rail as another wave of dizziness struck him. "That rum's mighty powerful after a time away from it," he laughed weakly.

"You're back for good?"

"Aye, Captain. We've been doing our best but I'm

fearing tis a lost battle. No opiates, no surgical tools, no bedding, no more tents nor sheds, nothing more but prayer and that's running out mighty fast, so it is." He paused to clear his throat. All of a sudden it felt closed and rough. "When are you free from quarantine and off-loading your passengers into the river steamers?"

"That's why we were awful glad to see you, Keane. What passengers are left can be leaving tomorrow."

"How many?"

"Out of the 257 who left the Shannon," Captain Swain said quietly, "there are only 89 left here. The rest are in their graves or on that cursed island."

"That's . . . that's . . ." Jack was unable to think clearly for a moment.

"One hundred and sixty-eight dead or wishing they were, God rest 'em."

Jack sighed then smiled at Matt. "Still the main thing is you're fine, lad. And so will I be after a night's rest. Then tis off to Montreal in the morning."

"It's bad there, Keane. The steamer captain who came aboard yesterday said the Irish were dying in their hundreds in the sheds along the old wharves. The fever's everywhere. Even the priests and politicians trying to ease the sick are catching the fever. You'll only be safe when you're in the barges for Kingston and beyond. Reach Lake Ontario, the captain said, and you're halfway safe. But not till then."

"Does it never end?" Jack asked despairingly. "Does it never end?"

But he cheered up a little after taking some more rum from the captain's private stock. For the passengers' last night in the *Egypt*, the captain had thrown all his usual financial caution overboard by purchasing a dozen wild turkeys from one of the boatmen. They were devoured voraciously by people who hadn't tasted fresh meat in two months or more but Jack could only pick at his portion.

"You're not sickening, Jack-Da?" Matt asked when they'd rolled themselves into their blankets under the deck awning.

Jack shivered. He didn't feel well, he had to admit, but he didn't want to alarm the lad. "Go to sleep, you gosseen," he said as lightly as he could. "These old bones need some rest after all their slaving on that island, that's all. Don't be worrying yourself."

Jack slept heavily, dreamlessly, for a few hours before waking. His body was burning, and there was something else, he realized with growing dread. A swelling feeling; a sense of his limbs bloating up, of becoming heavier. "Holy Mother of God," he whispered to himself, his eyes closed, his jaw clenched in awful fear. He gulped, unable to put his thoughts into words, even to form them in his brain. "Jesus, not me. Not me," he muttered.

Jack kicked his blanket aside and shifted a yard away from Matt who was soundly asleep. He held his hands in the dim light from the four lanterns hung round the deck. Was he imagining it? Were his hands turning darker? And swelling? Jack pressed them together as hard as he could. There was a definite numbness in them. He peered closely at his fingers one by one. Yes, they were rounder and their nails were darker.

There was no doubt in his mind. He had seen the symptoms too often for that. He had typhus fever. How long before he became a helpless, twitching victim, unable to think coherently or talk intelligibly? He had to speak to Matt before that happened. There was so much to tell him with so little time left. He leaned over and shook the youngster awake.

"What . . . what is it?" Matt woke, his eyes wide with alarm.

"I must speak to you, Matt."

"Now, Jack-Da? Tis the middle of the night. Why now?"

"Because there's not much time, lad. Don't be getting upset now with what I've to tell you."

Matt peered closely at him in the half light. His eyes reflected the shock of what he saw.

Jack watched the expression on his face. "There's little doubt, lad," he whispered hoarsely. "I've the fever."

"Oh, God! Jack-Da. Oh no!" Matt sobbed.

"Tis no respecter of age or person, lad. Be remembering that," he said gently.

Strangely, a weight had been lifted from him by confiding his fear, his certainty, to Matt. He felt calmer as he began to talk of the inevitable.

"When light comes, Matt, be seeing that I'm taken to the island. Make sure that the priests are knowing I'm there. I'm sure they'll do all they can for me."

"You're stronger than any man alive, Jack-Da. You'll beat the fever."

Jack smiled at the youngster's attempt to cheer him up. "Aye, lad, the old faction fighter's strong, so he is. Mighty strong. Twill take more than a rotten old fever to put him in a box, and that's the truth. But I still can't be going upriver. Don't you see I'd be infecting the others?"

"Then I won't be leaving, Jack-Da." Matt spoke firmly.

"And isn't that what I want to speak of, lad? If there's bad fever in Montreal, there's little point in going there or even to Kingston. We've no friends there. No, leave me on the island and strike out for Boston. Tis less than three hundred miles. A strong lad like you will stride it easily in two weeks or so."

"But how can I leave you alone here?"

Matt went to pat Jack's arm but the older man drew back.

"Don't be touching me, lad," he warned. "One of us has to be reaching Boston. You're the last of the Ahernes from Gortacrossane. Be remembering that." Jack lowered his voice. "Listen well, Matt. In my chest stowed below . . . you know it . . . there's a secret drawer at the bottom. The catch is one of the nails at the side. In the drawer there are twenty or more sovereigns. Enough for you to hire a boatman to take you to the south bank of the river. More than enough to see you through the journey. But be careful slipping ashore. I'm guessing there'll be Yankee guards posted all along the river and the border to stop any Irish crossing." Jack paused. He ran his tongue round his mouth to moisten it. His throat was closing fast. "When you reach Boston, and all trails east lead to it, go near the harbor and ask anyone for Matt Finucane. He'll help, so he will. I'll be joining you as soon as I can so tell Finucane to be saving a position for me."

Tears welled in Matt's eyes and began to roll down his cheeks.

"I can't be leaving you alone, Jack-Da," he said fiercely. "Not on that island. Not alone."

"Can't you be seeing that I'm not alone, lad." Jack lay back, his strength dissipating fast. "When you've had a life like mine, Matt," he continued, his words becoming slurred, "when you've seen the things I've seen, then you're not alone . . . when you're older you'll know that . . . you're not alone. Haven't I told you that the only life worth living, worth a fiddler's damn, is in your head? And that's where I'm not alone. So many people . . . so many . . . thoughts . . . memories . . . so many . . ." His voice trailed away. He was silent for a minute. Then he croaked, "Can you be getting me some water, lad. I'm awful hot and parched. Can hardly talk."

Matt hurried over to a pail of water lying on the deck and returned with a ladleful. He held the ladle steady for Jack to take a drink. Even this small effort seemed to exhaust the sick man. He groaned at his own weakness.

"Are you afeared, Jack-Da?" Matt asked tentatively, curiously.

"Afeared, lad?" Jack coughed again, his chest heaving painfully. It was now becoming difficult for him to speak. "No, there's no fear in me. When you're so near . . . maybe you're . . . no, tis not fear . . . only a mighty reluctance." Jack smiled and repeated, "Only a mighty reluctance, so it is." He held his right hand into the light again, looked at it closely, then screwed his eyes shut in his distress.

"Rest, Jack-Da," Matt implored. "Don't be speaking on. Rest your strength."

Jack waved his protests away. "Not long while I can speak, lad. Then will be the gibbering. Close your ears to that, for I'll be saying words from the fever . . . words that are in the dark parts of me . . . Be ignoring them, lad, while you're remembering what I'm saying now."

"You're a stubborn one, Jack-Da. You're real stubborn."

Jack tried to smile at the youngster but the grin was merely a grimace of swollen lips. "We Irish have to be stubborn, don't we? Else we'll never have our own land again. Once we possessed it but we fought each other and delivered Ireland to the English, so we did." Jack's eyes were closed now. His voice had become so much of a whisper that Matt was forced to lean closer in order to hear him at all. "Tis when we learn the value of freedom that we'll be uniting . . . and when that happens we'll be taking our land back from the English. It'll happen one day, lad. I'm praying twill be this suffering, this history, that'll be bringing the Irish together one day . . . Aye, together one day . . . together . . . together, Brigid . . . Brigid . . ."

Jack's voice died away and then, suddenly, he sat up, his eyes staring in alarm. "What was I saying, lad? Was I seeing your mam? Was she in my mind?"

Matt put an arm around his shoulders and pressed him gently back on to the blanket. The youngster started to cry silently as he realized his guardian's delirium had begun.

By morning, Matt could look quite calmly on Jack's swollen, twitching features and limbs. He felt that Jack had already gone from him. The sick man he and Captain Swain helped load into a boat to be taken to Grosse Island was no longer Jack Keane. Matt didn't want to—he wouldn't—remember him in this condition. He would remember him as he was; a brave, laughing man who had looked life squarely in the face and had regretted nothing.

Despite the pleadings of Captain Swain, Matt insisted on accompanying Jack to the island. There, he helped the priests nurse him through the fever for the next three days. He bathed and cleaned him and sat by his side, restraining him throughout his delirious agony.

On the fourth morning, just as first light crept across the island, Matt woke from a brief sleep on the floor of the church, next to the pew where his guardian lay. His heart leapt when he saw Jack's eyes were suddenly clear. He bent over him, smiling. The eyes smiled back from their ravaged sockets. For a moment they held all their old strength. Then they glazed over and rolled upwards. There were no tears left in Matt Aherne, none at all.

Chapter 5
June, 1847

The young man, black hair drooping over his forehead, sat on the edge of the bed and scuffed his bare feet in the rich pile of the carpet. He looked around the bedroom, his gaze lingering on the wardrobe, the dressing table, the two chairs, and the curtains half-pulled across the windows. He pushed himself off the bed, walked over to the dressing table and ran his hand gently, almost reverentially, round the neck of the china pitcher in its wide bowl before the mirror. He cocked his head a fraction, listening intently to the faint creaking noises of the house.

Matt Aherne thought that he'd never been so alone before. Being alone in a closed room was different from being alone in the fields or woods. He knew that there were people in the other bedrooms of Alderman Finucane's Dorchester home, but within his own room it was as if they did not exist. Here he felt master of his own destiny. He liked that. The thought filled him with tingling excitement.

His mind drifted back over the past three weeks or so of his journey from the St. Lawrence River to Massachusetts. Matt had little doubt that Jack-Da would have been proud of him. He had kept a wary eye for Yankee border patrols after being landed at a small settlement on the south bank some five miles upstream from Grosse Island. He'd come ashore dressed in the warmest of clothes from Jack-Da's sea chest with two rugs strapped on his back and the pair of pistols

373

round his waist. The sight of only one of his twenty-two gold sovereigns had brought instant, almost overwhelming service and advice from the owner of the log-built store at the little town perched between forest and river. Matt bought dried strips of venison, biscuits, beans and oatmeal and asked, as off-handedly as he could, directions towards the east.

"Just keep to the main tracks and paths, son," the storekeeper had advised. "That way you won't be getting lost in the forests and mountains or meeting any Redskins."

"And how will I be knowing if I'm heading in the right direction then?" Matt had asked, beginning to worry as he realized that he would be journeying through entirely wild territory. He knew that the West of Ireland was considered desolate and underpopulated by strangers but his new surroundings had the daunting magnificence peculiar to country virtually untrodden by man.

The storekeeper had laughed at his question. "Why, son, it's mighty easy to see you're no woodsman. Now all you do is face the sun in the morning—and the birds'll make sure you don't oversleep—then keep it at your right hand during the day and make certain it's on the back of your neck at dusk. That way you'll be heading roughly east. But don't be fretting yourself too much. If you do what I'm saying and stick to the main tracks you're bound to be meeting other travellers more versed than yourself."

Matt spent the first night of his journey alone, cold and extremely fearful, under a bush about ten miles along the track leading east from the settlement. The sounds of the forest, the night calls of the animals, ensured only fitful sleep and he was glad to leave his resting place at first light and chew a breakfast strip of venison as he continued along the main track through the trees. After an hour's trudging along the rutted surface of dried mud Matt heard the unmis-

takable creaking of wheels round the next bend. He broke in
to a run, pack bumping on his back, to catch up with an
uncovered wagon pulled sedately by two large workhorses.
A man wearing a broad-brimmed hat held the reins loosely
in his hands. A woman in a sun bonnet was beside him on
the driving seat, her arm casually around the shoulders of a
young boy. The rumblings of the swaying wagon forced
Matt to shout to gain their attention. The man immediately
dropped the reins and reached behind the driving box. Matt
found himself staring into the shining barrel of a flintlock
musket. He skidded to a halt. Still panting from his dash, he
moved his arms away from his own weapons. The middle-
aged man on the wagon studied him for interminable
moments, squinting through the crude musket sight.

"And where might you have sprung from, youngster?"
the man asked finally, his voice low and determined.

"Back there. Just back there, sir," Matt replied. "I heard
the wagon . . ."

"Squawking like a Redskin, you were," the man said
accusingly. "Near scared me britches off. What you be
wanting anyway?"

"Well, I was just thinking . . ." Matt began lamely.

"Thinking was it?"

". . . you're heading east, aren't you?"

"So?"

"Well I was just reckoning we . . . I'm going your
way."

"We?" The man's tone was still suspicious but he'd
lowered his musket. He glanced at the woman and child
beside him. They in turn gazed rather more sympathetically
at Matt.

"Don't bully so, Jebediah Wren," the woman said
sternly. "The lad's only looking for company. Aren't you,
young man?"

"Tis so, ma'am." Matt looked gratefully at her.

"How long on the road then?" The man put down his musket with studied reluctance.

"A day, sir."

Jebediah Wren snorted. "From the boats in the St. Lawrence then. An Irisher, I'm betting."

Matt nodded.

"And heading for your friends in Boston or New York."

"Boston, sir."

"Well, we're only travelling as far as Concord in New Hampshire but that's nearer Boston than you'd be reaching on your own with all that hollering. If you want you can tag along. But, mind you, no more screeching."

"I've food," said Matt but Jebediah Wren picked up the reins and nudged his horses into motion.

Matt walked behind the wagon as it jolted along the forest track. He was disconcerted by the man's suspicious attitude. An Irishman, he thought, would have been much friendlier than this Yankee.

After about an hour, he was invited to clamber up on to the wagon. "You'll be doing enough pushing and heaving over the mountains, youngster," the wagon-owner explained with a half-smile.

As the day's shadows lengthened, Matt and the Wren family swapped tales of their background and their travels. By nightfall, with a stew bubbling over the fire, they had become good companions.

"You can't afford to take a man on face value out here, Matt," confided Jebediah Wren. "This here ain't civilization. No, sir. Why a man'd shoot the kid, my woman and me just to get the wagon and team. And what them Redskins would do, don't bear thinking about. Always sleep with a firearm at your hand and one ear to the night.

That way you won't be waking up and finding you ain't gotten no hair on your head to comb.''

In the weeks that followed, Matt learned a deal from the hardy frontier family. He saw the virtues of self-discipline, of self-denial, of self-reliance. He compared them with the often feckless behavior of his old neighbors back in North Kerry and found himself agreeing with the Wren family that no person was owed a living. Jebediah Wren was particularly hard on the Irish when Matt described the way of life he'd left behind.

"A man has two choices, youngster," he'd said. "Either he uses his brains and muscles to change what he don't like or he uses them to up and go somewhere better. Them that do neither have no right to complain. And, begging your particular pardon, that's how many Yankees look on you Irishers as you'll find when you're reaching Boston.''

Matt saw many practical examples of that New World philosophy in his long journey. He passed through communities of a few houses carved out of mountainside forest where everyone seemed so busy that the wagon hardly merited a glance. He marvelled at the calm and prosperity of the small towns in the valleys and on the plains, their neat white-painted houses always built around a steepled church.

When he had left the Wrens at their new home in Concord and travelled alone the last miles to Boston, the small towns and villages seemed to get closer to one another. There were sizeable civic buildings and increasingly busy streets. Matt's anticipation grew with every stride, but his expectations were dwarfed by his first impressions of Boston itself. Everywhere there were people—dashing people, scurrying people—all apparently moving with a firm purpose in mind. Any one of the buildings, Matt thought, would have been regarded as a wonder back in the stony flatness of the West of Ireland. And after the buildings, the noise: from the horses, the carts, the carriages, the factories, the people themselves. They didn't talk but shouted. They didn't smile gently but laughed uproariously. They didn't weep but cried aloud. They appeared to have no inhibitions. Matt felt so cowed by everything around him that he had to pluck up all his courage to approach any of the people brushing past him on the rude sidewalks.

Then he saw the burly, uniformed figures of two constables ambling towards him, sticks twirling on their fingers and amiable smiles and greetings for all they passed. Matt ran up to them eagerly.

"I'm a stranger here . . ." he began.

"And wouldn't we be knowing that?" one of the constables interrupted. "What with your pack and your pistols and your dust even a man with his lanterns out would be seeing that."

"I'm trying to ask the way," Matt explained.

"And what way would that be?"

"To Alderman Matt Finucane."

"The alderman, eh? . . . a friend of his?"

"My da . . . I mean, my guardian was."

"Well, my friend and associate here and myself happen to be heading the way you're wanting so you'd better just come along."

The constables shepherded Matt through busy streets and alleys, pointing out places of interest to him while they asked questions to elicit the youngster's background. After a quarter of an hour they turned down yet another side alley. There, in a courtyard, Matt saw the gates of a small factory with a sign hung above them—"Finucane-Cooper." The constables hammered on the gates with their sticks until a fresh-faced boy pulled them squeakily open.

"The alderman here, lad?" the older constable demanded.

"In his office, sir."

Matt thanked the constables for their help before being led through the yard, littered with half-built casks, and up a narrow wooden staircase to a small office on the first floor of the building. His guide knocked on the grimy window set into the door, turned the handle without waiting for an answer and motioned for Matt to enter. To his surprise, he found himself looking down at the crown of a young woman's head. Her long fair hair almost totally obscured her face as she bent over a ledger on the desk. In another corner of the small office, Matt saw a man sitting with his back to him, also hunched over a desk.

"What is it?" the young woman asked without raising her head.

"I am wanting Alderman Finucane," Matt replied hesitantly. "They said he was here."

"Oh, you are, are you?" She looked up. Her clear green eyes took in Matt's dishevelled countenance and clothing, the pistols at his waist, the uncertainty in his expression. "You're wanting the foreman in the cooperage below if you're seeking work. The alderman doesn't hire labor."

The dismissiveness of the reply disconcerted Matt. He was about to turn and leave the office when he heard a half-suppressed guffaw from the man at the far desk.

"I'm from Jack Keane of Drombeg townland," he blurted out, suddenly finding a growing anger within him at the off-handedness of the Bostonians. "And I'll not be leaving here until I see the alderman. I'm no workman wanting hire."

The young woman's eyes showed her surprise. The middle-aged man at the desk swung around in his chair, laughter on his face.

"And who might you be, you cheeky spalpeen?"

"Mr. Keane's ward . . ."

"Matthew Aherne?" the man asked, the amusement leaving his expression.

"The same."

The man jumped from his chair, crossed the floor in two strides and gripped Matt's arm below the elbow. "And Jack?" he continued urgently.

"Dead these three weeks or more."

"Dead?"

"And buried on an island in the St. Lawrence along with thousands of other poor souls."

The man turned away. He pressed a hand across his mouth. "God rest him. Holy Mary, he was the truest friend a man could have," he muttered.

"You're Alderman Finucane?" Matt asked quietly, recognizing the man's genuine emotion. Matt Finucane shrugged his shoulders as if throwing off his grief. When he turned again to his young visitor a broad smile of welcome pointed up a sudden bleakness in his eyes.

"Two days running her da's office and she thinks she's the head man already. That's the female for you, lad," he said in a mock serious tone. "Welcome, Matthew Aherne. *Cead mille failte.*" They shook hands firmly. The young woman rose gracefully from behind her desk and offered her hand. Matt was aware of its softness, of its fine bones, as he held it for a second.

"My youngest, Mary," explained the Alderman, brushing a hand through the grey hair at his temples. "And was any hard-working man so cursed with a girl-child?"

Mary pouted, then laughed.

"That's it, daughter, mock me, will you? Now lock up the office and call the trap. It's straight home for us or your mam'll be giving me her tongue for holding him here and him exhausted from his travels."

Despite his protests that he wasn't tired, Matt was

ushered from the office, helped into the trap and almost rushed to the Finucanes' spacious, airy home at Dorchester. In fact, Matt felt so excited by the sights of his short journey across the Boston Neck—the sea on one side, the Charles River on the other—that he forgot the deep fatigue within him. But, within an hour of his rapturous welcome by the alderman's wife, Alice, he felt his eyelids beginning to droop. He sat in a high-backed chair, his stomach full from a huge plate of cold cuts, and tried desperately to stay awake as the family fired question after question at him. Eventually, he was unable to suppress a wide yawn much as he attempted to disguise it with a fit of coughing.

"Bless me, Father," exclaimed Alice Finucane, "you're blathering away and all that Matt's wanting is his bed. The talking can wait till morning."

Matt smiled to himself as he dressed for breakfast the next morning, remembering the family's solicitude. Jack-Da, he thought, had been wise in his choice of friends. He felt thoroughly at home with them.

He was aware of darting, curious glances from Mary Finucane during the family's breakfast, and reddened perceptibly under the girl's inspection. He sighed almost audibly with relief when the alderman drained his third cup of coffee and announced that Matt and himself would retire to the drawing room.

The alderman settled back in his favorite cushioned rocking chair, twined his fingers over his thickening paunch, and smiled reassuringly at Matt. "When you're well settled in, lad, I'll be wanting to hear all about the last days of my old friend, Jack, but right now I'm more exercised about your future. If I'm a mite impertinent just tell me so but starting from now I'm regarding myself as filling Jack's shoes. You can clearly look after yourself and I guess you know where you're headed, but I feel duty bound to help you along the path. We Irish aren't the novelty we were when Jack or my folks came here. Indeed, there are Boston people who'd be quite happy to dump us all back in the sea. The Irish who've arrived over the past year or so haven't exactly been the pick of the crop—and that's this Irishman's opinion. So however tough you are, Matt, you'll still be needing all the help I can give you."

Matt lowered his eyes, embarrassed for a moment at the older man's obvious sincerity.

"Come on, lad," the alderman urged. "The little people haven't got your tongue, have they?"

"Well, for a start, before we left Kerry Jack-Da arranged for me to keep the cabin and fields at Drombeg in case I ever wanted to return to them. I'm sure I'll want to one day."

"Then I'll be contacting the landlord's agent. Who is he?"

"Well, that's one problem. His name is Sandes . . ."

The alderman held up a hand to interrupt Matt. "I know of him from Jack's letters . . . and of your kinship with him. Have no fear, lad. We'll arrange to keep your cabin and land safe. But what's puzzling me is why you should want to return. There's so much opportunity here for a youngster like you and, of course, I'd be insisting on giving you a start in business."

"'Tis hard to explain, but I know I shall be going back. I don't know when or why precisely but I'm sure Ireland can't be helped by people like me leaving her for good."

Alderman Finucane nodded. "I reckon Jack talked of politics and such with you."

"He did that. Aye, he did. The ways of landlords and their agents like Mr. Sandes have to change if Ireland is ever to be more than a cat's paw for the English."

"And you'll be wanting to help?"

"Aye, I shall. Although I've no idea yet about how."

"Well, then, young Matt, how's this for a proposal? Be my assistant, my secretary if you like, in the business and in the politicking. You'll find out how Boston town works and maybe you'll discover a way to help Ireland. You'll get a wage. You'll live here with us. You'll be one of us."

Matt's face shone with excitement at the offer, and before he could speak, the older man said, "I see you're liking the idea. We'll take it as settled then. And what better time to be starting than now, today?"

Matt nodded quickly in agreement, then frowned. "One thing's worrying me."

"What's that?"

"How do I call you?"

The alderman slapped his thigh and laughed. "And now isn't that a problem. You can't be calling me da, can you? And two Matts together will confuse everyone. And Alderman's a bit high-falutin' . . ."

He thought for a moment before announcing, "You'll call me Finny. That's what. That's how I'm known to my cronies and you've just signed on with them."

Alderman Finucane stood up and held his hand out to Matt. "A deal then, Matt Aherne?"

"A deal. Aye, a deal, Alder . . . I mean, Finny," replied Matt.

The two women next door looked round in surprise, then smiled at each other, as they heard the burst of laughter from the drawing room.

The owner of the boarding house in Oliver Street shifted his feet uneasily under the remorseless questioning of the visiting committee's chairman, Lemuel Shattuck.

"Only three to a room, Cahill?"

"At the very most, your honor, the very most."

"But we counted six straw sacks in the small room. Presumably they pass as mattresses."

"Just storing them, your worship."

"Mr. Cahill, you are prevaricating. In all the ten rooms you let to those brought here by your runners this committee found sixty-eight mattresses of palliasses or what you will. Surely you couldn't have been simply storing all of them?"

The boarding house keeper didn't reply. He stared sullenly at the six men confronting him in the small entrance hall of his rickety three-story premises which had been converted from a warehouse only a few months before. Although he tried not to show it, Paddy Cahill was thoroughly overawed and frightened by the gentlemen in their tall hats and somber clothes.

Shattuck paused for a moment. "Very well, Cahill, this committee shall merely record the facts about your establishment in its report. Now, how much do you charge the poor wretches here?"

Paddy Cahill fingered his broken nose thoughtfully. "Fifty cents per person per room?" he offered tentatively.

Matt Aherne, standing behind the committee's members, found this so ridiculous that he laughed openly. The committee swung around, wondering at his impertinence and levity.

"It's no laughing matter, Matt," Alderman Finucane warned sternly. Matt stepped away from the wall, revealing two notices hanging there.

One was headed simply "Rules." In large, uneven print it warned occupants of the room that they faced instant eviction and forfeiture of their baggage if they were the slightest tardy with payments of their rents of two dollars.

Lemuel Shattuck turned back to the hapless Cahill. "I think a constable posted outside these doors to warn any of your would-be guests will cramp your business enough,

Cahill. There are already too many of you living off the miseries of your less fortunate countrymen. You should be ashamed of your vile trade. Ashamed, sir.''

As the committee members murmured assent and the boarding house keeper began to protest, Matt peered closely at the second notice on the wall. It hung beneath small etched portraits of Daniel O'Connell and George Washington.

Robert Emmet's last words from the scaffold: ''. . . . Let no man write my epitaph; for as no man who knows my motives dare now vindicate them, let not prejudice or ignorance asperse them. Let them rest in obscurity and peace, my memory be left in oblivion and my tomb remain uninscribed, until other times and other men can do justice to my character. When my country takes her place among the nations of the earth then and not till then, let my epitaph be written.''

The exploitation was pathetic, Matt thought, but typical of the Irish in Boston in this year of 1848, forty-six years since Emmet had been hung and then beheaded.

Alderman Finucane had insisted that he accompany the state legislature's committee during their investigation, which had interrupted his training in book-keeping at the cooperage factory. The youngster, now eighteen years old, supposed the alderman had wanted to make clear to him now fortunate he was to be in a privileged position among Boston's middle class. Certainly, Matt had been shocked and disturbed by the awful conditions of most of the sixty to seventy thousand Irish who'd arrived in Boston during the previous two years.

To leave the city for the small towns on the mainland you had to cross bridges, paying tolls of up to ten cents in each direction. The wretched emigrants with little enough money and hardly any spirit left were stranded in the districts near the docks, particularly Matt Finucane's Ward 8, Fort Hill, and in the North End. As the human flood increased so Boston's old families moved inland across the peninsula. The gardens and courtyards of once-fine houses became covered with shacks; backyards and alleyways were built over; rooms were divided and divided again. Disused warehouses, lacking water and drainage, were leased by get-rich-quick speculators, mainly Bostonians, and split with flimsy partitions into living compartments, most without windows.

Each new address visited by Lemuel Shattuck's committee provided a new insight into the hellish conditions. After the third week of the investigation, the committee had still not grown used to the cramped rooms, to the cellars barely 100 feet square inhabited by twenty people, to the smells of excrement and stale urine, to the foul-running open drains. In such conditions the newly-arrived Irish sank into apathetic despair: they had little strength to resist the New World's rape of their consciences and sensibilities. Each day, the investigating committee found new evidence of their almost total moral disintegration.

In Hamilton Street, one crisp March day, the committee, with Matt tagging along to take notes as usual, pushed their way through at least a dozen child beggars before they could enter one house. From the outside it still bore the decorative fineries and fripperies which had marked it as the residence of a prosperous merchant family.

A woman, eyes bleary with drink, swayed against the doorway of the first tiny room along the dim and dirty hallway.

"Have you children inside?" Alderman Finucane asked her courteously.

The woman patted her long dark hair, knotted with filth. She smiled coquettishly. Her mouth was filled with brown stumps of teeth, where teeth there were.

"Why . . . a fine gentleman like you wanting such things . . ."

Before the alderman could explain she continued, winking at Matt at the same time, "And wouldn't you prefer a woman of experience like me, sir? Your lad there can be having the girl at the same price of a dollar."

Without turning her head, leering grotesquely, the woman shouted back into the dark recesses of the tiny box of a room, "Bernadette, Bernadette, get your pretty self out here. Some fine gentlemen have come calling."

A girl of about twelve years appeared at her side, smiling shyly. Her thin body, grimed with dirt, showed through a tear in the grubby shift she was wearing . Matt saw the pink tip of a budding breast. He looked away in shame.

"Madam, I do protest," the alderman said sternly when he had recovered his composure. "Your husband, madam. Where's your husband? Get your husband! Find the man this instant!"

"Him?" The woman spat contemptuously. The spittle dribbled down the flaking plaster on the wall. "He's so bottled in the groggery below that he won't be disturbing your pleasures."

She lunged drunkenly at the alderman, trying to grab his arm and pull him inside the room. Matt, who saw what was happening, stuck out a foot. The woman tripped and slid to the floor in an ungainly flurry of stained petticoats.

The committee voted with their feet and headed down the hallway toward the first upward flight of stairs. Alderman Finucane and Matt were pursued by a stream of obscenities, much of them in the piping voice of the little girl.

The upper three floors of the house were much as they'd seen elsewhere; airless, windowless rooms crowded with young children, many of them visibly sick. Some were on their own, screaming in their distress, others were being cared for by their older brothers and sisters. The absence of grown-ups puzzled the committee. The invariable answer from the children was that their parents were "down below."

"The groggery?" Matt suggested.

Lemuel Shattuck nodded grimly. "I fear so, young man. This is the first time I've heard of a groggery in the cellars catering just for the occupants of one of these hell holes."

"And what else can the wretches do?" Alderman Finucane interrupted, shaking his head resignedly. "They sell their children's bodies or put them on the streets to beg to raise some money, then spend it on drink to dull their consciences at what they're doing."

The committee was silent for a moment. There was little to say.

"Do we go below, Finny?" Matt asked.

"Aye, lad. We do," the alderman replied with a weary sigh. "But you go first and keep a weather eye for that harridan and her she-child. Lord above, I've had some offers in my time but that one's enough to turn me away from the ladies for life."

Matt couldn't stop himself guffawing at the expression of total dismay and distaste on the alderman's face. In return he received a hefty shove in the small of the back which sent him stumbling down the stairs. He grabbed the banisters to ease his descent and poked his head around the stairwell to see if the hallway was clear. There was no sign of the woman or the girl. The committee members, some on tip-toe, descended the stairs quietly, turned a bend and then with more boldness, started down some more steps toward the cellar.

The first thing they noticed were the keening, ill-played notes of a fiddle coming from somewhere below, rising above a peal of men's drunken laughter and a shriek of female mirth. They stood on the top steps until their eyes became accustomed to the flickering yellow light thrown by the oil lamp hung on the wall.

Matt heard a grunting, panting sound from under the stairway beneath his feet. He craned over the rail and, to his astonishment, looked straight down on to a man's naked buttocks, rising and falling, thrusting and twisting. For a moment, the youngster was completely nonplussed. Then he noticed the slimmer legs wrapped, ankles interlocked, around the man's thighs. He'd heard of it. He'd dreamed of it. Now he was seeing it at close quarters. Matt watched, fascinated, as the man's thrusting became quicker and more vigorous. The woman's ankles beat a frenzied tattoo as his movements juddered to a halt.

So that was it, Matt thought. That was what it's about.

There was no doubt that the love-making had excited him. He ran one hand quickly, surreptitiously, over the front of his breeches to feel the bulging proof of his arousal. As he straightened up, Matt found himself looking into the flushed features of Lemuel Shattuck and, above him on the stairs, the narrowed eyes of Alderman Finucane.

"Herrumph . . . gentlemen, let us proceed."

When they reached the foot of the stairs a couple staggered past them, their clothes still in disarray. Matt thought he recognized the woman as the one they'd met earlier.

They followed the couple along a short passageway into a large room lit by two smoky oil lamps. The lights threw long shadows across the cellar. A plank had been placed on two upturned barrels across the angle of one corner. It was covered with stone bottles, some lying on their side and dripping the last of their contents on to the dirty straw on the ground. About fifty men and women sat on the cellar floor with their backs to the walls, most drinking from broken cups and mugs, some fast asleep and snoring in their drunken stupors, heads resting on their neighbors' shoulders. Three couples were on their feet attempting to dance a reel to the discordant tune of a fiddler who was as drunk as they were. They kept slipping and sliding on drying pools of vomit on the hard-packed earth floor, screeching with laughter.

In another corner, Matt saw a middle-aged man, face blotched with drink, fondling Bernadette, the young girl he'd seen upstairs. Her shift was bunched around her waist, her head tossing, as the man's thick fingers sawed back and forth between her thighs.

The man and the woman whom Matt had seen under the stairs looked around the cellar room before walking over toward the girl. They slumped against the wall beside her. The woman—her mother, Matt presumed—looked up at her once, dully, before accepting the stone bottle offered by her companion.

As she took her first swig, the girl was lifted by the man until she hung monkey-like around his neck, her legs almost encircling him. He fumbled with his breeches, adjusted Bernadette's position, and began moving upwards and inwards against her. The girl whimpered thinly. Her moans hardly carried against the cacophony of noise in the cellar. Those nearest her glanced up once then looked away or busied themselves with their drinking.

The stench in the cellar of unwashed bodies, vomit and rot-gut alcohol bit into Matt's throat. He stumbled out of the room, retching bile deep from his stomach. Alderman Finucane followed him and put a comforting arm around the youngster's shoulders as he leaned, shaking helplessly, against the stairway upwards.

"Come on, lad," the alderman urged. "Hold on till we

leave here. Don't let them see. Never let them see weakness."

"How can it be?" whispered Matt. "They're our people, Finny. They're Irish. Our people."

"I know, Matt. Whatever they might be now, they're still our people."

"How can it be?" Matt repeated. "Oh, Mother of God, how can it be?"

A roar of laughter and applause came from the makeshift groggery. Matt looked up just in time to see the little girl disappearing naked up the stairs.

Chapter 6
July, 1848

The good people of Boston were properly shocked by the report of the Committee of Internal Health. It was explicit in its descriptions of how the Irish were living. It spared few details of how they had been exploited, deserted, brutalized. Many Bostonians had known about their condition but had preferred to ignore it. As they said to themselves with no little self-satisfaction, the state of affairs seemed much worse in New York. The report was a heavy blow to their civic pride.

Matt Aherne and Alderman Finucane were particularly pleased with the report's concluding paragraph about the emigrants' lives. "Under such circumstances, self-respect, forethought, all the high and noble virtues soon die out, and sullen indifference and despair or disorder, intemperance and utter degradation reign supreme."

The "utter degradation" was left to the imagination but the phrase had been written with the scenes in the Hamilton Street groggery firmly in mind.

Newspaper editorials and charity organizations urged the emigrants to uproot their families from the slums and strike out for the opportunities further to the west. The Irish preferred to hug the stink and misery of their existence in Boston.

Their obstinacy began to sour any sympathy aroused on their behalf by the efforts of Alderman Finucane and his friends. Other official reports which followed soon transformed any remaining sympathy into resentment against the Irish.

Every citizen knew that violence and crime had increased in Boston since the mass arrival of the Irish. The Clerk of Boston Police Court disclosed that in the five years since 1843, the number of murders had nearly trebled; cases of attempted murder had increased 170 times; assaults on constables had quadrupled, as had aggravated assaults with weapons ranging from knives, dirks, pistols, slingshots, razors, pokers and clubs to flatirons and bricks.

"Trouble's coming, Matt. There'll be trouble, mark my words," Alderman Finucane said gloomily as he perused the columns of the *Boston Pilot*. "Word's already reaching me of some night hawks ganging up to attack our people. If they retaliate . . . well, we'll be having riots in the streets and the work of years'll be undone."

"Do you think we'll ever be accepted, Finny? Will we never belong here?" Matt asked earnestly.

"Oh, there's no fear of that, boy. No fear at all. The Yankees might have the high ideals but they haven't our native cunning or ruthlessness." The alderman smiled suddenly. "They haven't our sense of belonging to each other either. One thing we Irish do well is stick together. Oh no, we'll survive here. The next generation or so will have hard times, make no mistake. They'll take a buffeting but in the final day the Yankees will need us. They'll appreciate our muscles and our like of a fight, you see."

Matt laughed at his optimism, his lightening of spirit. "You're almost talking like a Yankee, Finny."

"And isn't that the truth?" The alderman joined in the amusement. "And what young spalpeen, may I ask, is learning the Yankees' talk mighty quick? Why I've hardly heard a tis or a twas out of you for weeks. And that's the truth as well."

"Twas Mary . . ." Matt stopped, smiled and began again. "Mary said I'd soon lose the habit if I thought of what I was going to say before I opened my gob."

"She did, did she?" The alderman had a broad grin on his homely face. "And what else has she been saying, young man, while you've been walking out together?"

Matt lowered his eyes, embarrassed for a moment. "Oh, not much, Finny. Just this and that. Really, she's only been showing me around the town when we've finished at the cooperage." He tried to steer the conversation into more political avenues, anxious not to discuss his deepening friendship with Mary Finucane. "One thing she did say, though, was that the only matter uniting the Irish and the old Boston Yankees was our hating of the English."

"Dislike them, maybe. Distrust them, certainly. Not hate though. There's too much between us in history for that. But you know, Matt, I often think, with the world as it is, that God made the English first, looked at them, examined them, turned them this way and that and then changed his mind for the rest of us."

The yellow light of the single oil lamp reflected back into the office from the windows which were covered with specks of sawdust and glue. The late autumn sun had disappeared long since and the half moon was too busy dodging in and out of the ragged clouds to shed much light.

Matt Aherne shivered suddenly in the chilly office. He glanced across at the desk where Mary Finucane was still poring over the account books and saw that she had tucked a heavy shawl around her shoulders. His eyes softened as he gazed on her. The cold seemed to lift from him. His thoughts drifted from the pile of invoices in front of him to warmer times spent with Mary, particularly the day a week before when their hands brushed as they walked together across Boston Common. He could swear that she momentarily ran her little finger across the back of his hand. Matt was certain that it had been deliberate. Why else had she not looked directly at him for the next minute or so but walked on with head demurely bent, a slight blush spreading on her cheeks? He smiled to himself as the side of her mouth flicked up a little in a grimace of impatience caused, no doubt, by the columns of figures she was trying to add up. She rubbed her hand wearily across her eyes. Soon, Matt thought, her father would return from his weekly tour of the six "Mother McCarthy" bars and restaurants. Then, the two youngsters could finish their tiresome work on the accounts of the cooperage factory. He cupped his chin in his hands, preferring to surrender his thoughts to Mary. There had been no formal courtship, he realized. How could there be when their closeness had pushed them into a relationship near to that of brother and sister? He had sensed a definite tension in recent months. It was as if there was a barrier between them which neither had the experience nor confidence to attempt to cross. There was also a rough mateyness in their conduct together which Matt, at least, used to disguise his increasingly romantic feelings for the alderman's daughter.

But Matt's state of mind hadn't been helped by the deep humiliation he'd felt at the debacle of William Smith O'Brien's uprising in Ireland in late July. Mary had been particularly caustic about that.

"Can't you Irishers never do anything right?" she'd asked cuttingly. "You blow your tin trumpets hard enough, wave your flags and pistols in the air, then run for your lives when the English say 'boo' to you."

Matt hadn't replied. Indeed, he didn't know what to say. Even the *Boston Pilot* had been markedly unenthusiastic about the uprising although it had uttered, for its readership's sake, the usual condemnations of the English rule in Ireland.

The final humiliation for Matt had been the news that the English, learning from earlier mistakes, had not even created martyrs from the rebel leaders they'd captured. Try as they might even the most rabid among the new Irish-Americans could raise little indignation that William Smith O'Brien, Thomas Meagher, and Tom McManus had been transported to Tasmania after their trials. Unpleasant as that fate was, it was not the stuff of martyrdom. The later news that some of the others, including James Stephens, had escaped successfully to France went almost unreported as everyone with an Irish background tried to draw a veil over the bungled affair. Unhappily, they were not allowed to do so. The rising's failure had given added impetus to anti-Irish feeling throughout the eastern states of America.

As Alderman Finucane had feared, gangs of thugs now regarded the Irish as legitimate targets for their drunken attacks. The Irish had retaliated and already there had been two full-scale riots in Boston. The town's constables had been ordered to keep special watch on any Irish business premises but many of the constables were only too happy to nip down an alley for a quick smoke while the gangs smashed up Irish-owned shops and warehouses. The outbreaks of violence, although sporadic, were increasing in number. That was why this evening Matt Aherne and Mary Finucane had not ventured home on their own from the cooperage factory but had waited for Alderman Finucane and his carriage driver, newly employed for his brawn as well as his skill with horses.

"Back in the mists again, Matthew?"

Mary's voice cut low into the young man's thoughts. He jerked his head out of his hands and looked around at her.

"What, Mary?"

"Thinking again, then? Away back in Kerry?"

"No, but twas of Ireland I was thinking."

"It was of Ireland," she corrected.

He smiled at her. "It was . . ."

"Aren't you happy here?"

"Oh, yes. But . . ."

"You're doing so well," she interrupted. "Father's extremely pleased with your advancement."

Matt stood up, stretching himself. His shoes echoed on the office's wooden floor as he walked over to Mary's desk. Her face glowed in the light from the oil lamp. He gazed down at her. "Sometimes I'm knowing clearly what I want to do, what I have to do with my life. Then . . ." he spread his arms. "Then it all becomes confused and I'm not sure."

Mary lowered her eyes to the ledger on her desk. "Mother says you've always to do what's in your heart and there's so much to be done here for the Irish. You and Father both say that."

"We do and there is. Sure there is. But I'm thinking we'll maybe never really succeed here until Ireland's a free nation again. Until then the Irish'll always be refugees, always be looked down on. And isn't that what's happening here and now in Boston. After the uprising . . ."

"That again. That silly nonsense," Mary said scornfully. "I knew we'd return to that."

Matt shrugged his shoulders. "How can you forget it?" he asked. "It happened so it did. And made us the laughing stock again. And ruined a deal of the alderman's work."

"It did that," said Mary as she stood up and adjusted the shawl around her shoulders.

"I wish Father would hurry up," she declared rather petulantly. "It's a mite cold in this office."

She moved out from behind her desk and brushed past Matt as she went to the window. For a moment, Matt thought of clasping her in his arms. He cursed inwardly at his timidity.

Mary rubbed the window with her hand and peered out. Then she cocked her head slightly. "I can hear something," she said.

"Your father's carriage?" Matt asked.

"No, it's not that. More like a parade. A deal of people by the sound of it."

Matt took two paces to the window. Mary was right. He could hear the tramp of feet, the low grumble of voices. The sounds were still some distance away, perhaps two or three streets, but they seemed to be coming nearer.

"What is it, Matt?" There was anxiety in her voice.

"A crowd of some kind, that's for sure, but what kind is anyone's guess." Matt was puzzled but unconcerned.

He was more concerned by his closeness to Mary. They were barely six inches apart as they pressed their ears to the window, then tried to peer through the encrusted grime on the outside of the glass.

Her green eyes were huge, luminous, at such a distance. Suddenly, they flicked upwards and gazed directly into Matt's. The approaching sounds of the crowd, whatever it was, seemed to vanish. He was aware only of the stillness in the office and the warmth flowing from Mary. It was as if he and she were cocooned together in a world of infinite, unspoken yearning. The feeling of wonder, a definite physical feeling clutching at his chest, grew inside him like a bubble. Matt could smell her sweet breath on his face. Her eyes, serious, wondering, drew him still closer until they filled his vision. Their lips touched, then pressed fleetingly against each other. Matt lifted his arms to encircle Mary, to hold her closer, but after an instant, she turned away, her head bowed.

"Mary . . . Mary . . ." Matt whispered. "Oh, Mary."

She didn't reply. Her right hand groped backwards searching for his. Their fingers met and entwined, softly at first, then more fiercely. Mary turned and pushed her face against Matt's chest as though listening to his heart. Matt smelt the freshness of her hair, felt the softness of her body, marvelled at the cool smoothness of her hand in his.

They stood profiled against the window for long seconds, wrapped in each other's warmth and love.

Distantly, as if from another time and place, Matt heard a rough hammering mingled with harsh, raised voices. He wanted them to go away, to leave him in the peace of newly-declared love, but they persisted, even grew stronger. He shook his head, attempting to make the sounds vanish, trying to remain in his and Mary's tender world. She looked up at him as she felt his movement and heard the noises too. The spell binding them was broken. They stepped slightly apart and peered through the window again.

"Holy Mother of God!" Matt breathed.

Below them, outside the factory gates, was a large semi-circle of torches flickering in the night. The noises they'd heard was a crowd trying to break through the stout gates.

The baying of the mob flooded into the upstairs office.

"Irisher scum . . . Irisher scum . . . Irisher scum . . ."

Matt and Mary could see the gates bending and swaying under the pressure of the men outside. They heard, rather than saw, a fusillade of bricks and stones hurtle over the factory walls, clattering into the courtyard below, smashing into the wooden building.

Matt pulled Mary away from the window and fell with her to the floor.

As they did, a brick crashed through the office window, showering them with shards of glass.

Mary screamed shrilly.

Chapter 7
August, 1848

The drunken mob attacking the Finucane cooperage was out for blood. Each brick hurled against the slatted wooden walls was a protest against the Irish influx and against the spreading slums. Every wave of a flaming torch was angry defiance against the authoritarian meddling by the Roman Catholic hierarchy in the traditionally liberal politics of Massachusetts. Every curse and chant was a cry of fear that one day the alien minority might hold the balance of political power, might even become the majority. The fact that Alderman Finucane was a prime mover in attempting to reconcile the two cultures made his factory a target. Reconciliation meant compromise and the mob was in no mood for that.

The constable manning the factory gates had run the other way as soon as the mob had flooded into the narrow street. Now he watched from a safe distance while a group of men rammed a cart repeatedly against the factory gates. The rest either threw bricks and stones or vainly tried to scale the high walls topped with sharp, pointed flints. The constable noticed a flicker of flame on the first floor of the factory and decided he ought to hurry off to alert the nearest fire brigade. The thought that any people might still be in the factory so late in the evening simply did not occur to him.

Matt Aherne pulled Mary into the corner of the upstairs office furthest away from the spreading pool of burning oil spilt from the lamp which had topped off the desk when the youngsters fell to the floor.

Mary was sobbing more from shock than from fright. Matt tried to comfort her, holding her close, patting her hair, while he surveyed their desperate situation. The flaming oil licked hungrily at the cane seats of the office chairs and devoured the pieces of paper in the waste bin. Within seconds, it threw a leaping barrier of heat and fire across the office in front of the door. Matt realized their only route to safety would have to take them through the flames.

"Quickly, Mary!" he gasped, acrid smoke already beginning to bite into his lungs. "The door . . . the door . . . we must reach it or we're done for!"

Mary shrank back into the corner, panic in her wide eyes.

"Holy Mother . . . Holy Mother . . ." she kept repeating as she clung to Matt.

He forced himself away from her. He realized they had only seconds in which to save themselves. Matt shrugged off his coat. He flung it over Mary's head, covering her face and long hair. "'Tis the only way . . . through the flames," he shouted, his voice hoarse with smoke and fear. "Come on . . . come on now!"

He gripped Mary's wrist tightly to heave her to her feet. She hung back, coughing and sobbing, one arm flung upwards as if warding off the heat of the flames.

"Come on!" Matt implored. He wrenched harder but she would not budge from the corner, immobilized by panic.

There was only one thing for Matt to do. He bent down, circled his arms around Mary's thighs and lifted her bodily over his shoulder.

With one arm gripping Mary and the other across his eyes, he plunged towards the flames, now waist high.

For a moment, his world was one of unbearable heat. The rays of a thousand suns pierced his body. He felt as if his very blood would boil, as if molten lead was being poured into his nostrils and down his throat. His scalp and skull seemed to shrivel and tighten, squeezing his brain in a vise.

The fleeting parts of a second were more like hours. And then he and Mary were through the flames and by the door. Matt fumbled for the catch and thrust it upwards. As the door flew open under his frenzied strength, the inrushing air bellowed the flames behind him. The heat flared terrifyingly on his back before he managed to negotiate two or three steps down the rough staircase to the factory yard. He turned his head to look back just as a ball of fire exploded from the shattered window of the office. Jagged flames shot upwards and outwards in the night, curling around the outside of the upper floor of the factory, searching voraciously for the sloping roof timbers.

Matt stumbled under another engulfing wave of intense heat. He put Mary down, holding tightly on to her until he was certain that she had a steady footing on the stairway, and slipped the coat from over her head.

"Oh, Matt!" she gasped. "Are we safe now?" Long strands of hair covered her features. She brushed them aside impatiently. An expression of horror mingled with disbelief grew on her face when she saw how fast the fire had spread.

The inside of the office they'd escaped from only seconds before was a mass of whirling, crackling fire. Fingers of flame were even now reaching for the first step of the stairway.

"Oh, no," Mary whispered. "Oh, no, Holy Mother." The factory was doomed.

"Quickly!" Matt urged. "Before these steps go."

The youngsters hurried down the staircase, hand in hand, oblivious to the stones and bricks still smashing around them into the walls of the factory. It was only when they reached the courtyard they became aware again of the baying sound of the men outside. The factory gates were starting to give way under the continuous battering.

"This way," Matt ordered, pulling Mary away from the gates and towards the end of the wide courtyard. He realized the mob would soon break through. The cries and shouts from beyond the walls already contained a note of exultation, of triumph, as the men saw that their work of destruction was well under way. Like the constable, they too thought the factory was unoccupied and assumed one of their own number had started the fire with a torch flung over the walls.

Matt searched his mind desperately for a way out of the courtyard while they cowered in a corner of the wall. Mary held Matt's coat above their heads to protect them from the fiery clouds of sparks and glowing splinters of wood billowing from the factory. The flames were well on to the roof and had spread already to the lower floor. The pile of barrels stacked outside the main door to the factory were colored a dull red in the fierce light of the blaze.

Matt looked at the barrels and realized there was a chance, a slim one, but still a chance if he was quick enough. "Stay there," he shouted to Mary over his shoulder as he sprinted across the yard towards the barrels. They were stacked according to their different sizes. First, Matt flipped one of the largest on to its side and rolled it back towards the wall, its metal bands clattering on the cobblestones. He levered it upright before hurrying back again to the stack. This time he selected a taller but narrower barrel to roll back to the wall. He clambered on to the first, larger barrel. "Quick. Hand me the other," he called to Mary.

She nodded, her shock replaced by her usual resourcefulness and understanding.

It was a strain for her to lift the narrower barrel but she managed to raise it high enough for Matt's groping fingers to fasten on the rim. He pulled it on the larger, wider barrel, before scrambling gingerly on to it. Now he could reach the top of the wall with his hands.

"Tis I shall go first, then pull you up. But quick for they're coming."

Mary caught her breath as Matt teetered on the barrels, searching for a hold on the wall away from the jagged flints. She looked anxiously round at the factory gates. Already one of the panels had been smashed. Through it, she could see the waving torches of the mob. Her lips moved in a silent prayer for their safety while she watched Matt haul himself painfully onto the top of the wall.

"My coat," he called down, his voice cracking with pain. The flints cut into the inside of his thighs as his legs straddled the wall. "Hand up the coat, then on to the barrels."

Mary peered at him, silhouetted by the dancing glare of the burning factory. The height frightened her but she knew there was no alternative. She handed up the coat before managing to crouch first on the large barrel and then pull herself up again. She winced with pain from the raised rims of the barrels cutting into her knees.

Matt folded the coat into a pad. He groaned from the pain of the flints gashing his legs. Eventually, after more painful maneuvering, he succeeded in balancing himself on top of the wall. He lay flat on his stomach, partially protected by the coat beneath him. He leaned over as far as he dared, his legs dangling into empty space acting as a balance. His hands searched for those stretched upwards by Mary. He caught her wrists, holding them gently at first. Matt felt their small, fine bones. His grip tightened. Mary gasped with pain.

"A moment, mavourneen," he whispered, using his first

word of endearment towards Mary. "Twill only be a moment."

She smiled up at him although the strength of his grip was almost unbearable.

Matt looked quickly down the yard. One of the mob was squeezing through the widening hole in the gates. His arm was reaching to lift the stout wooden plank which held the gates shut.

He began to pull Mary upwards. As he took the strain, the flints in the wall pressed, jagged, into his stomach through the protection of the coat. Mary's shoes scrabbled at the wall, trying for a foothold, the smallest ledge, to help lift herself.

Matt gave a convulsive heave, almost toppling over in the effort, and then Mary's face was level with his. He couldn't resist brushing his lips across hers before starting the agonizing maneuver to help lift her firmly on to the wall.

"Ooh! . . . Ouch!" Mary complained, the flints bruising into her through her skirt and petticoats. But there was a lightness in her voice. She realized she was safe.

With Mary perched safely on the wall, Matt took a deep breath before pushing himself into the darkness on the other side of the high wall.

He was ready for a jarring fall on hard ground but instead landed squelchily up to his knees in a pile of rotting straw. The immediately overpowering stench of horse dung flared into his nostrils, making him cough and retch.

"What is it? Are you safe?" Mary called down, concerned and alarmed by the noises from below.

"Jump now," Matt spluttered. "I'll catch you."

Mary hesitated. She couldn't see into the dark shadows under the wall.

"Is it safe?" she asked tremulously, shutting her eyes and pushing herself off the wall.

"For horses, at least, mavourneen," Matt laughed, catching Mary around the waist to stop her falling headlong on to the pile of well-rotted manure.

"Oh, no!" Mary shrieked. "Horse dung! My shoes . . . my dress! You've ruined them, Matthew Aherne. You've ruined them . . . you . . . you ignorant spalpeen!" Her protests died and were reborn as chuckles, then peals of laughter when the ridiculousness of their plight dawned on her.

They clung to each other, arms around waists, still laughing.

The street outside the factory had quietened when they looked round the corner of the alley. Some men were still entering the gates but their shouting was drowned by the crackling of the giant bonfire that was the once-thriving cooperage. A red glow was reflected in the windows of the houses and warehouses opposite. As the youngsters watched, a dozen constables ran into the street, truncheons drawn. They were followed by two horse-drawn insurance company fire wagons, flanked by men whose efforts would clearly be in vain.

Emboldened by the constables' presence, Matt and Mary ventured out into the street, walking nearer to the factory entrance. The mob were pressed into the courtyard and around the shattered gates.

The crowd cheered when the factory collapsed upon itself with a grinding explosion, but those near the front yelped as large splinters of burning wood whirled among them.

The youngsters began to walk away, unable to watch any more, and were just turning the corner when they heard a commotion behind them.

Alderman Finucane had been enjoying his weekly tour of the "Mother McCarthy's" bars and restaurants when news of the fire had reached him. He had been taking a few glasses with two particularly old friends, Padraig Costelloe and Timmy Brehoney, and the three of them had run nearly a mile to reach the scene.

"Where are they?" the alderman shouted at one of the constables, nearly hysterical with anxiety.

"Who, sir?" The constable had immediately recognized the distraught politician and businessman.

"Mary and Matt, they were inside. Are they here? Are they safe?"

"Inside there, sir?" The constable, horror spreading on his face, nodded towards the twisted, broken factory, still covered with dancing flames. "In there?"

"Yes, in there, you gobbeen. In there . . ."

"No one came out as far as we know. This mob were everywhere, just everywhere around the building . . . oh my God . . . in there . . ."

Alderman Finucane staggered fractionally as if he'd been punched in the chest. Costelloe moved to his side, ready to comfort him, while Brehoney began shouldering his way through the mob. Many of them were turning away, leaving for their homes, content with their night's work.

"Have any of you swabs seen the youngsters from the factory? Have you seen them?" he kept bellowing. Nobody answered him or even attempted to. They looked at him dully, sated by the destruction they had wrought.

"Father! Father!" cried Mary, pushing her way against the tide of men ebbing from the street.

"Over here, Alderman!" Matt shouted. "Tis safe we are." He held Mary's hand tightly as they struggled through the crowd.

The alderman's face told of his delight at their safety. He hugged them closely and then stepped back, sniffing the air. "By the saints!" he exclaimed, a quizzical smile on his face. "And what have you two been grovelling in?"

"Twas out of the fire, Finny, and into the horse sh—"

"Manure," Mary interrupted sharply. "And there's that 'twas' again, Matthew Aherne."

The alderman and his companions roared with laughter.

"That's the female for you, Matt. You'll learn, lad. You'll learn. Even in the state she is, she won't be letting you be."

"State, Father?"

"Just look at the pair of you, lass."

Matt gazed at Mary. Her face was streaked with black, the ends of her long hair were singed, her dress was soaked and covered with evil-smelling straw up to her thighs.

"And you're a pretty sight too, Matthew Aherne," she snapped. "Filthy, smelly, and with hardly an eyebrow left." Then her tone softened. "But you saved my life, so you did, with all your tis and twas . . ."

She stretched up, put her arms around Matt's neck, and kissed him firmly on the mouth. She wasn't able to see her father wink broadly at Costelloe and Brehoney.

The next morning there was a feeling of subdued tension around the breakfast table at the Finucane household. The alderman was worried about meeting his insurance company; whether they would pay his claim in full and whether that amount would be sufficient to rebuild the factory. His wife was more concerned with the previous night's public show of affection between Mary and Matt.

The alderman pushed aside his business worries when his wife, with a shrewd nod, drew his attention to the young people's evident preoccupation with each other. "Mother," he announced, "I'm thinking before we consider the question of a new factory, we should be looking at some matters closer to home, don't you?"

"As you decide, dear."

Matt and Mary exchanged quick glances. Two small red spots appeared high on Mary's cheeks.

"Then, when the table's finished, perhaps you'll talk with your daughter here, while I take this young man into the drawing room. I've a liking to know his intentions."

When they were seated in the drawing room, the alderman began speaking, his voice as soft and concerned as he could manage.

"The question, Matt, is quite simple. What's there between you and Mary? Was last night's display just in the heat of the moment?" He began laughing. The tension eased. "What a gobbeen way to put it, eh? In the heat of the . . . well, was it anyway? Or is there something deeper?"

"Deeper, I think," Matt replied quietly.

"You think?"

"Well, for me, tis knowing I am."

The alderman tut-tutted.

Matt smiled. "I know it's deeper on my side, Finny."

"Then, your intentions?"

"Marriage, if she'll have me. And if you're approving, of course."

Matt looked appealingly at the older man, who hesitated deliberately. The tension grew. Then the alderman smiled broadly, pushed himself out of his chair and crossed the room to shake Matt's hand.

"Of course, I'm approving, lad. Fact is, I was guessing this would happen for some time back."

"But what of Mary?"

"We'll be knowing soon enough, I'm thinking. But, what if she does say 'Yes.' What then? You'll not marry yet, will you? Eighteen is young, so it is. Wait till you're twenty, eh? The years'll help you be certain in your minds."

"They will?"

"Aye, they will. And we'll be wanting to rebuild the business, won't we?" The alderman guffawed. "And I'll be needing all your strength and concentration for that, I'll be bound."

Matt reddened and changed the subject. "As you like then, Finny. I'll be waiting if she'll have me. But I'm wondering if the factory's worth rebuilding. Won't they burn it again?"

"They might, lad, but that's hardly the point. The Ursuline nuns didn't leave town, when the mob burned down the convent a few years back, did they?"

"No."

"Well, then, neither shall we. If we're to stay and grow in this town, we've got to fight back. The factory's of no matter in itself. It's our determination that counts. As I've told you time and time again, if we stay together, we'll survive and prosper."

The door opened behind him. His wife came into the room with Mary hovering behind her.

"Ah, Mother!" the alderman exclaimed, moving to her side. "And what does the daughter say?"

"More to the point," his wife replied, nodding at Matt, "what's he saying?"

"His intentions are perfectly honorable."

Mary's mother beamed. "Then, Father, I'm sure we can leave them to discuss the future themselves." She turned back to the door. "Don't you agree?" she added pointedly.

"Oh, yes, dear." The alderman hurried to join her, pausing only to give Mary a light kiss on her forehead.

The young people stood at opposite ends of the room, looking serious and slightly embarrassed. There was silence for long seconds. Then they began speaking at the same time.

"Mary, what . . . ?"

"Matthew Aherne, did you . . . ?"

They laughed, their eyes softening towards each other. Matt walked up to Mary and took her hands in his.

She spoke softly without looking up at him. "So your intentions are perfectly honorable are they, Matt?"

"You know they are, mavourneen," he replied quietly, smelling her freshly-washed hair.

"And what are they then?"

"To marry, if you'll have me."

"Then you'd better ask, hadn't you?"

"Will you?"

"Will I what?"

Matt sighed. "Mary Finucane . . . mavourneen . . . will you be accepting my hand in marriage?"

"Of course, Matthew Aherne. I will," she said simply. She lifted her face towards his. They kissed without embracing. It was a chaste kiss, the sealing of a bargain rather than a passionate avowal.

Two years later, in the autumn of 1850, Matt and Alderman Finucane stood beside a grave in the Granary Burying Ground alongside the church in Park Street.

The grass on the slight rectangular mound was well clipped. The gravestone was free from the moss that disfigured some of its neighbors. Matt could read the inscription easily: "Elizabeth Kilfedder—1797–1826" and underneath the single word "Beloved."

"Jack-Da said there'd been someone else apart from my mam, Finny," the young man said. "Just before the fever took him, it was."

"Theirs was a mighty love, lad."

The alderman stood on the opposite side of the grave to Matt. They spoke in hushed tones although there was no one else in the yard.

"Strange to think but I'm doubting if you'd be here today, Matt, if Elizabeth hadn't died. I'm guessing Jack would have stayed his time in Boston and never returned home."

"And I would still be in poverty with them Cooleens."

"Or worse."

"Aye."

Matt bent down to place a spray of red roses at the head of the grave.

"Did they ever catch him, Finny?"

"J. P.? Not that we ever heard. There was tell though that he'd been sighted in Natchez and then later that he'd been tumbled off one of them riverboats after being caught with one too many aces up his sleeve. That divil deserved an end like that after all the misery he brought on people. And yet if it hadn't been for all his conniving I might never have been elected."

"So it didn't end here," Matt replied, pointing at the grave.

The alderman nodded. "Everyone's dying alters life here and now. Elizabeth's altered Jack's and yours, now didn't it? And that means it's going to change the lives of mother and me when you marry Mary. There'll be a new family in the world. The Ahernes. Not the Finucanes. That's what the churching means this afternoon. You'll have to build your own life as a family just as we Finucanes did ours, just as Jack Keane did his. It won't be easy. It doesn't happen natural. There'll be times when you and Mary'll gladly strangle each other. But you'll stay as one if you never forget you're building your own piece of history."

Later that evening, it was as bridegroom and father of the bride that they stood beside each other toasting themselves and the two hundred wedding guests in the ballroom of the

United States Hotel in Beach Street, just across from the depot of the Worcester Railroad.

Matt's head was in a whirl. The champagne, the dancing, the strangers to be greeted and hopefully committed to memory, the wedding ceremony itself, had all conspired to draw a veil over his mind. Even words of a moment before seemed to have been heard in the distant past. The only clear image was of Mary approaching him along the aisle on the arm of her father, her face covered by the tucks of a white veil. The short, tulle train of her dress had been carried by the small daughter of her only sister, Kathleen, who, as matron of honor, assumed the proprietorial air of someone who'd seen it all before.

She'd arrived from her home in Philadelphia three days before the wedding and had set to gleefully helping her mother in all those last-minute panics of a family marriage so beloved of women. Her husband, a physician and budding surgeon, had offered to be best man but Matt had preferred, as a gesture in memory of Jack Keane, to ask Padraig Costelloe. And to give Costelloe full credit, he'd avoided becoming too drunk until after his speech at the crowded reception.

Now the toasts and speeches were done, the relatives and guests began to relax. The jigs became wilder, the drink stronger and the songs more fervently Irish or tearfully sentimental as the evening wore on.

Matt glanced sideways at Mary sitting beside him. Her face was slightly flushed from the heat and the champagne. Her eyes were following the whirling dancers. Matt nudged her under the table with his knee. He leaned closer to her.

"I'm thinking they wouldn't be missing us, mavourneen," he breathed into her ear.

Mary didn't reply. Her tongue flicked out once and

moistened her lips. Her eyes turned toward his. She nodded almost imperceptibly.

Alderman Finucane had been watching the exchange of glances. He tried not to smile, remembering his own feelings on his wedding night. He tapped Matt lightly on the forearm.

"Slip away now, lad," he whispered. "They're too addled to be noticing much. Use the serving door behind you, eh?"

"But there are many to thank. Is it being right?" Matt protested, looking about him to ensure that he wasn't overheard.

"Just go, lad. Don't be worrying about them. Be off and God bless you both!"

Matt took Mary's hand. They rose quickly together and disappeared through the kitchen door without daring even a backward look to see if any of their guests had seen their leaving.

A plump, middle-aged waitress, stacking dishes, started with surprise as the newlyweds burst into the kitchen. Then her face broke into a large, welcoming grin. Having served at many weddings before, she instinctively understood the young people's predicament. "This way, my loves," she giggled, beckoning them through another door. "The suite is it?" she asked over her shoulder as she scurried on.

After climbing three flights of stairs the waitress stopped outside a door. She pressed her ear against it, listening. She opened the door only when she was satisfied that no one was passing along the corridor outside. "There it is," she reported in a conspiratorial whisper. "It's unlocked with the key inside. We always do that so you poor loves won't be having to stand around the night-clerk's desk."

"Thanks for that," Matt muttered.

Mary gave the waitress a quick peck on the cheek before she and Matt slipped across the corridor and into the bridal suite reserved for them.

The red velvet curtains were drawn. They threw back the light from the oil lamp, bathing the large room in a pinkish glow. A silver ice bucket containing an unopened bottle of champagne stood shinily by the side of the high double bed. Across the rich coverlet lay two nightgowns.

Matt turned to Mary, his arms circling her slim waist.

"Well, Mrs. Aherne?" he said softly.

"Well, Mr. Aherne," she whispered in reply. She lifted her lips to his. They kissed, softly at first then more fiercely. Their breaths, sweet with champagne, mingled. They clung to each other for a second until Mary pushed Matt lightly away.

"I'll change in the bathroom," she said matter-of-factly. She smiled up at him. There was no hint of nervousness in her voice or expression.

While Matt stayed near the door, Mary lit another lamp on the dressing table and carried it into the adjoining bathroom. She left the door ajar. Matt quickly stripped off his clothes, kicking them under the bed, pulled his fine linen nightgown over his head, and sat down on the side of the bed. He was uncertain what happened next.

Suddenly, he realized Mary had left her nightdress, all lace and frills, lying across the bed. He picked it up, wondering what to do.

"Matt?" Her voice came softly from the bathroom.

"Mavourneen?"

"Blow out the lamp will you, avourneen."

Matt crossed the room, doused the light and felt his way back toward the bed in the dark.

The door of the bathroom opened wide. Mary stood in the entrance, her long hair flowing over her shoulders, the slim curves of her body outlined in the light of the lamp she'd left burning behind her.

Matt stood up, still clutching her nightdress. He stepped toward her, offering it to her, but Mary waved it away.

"Have you ever been with a woman?" she asked, her voice breathy and slightly hoarse.

"No. Never."

She took a step toward him. Her arms were raised a little, palms turned toward Matt in a compliant gesture.

He gasped audibly as his eyes took in the roundness of her raised hard-tipped breasts, the slimness of her waist, the dark triangle beneath her flat stomach.

Mary allowed him to gaze on her for breathless seconds before she moved toward him.

"Then we'll have to learn how to make babies together, won't we?" she said with an almost joyous lilt in her voice as Matt swept her into his arms and on to the bed.

There were no more words for a while, nor any need for them.

Chapter 8
February, 1858

The atmosphere seemed to grow colder in the master bedroom of the Aherne household in South Boston.

"Do you really have to go?"

The concern was apparent in Mary Aherne's voice.

Matt stirred slightly on the pillow beside her. He'd pretended to be dozing when Mary had come to bed. He knew too well what her tactics would be. "Uh-huh," he murmured.

"You're leaving us then?" Mary Aherne's tone sharpened.

"Just for a month or so," Matt answered sleepily.

It was no good, he thought. There was no escape. He turned to look at his wife. She stared straight up at the ceiling, her hair spread like a brown halo on the white bed linen of the pillow. Her profile was as beautiful as ever. Her body still excited him even after eight years of marriage and three children. A candle flickered on the bedside table. In its light, Matt could see that his wife's mouth was set in a firm line.

"You'll do us the honor of coming back?"

"Of course, darling."

"But why you? Why do you have to go?" she persisted.

"Because I was asked, that's why. Because the association wanted Joe Denieffe and me to go to Dublin."

421

Mary sniffed. "It's all right for him. He's no responsibilities. You've a family to look after and a business to run."

"You and Finny can manage, dearest. You've been fine before when I've had to go to New York or Philadelphia on business."

"That was only a week or two. Not months."

"Won't make a mite of difference, you'll see." Matt tried to keep his temper under control. It was the third time in as many days that Mary had mounted a campaign to dissuade him from going to Ireland on behalf of the Emmet Monument Association. He regarded the invitation to meet James Stephens as a singular honor.

After taking part in the failed uprising of 1848, James Stephens had spent years in exile in Paris. There he had learned a great deal from continental revolutionaries, and had accepted many of their views. John O'Mahony, another rebel, had fought alongside him on the barricades during Louis Napoleon's *coup d'état* of 1851.

When memories of the '48 fiasco had had time to dim, Stephens had set off for Ireland once more. O'Mahony had gone to the United States with their comrade Michael Doheny.

Stephens had travelled the length and breadth of Ireland, assessing the state of nationalist sentiment, and planning a secret rebel organization, to be divided into cells for the sake of security, with himself at the head. This was the man Matt and Joe were going to see. What Matt saw as an honor, Mary saw as an imposition.

"It'll be dangerous mixing with all those revolutionaries . . . that Stephens." Mary switched her attack.

"Why should it be? All we're doing is taking messages to him."

"Messages pledging support if he starts his revolt."

"Yes, but . . ."

"And money, I guess. You've been holding enough money-on-the-plate dinners, haven't you?"

"Not a deal. Only £80. The very minimum he wanted."

Mary sniffed again. "Fat lot that'll do. If the English get hold of you, it'll mean prison more than likely."

"They won't." Exasperation was creeping into Matt's voice. Mary sensed it. She turned to him and buried her head against his chest.

"Please, darling. Just for me." She begged like a little girl denied her favorite doll. Then she started to sob. Matt could feel the damp tears seeping through his nightgown. He raised his eyes to the ceiling in silent prayer.

"It has to be, Mary love," he said quietly.

Her sobs grew. He put his arms around her and was instantly aroused.

"Hush dearest. You'll be waking the wee ones."

"Oh, damn them!" Mary said fiercely. "I'm married to you, not them."

Matt bent his head and nuzzled her cheek before kissing her gently on the lips. Her mouth, wet and salty with tears, opened under his. Their tongues flicked together.

"Please, Matt," she whispered.

"I have to, dear one. You know that."

He silenced her reply with another kiss. His hand slid down her back to caress her buttocks. His fingers gripped the folds of her nightgown and pulled it upwards. She lifted herself slightly to allow it to slide around her waist. Matt did the same. Their lower bodies pressed nakedly against each other. Her hand, moving gently to and fro, gripped his stiffness.

"It's always your solution, Matthew Aherne, isn't it?"

"What is?"

Her sobbing had ceased. Their voices were low and husky with passion.

"This." She squeezed softly.

"So?"

"Well, it is, isn't it?"

"Do you mind?"

"No."

"Is it safe?"

"Should be."

Their caresses became more urgent until he lifted himself on his arms and moved over her. The silk-smooth inside of her legs gripped his hips tightly and he entered her, smoothly, warmly.

"Do you really love me?" Her breath was coming in short gasps.

"You know I do."

"You never say it."

"I love you."

"Won't you miss me?"

"Mavourneen . . ."

"Will you miss . . . this?" The last word was an effort. The slow, deep, deeper rhythm quickened. He didn't, couldn't answer.

Mary's head tossed from side to side on the pillow. Matt's lips were fastened to the smooth skin between her neck and her shoulder. The moans grew low in her throat. Her heels tattooed on his buttocks. Matt felt the contractions inside her, her liquid flooding, before, moments later, climaxing himself.

His weight pressed down on her as the strength went from his arms. They lay together, warm, close, while he softened and shrank inside her. Then he pulled back and shifted sideways off her. He put an arm across to ease her nearer to him. His mouth was buried in the pillow. He could feel a few beads of sweat on his forehead.

"Love you," he murmured.

"Love you," Mary replied, running her nails down the small of his back to the crease in his buttocks. The muscles under his skin twitched. She giggled and repeated the caress. Matt turned back to her. She felt his new tumescence press against her thighs.

"No . . . no," she protested softly, pushing him away. "Do you ever have enough?"

"Do you?"

"That's quite enough, Matthew Aherne," she scolded, though without any rancor. "Else you'll be coming home to another babbie when you've finished your gallivanting across the Atlantic."

He continued to hold her close. "You don't mind then?"

"Mind? Of course I mind. But you're set on it and you're as stubborn as only the shanty-Irish can be, so what's the point?"

"As stubborn as you."

"Go to sleep, lummock," she whispered affectionately. Mary twisted away but still thrust her nudity into the angle of his body and his thighs. "Go to sleep." She had conceded as gracefully as she could. Matt knew that and loved her even more.

Usually he fell asleep quickly after love-making, but this night early in February, 1858, he lay awake for a long time, his mind still whirling at the prospect of his return to Ireland.

Would it be as dangerous as Mary feared, he wondered? How far ahead in his planning for revolution had Stephens got? What would Dublin be like? Would he have time to journey to Kerry? What help would the Irish-Americans provide in any rebellion?

Nationalism had been rekindled among the emigrant Irish living in the eastern states. The living conditions for the vast majority of them had not improved overly in the past ten years. And, try as they might, he and Alderman Finucane hadn't found great success in their attempts to reconcile the two cultures. Under the influence of the Catholic Church, the Irish settlers had opposed almost every liberal policy put forward in Massachusetts. They'd upheld Negro slavery, opposed temperance laws, voted for the Democrat Party, clamored for more places of worship, and generally made themselves an object of dislike to the native Bostonians. Resentment had shown itself in a flood of vicious, nearly obscene, anti-Papist pamphlets and books, then more violently, in riots and attacks against Catholic churches. Finally, for four years until 1857, Massachusetts had been run by the Order of the Star-Spangled Banner, a secret society opposed to the emigrants and whose members were commonly called Know-Nothings. Under their administration, the Irish were fired from jobs on the police force and in state agencies; Irish military clubs—although more social than military—were officially disbanded; laws were passed affecting Irish voting rights; and, as a final blow to many Irish, the temperance laws were strengthened.

In the face of such determined and organized opposition the Irish had turned in on themselves. The emigrants began devoting their energies to the common enemy across the Atlantic and away from their entrenched opponents who were making their lives such a misery in their new home. Ironically, Matt thought in his half-dozing state, the resurgence of Irish nationalism had sprung directly from the anti-Irish campaign in Massachusetts.

The Irish Emigrant Aid Society, along with its Massachusetts Lodge, had been formed initially to combat the Know-Nothings before that organization was absorbed into the stripling Republican Party. But within months, a society convention, attended by Matt and Alderman Finucane, was discussing a resolution to decide "the speediest and most effective means of promoting action leading to ensure the success of the cause of liberty in our native land."

Matt had looked around the faces of the people at the convention. Most were those of white-faced groggery owners, frightened small businessmen, avaricious lawyers, itinerant journalists, and young, genuflecting priests. None of them, Matt had thought, at all capable of aiding the success of any project, let alone a rebellion against the mighty British Empire. In fact, he'd stood up and said so. He smiled to himself in the dark of the bedroom as he recalled the stony, outraged silence which had greeted his remarks.

The very next day, he was contacted at the cooperage by an Irishman called Joseph Denieffe, who'd apparently been at the same convention and had listened to Matt's withering comments.

Denieffe had sounded Matt out about the strength of his nationalist views then, satisfied, had invited him to join an organization recently founded in New York called the Emmet Monument Association, in memory of that disastrously misled rebel, Robert Emmet. It wasn't until two months later that Matt discovered the driving forces behind this vehemently anti-English society were John O'Mahony and Michael Doheny, the companions in exile of James Stephens, who had fled to Paris after the '48. By then, though, the inflammatory words of O'Mahony and Doheny had filled his brain. It was as if his guardian, his beloved

Jack-Da, was speaking directly to him. The association's secret meetings drew upon the well of revolt dug deep within him long before. He looked upon his mission to Dublin with Denieffe almost in terms of a pilgrimage.

This spiritual longing for nationalistic fulfillment added to the emotions of his farewells a fortnight later. His family gathered in the spacious entrance hall to say their goodbyes while Alderman Finucane's best carriage waited outside. Matt clasped each of his children to him in turn.

Firstly, there was seven-year-old Brigid, long black hair tumbling down her back. She, being the eldest, had sensed the tensions and misgivings between her parents about this journey. Once, she'd discovered her mother crying to herself as she sat in front of her vanity mirror. Brigid was determined not to cry but the tears still moistened her wide, green eyes when her father hugged her.

"You and your mam are in charge now, little one," Matt whispered to her before turning to her sister, Bernadette, just eighteen months younger. She looked up at him with solemn, unblinking eyes. To lighten the moment, Matt swirled the folds of his heavy travelling cape around her and pulled her to him. He uncovered her, hair all tousled, then knelt to be at a level with her face.

"You be good, mind," he warned in a mock-serious tone.

"Yes, da," she piped, her voice a little unsteady.

"That's the girl." He began to rise from his knees.

"Da . . . you won't be gone for ever, will you?"

Matt laughed. "Before you know, I'll be back to read you the bedtime story."

He ruffled her hair as he moved towards Mary. She was holding their little boy, born three years before. He pushed his face between theirs. His embrace pulled them close.

"Goodbye, Mother. Don't be worrying too much. All will be well."

He felt a tear slide down Mary's cheek. Little Jack's lips fastened on the lobe of his ear in a misdirected kiss.

"Be careful, dearest, and the Holy Mother bless you and watch over you," Mary murmured.

Matt felt the emotion rising in his throat. He turned to leave, unwilling for his family to witness his tears. He was passing through the door when Mary called to him.

"Take this as your talisman, Matthew Aherne."

She held out to him the dried sprig of hawthorn that, so many years before, had grown on a hedge in Drombeg townland. Matt took it without a word, a tight, forced smile on his features.

The last sight of his family on the front steps of his home, grouped protectively around Mary, stayed with him during the long days of the winter crossing of the Atlantic. The comparative comfort of his own cabin did little to ease Matt's misery at being without their love and support. It was not until the Irish coast was sighted that his imagination became fired again at the prospect of the mission before him.

He and Denieffe stood at the ship's rail, fine spray billowing around them, while the grey smudge on the horizon gradually took on the distinct image of a coastline.

Two days later, Matt looked apprehensively down on the bustling crowds along Customs House Quay in the center of Dublin. From Dublin Bay, the Irish capital had appeared small and rather flat. From the River Liffey, stabbing through Dublin's heart, he had noticed the perfect, almost model-like proportions of the public buildings. Now close up, he had the immediate feeling of being in a great capital city, an important outpost of a thriving empire. There was a sense of assurance, of self-confidence, among the people on the quay.

Much to Matt's relief, the customs officers showed little interest in himself and Denieffe and, within the hour, their baggage had been loaded on to carts to follow them to Buswell's Hotel. Despite his companion's entreaties to behave like the well-off Irish-American businessman that he was, Matt still flinched inwardly whenever he caught sight of a constable's blue uniform or the red jacket and black helmet of an Army officer. Indeed, it was a full twenty-four hours before he was entirely convinced that nobody was paying any undue attention to him. Denieffe had been watching him closely, waiting for Matt to relax and behave normally, before suggesting they make contact with James Stephens at his lodgings behind Lombard Street, not far from the center of the Irish capital.

Matt saw another side of Dublin's life in their walk through the damp March evening. Groups of child beggars, ragged and shivering, pulled at his clothes. Prostitutes, half-drunk and predatory, advertised their blowsy wares openly, vocally. Human filth and waste ran in the gutters from the breeding pens for degradation which were the dilapidated tenement buildings. Well-dressed Dubliners walked past these scenes without a second glance. It was an everyday part of their lives.

The welcome from James Stephens was as warm as the brandy punch he poured for them as soon as they'd settled in the comfortable, if small, sitting room at his lodgings.

"I'd heard the ship had arrived," he told Matt and Denieffe, hands thrust deep into the pockets of a silk smoking jacket. "I'd an awful temptation to come down and meet you but that would have been breaking my own rules, wouldn't it? A commander should never do that, should he?"

Stephens tried to make light conversation, inquiring about their voyage and their health. It was obvious to Matt, though, that his host was bursting for news and messages from America. Eventually, after about ten minutes, he could contain himself no longer.

"Well, Joe," Stephens said as casually as he could. "What's for me then? What have you brought?"

"Messages from all your friends in the New World, James."

The sides of Stephens' mouth was creased in disappointment.

"And this," Denieffe added with a smile, reaching into his jacket pocket and pulling out a large chamois leather purse the contents of which clinked as he handed it over. Stephens tore at its neck and spilled a cascade of gold sovereigns into his lap.

"How much?" he asked eagerly.

"What you asked, James. £80. A month's funding from your supporters. A sign of their faith in you, their belief."

"Oh, very good. Very good. Well done!" Stephens exclaimed gleefully, tinkling the money through his fingers. "And easily raised?"

"Without trying," Matt interrupted. "Well, not very hard."

"And the remainder?"

"The remainder?" Matt didn't understand.

Denieffe nodded reassuringly, almost patronizingly, in his direction before speaking. "Matt here is something of a newcomer to the association but we've great hopes for him," he told Stephens. "That's why he came. A blooding, as it were. But he hasn't been fully involved in the councils yet."

"Admirable, admirable," Stephens commented. "Discretion. Secrecy. Very worthy. Very."

"Well, he doesn't know what you're asking and wanting, James."

Stephens grunted to himself before speaking. "As I told you last time we met, Joe, give me five hundred Irish patriots from the States, fully armed with those Lee-Enfield rifles, and I'll undertake to have an army of ten thousand men organized here within three months. Most will have pikes but I guarantee at least fifteen hundred will have firing pieces of some kind. And didn't I pledge that when I have them, they'll be ready to rise and fight at a day's notice?"

"You did, James. You did."

"Well?"

Denieffe spread his hands and shrugged his shoulders. Stephens sank back into his chair. Matt looked at each of them in turn. His mind was still trying to absorb all this sudden talk of arms and armies.

"There's support, James," Denieffe said deliberately, stroking his dark beard. "There's support all right but there's no proper organization yet in America. There's the clubs, the societies, the association, but no organization. So we can't give you the men for certain. O'Mahony and Doheny think you should form the organization here in secret and then we'll found a similar body over there."

"Why so?" Stephens replied shortly, disappointed at the obvious lack of material pledges.

"Well, they're thinking—and I agree with them—that we'll find a stronger response if the Irish-Americans can be told of a secret, suppressed organization over here. They'll give themselves and their monies more readily if they think they're supporting the actual men at the barricades, as it were. The men doing the stern work, as you put it yourself, James. Anything founded in America must be rather nebulous while here—why you're under threat of exposure and arrest all the time."

"Makes an awful sense," Matt interrupted.

"Well, I do have a detailed plan for an organization," Stephens laughed. He leaned forward in his chair, warming his hands against the heat of the coal fire in the grate, while he began to explain his ideas. Matt and Denieffe listened with silent approval.

"That's it!" Denieffe exclaimed when Stephens had finished. "Every unit watertight from the other. The police agents'll never penetrate us."

"Precisely. They won't know who are the men and who the officers."

"It'll survive, Matt. You'll see."

"What are you calling it then, James?" asked Denieffe, his face glowing with fervor.

Stephens waved a hand deprecatingly. "I'm just thinking of it as 'Our Organization' or 'Our Movement.' I've nothing firm in mind."

"Didn't O'Mahony have an idea for a name?" asked Matt. "I remember it from one of his speeches."

"And isn't he the Gaelic scholar?" Stephens broke in.

Denieffe ignored the implied sarcasm. "Matt's right. O'Mahony talked of the warrior Fiona MacCumhail and his legion of Fianna."

"The Knights," Matt murmured.

"I have the Gaelic," Stephens said testily.

"Well, from the Fianna, O'Mahony took the name, Fenians," Denieffe continued. "He reckons the organization should be called The Fenian Society, or perhaps The Fenian Brotherhood."

Stephens thought for a few moments, looking deeply into the fire. Then he nodded enthusiastically.

"It sounds right. The Fenians." He rolled the name around his tongue several times. "Yes, the Fenians." He paused for a second before going on. His voice was quiet and determined. "Two things, though. Or perhaps three. I'm absolutely certain that what I'm called, the Head Center or Chief Organizer, if you like, should be utterly free, totally unshackled in making decisions. He'll have to be a sort of provisional dictator of Ireland. Definitely a provisional dictator."

Denieffe nodded. "I think O'Mahony and Doheny'll accept that. Discipline is needed."

"Then, there'll have to be the same oath both here and in America."

"Agreed!"

"And thirdly, I want one of you two to become vice-centers or centers over here in Ireland. It'll be a gesture of faith from America. It'll inspire our men. It'll cement the link between us. And it'll help me in my approaches to our friends on the Continent."

Matt and Denieffe looked at each other in bewilderment. They began speaking at the same time, their voices rising.

"But I'm too well-known as an agitator," said Denieffe.

"My family . . . my business," Matt protested.

Stephens sat calmly back in his chair. "I can yield nothing on this point. It must be agreed or there'll be no Fenians—or what you will—formed here. From the very start, you Irish-Americans must supply more than fine words."

"I'll be a danger, James. They'll spot me for sure. Can't you see that?"

"Perhaps, Joe. Perhaps. What about Matt?"

"No one knows him," Denieffe continued quickly. "And you do have land in the West to settle, don't you, Matt? You told me yourself."

"But my family, the wee ones." Matt was becoming

angry and flustered. He realized he was being forced into an impossible situation. "They're born and bred in Boston. They're Americans."

"Of an Irish father and a half-Irish mother," Denieffe snapped.

"Gentlemen, gentlemen," murmured Stephens, scenting eventual victory. "There is a solution."

"What?" Matt and Denieffe echoed.

"A coin, of course. The toss of a coin."

"No!" exclaimed Matt.

Stephens shrugged. "Then there'll be no . . ."

"Come on Matt," pleaded Denieffe. "I don't like it any more than you do. But it'll be the fairest way."

"Well, gentlemen?"

It seemed to Matt as if the dark walls of the sitting room were closing in on him. Stephens took a cigar from a pocket in his waistcoat and started preparing it for lighting. Denieffe appeared to be studying the heavy, faded velvet curtains. Matt knew he was trapped, and that whatever his call, the outcome would be equally inevitable.

Stephens flipped a sovereign into the air.

Denieffe called, "Royal."

The coin slapped back on to Stephen's palm with Queen Victoria's profile upwards.

Denieffe was quick to try to alleviate Matt's discomfort.

"Are you sure, Matt?" he asked.

Matt nodded. He felt numb all over.

"It'll be my duty to help you bring Mary round, for I'm sure she'll be having misgivings."

"You're too proper, Joe," Matt said sourly. "Misgivings? Her? Mary? Leaving Boston to live in Ireland with a man committed to rebellion? She'll be as pleased as when I jumped her into a pile of horse shit."

"Horse shit?" Stephens tried not to laugh but the amusement was in his voice.

"Doesn't matter," Matt replied disconsolately. "Matters not at all."

Denieffe couldn't keep the elation he felt out of his remarks. "Well, now that's settled, James. What now? What's halting the Fenians? You've your first vice-center."

Stephens stretched up from his chair, satisfied with the evening's work. He leaned over Matt to pat his shoulder. "Don't be worrying," he said reassuringly. "I'll help explain to your good lady the need for your return to the old country. Don't be worrying about that." He straightened, walked to the narrow mantelpiece, turned and clapped his hands decisively. "Well, the next matter of moment is the oath taking. Tomorrow would be propitious. Yes, tomorrow would indeed be entirely propitious." Clearly, James Stephens would brook no argument.

The next evening, Matt Aherne stood opposite him across a dining table covered with a ragged piece of green cloth. A rusty-looking flintlock pistol lay diagonally on the table.

"Place your right hand on the firearm," intoned Stephens, remembering the way of the oaths of the Phoenix Literary Society of Skibbereen. "And recite after me . . ."

Matt gazed around the room. He saw Joe Denieffe standing stiffly to attention, beard bristling, alongside two other men whom Stephens had introduced only a few minutes before as Tom Luby and Owen Considine. They were looking at him with an expression Matt had seen before on the faces of women about to take Holy Communion, one of great expectancy, of untried belief. Matt spoke automatically in a low voice.

"I, Matthew Aherne, do solemnly swear in the presence

of Almighty God, that I will do my utmost, at every risk, while life lasts, to make Ireland an independent Democratic Republic; that I will yield implicit obedience, in all things not contrary to the laws of God, to the commands of my superior officers, and that I shall preserve inviolable secrecy regarding all transactions of the society that may be confided in me. So help me God. Amen.''

The Fenian Society, the Irish Republican Brotherhood, was in being. It was March 17th, 1858. St. Patrick's Day.

Chapter 9
December, 1866

"Come on, me boyos. Smarten yourselves."

Matt Aherne's voice carried into the biting Atlantic wind blowing across the sands at the mouth of the River Cashen on the North Kerry coast.

He was perched on one of the dunes towering over the beach. His vantage point enabled him, even in the fast-fading winter dusk, to watch and judge the drilling of the Listowel Company of the Fenian Brotherhood.

Lookouts were posted on top of the dunes to warn of any strangers, of any nosy constables, but Matt wasn't worried in the least about that particular danger. The authorities hadn't stumbled across the secret drilling ground in all its years of use by the Fenians. The high dunes protected it from the gaze of anyone wandering along the nearest track and the slapping waves forcing their way through the narrow mouth of the river drowned most noises.

The men below him on the smooth beach marched and wheeled and halted to the commands of a former private in the British Army. He was one of nearly twenty regular soldiers who had deserted the ranks to become Fenian drillmasters for the sum of one shilling and sixpence a day, twopence more than they received for serving the Colors.

As he watched his men go through their paces, Matt had to admit that they did not look anything like fierce rebels against Queen Victoria's Empire, even under the drillmas-

439

ter's professional tuition. Their clothes were ragged, their step uneven, and their pikes at every angle except the correct one. Their "pikes" consisted of staves cut from tree branches with any piece of metal sharpened and lashed to the end. They were adequate instruments of death and mutilation in a racetrack brawl or an old-fashioned faction fight, Matt thought, but he dreaded to think what would happen against properly armed soldiers or police. Surprisingly, though, the ordinary Fenian's keenness and appetite for drill hadn't diminished during the long years of waiting for the call to action.

"Let's have a song then, drillmaster," Matt bawled, his voice echoing off the wall of the dunes. The men heard his shout. Their faces brightened as they broke into the Fenian marching song. The words, slightly out of tune, mingled with the gurgling, choppy waves of the river.

"See who comes over the red-blossomed heather,
  Their green banners kissing the pure mountain air,
  Heads erect! Eyes to the front! Stepping proudly together,
  Out and make way for the bold Fenian men.
  Side by side for the cause have our forefathers battled,
  On our hills never echoed the tread of a slave,
  In many a field where the leaden hail rattled,
  Through the red gap of glory they marched to the grave.
  All those who inherit their name and their spirit
  Will march with the banners of liberty then.
  All who love foreign law, native or Sassenach,
  Must out and make way for the bold Fenian men."

Matt found the words stirring, although he realized only too well that the history of the Fenian Brotherhood had scarcely been one of glorious revolution in the eight years since its founding. Indeed, it had nearly sunk into total obscurity at times. But, by this December afternoon in

1866, the movement was in the ascendancy once more. There had been a power struggle among the hierarchy which had diverted attention from the Fenians' main aims.

During the American Civil War, both sides had sported Irish Brigades. Sometimes Irishmen had fought against Irishmen, gaining, at least, grudging acceptance from the native Americans as well as a deal of much-needed experience in modern warfare. The Civil War also increased the Irish-American thirst for action against the British, a thirst that James Stephens was unable to quench. He urged caution and preparation while the war-hardened Fenians across the Atlantic wanted immediate revolution in Ireland.

The previous year, the American Fenians had strained at the leash when they met for their annual convention in Cincinnati. Stephens' old friend, John O'Mahony, didn't even have to disguise his fiery intentions since the Fenians had been declared a legal organization in the United States.

"This brotherhood," O'Mahony had told the wildly enthusiastic delegates, "is virtually at war with the oligarchy of Great Britain. The Fenian Congress acts the part of a national assembly of an Irish Republic. Our organized friends in Ireland constitute its army!"

The leaders of Irish society began packing their silver and gold into boxes and sending it to banks in London. Reports from boatmen along the Shannon spoke of large boatloads of Fenians crossing to the Limerick side of the river from County Clare. The country grew tense, expecting the long-anticipated rebellion at any moment.

James Stephens sent a letter to the Fenian cell in Clonmel telling his volunteers that the uprising would come in a few months, in the autumn of 1865. His messenger got drunk before leaving Dublin and decided to sleep it off in the offices of the pro-Fenian newspaper, the *Irish Post*. While he was relieving himself into a chamber pot the next morning, the letter was stolen from his coat pocket by a police informer who'd been working undercover at the newspaper for more than eighteen months.

The *Irish Post* was suppressed and, in a carefully coordinated operation, the police arrested dozens of Fenians. Stephens himself was picked up nearly two months later but managed to escape from gaol with the help of Fenian prison warders. Cheekily, he went into hiding in the center of Dublin, in lodgings almost directly opposite the staunchly Unionist gentlemen's club in Kildare Street. His actions were as bold as his future strategy was timid.

A meeting was held at Stephens' secret address, which Matt attended, and the Irish-American Fenians pressed for immediate action.

"No! No! It would be wrong," Stephens argued. "It would seem as if we were striking out of desperation, that we were in a corner after the arrests."

"But you've the men, haven't you, James?" persisted Michael Kelly, the Irish-American who'd been lately titled "Colonel" and voted Fenian chief of staff.

"We have that, sir. Almost two hundred thousand of them in Ireland alone," Stephens replied, banging the table enthusiastically in an effort to appear more confident and decisive than he himself felt. "Fifty thousand of them are thoroughly armed and add to that my intelligence reports which say a third of the British garrison here are on our side. Oh yes, colonel, we have the men alright."

"Then, strike now, dammit," urged Kelly, furiously stubbing a half-smoked cigar into an ash tray. "Let the rising begin!"

Stephens leapt to his feet, realizing that Kelly carried support around the table. He leaned over, fingertips spread on the brocade cloth. "And how many times have risings failed just because of that attitude?'' he exclaimed. ''When we rise against the British, we must be certain of our organization. I don't believe Ireland can stomach another bungled affair. There have been too many, draining the resolve and spirit of the people. We must be sure of success this time.''

Kelly wagged his beard in dismay. His argument with Stephens continued throughout the two days of the meeting. Eventually, more from weariness than conviction, he conceded the point. The rising would be postponed. Kelly and his supporters returned to America with doubts growing in their minds about Stephens' qualities of leadership.

The truth, if the Fenian founder would recognize it, was that Stephens was besotted with the concept of revolution but his years in the wilderness had almost completely blunted his desire for action. If his rebellion failed, then he knew his power was over. While the revolt was still theoretical, he remained in command. Or so his mind instinctively worked. But he was driven out of his ivory tower by a further move by the authorities against the Fenians in February 1866. It forced Stephens to flee Ireland and seek sanctuary with Colonel Kelly in New York. Kelly lost little time in demonstrating his influence over the Irish-American Fenians and their desire for swift action.

On May 31st, about two hundred armed Fenians rowed across the Niagara River and took over the small Canadian village of Fort Erie. The inhabitants were quite bemused when the Fenians paraded with rifles along the hard-packed mud of their one and only street, a green flag with an embroidered yellow harp fluttering before their columns. That was all the Fenians could do since the only representative of the British Empire's far-flung authority was the part-time village constable who promptly surrendered and insisted on buying liquor for his captors.

Within forty-eight hours, though, a company of Canadian volunteers, mainly students, moved against the Fenians. Both sides' experience in such matters led to a circumspect battle fought at rifle range at a local landmark called Lime Ridge. The marksmanship was of a surprising quality. After three hours, the Canadians had lost twelve killed and forty wounded; the Fenians, eight dead and twenty wounded. The Fenian leaders decided they'd had the best of the day and withdrew, fearing they might not do so well against regular troops if they were cut off from the river and their route back into the United States.

Colonel Kelly, from his campaign headquarters at Buffalo, issued a triumphant statement to the gathered newspaper representatives. "The Irish Republican Army has been in action for the first time," he announced. "Arise Irishmen, a glorious career has opened for you. The Green Flag has waved once more in triumph over England's hated emblem."

The success of the invasion of British soil meant the virtual end of James Stephens' influence over the Fenian movement. His counsels of caution were ridiculed as Kelly was voted head of the Fenians' "military" sector with the grandiose title of Acting Chief Executive of the Irish Republic. In an hysterical attempt to regain favor, Stephens even offered to return to Ireland "to get hung." There were no takers. The leaders of the self-styled Irish Republican Army were firmly in control of any future revolution in Ireland.

"Perhaps there'll be action at last," Matt remarked to his wife late that summer as he read of Stephens' eclipse in a letter sent from Boston by Joe Denieffe.

Mary gave him a sour look.

"And how long have you been waiting? Eight years, is it?" she said, complaint in her voice. "An awful lot of parading up and down the sands with your long sticks that is."

"You know there've been problems, dear," Matt said soothingly.

"Problems, is it?" Mary put her sewing down in her lap and removed her glasses. "Problems . . . So now they've got rid of your precious James Stephens, have they? The friend who deceived you into leaving our future behind in Boston. Fine friend, he was!"

Matt sighed inwardly. He really had thought that, at long last, the subject had been closed. But then, Mary had been increasingly tetchy recently.

"You know it wasn't like that, dear."

"And what was it like then, Matthew Aherne?"

He looked round the sitting room of the house in Church Street. It was a solid-stoned, high-ceilinged concession to Mary's aversion to living in the old cabin at Drombeg townland. It was a concession he'd felt bound to make in the trauma of moving her and their children from the comfortable Boston suburbs to what Mary still regarded as the most backward part of a backward country. He sighed again, audibly this time.

"It had to be. You know that."

He thought Mary had realized that inevitability those years ago when he'd returned to Boston to tell her of his oath-taking with the Fenian Brotherhood. Strangely and surprisingly, she'd said very little. No violent tantrum of objection had occurred. The sea voyage had been like a second honeymoon with Mary's sexual passions undoubtedly aroused by her journey into the unknown. They had explored each other's minds and bodies as if for the first time. The doubts had set in, though, within a few days of arriving in Kerry.

Alderman Finucane had been as good as his word in

ensuring that the Ahernes could return to the cabin and two
fields where the Keanes had lived and where Matt's mother
was buried.

Matt's first meeting with the land agent, George Sandes,
had been agreeable enough despite the awkwardness between the two men as they tried not to mention—or even
acknowledge—the fact that they were half-brothers.

They were not dissimilar in build, both lean and tall, but
there was a weakness around Sandes' almost feminine
mouth and chin. His eyes were watery and bloodshot, the
pupils colored an unusually pale blue. His voice, as he
greeted Matt, bore little trace of an Irish accent.

"My dear fellow," he said, shaking Matt's outstretched
hand and guiding him at the same time to an armchair next
to the desk in his study. "My very dear fellow," he
repeated. "On his deathbed, my father . . ." He smiled
faintly to himself. "Jonathan Sandes told me of you. Oh,
indeed he did. He said you might return here one day and
then, lo and behold, your letter of last month announcing
your intentions. So unexpected. So very pleasurable."

Sandes rubbed his hands together as if washing them. His
eyes flicked to some documents on his desk.

"Your family?" he inquired. "Are they with you?"

"In the hostelry next door."

"Ah, the dear old Listowel Arms. Many an evening in
their private room . . ." Sandes laughed. Matt sensed his
nervousness, his unease. "Are you comfortable?"

"Well enough for the present."

"Wanting to take possession of the Keane cabin again?"

"Indeed."

"Well, everything's in order, of course. The rents were
properly remitted by your patron, Finucane, and so you can
go in directly. But I must warn you the years have taken a
toll. The roof . . . the outhouses . . . the fields. Plenty

of work there, Mr. Aherne, a sufficiency indeed . . . now that's silly, isn't it? . . . Mr. Aherne . . . Matthew, I meant . . . or is it Matt?"

"Matt."

"Matt, then. You don't mind?"

"No."

"Good. Capital. Well, as I was remarking, there's work a-plenty there but I'm sure you're used to that. Have to be tough to survive in the colonies, or rather the former colonies, what? And we're just approaching our prime, aren't we?"

"Not yet thirty."

"Of course."

"And you?" Matt asked curiously.

Sandes' eyes flicked again to the table. "Some five years after you, I believe. Can't be precise, I think . . . about you, I mean."

"No. I think not, George."

Matt placed a heavy emphasis on his half-brother's given name.

"The documents, Matt," Sandes said quickly, seeming to wish a change of subject.

"Yes."

"I've had them put in order. A proper agreement is needed now. Not like the old days."

"Security of tenure?"

"Not quite. But having everything in writing is a step in the right direction, isn't it?"

"You can still put us in the ditch when you like." Matt made a flat statement of fact.

Sandes looked sideways at him, not sure how to take the remark. Then he laughed.

"Come now. How could I do that? Hardly with you. Hardly."

It became clear, though, at the family's first sight of the

cabin that to live there was out of the question. The property was overgrown and almost completely tumbledown. The Ahernes' natural excitement at being in a strange country, of returning to their father's birthplace, long told on in bedtime stories, vanished in a torrent of dismay. Even Matt felt abject with disappointment.

The long silence of the journey back to Listowel in a cramped jaunty cart remained in Matt's memory for years afterwards.

Within weeks, he'd moved the family into 36 Church Street, Listowel. The next problem had been to make a living.

He and Mary took stock of their experience with the Finucane cooperage and tavern business and eventually settled on opening a hostelry further up Church Street, just opposite Forge Lane and the police barracks. It was named "The Boston Tavern" although people were soon calling it simply "Aherne's." The customers were attracted by Mary's New England cooking and Matt's brainwave of making the hostelry the clearing house of any news and gossip about all those Kerry families who'd sought a new life as emigrants.

Soon, the establishment became a necessary port of call for anyone whose relatives had left the district as well as the "local" for the police constables of the town. Matt knew he would never make his fortune there but, then again, he was certain the business would always provide a comfortable, sociable existence. He also realized that the hostelry gave him an ideal cover for his Fenian activities. Who would, after all, suspect someone who was on such good terms with so many police constables? From their alcoholically indiscreet comments, Matt was able to glean many snippets of information which were invaluable in establishing a Fenian network in Kerry. And by observing his customers in their unguarded moments of relaxation he was in a good position to weigh up who were potential recruits. Once they had been recruited, though, the firm rule was that they should stop drinking in "Aherne's" and take their custom to another of Listowel's many hostelries. Only his two most trusted lieutenants who passed all orders to the rank and file members, Paddy Sugrue and Bryan Stack, were allowed near his home or the tavern. Indeed, Matt attempted to keep his involvement with the Fenian cause as far as possible from his home and business lives. He knew only too well that Mary's dislike of it was never far below the surface. That it should emerge again with the news of the hawkish elements assuming control of the Fenians was unfortunate but, with hindsight, not unexpected.

"So when's all this action you're braying about going to commence?" Mary's questions remained sour and pointed. "Is it tomorrow you'll be picking up your pointed sticks and beginning the war against the English?"

"What war, Mama?" Brigid Aherne, now a burgeoning fifteen-year-old, caught her mother's last remark as she entered the sitting room. "Mama, you said war against the English," the girl persisted.

"Mama was only joking," Matt interrupted. He and Mary exchanged frosty glances.

"Run along, dear," said Mary. "Your father and I are talking of matters not for your ears. You were supposed to be making tomorrow's pig's pudding, weren't you?"

"Yes, mama but I'm thinking the blood isn't smelling fresh."

"The pig was fresh killed yesterday, Brigid," her mother replied. "It'll be fresh enough. Be off with you now, will you?"

Brigid, suitably chastened, returned to the kitchen to set about mixing the blood with grated pig's liver, bread, wheatmeal, oatmeal, lard, and onion. The smell of the pudding as it steamed would fill the house for hours. So would the acrimonious words between Matt and Mary.

The Fenians began to drill in earnest again, three times a week at Ballyeagh Strand, whatever the weather. Matt knew that with Kelly in charge of the movement action would not be far away.

The call came shortly after Stephen's Day that year. Matt was woken at home by a banging on the kitchen door. He opened it, grumbling audibly, to be confronted by an apparent stranger, a tall clean-shaven man.

"I'm sorry to be rousing the house, Matt." The man smiled, clearly not sorry at all.

"It won't be helping me back into Mary's good books, I'm reckoning."

Matt peered closely at him in the grey, early morning light. There was a familiar smile in the caller's eyes but surely it wasn't . . . ?

The stranger's smile broadened as he noticed Matt's bewilderment. "Put some weight on me, Matt, a fair weight, and then a beard."

"Joe. Good Lord, Joe Denieffe, by all that's holy. But why? When?"

Denieffe looked quickly over his shoulder. "Hush, Matt." He pressed a finger to his lips. "Don't be spoiling the disguise by telling the town who I am."

Matt pulled him into the kitchen and swiftly bolted the door again. "It's mad you are, Joe, coming here yourself. Mad!" he exclaimed. "And us just opposite the police."

"Had to, old friend. Orders for me and orders for you. And anyway even yourself wasn't knowing me without the whiskers."

"But still a risk, Joe. Are you straight here from Boston?"

"Not directly. I've been in London making arrangements, then in Liverpool, and finally a few stops over here."

"With the orders?"

"Aye."

Matt looked at Denieffe across the kitchen table, excitement growing within him. "Then it's really happening?"

"It is that. You've some travelling to do in the next weeks, so you have, Matt."

The next morning, after strained family farewells, Matt and Denieffe set off to visit Fenian cells in Limerick, Cork, Tipperary and Waterford, before journeying to the northwest of England and North Wales. They spent a week there together before Matt broke away. He took a train from Crewe to London, arriving in the heart of the great Victorian empire late on January 25th.

He took temporary lodgings off Bloomsbury Square. For the first time in his life, he had seen his sworn enemies at close quarters, in their natural surroundings, and had recognized them as human beings like himself with similar aspirations and emotions. The experience unnerved him so much that he hardly slept that night. But the next morning, January 26th, 1867, he was at the rendezvous at the appointed time to meet the Irish-Americans who were to lead the revolt.

He stood outside the entrance to the Langham Hotel in Portland Place with its lofty statues dotted along the wide thoroughfare toward Regents Park. Matt felt unnaturally conspicuous in his heavy tweed suit, cloak and long green muffler beside the elegantly dressed men and women entering and leaving the hotel. He waited on the edge of the pavement for ten or more minutes, pretending to be absorbed in the study of Christopher Wren's small master-piece of church building, All Souls, just across the busy road. Light flurries of snow stung his cheek and dampened his hair.

"The day is coming."

A drawling voice beside him dragged Matt out of his thoughts.

"When Ireland's woes are done," he replied automatically, smiling into the heavily bearded face of the man who'd stolen up behind him. They shook hands, introducing themselves.

"Aherne. Matt Aherne from Kerry."

"I know, Matt. I'm Gordon Massey from New York."

"Joe Denieffe told me of you."

"Good. Well, let's be off and meet the others. You haven't been watched, have you?"

"Not that I've seen."

"No, I think not as well. I was watching from across the street and no one was paying too much attention."

"Where are the rest?"

"Just a cock's stride from here. No. 137, Great Portland Street. At least, that's where Cliseret is. The colonel's been staying near Tottenham Court Road. General Halpin and Dick Burke and myself are in Tavistock Square. Spread all over the area we are under a variety of names. Safer that way. But this address we're going to is our main headquarters, as it were."

It took them less than five minutes to reach the house, as tall and imposing as its neighbors along the fashionable street in the heart of London. The Irish-Americans, who'd apparently rented the entire premises, were gathered in a drawing room downstairs when Matt arrived. Some he remembered from past meetings in America and Ireland. The others clearly had been recruited into the Fenians

during the American Civil War. Most of them were
introduced to him with military titles but Matt had no way
of knowing if the titles had been assumed or awarded in
other armies.

". . . Colonel Kelly you know, of course . . . General Halpin . . . Captain O'Sullivan Burke . . . Brigadier-
General Cliseret . . . Major Fariola . . . Major Vifquain . . . Captain McCafferty . . . Captain O'Brien
. . . and finally, last but not least, Mr. Corydon . . ."

Matt shook hands or merely nodded at the men gathered
around the large table, strewn with maps, railway time-
tables and piles of paper.

"And my rank is general," said Massey rather self-
consciously when he'd finished the introductions. "I'm to
be senior commander of our forces on Irish soil." He
gestured for Matt to be seated.

"You know the plan, Aherne?" asked Kelly at the head
of the table.

"Aye. Denieffe acquainted me, Colonel."

"What chances of it in your estimation?"

"Good, I hazard. Joe and I have studied the terrain and
there's no reason why we shouldn't have success . . . that
is, if . . ."

"What?"

"If there's complete surprise, and that means total
secrecy."

"There has been and there is," interjected Massey. "I'll
stake my life on that."

"You might have to," Kelly added with a harsh, throaty
laugh. "We all might have to."

He turned back to Matt.

"Your men are ready?"

"Not only mine but all those you've called for."

"Excellent. Excellent."

Massey broke in again. "Can we move on, Colonel, to the proclamation?"

"But the plan?"

"Can't we return to that in detail later?"

"Indeed, yes. Perhaps it would be more advantageous. There has to be final discussion and approval and better that it should be as the last item on the agenda. It will remain fresh with us that way."

Kelly riffled through a stack of papers in front of him then began passing them around the table.

"Gentlemen," he explained. "This is a draft of what will be delivered to the newspapers within the next few days. As you will see, it has had careful consideration."

Matt read the three pages handed to him. He felt distinctly uncomfortable on reading the appeal from the Fenians to the British public at large. Where were the grand phrases of previous proclamations? Where was the disinterested note of scholarship? These words in front of him seemed to be a demand for total revolution in social thinking and attitudes, rather than a simple explanation of Fenian aims.

Certainly, the first part of the proclamation from what was termed "The Provisional Government of the Irish Republic" was conventional enough. "We have suffered centuries of outrage, enforced poverty and bitter misery," it read. "Our rights and liberties have been trampled on by an alien aristocracy who, treating us as foes, usurped our lands and drew away from an unfortunate country all material riches."

But it was the concluding paragraph which worried Matt.

"As for you, workmen of England, it is not your hearts we wish but your arms. Remember the starvation and degradation brought to your firesides by the oppression of labor. Remember the past, look well to the future, and avenge yourselves by giving liberty to your children in the coming struggle for human freedom.''

The draft statement ended, "Herewith we proclaim the Irish Republic.''

"Well, gentlemen?" Kelly inquired after a few minutes.

A variety of approving remarks spread around the table.

"Everyone in agreement, then?" the colonel asked.

Matt looked at his companions, seeking some moral support for his doubts. By the smiles on their faces, it seemed he was in a minority of one. He raised his hand reluctantly.

"Aherne?"

"It's these phrases about the workmen of England and the oppression of labor."

"Yes?"

"We're after the freedom of Ireland yet here we're talking about English workers, urging them to rise against their masters."

"So?"

"Are we not confusing the issues?"

Kelly's pitying look added to Matt's discomfort.

"The issues are indivisible, my dear sir. One and the same. Ireland can never be free until the peasants are, until the people are."

"I can understand that, but the proclamation mentions English workmen as well."

"The struggle in Ireland is but part of the greater struggle for freedom among working men and women in all the countries in Europe. Surely you know that?"

"But . . ."

"But nothing, sir." Kelly's voice held traces of frustration and anger. "You are a friend of Stephens, aren't you? A good friend?"

"Yes."

"Then you should know his philosophy. Dammit, Aherne, he founded the movement even if he did lose his resolve. His principles remain. They predominate. All he learned during those years on the Continent. The match to our flame. The steel to our sword arm. Oh yes, sir. His are our principles. They are why we shall succeed. Have no doubt. None at all. The Fenians are in the vanguard of a great historical movement sweeping across the civilized world. Established orders must be overthrown before there is real freedom."

"Isn't that the belief of the anarchists?"

Matt continued his questions although he saw a growing restlessness and resentment from his companions. Kelly's face began to whiten with anger.

"Anarchists?" he boomed. "Anarchists?"

Massey tried to mediate.

"Matt," he said soothingly, "that's just a name the authorities give to anyone or anything they see as a threat to the traditional ways. We are patriots, nationalists if you like, whatever label others might attach to us."

"That's correct, Matt," McCafferty murmured beside him. "Let the matter rest."

"Colonel, I propose we move on," Massey urged. The slapping of hands on the table drowned any question on Matt's lips. He bowed to the inevitable and sat back in his chair, his doubts unresolved.

Chapter 10
February, 1867

Down the centuries, more than one invader bent on plunder had come to the town of Chester in northwest England. The Romans had recognized the site's strategic importance as far back as A.D. 79, sending the XX Legion to establish a camp where the broad River Dee narrowed to a fordable stream. From there, they dominated the valuable salt mines in central Cheshire and protected the rich farmland of the plain against the marauders from Wales and Yorkshire. When the legion moved on after two hundred years, the Saxons renamed the settlement "Chester" from the Roman word for camp. The town could not fail to prosper with its direct access to the Irish Sea, the rich agricultural lands and the lusty industrial towns further to the north. And being such a prize, it had been properly fortified over the years with stout, red sandstone walls and a fine castle high on the banks of the salmon-rich river.

Matt Aherne and John McCafferty stood on the side of the bridge over the river on the morning of February 11th, 1867, pretending to study the layout of the racetrack set in the meadows below. Their vantage point also gave them a good view of the sentries at the castle entrance on the other side of the bridge. They stood in huts by the wrought iron gates leading to the cobbled square in front of the castle.

"The most action they've seen is someone dropping their musket on Sunday church parade!" muttered McCafferty.

"And isn't that just why we're here?" Matt replied, leaning on his elbows over the balustrade of the bridge.

"Sure and they'll be in for a fine surprise when the boys come calling. They'll be dropping more than their guns then, I'm guessing."

Both men laughed and began strolling back over the bridge into the maze of the town's narrow streets. Chester wore that air of well-ordered gentility common to most towns steeped in history and benign feudalism. The citizens instinctively knew their place in the order of things. The soldiers and constables were to remind and reassure the gentry of their own superiority, the outward proof that Victoria was on the throne and all was well with the world.

It was one of the reasons why the Fenians had chosen the town; that and Chester's importance as a railway junction with tracks running along the Welsh bank of the Dee to Holyhead on the Isle of Anglesey, the departure point for mailboats bound for Ireland.

The land was so breathtakingly bold that, even at first hearing, Matt had been convinced of its chances of success.

First, the Fenians would overpower the castle sentries and seize all the available arms and ammunition in the barracks. Then, at gunpoint, they would commandeer trains to carry the weapons to Holyhead, having cut all telegraphic links to and from Chester and the Welsh seaport. Once there, the Fenians would capture the mailboat and set sail for Kingstown, just south of Dublin. Simultaneously, the uprising would begin on Irish soil.

Matt had arrived in Chester two nights previously, taking cheap lodgings near the station. McCafferty had joined him the next morning. They had checked all the back alleys for the most unobtrusive routes to the castle entrance, and for possible escape routes. Their confidence grew. The town was clearly going about its business as usual. Surprise, the plan's supreme element, seemed to remain with them.

Despite his warm tweed clothes, Matt shivered suddenly just as they'd completed their tour of the town's center and had retraced their steps in Lower Bridge Street.

McCafferty noticed Matt rubbing his hands together and felt the frosty nip in the air himself. "At last jar then?" he asked, pointing to the long rows of casement windows of the Bear and Billet Inn further down the street.

The two hundred-year-old inn had a dozen customers scattered about its gloomy bar when the two Irishmen entered. They ordered a jug of porter with two large glasses of cognac and took their drinks to a well-scrubbed bench table.

"Nervous then?" McCafferty asked after they had their first mouthfuls.

"Not much, John. There's too much in my mind at present for nervousness to slip in."

McCafferty peered closely into Matt's face. "Well, you can say better than I can. The porter's jumping around my insides like it's alive."

"Take the cognac."

"I will that but I'm thinking now of what can go wrong, Matt."

"Nothing, friend."

"I'm trusting so, but last night an awful strange feeling took me. For want of a better word, Matt, I had a foreboding."

"That it wouldn't go well? Oh come on, man," Matt urged. "Isn't it your plan and haven't we discussed it often enough?"

"We have."

"And could we see a weakness?"

"Not one."

"There you are, John," Matt said cheeringly. "A bad dream. That's all you had."

McCafferty brightened slightly. "Aye, you're right. Didn't I have the feeling enough during the war between the states and aren't I still here to be blathering away?"

"You are that."

Although he tried not to show it, Matt felt some of his companion's unease begin to creep over him. But he tried to reassure himself. The Fenians would start arriving in town within an hour or so and wasn't Chester quiet enough? He slipped his hand into his jacket pocket to feel the comforting weight of the small Remington revolver McCafferty had given him the day before.

"Not long now." McCafferty spoke suddenly, breaking into Matt's thoughts. Automatically, they both pulled out their fob watches. McCafferty's was inscribed inside.

"An hour," Matt said quietly.

"Aye."

"A last cognac?"

"To settle my nerves, eh?"

"No," Matt smiled. "To settle the ones I've been catching from you."

Matt called his order to a rotund, jolly-faced man in a stained apron.

"Busier now," he remarked casually as the man started filling the glasses on the counter.

"It is, sir. Always around this time before midday."

Matt nodded.

"But you'll be seeing it busier later," the man continued.

"I expect so."

"Yes, them maneuvers are always good for trade."

"Maneuvers?" Matt said, not thinking for a moment.

"A little early this year. They're usually in the spring. The soldier boys from London or wherever bring their camp followers with 'em more often than not. Trollops but good for trade. You'll see. Just you wait and see. Like bees round the honey, my regulars are. All wanting a dip, if you'll pardon the expression."

A pang of alarm gripped Matt. "You mean military maneuvers? Here?" He tried to sound as casual as he could.

"That's what Constable Skidmore reckoned when he came for his breakfast. The Volunteers are called out and the Welsh Guards entrained from London. That's what the constable said."

"Why?" Matt realized the question was too urgent. He softened his tone. "Did the constable say why?"

"That's the strange thing, sir. He didn't know. Leastways he said he didn't. Special maneuvers at the castle. That's all he knew. That's fourpence, sir."

Matt fumbled in his pocket and handed over the coins before striding across to McCafferty with the glasses.

"There's trouble, John," he whispered urgently. "Sink this quick and outside. Hurry now!"

They gulped their glasses and walked swiftly outside. Matt glanced up and down the cobbled street.

"What the devil is it, man?" McCafferty demanded.

In three clipped sentences, Matt repeated what he'd been told in the Bear and Billet. Although the street was virtually deserted his voice was so low that McCafferty strained to hear.

"Oh God, no!" he muttered. "They're on to us then . . . Holy Mother!"

Matt pulled him by the arm away from the inn.

"We don't know that yet, John. It could be coincidence."

"You think so," McCafferty said bitterly. "You really think so. Someone's talked, that's what. We're dished right and proper, that's what."

The Irish-American seemed stunned by the news. His complexion had turned ashen, muscles working high on his cheekbones, eyes blinking rapidly. Matt saw that he was scarcely capable of thought.

"The castle!" Matt exclaimed. "That's where we'll see."

McCafferty stood motionless. "Dished . . . dished . . . dished," he kept murmuring.

"Come on, John." Matt almost dragged him down the street. "The others'll be here soon. We must get to the castle."

"But the boys . . ." McCafferty protested, apparently still in a daze.

"The boys are coming in now," Matt half-screamed at him through clenched teeth. His companion's panic was beginning to affect him. "That's why we must go to the castle. To see what's happening there. We must find if the game's up."

"It's too late."

"'Tis not. Come on, for God's sake. We'll still be having time for the others."

Matt put his hand under McCafferty's elbow to force him into a stumbling walk. After a few yards, the Irish-American seemed to regain his composure. He began to stride out through the narrow streets, now busier, up and down the alleys and narrow flights of stairs, his pace keeping up with Matt. Neither spoke. Here and there, they noticed small groups of constables where before, hardly an hour before, there had been none.

Their deepest fears were realized when they burst out of a side street and came in sight of Chester Castle. Instead of just two soldiers guarding the entrance, there was now a cordon of troops spaced a yard apart inside the perimeter railings, fixed bayonets twinkling in the watery sunlight. Four gleaming pieces of artillery were positioned by the castle building itself, muzzles pointing across the parade square toward the now-padlocked gates. The men stood at ease. They looked impassively through the railings but the constant pacing to and fro of the officers and sergeants behind them gave little doubt about their state of preparedness.

Curious crowds had gathered to watch this unexpected and, as yet, unexplained show of strength by the military. Dozens of constables and what looked like part-time volunteer soldiers were pushing them back away from the railings and gates. The Union Jack fluttered limply from the flagpole on the castle's gently sloping roof. Its presence seemed to warn any would-be attackers of the garrison's strength under the flag of empire.

Matt's first instinct was to turn tail immediately. McCafferty skidded to a halt on the cobbles, his feet nearly going from under him, spun around and started back the way he'd come. But Matt realized instinctively that this would be a mistake, would draw attention to both of them. He grabbed McCafferty by the arm again and almost forced him to saunter to the edge of the milling crowd. The snatches of conversation were enough to discover what was happening.

"Where's the guards then?"

"There . . . behind the railings."

"No, not them. I mean the Welsh Guards."

"Oh, them . . . they're nearly here. Our Albert says they're past Crewe."

"Your Albert?"

"Him with the mustache and rifle down by the gates."

"They've all mustaches and . . ."

"The tall 'un . . ."

"Oh, I see 'im . . . when's the navvies coming then?"

"Navvies?"

"Them Irish your Albert told you."

"They're not navvies."

"What are they when they're at home then? Irish are navvies, ain't they?"

"Maybe, but these are rebels so Albert says."

"Rum sort of rebels, if you ask me: navvies."

"They might be navvies but Albert says they're rebels and they're planning to raid the castle . . ."

"Raid the castle? They must be off their chump. Proper mad, they must be. What they want to do that for anyway?"

"Dunno. Albert didn't say."

Matt and McCafferty turned away, despairing. They hurried back down a side street and stood, backs pressed against the wall of a house.

"What now then?" McCafferty spoke first, his voice strangely even and calm.

"We must warn the others."

"And in Ireland. Not only warn them but call off the whole rising."

"But how?"

"I'll telegraph them and head there straight off. I've the escape route. You know that."

"They'll be waiting for Irishers."

"They will that. But I've my American papers. They'll not be harming me too much. Catch you and you'll be doing the rope dance, more than likely."

"Nothing's happened though."

McCafferty snorted derisively. "You think that'll stop them. We're rebels, Matt, whether there's a rebellion or not. And I'm reckoning we haven't even that now. No, you warn the boys here and I'll signal the rest. We've to be quick though."

Matt glanced at the Irish-American. "You've not the nerves now, have you?" he asked curiously.

"Friend," McCafferty smiled wanly, "when the worst you've feared happens, there's nought to be feared about. Believe me."

The two men shook hands, their grips strong as if trying to reassure and strengthen each other, before parting in opposite directions.

"For Ireland," McCafferty whispered.

"Aye," said Matt. "The blessed saints save her. And us."

He ran down the streets towards the inns where meeting places had been previously arranged, slowing to a walk only when he spied the knots of constables dotted around Chester. Some inns were still empty but in others small groups of men, fellow Fenians, mostly young, stood expectantly in small groups.

Swiftly and in lowered tones, Matt told them what had happened, that the action at the castle was cancelled, before rushing off to the next rendezvous point. The rank and file were urged to dump what weapons they possessed and disperse discreetly on foot to make their way home as best they could. All but a few of them needed no second bidding. Some objected.

"I've not been coming from Manchester to be scared off now," one protested. "The women'll not let me in the house. And the boys'll be thinking what a fine da they've got after all the big words."

"How can I be going home without one shot fired?" another remonstrated. "We'll take a crack and the divil have the soldier boys!"

But a few minutes' muttered argument—and the departures of their friends—soon convinced them that nothing but hopeless bloodshed would come of any attack on the castle.

Matt enlisted the aid of their "captains" to contact as many as possible of the Fenians who'd arrived in the town that morning from all over Lancashire. He decided himself to make for the railway station to see if others could be stopped in time but it quickly became apparent that it was an impossible task.

He saw dozens of what he knew from his previous visit to the area to be young Fenians scurrying down the streets leading from the station. One looked round to check if any police were watching before he dropped a handful of bullets down an open drain. Another tossed a revolver surreptitiously into an untended brewer's dray. Matt wondered if McCafferty had had time to warn them. There were so many of them that even the large numbers of police on the streets had little chance of stopping and questioning more than a few. But when Matt came in sight of the station he realized immediately what had alerted them. The train from London had arrived with the reinforcements from the Welsh Guards. The elite soldiers, immaculate in their red and black uniforms even after their journey, were drawn up in ranks on the station forecourt, ready to parade through Chester to the castle.

"By the left, quick march!" bawled a sergeant and the men moved off as one, rifles sloped precisely over their shoulders, a line of constables on each side of them.

Matt shrank into a side alley. His eyes darted round for any way of escape. There was none. The small alley ended in a high wall topped with iron spikes. The sound of boots tramping on cobbles came nearer and nearer. Matt was trapped. Instinctively, without a conscious thought, he did the only thing he could. He stepped boldly out of the alley and stood in full view. He swept off his tweed cap and waved it enthusiastically above his head.

"Hurrah!" he cried, trying to sound as English as possible. And again, "Hurrah!"

His cheers mingled with those of the citizens of Chester who watched the impressive progress of the two hundred or so guardsmen.

The crowd began drifting away when the troops had wheeled out of sight into the next street. Matt realized suddenly that he was almost alone and under the surveillance of the half dozen constables remaining on the station forecourt. He feared that any moment one of them would walk over and ask a routine question which might lead to inevitable exposure and arrest. The revolver in his pocket felt like a ton weight. Again his instincts took over.

Matt strode out firmly towards the constables. "Could any of you gentlemen tell me the next train to London and which platform I need?" he asked.

The constables looked at each other.

"You're lucky, sir," one said. "I think there's one in fifteen minutes but the conductor in the station'll tell you better."

Matt touched the peak of his cap. "Thank you for that."

"You're welcome, sir. Been watching the Guards, have you?"

"Indeed I have."

"Thought I saw you there. Fine body of men, aren't they?"

"They are that. The finest. We're fortunate to have them."

"We are that."

Matt decided to risk a question. "But why were they here today? They weren't due, were they?"

"Oh, no, sir. There were rumors of some trouble coming at the castle."

"Trouble? Really?"

"Some hotheads from Ireland, they say, but it's scotched now and no mistake what with the troops and all."

Matt nodded, forcing himself to smile agreeably at the constables. "Well then," he said, "I can go about my business without worry, thanks to the Guards and you gentlemen."

As he settled back into his empty carriage he wondered how McCafferty had fared and whether many of the Fenians had been arrested after that morning's debacle. Most, he reckoned, would have been safe unless they'd been caught red-handed, carrying firearms. The Irish population in the northwest of England was so large—after successive famines—that the police would have been hard-pressed to choose between a law-abiding Irishman and a Fenian.

The longer the journey went on, the more depressed Matt became, swearing at himself for ever becoming involved with the Fenians. How could they hope to overthrow the British in Ireland? How on earth had he been persuaded to endanger Mary's and the children's futures in Boston by joining such a hare-brained enterprise? He felt ashamed and angry with himself. When he reached London, he decided, he'd go directly to Kelly and the others in Great Portland Street and tell them he was finished with the brotherhood.

London was still busy, despite the chill evening, when the train pulled in. Matt welcomed the anonymity of the crowds on the pavements as he walked out of Euston Station. Here, he thought, not many people, if any at all, had heard of the day's events in Chester. He turned into the tavern nearest the station, drawn by its beckoning lights, and ordered a plate of cold beef and porter with cognac. His meal was served well away from the bar and the energetically out-of-tune pianist. Matt signalled for more drink. He closed his eyes for a moment, leaning his head against the alcove's greasy upholstery, shutting his mind to the tensions of the day.

"Ullo, sir. All on your own?"

It happened so quickly. One moment, Matt was alone, his thoughts far away. The next, a young woman had slid into the alcove on the opposite side of the narrow table. A dark green straw hat, sporting a white flower, was perched on top of her mop of curly blonde hair. She shrugged a black shawl off her shoulders and settled into the seat. Her painted lips smiled glisteningly. Blue eyes looked straight into his, challenging and assessing at the same time.

Matt stared blankly at her for a second, then opened his mouth to protest, to send her away.

"Just a port and lemon, sir," she continued quickly, anticipating his rejection. "And another slosh of brandy for you?"

Before he could speak, her right arm shot above the back of the alcove and waved.

"Nellie, Nellie Shaw, that's me."

"But . . ."

"I saw you on your own, sir, and thought to myself, Nellie, I thought, that gentleman's on his own and needing some cheering up."

"I'm not . . ."

But before Matt could continue, a barman appeared carrying a tray.

"Port and lemon, Nellie, and a brandy for your gentleman friend?"

"Ta, Alf."

The glasses were slapped on the table before Matt could object.

"He'll pay later, Alf," the girl said. "Won't you dear?"

Her manner oozed brisk confidence with, perhaps, a slight note of pleading. Matt smiled resignedly at the barman, shrugging his shoulders. He'd had enough experience of tavern life in the various Finucane establishments in Boston to realize he'd been accosted by what polite society termed a lady of the night. Looking more closely at her, he saw that she was rather pretty with delicate features beneath the mandatory rouge and paint. Probably, he thought, she wasn't much older than seventeen or eighteen. They each raised their glasses at the same moment, their eyes meeting over the rims. The idea struck Matt that it was ludicrous that such a supposedly epoch-making day in his and Ireland's history should end with him drinking in a London tavern with a whore, and an attractive one at that.

The girl mistook the bitter laugh as a sign of friendliness, of acceptance, of a bargain sealed even before negotiation.

"Far from home after a busy day, then . . . you're?"

Matt waved at the barman. Another two glasses arrived.

"Matt."

"Irish?"

"Uh-huh."

"And a bit of a toff from your duds."

"Not really."

"Anywhere to stay?" She looked shrewdly at him, a tiny smile playing at the corner of her mouth.

"No," Matt replied. He paused for what seemed long seconds. His mind, beginning to fume with brandy and the acrid tobacco smoke clouding the bar, was tired of trying to think rationally any more. It didn't matter after all, did it? he thought. Nothing much mattered now, he decided, not even Mary and the children. They were in another world, nothing to do with this girl or this tavern. The rising had failed. He had failed. Or so it appeared to him in his deep depression. "No," he repeated. "Tis I've nowhere to stay."

He drained his glass again.

"Well now, fancy that, duckie," she giggled triumphantly. "And there's me with a cozy little gaff just round the corner."

"Fancy that." Matt signalled for another two drinks, then leaned across the table and lightly touched the girl's left hand.

By the time he left the tavern, nearly two hours later, his legs were so unsteady that he was forced to lean on the girl for support while they weaved the fifty yards to her room. His nostrils were filled with the smell of cheap brandy and her even cheaper scent. He tumbled on to her squeaky brass bed and watched through bleary eyes as she shrugged off her clothes. Her body, he was to recall later, was slim and pink in the light of the bedside candle. He was to remember her pushing one finger deep into the downy triangle between her legs before holding it, moist, out to him in offering. He was not to remember, though, how tears dripped down his cheeks to fall on to her soft-spread nipples while she writhed beneath his thrusting, twisting hips or how he cried out Mary's name when he eventually climaxed deep inside her.

The next morning, he left the small room as soon as light shone through the begrimed curtains. The girl protested, kicking back the stained sheets to offer her gleaming sex to him. Matt merely shook his head, not speaking, and placed a single gold sovereign between her wide-stretched thighs. As he went through the door, he looked back once. The girl's scrabbling fingers had closed round the coin.

A wave of nausea and self-disgust gripped him when he reached the street below. He wandered through the early-morning crowds not caring where he was headed and swore at himself for his weakness, his infidelity.

He saw a red and white striped barber's pole poking out of a narrow alley, rubbed the stubble on his face and decided a shave with hot towels would ease his feeling of wretched-ness. The chatter in the barber's was mainly of steeple-chasing and the murder of a whore near Fleet Street. Presumably the news of the previous day's events in Chester had not yet reached London. From his greeting an hour later at 137 Great Portland Street, though, it was clear that the Fenian leadership had heard. Richard O'Sullivan Burke, the armaments organizer, opened the front door, starting with surprise when he saw Matt.

"Good God, Aherne! You! What the devil . . . ?" Burke leaned out of the doorway and looked swiftly up and down the street. "You're not followed?"

"No. Not as far as . . ."

"Come in quickly, then, man."

Burke called up the stairs before ushering Matt into the drawing room, its table covered with maps and papers as before.

"You look done in." Burke's tone was concerned.

"A hard journey and a long night," Matt said shortly. "Where are the others?"

"All over the place, frankly, but the colonel's here. He'll be with you in a trice."

Kelly's greeting seemed genuinely effusive. "My dear chap," he exclaimed. "We were fearing you'd suffered the same fate as poor McCafferty."

Matt's face showed his dismay.

"You hadn't heard? No, that's silly of me. Of course, you wouldn't have. Nabbed good and proper, I'm afraid," Kelly went on, pulling at his beard. "Picked up off a collier from the Dee—Connah's Quay, I think. His false papers were good, mind you . . . in the name of William Jackson, I recall . . . but he would insist on carrying his ring everywhere. The police found it in the lining of his coat."

"His ring?"

"The one inscribed by our circle in Detroit. Quite damning, I fear. Straight into the hoosegow for him."

"And the others?"

"McCafferty's warning was in time, thank the Lord. None took to the field except in Kerry—Cahirciveen, wasn't it?—but the few hundred there dispersed quickly enough when they realized they were alone."

"In Chester?"

Kelly gave a short laugh.

"Thanks to your presence of mind, only a few arrests compared to what there could have been. But the police'll have to search the ponds and canals for quite a time, I'm guessing, if they want to find all the guns and bullets that were abandoned."

Matt had to smile, despite his grim mood. "I know. I saw some being tossed away myself. A mighty panic that was when the Welsh Guards arrived."

"But how did you escape?" Burke interrupted.

In a few sentences, Matt offered a censored version of his movements. ". . . it was a total fiasco," he ended bitterly. "Total and utter."

"Come along now, Matt," Kelly said, putting a hand on his shoulder. "It could have been much worse, you know."

"Worse. What could be worse? The entire rising is finished. The government is alerted. We've lost weapons and men for nothing. And what about the informer amongst us? What about . . ."

Kelly's face whitened during the angry tirade. His voice rose above Matt's to interrupt. "No, sir. Definitely not. No informer," he roared. "Idle chatter from the men over a jar of porter maybe, but no informer."

"But they knew the very day, the very time . . ."

"Coincidence, my dear sir. I can understand your feelings but pray remember whom you are addressing."

Burke went to put a conciliatory hand on Matt's forearm but he brushed it away. "There's no point in continuing, Colonel. You're blind to the facts. I want no more of it."

Kelly looked him directly in the face, eyes staring with rage. "No more, sir! No more! What do you mean, sir? Here I greet you as a hero of the brotherhood and you throw this at me. Explain yourself, sir. Now!"

"I mean I'm leaving the brotherhood, Colonel," Matt said, trying to make his voice as firm as possible although it rasped in his brandy-dry throat. "I cannot go on. I've sacrificed enough, transporting my family from Boston, working these long years, and for what? There's no point any more in the brotherhood. It's as hollow as all the other so-called secret societies which have failed Ireland time after time."

"Be careful, Matt," Burke warned quietly, moving to his shoulder. "You're tired and disappointed. We know that. But think of what you're saying."

"I know what I'm at."

"Do you, sir? Do you?" Kelly swung round, his piercing gaze reaching out across the room. "When you took your oath to the brotherhood, Aherne, you made a vow of loyalty, a vow to be broken on pain of punishment." The colonel took three steps towards Matt before flinging out his right arm and pointing dramatically into his face. "Punishment, sir, I said, and punishment I mean. You might have heard of how informers in New York have disappeared to be found in the Hudson River. Let me inform you that the punishment didn't end with them. Their families suffered too. They became virtual pariahs, outcasts in their own communities. They didn't bless the names of their dead believe me. Rather they cursed them and spat on their headstones. That, sir, is the Fenian punishment for disloyalty. It is swift and terrible."

Matt tried not to flinch under Kelly's vicious words and stern gaze but, after a moment, his eyes flicked downwards toward the carpet. He attempted to clear his parched throat. "I cannot be going on, Colonel, whatever you're threatening," he said quietly, hesitantly.

Kelly's tone softened. He took another three paces and thrust out his hand, taking Matt's in his. "Now Aherne, you've had a bad time. We all realize that. I'm not wanting to be too hard on you, you should know that.''

Matt looked up in some bewilderment as the colonel continued.

"Loyalty cuts two ways. As you must be loyal to the brotherhood, so we must be loyal to you. That's only fair. I'm certain you'd never desert us just as I'm certain we must find you a role here at headquarters. You're too valuable to risk in the field, don't you agree, Burke?''

"I do indeed, Colonel."

"Well, let's be forgetting our hasty words and settle down to our unfinished business.''

"Unfinished?" The surprise was clear in Matt's voice.

"Oh, yes, Aherne," the colonel replied confidently. "Chester was a mere hiccup in the rising. The rebellion will still go ahead and will be even more deserving of success if we learn the lessons of yesterday's unfortunate episode.''

"The main one must be secrecy.''

"You're correct, of course, Matt," Burke cut in hastily. "We've already decided that only the inner council will discuss strategy and timing. The vice-centers and centers will be told only the general outlines until the actual day.''

"It's a beginning," Matt sniffed.

"That's so, Aherne. I look forward to having you work alongside us here. Your advice will be invaluable.''

"Thank you, Colonel. I'll be waiting a few days in London before going home to tell my family what's transpired. Then I'll return.''

Kelly's features hardened. "I really don't think that would be wise. Better to write to them, I'm sure. They'll understand, you'll see.''

"I must . . ." Matt interrupted.

"No, Aherne. You stay here. And you, Burke, become our friend's closest companion. Day and night."

"You're making me a prisoner, Colonel?" Matt felt a lump coming in his throat.

"Just ensuring that nothing goes amiss. My words about punishment were not light ones, sir."

Matt shook his head, hardly believing what was happening to him. The set expression on Kelly's face left him in little doubt, however, that his loyalty was in question after his threats to leave the Fenians.

"Have you your revolver still?" Burke asked quietly, almost apologetically.

"Yes," Matt muttered, anticipating what was to happen next.

"I think it would be better if I took it." Burke was obviously embarrassed about his new role as, in effect, Matt's gaoler.

Without a word, Matt lifted the Remington from his pocket and handed it to Burke.

Kelly clapped his hands, rubbing them together, as if washing away the unpleasant, strained atmosphere. "Good. Capital. I'm sure that in the fullness of time you'll come to accept my decision as the correct one. But, now, to business. The inner council meets this afternoon. It'll want a full report from you about Chester."

To Matt's amazement, the council did, indeed, regard the previous day's events as no more than an unfortunate setback. The leading Fenians went on to discuss mobilizing their members again. No exact date was mentioned but Matt gained the firm impression that it would be within a matter of weeks.

During the meeting, he looked continually around the

table at the members of the council, wondering which one could be an informer. Massey? Cliseret? Vifquain? Which one? He was convinced that one of the men in that room was a government spy. Joe Denieffe even? Why hadn't he been in Chester after working so closely on the plan? And Corydon? He was out of the ordinary all right, almost disinterested in the meeting but not so disinterested as not to listen.

The next two weeks were miserable. Matt's letter to Mary eventually brought a cool reply filled with complaints and veiled threats about the future of their marriage. He could only leave the house with Burke as an escort, invariably to walk in Regent's Park. Council meetings were held daily and, more often than not, his attendance wasn't even requested. He spent many hours sitting in his attic room sharing bottles of cognac with Burke. At least the drink numbed his despair and made the hours appear to pass more quickly. Although his friendship with Burke grew quite naturally in their enforced proximity, his escort never once relaxed his vigilance. Even if Burke had, Matt mused, it wouldn't have made much difference. He felt completely drained and apathetic. In his moments of lucidity, usually filled with self-recrimination, Matt wondered if he had become what he described to himself as a "broken man." But, after a few glasses, he didn't really care one way or the other.

In the first week in March, the arrival and departures increased at Great Portland Street. A fever of activity and expectancy was everywhere. On the afternoon of March 3rd, Matt was summoned at last with Richard O'Sullivan Burke to the drawing room. Only three members of the inner council were seated around the table.

Colonel Kelly appeared, for him, light-hearted as he handed Burke an envelope. "The moment has come, Richard," he said with an all-embracing smile. "You know what to do and where to go, don't you?"

Burke nodded.

"Take Aherne with you. Of necessity he's had a trying time. He deserves to be part of this time of destiny."

Outside the house, Burke hailed a cab and directed it to Ludgate Circus.

"What is it, Richard?" Matt murmured. "What's happening?"

Burke held up the envelope, tapping it in the palm of his hand. "For *The Times* and the English government. Tomorrow, when it's printed, the Irish Republic is in being."

"The proclamation?"

"Aye. You know the wording?"

"I read a draft. And the rising?"

"The day after tomorrow. All Ireland will be on the march, thanks be to God!"

"Thanks be," Matt responded dispiritedly.

Chapter 11
March, 1867

From the crest of the hill not two hundred yards away, the Fenian pickets could see the smoking chimneys of Tipperary. The townland of Ballyhurst had been chosen as the rendezvous point and the battleground for the one thousand Fenians in the district. Here, on March 5th, they would confront the British troops garrisoned in Tipperary.

The news had not yet reached Tipperary—or anywhere else for that matter—that Massey and John Corydon had been detained by the police the night before at Limerick Junction nor that the entire battle plan was in the hands of the authorities.

The motley Fenian ranks were silent except for nervous coughing and feet-stamping here and there. They watched the precise wheeling and flanking of the professional soldiers before them. As if by magic, with hardly a spoken command, their files fanned out into long ranks. The soldiers marched steadily toward the Fenians, spotless rifles at the port, bayonets fixed.

Suddenly, from the front rank of Fenians a cloud of smoke puffed upwards, followed by the crash of a musket discharge.

"Wait till they're in range!" screamed an officer.

His voice was drowned by the rippling crash of a ragged volley. Tiny pieces of earth and grass flicked up twenty yards in front of the British soldiers. One soldier on the

481

right flank leapt visibly off the ground. His rifle fell at his feet. He clapped a hand to his shoulder, stung, perhaps even bruised by a piece of shot which had somehow outdistanced the rest. With hardly a break in their stride, the soldiers continued their advance.

A light drizzle began to blanket the scene. The Fenians swore aloud, trying to reload their weapons, hands slipping on wet metal. They could hear now as well as see the measured tread of the troops. It was a relentless sound, grass and divot crushed under boot. It came on and on.

An unexpected silence made the Fenians straighten up. The first of the two ranks of troops had knelt, rifles now pressed into shoulders. The second rank's weapons pointed straight ahead over the heads of the first rank.

Some of the Fenians redoubled their efforts to prime their ancient guns, fumbling in desperation. Others shuffled around so that their backs were toward the troops. The movement spread through the ranks.

It wasn't an accurate volley. Perhaps the soldiers were more excited than their ordered drill suggested. Some bullets hit targets, thudding soggily into body flesh, or shattering bones, the dry, echoing snaps mingling with agonized cries.

It was too much for the Fenians. This wasn't the glorious death depicted in paintings and legend. This was slaughter of the untrained by the skilled.

Who broke rank first didn't really matter. Within a minute, most of the thousand Fenians were fleeing in every direction away from the soldiers.

The British troops, confident of the route before them, resumed their measured advance, not even attempting to chase their fleeing enemy. That, their officers knew, could be left to the Royal Irish Constabulary.

The disaster at Ballyhurst was just one of many. At

Drogheda, a thousand rebels were routed by thirty-seven constables. Worse, at Tallagh, seven hundred Fenians fled after the first volley from just fourteen constables. Only around Cork did the rebels acquit themselves with anything approaching honor.

The gloom of the Fenian headquarters in Great Portland Street deepened perceptibly with news of each successive disaster. Colonel Kelly locked himself in the drawing room, refusing to talk to any of his aides for the whole afternoon.

"You go where you like, when you like, from now on, friend," Richard O'Sullivan Burke told Matt as the day wore on.

"It's over, isn't it, Richard?"

"All over. Finished. Perhaps for ever."

Although he'd opposed the Fenian plans, Matt couldn't help but feel sadness for them. After all, he still agreed with their aspirations. He tried to comfort Burke. "The Fenians will never die. It's not all over, you know."

"It is for many years."

"Possibly. But if we remember the oath, we can stay together. We must go underground, become a secret society again."

"You were the one who wanted to cut and run," Burke reminded him sourly.

"Not from the ideals of Fenianism," said Matt. "I was against precipitant action. There have been too many bungled rebellions already."

"And now this . . ."

"Yes, and now this. We must wait for a proper cause we can make our own. Something that the people can understand, something that affects their very lives. If we can unite them in such a cause, then we can lead them into the greater fight against the English."

"All very fine, Matt," said Burke, slumped disconsolately in his chair. "But what are we to do in the meantime?"

"We must stay close to the people, identify with them. We've overestimated their resolve, their stomach for fighting. We must never lead from in front again. We must guide the people to do what we want them to do. Allow them to think that rebellion is their idea, not ours. When there's an issue, a dispute, which concerns them, angers them even, we can turn it to our advantage."

"Mislead them, you mean?"

"Of course. Our fight now should be one of stealth, not of standing and waving flags before a British Army. That's never worked and probably never will."

"Have you been listening to James Stephens recently? Is that what you're about?" asked Burke suspiciously.

"Well, Stephens was right, wasn't he? He counselled against open revolt. England's struggle will be Ireland's opportunity. That's what he said. But no one listened and now we've failed."

"Tell that to Kelly," Burke said flippantly.

"No, you tell him, Richard, if you want to. There are other bridges for me to build."

"Mrs. Aherne?"

"Uh-huh. I should have said fences to mend, really," Matt smiled. He felt his depression lifting for the first time since that day in Chester more than three weeks before.

When he arrived back in Ireland two days later, Matt found little or no sign that the country had just undergone a major attempt at rebellion, however inept. None of his travelling companions spoke about it and, in Ireland herself, the people seemed too ashamed to mention it. The newspapers he read during the train journey from Dublin were still praising the authorities for their swift action and castigating the Fenians as being unrepresentative of the Irish. Only one editorial noted that the Fenians would have had no support if there were not still discriminatory laws against the Irish in Ireland. In general, the newspapers expressed total satisfaction at the outcome. They welcomed the authorities' policy of charging captured Fenian leaders with treason but dealing with the small fry more leniently. The government was clearly determined not to create any more martyrs.

In the last few miles of his journey, Matt wondered continually what sort of welcome he would receive in Listowel. He prepared for a cheery one from the town and a frosty one from Mary. In the event, it was almost exactly the reverse.

During his walk from the station to Church Street, he passed several Fenian colleagues, among them Tom Luby, Jim Bunyan and Mike Quille. He started to greet them, to ask what had happened around Listowel, but they seemed embarrassed to meet him. After a few stilted words, they hurried on their way, promising to see him later at the tavern.

Matt was still perplexed by their attitudes when he flung open his own front door. "I'm home, everyone," he called, trying to sound more cheerful and confident than he felt. "Mary. Children. I'm home!"

The door to the kitchen burst wide. Mary ran out, wiping her hands on an apron, followed by Brigid, Bernadette and Jack. "Dearest husband, you're back," she cried, throwing her arms around his neck. "You're safe. Oh, you're safe."

Matt felt a wetness on his cheek as Mary pressed her face against his. It took him a moment to realize that the tears were his own.

Much later, in the hushed warmth of the bedroom, Mary asked only one question when he had finished recounting his adventures. "Your heart is here?" she whispered.

"Aye. With you and ours. It was madness but I'm thinking it's over. Oh God, I hope it is!"

Mary placed a finger gently on his lips. "And didn't I realize that in these last weeks? Sure and I was awful upset when you didn't come home but I knew it wouldn't be your doing."

He nodded, then gathered her to him.

In the months that followed, Matt slipped back into the quiet, ordered life of the small market town. It was as if the rebellion had never happened. The only outward sign of it was the company of infantry still garrisoned in Listowel. The soldiers had arrived at the magistrate's request following the Chester fiasco when the local Fenians, not receiving the news of the rising's postponement, had mobilized at Cahirciveen. The actual day of the rebellion had passed off in Listowel virtually unnoticed. Some Fenians had congregated but the overwhelming presence of troops and two hundred and fifty armed constables had persuaded them that discretion was the better part of valor. Those who had been arrested were merely charged under the law dating from the Whiteboys troubles. Most were bound over in their own assurances of future good behavior.

Matt's only source of information now was the occasional letter from Joe Denieffe, still hiding out in London. It seemed that the Fenian leadership had decided to adopt, after all, the policy of James Stephens and regroup as a smaller secret society comprising only the most fanatical, the most dedicated, members. The final blow to any lingering hopes of open revolution was the lack of effective support from the Fenians in America.

They'd chartered a ship, optimistically renamed *Erin's Hope*, which sailed from New York with five thousand repeating rifles and one and a half million rounds of ammunition. The ship didn't arrive off Sligo until two months after the abortive rising.

"Too much, too late," Denieffe wrote sarcastically.

A subsequent letter from him saying that, at long last, the informer had been identified as John Corydon served only to strengthen Matt's opinion of the brotherhood's incompetent leadership. Corydon had steadily fed the authorities in New York and London with every twist and turn of Fenian planning. He was now, according to Denieffe, under heavy guard, available to identify and give evidence against captured Fenians. His arrest earlier with General Massey had merely been a subterfuge.

The final confirmation for Matt that he was well out of it was the news that Colonel Kelly had been arrested in Manchester along with Captain Deasey, his diehard commander in Cork during the rising. They'd been trying to reorganize their units in the northwest of England. They gave their names as Wright and Williams but soon, thanks to information from John Corydon, their real names were known. It was in this ignominious capture that Kelly, named chief executive of the Irish Republic by the Fenians, was to serve his cause best.

A week later, September 18th, 1867, a horsedrawn prison van rattled and jolted its way through the Ardwick district of Manchester, an area of grimy little streets and small workshops, traditionally one of the main homes of the Irish who'd settled in the city closest to Britain's industrial revolution. In the back of the van, a police sergeant watched over the crude cells containing the two handcuffed Fenian leaders and some common criminals, including women, while they were returned from police court to Belle Vue Prison.

Suddenly, as the unescorted van passed under a sooty

railway bridge, thirty Fenians leapt, whooping and yelling, from the side streets.

Brandishing revolvers, they held back passersby and ordered two constables down from the driving seat. Then they began battering the van with heavy stones in an attempt to break it open. The police sergeant drew his wooden truncheon and stood by the doors, prepared to fight off the attackers if they should break through.

One Fenian, Peter Rice, pointed his revolver through the ventilator and jerked the trigger. The bullet smashed through the thin metal slats and into the police sergeant's temple. With only a sob of surprise, he fell back, blood and brains jetting upwards, spraying the walls of the van. A few seconds later, the van door swung open. The Fenians pulled Kelly and Deasey, still handcuffed, into the street, over a wall and across a railway line on the start of a long journey which eventually took them—and Peter Rice—to freedom in the United States.

The police action was immediate and draconian. Hundreds of Irishmen were picked up for questioning before five were charged with the police sergeant's murder. One was later to be granted a free pardon when it was admitted that he was nowhere near the scene of the rescue at all. Edward Condon, of Irish descent but an American citizen, was reprieved after diplomatic pressure, although he was, in fact, the person who planned the rescue. The remaining three were destined for the scaffold. None of them had fired the fatal shot but legally they were all accessories to murder.

Matt Aherne read the reports of the trial in his copy of *Freeman's Journal* while he stood behind his tavern bar. His first reaction was of cold anger. The few customers at that time in the morning had read the statements from the dock as well. The feelings of pride and anger and shame and resentment were, perhaps, too strong to be expressed. Matt, within his heart, rededicated himself to Ireland's fight, to the Fenian Brotherhood. So did thousands of others. Three Fenians, William Allen, Philip Larkin and Michael O'Brien, were executed before the people of Manchester on November 24th. Larkin and O'Brien jumped and twisted for ghastly, agonizing minutes at the end of the hemp rope because of the executioner's incompetence. Matt had no doubt—nor had many in Ireland—that they had died not because they were involved in the death of a gallant policeman but simply because they were rebels against British rule. They were martyrs, of that Matt was certain. He cursed his inability to express his feelings. His depression was all too clear to Mary.

"You shouldn't be taking it so hard, Matt," she said one late November night after the bar had closed and they sat alone by the glowing peat fire in their front room. "There's nothing you could have done."

"I could have believed like they believed," Matt said. "I could have done that, at least. All of us carry blame for their deaths. We're fine ones for talking and plotting but not many of us are good at dying. That takes something special in a man."

Mary rose from her chair and knelt by Matt's knee, resting her head on his thigh, gazing into the fire, shadows flickering across her face. "You tried at Chester, didn't you?" she said soothingly.

"Yes," Matt conceded. "I was ready then. For an hour I was prepared for anything that came. But after that, resolve went from me. Perhaps a man has only one chance, a certain time, to offer himself. And when that moment's gone . . . well, he's only left with a lifetime of regrets. Isn't most of living, anyway, an apology for not having done something or regretting what was done?"

He traced a finger gently through the fine hairs at the nape of her neck.

"Women have a truer notion," he continued. "They have the way of living for the present, for knowing what's important and what's so much dross. They regret very little. They know there's little enough time for that when there's all life to be savored, to be fought for."

"I wouldn't stop you. You know that," Mary said quietly. "If you want to go on with the brotherhood, well, that's fine."

"A little late, isn't it?" Matt said bitterly. "More than a little late, I'd say. The dying's done and that's that."

Mary tried to comfort him. She had seen how his feelings were gnawing at him, his increased drinking, his growing irritability with his customers and the children. He had been so certain of himself once. Now he seemed unsure and questioning.

Matt's depression deepened when the newspapers reported that Richard O'Sullivan Burke had been arrested and was being held, pending trial, in Clerkenwell Prison in London.

Then, three days after his friend's arrest, Matt's spirits soared with the arrival of a cryptic message from Joe Denieffe. "Help needed to open locked door," it read. "Come to usual place."

Matt showed it immediately to Mary, his hands trembling slightly with excitement. Her expression didn't alter. "Burke?" she asked calmly, quietly.

He nodded, eyes pleading.

"Well, you'll have to go, won't you," she decided briskly, turning away from him.

"Sure and it'll only be a few days, Mary." He stood behind her, folding her into his arms and pulling her close. She rested her head back on his shoulder.

"Will it?"

"I know things have been wrong between us," he said
softly. "But nothing will keep me away from you and the
children longer than necessary. Helping Joe is something I
must do."

"I know that."

"And when it's over, there'll be no more, I promise. Just
here and the tavern. But this time it's awful important to
me."

"I know that, Matt," she repeated.

"More than . . ." he went on, then stopped.

"I know," she repeated before tearing herself out of his
embrace and rushing into the kitchen, hands clasped across
her face.

Two days later, December 11th, 1867, Matt stood under
light falling snow outside the Langham Hotel in London.
After an hour's wait, stamping his boots in the slush, he
began to wonder if he'd chosen the correct rendezvous. He
was just considering whether to chance the house in Great
Portland Street when a cab jangled up to the hotel entrance.
Denieffe leaned through the window and beckoned Matt to
get in.

"No words now, friend," he said. "We'll talk at the
lodgings."

The cab clattered its way east toward the oldest part of
London. Here, poverty existed within spitting distance of
the great financial institutions which extracted the maximum wealth from the new colonies claimed in the name of
Queen Victoria. Denieffe halted and paid off the cab within
sight of the dome of St. Paul's.

"We'll walk a bit now," Denieffe grunted. The pavements were crowded with people in spite of the chilling
flurries of snow.

"You're well?" Matt inquired.

"As can be, what with all the changing of lodgings I've had since the affair at Manchester."

"You weren't there?"

"No, but the way the police are out looking for me, I might just as well have been. That bastard Corydon gave them most descriptions."

"Mine?"

"They haven't been to see you?"

"No."

"Well then, I'm reckoning he thought you weren't important enough to bother with."

"We'll be rectifying that, won't we, Joe?" Matt said grimly.

"Aye. We will that."

After twenty minutes of brisk walking, occasionally checking to see if anyone was behind them, they rounded a corner into a depressing row of terraced houses called Warner Street. Halfway down, Denieffe stopped at a door, looked around once more, and then entered using his own key. Matt followed him up the rickety stairs into a small room furnished only with a cot bed and an armchair.

"Not much, is it?" commented Denieffe, sensing Matt's dismay. "But it's cheap and the landlord doesn't ask questions."

"Do I stay here?"

"You have the armchair. It's more comfortable than that damned bed. It's only for a night anyway. We strike tomorrow."

"So soon?"

"The planning's been done. Our man, a fella called Mick Barrett, has been to see Burke in prison. And he's arranged the explosives from our friends in the gravel quarries in Middlesex. Everything's ready. All I've been wanting was someone I could trust and now you're here. So why not tomorrow?''

"Why not indeed?"

Denieffe pulled a large street map from under the straw palliasse on the bed and spread it on the floor. For the next two hours, he led Matt through the plan. In the late afternoon, when they'd finished, both men changed into ragged and stained sets of clothes which Denieffe had bought off a stall in Club Row market.

"That's what you are now, Matt, my boy," Denieffe said cheerfully, jamming a cap with a torn peak on to the side of his head. "An honest Irish navvie working on the underground railway."

He bent down, rubbed his palm in the dust on the bare floorboards, then wiped it across Matt's cheek.

"With that and a night's stubble even your Mary wouldn't be knowing you. Or wanting to," he laughed.

Before they went to a hostelry nearby for some food and drink, Denieffe showed Matt a large wooden barrel full of gunpowder—firing powder, he called it—which had been securely locked and padlocked into a small shed beside the earth privy in the backyard of the house. He'd also purchased a cart from the same market where he'd acquired their clothes.

The next afternoon, they maneuvered the cart out of the yard in Warner Street, the barrel of gunpowder safely roped down, and pushed it the quarter of a mile to the cobbled lane behind the granite walls and towers of Clerkenwell Prison. It was set in the middle of a small common, within range of the sweet fumes coming from the gin distillery just opposite.

Matt and Denieffe pretended to be exhausted and half-drunk, leaning over the shafts of the cart while they waited for the agreed signal from Richard O'Sullivan Burke.

They strained to listen for any sound coming from behind the high walls but all they could hear was the sound of men's tramping feet, presumably the prisoners exercising, and an occasional shout from a prison guard.

"There it is!" Denieffe exclaimed all of a sudden. "That's the signal!"

Something hollow, perhaps wooden, banged against the wall about ten yards from them.

"That's it!" Denieffe said excitedly. "The signal. It is. He's knocking with his shoe."

Both men looked around. The only person within thirty yards was standing outside a stable building, ignoring the couple of drunks apparently struggling with their cart.

"Now?" asked Matt.

"For God's sake hurry. Burke's only got a minute."

Matt leaned under the tarpaulin covering the gunpowder, struck a safety match and held it to the length of fuse. It spluttered for a second, then went out. He struck a second match. The same thing happened. It wouldn't ignite.

"Joe . . . for Christ's sake." His muffled voice was urgent from beneath the tarpaulin.

"What?"

The question echoed into Matt's ear as Denieffe's face, surprised and worried, appeared next to his under the covering.

"It won't light, dammit!"

"It must. Give me the lucifers."

Denieffe took the matches and struck one. It blew out and he swore and struck another one. The fuse smoked for a second before going out. There was no doubt now. It hadn't been properly prepared. It wouldn't light.

"On the back arse of a whore!" Denieffe stormed.

"There's not time," Matt said, his voice surprisingly matter of fact.

"And don't I know that?" Denieffe shouted, pulling his head from under the tarpaulin. "Get the bloody thing away."

As Matt frantically pushed the cart down the lane, he saw Denieffe pull a small white ball from his pocket, lean back and toss it over the prison wall.

"What the devil was that?" he asked breathlessly when Denieffe had caught up with him.

"A signal, you ignorant spalpeen. Burke'll know it's off till tomorrow."

"But won't the guards . . . ?"

"Not they. They've rotting cats and rats and pigeons over those walls all the time. It's the children's way of having a wee bit of fun in this neighborhood."

Denieffe spent most of that evening preparing a new fuse in the seclusion of the room in Warner Street. Matt watched him from the armchair, occasionally sipping from the bottle of cognac they'd bought the night before. It was strange, he thought, how detached he felt about everything. He knew the enterprise was extremely dangerous, yet he had no fear, no excitement. Perhaps, he wondered, it had been pre-ordained. Matt slept well and dreamlessly that night despite the uncomfortable armchair.

The area around the prison was slightly busier than it had been the previous day. Some children were playing about forty yards away at the end of the lane. By then, a woman was chatting to a milkman. The two men rested the cart in exactly the same position as before and waited. This time, however, they could hear no sound from beyond the walls.

They waited, nerves beginning to tighten, for a good five minutes. There was still no sound nor any signal.

Matt and Denieffe exchanged uneasy glances.

"Do we call it off again?" Matt asked.

Denieffe scratched the stubble on his chin.

"Twice we haven't been spotted," he grunted. "A third time would be asking too much. No, we'll do it now. Burke'll be ready."

Matt shrugged his shoulders, starting to lift the tarpaulin which covered the barrel of gunpowder. He looked casually up the lane to check that the children had come no nearer. To his horror, he saw that a patrolling constable had joined the woman and the milkman.

"Joe!" he called, almost shouting. "Joe . . . behind you. Trouble!"

Suddenly, the constable started toward them, breaking into a run, obviously suspicious.

"Oh, Jesus!" yelped Denieffe. He tore the tarpaulin off the cart. "The matches, for God's sake."

Instinctively, Matt tossed them to him, his eyes remaining fixed on the advancing constable. Everything seemed to be in slow motion.

The sound of Denieffe striking matches desperately jerked him out of his revery.

Matt saw that the fuse had started to splutter and smoke. His eyes switched to the constable and, beyond him, the children down the lane.

"No!" he cried. "No!"

He ran around the cart, almost colliding with Denieffe who was haring off in the opposite direction.

Matt waved his arms, urging the constable away from the cart, trying to attract the children's attention to warn them.

He opened his mouth to shout again but whatever words came out were drowned by the massive explosion.

Matt Aherne was engulfed by the blast and the roaring fireball. He ceased to exist.

Pitch torches and candle lamps threw smoking, grotesquely jagged shadows across the rubble of the slums near

Clerkenwell Prison while the police searched throughout the night of December 13th, 1867, for any further survivors from the Fenian bomb.

It was grim work. Many a young constable turned pale and vomited his horror over the shattered bricks as he uncovered the leg of a child, a woman's arm or in one instance a policeman's helmet containing the upper half of a human head, bloodied eyes still open and staring.

The explosion had, as intended, blown a large gap in the prison wall but the blast had also demolished most of the houses in the immediate vicinity and taken the roof slates of others within a radius of a quarter of a mile.

When the final count was done, the authorities announced to an aghast capital that twelve of its citizens had died and thirty-one had been blinded, disfigured or permanently crippled by the loss of limb.

Matt Aherne was not included among the number of dead for the simple reason that nothing tangible remained of him except a few splashes of drying blood on some pieces of shattered prison wall. The fragments and lumps of his body discovered at varying distances from the seat of the explosion were presumed to belong to other victims. Thus Matt was buried in at least half a dozen coffins.

By a fluke of the blast wave, Joe Denieffe was unscathed. He lived with the knowledge that the devastating bomb had been completely purposeless.

A security alert the night before had caused the governor of Clerkenwell Prison to change the prisoner's routine. Richard O'Sullivan Burke had heard the explosion from the locked confines of his cell.

But the deaths of Matt Aherne and his innocent victims brought the discontents of Ireland searingly into the consciousness of the British public.

At first, all over England, thousands enrolled into the

special constabulary to guard against what was seen as the hideous threat from the Fenians. Five thousand or so joined in the City of London alone. Even the sleepy Channel Island of Jersey established a force to take on the Irish at a signal from the guns of Fort Regent above St. Helier.

One of the instigators of the Clerkenwell outrage, Michael "Mick" Barrett, apprehended later by chance, faced a jeering, partisan crowd when he was allowed the dubious historical footnote of being the last person publicly executed in Britain.

The shrewder politicians, like William Ewart Gladstone, saw these reactions as the chance to focus public opinion on the Irish problem.

In 1868, when he became Prime Minister, Mr. Gladstone made an unequivocal statement on assuming office. "My mission," he proclaimed, "is to pacify Ireland."

Within months, his government disestablished the Protestant Church throughout Ireland, and, in 1870, enacted a Land Bill which provided legal recourse against landlords who arbitrarily evicted their tenants, although the three "Fs"—fair rent, freedom of sale and fixity of tenure—were not to become law for another eleven years.

Mr. Gladstone's ability to maneuver laws concerning Ireland through the Westminster Parliament, however, was certainly helped by the understanding now clear in the British mind that something had to be done about the Irish if further terrorist outrages like Clerkenwell were to be avoided.

The often misguided and inept Fenians had achieved something, not that it was of the slightest comfort to Mary Aherne.

She read of the bomb attack the day afterwards and knew that her husband was dead. Outwardly she tried to pretend that he was still alive, possibly in hiding and unable to write, and was partly aided by the newspaper reports which naturally failed to list Matt among the casualties. The worst part, she found, was her inability to confide in anyone during her torment.

To inquiries, Mary could only say that her husband was away on business.

The letter from Joe Denieffe was a blessing of sorts when it arrived six days after the explosion, less than a week before St. Stephen's Day.

Mary scanned the first few lines, giving the barest details, uttered a heart-wracking cry and swooned. She recovered her senses to find herself being comforted by the town's priest, Father Michael McDonnell, who'd been summoned by Bernadette after she'd read her mother's letter and understood its harsh message.

The sorrow deepened though the pain lessened as Mary confided in the priest. They went through the letter together, seeking any comfort in the words.

"He couldn't have suffered or known a thing of this, Mary," Father McConnell said softly, his hands folded over hers.

"No," she replied dully. "No pain for him."

"He believed in what he was at?"

"Oh, yes, Father. Sometimes, I think he wanted to die for Ireland rather than live with all his dreams and ambitions gone."

"Many men have desired that. Who's to blame them or say they're wrong? Not I, Mary, nor the blessed Church. He was a brave man and you can be proud of him."

"You really think so?"

"You must think so and you must tell your children so."

A thought struck Mary. "But how can we bury him or give him the sacraments? He'd want that, I'm sure. And how do we tell the town he died?"

The priest nodded, understanding her dilemma. "The Almighty will hear our prayers, will accept my blessing on the departed, I'm certain. And He'll forgive us if we don't tell all the truth. Your Matt died just in an accident while he was away in England and his remains couldn't be got home. That's what I know and that's what I'll say. You must counsel your own family in their answers."

"You'll bless him in death despite all those poor people dying?"

The priest shifted uncomfortably in his chair. "I'll commend his soul to Our Lord for being the loving husband and father that he was. But I cannot be condoning what he seems to have been involved in because I'm not knowing what was in his mind at the very time. Only the Almighty can know that. But I'm sure, Mary, that Matt wouldn't have been wanting those deaths."

"No, I don't think so," she said quietly, then more strongly, "No, I'm certain he wouldn't!"

"Then the Lord will know and understand too."

Mary's story of her husband's death in an accident in England—a story echoed, when asked, by Listowel's priest—was accepted without question in the market town.

Indeed, the news dampened the season's celebrations throughout the district. Many a child wondered why the grown-ups stood solemnly for a moment during the traditional feast on St. Stephen's Day before silently draining their glasses.

Tom Luby and Mike Quille, Matt's Fenian comrades, didn't hesitate when Mary asked them for an afternoon's work. In consequence, the undergrowth around the Aherne's tumbledown cabin at Drombeg townland was neatly scythed on New Year's Eve when Mary and the children stood in a biting wind off the Atlantic while Father

McDonnell blessed the small headstone set next to Brigid Aherne's grave and the three others.

Next spring, during one of her weekly visits, Mary noticed a wild rose bush, released from the undergrowth, rising above the tufts of coarse grass by the headstone. As the weeks passed, its buds opened, spreading a sweet perfume. In the autumn, the petals fell, creating a carpet of crimson over the small graveyard.

Sometimes, the wind, capricious as ever, piled the petals so high against the headstone that Mary had to brush them away in order to see the inscription which simply read: "Matthew Aherne—1867. Beloved of his Family."

Underneath were two words: "For Ireland."

It became Mary's habit over the years to pick up some of the petals after she had gazed for long minutes on the stonemason's work. She would crush them in her palm and then sniff the scent deeply.

Finally, she would brush her hand against the headstone, touching the indentations of its words, knowing once more the love in her heart that would never die.

BESTSELLING BOOKS FROM TOR

MORE BESTSELLERS FROM TOR